UNLEASH

LAUREN HARRIS

A Pendragon Press & True North Studios Novel

For information address: pendragonvariety@gmail.com

PUBLISHED IN THE UNITED STATES OF AMERICA AND CANADA

ABOUT THE AUTHOR

 Lauren was raised by an impulsive furniture mover and an itinerant TV News professional in a string of homes up and down the East Coast of the United States. Eventually settling (sort of) in Raleigh, NC, Lauren befriended a band of whimsical nerds who found themselves de-facto beta readers for her scribblings.

Now, Lauren balances a day-job of Cardiac Ultrasound with her passion for writing and other creative pursuits. She is the author of The Millroad Academy Exorcists novella series and an Assistant Editor at Orson Scott Card's Intergalactic Medicine Show. Her narration and voice acting can be heard on Audible.com, EscapePod, and various short fiction podcasts.

www.laurenbharris.com

ALSO BY LAUREN HARRIS

The Millroad Academy Exorcists Series
(*Young Adult Paranormal Novellas*)

Exorcising Aaron Nguyen

The Girl in Acid Park

The Spellhounds Series

UNLEASH

UNMAKE

Unjust (Short Story)

The Sea King's Daughters
Linked Standalone in Shared World

SIREN'S SURGE

Sign up for my mailing list for a FREE Spellhounds prequel

This book is dedicated to the Smoky Writers posse.
Food. Booze. Words.
Family.

CHAPTER ONE

No matter how many times I did it, my hands shook every time Gwydian made me kill. Never during the act. If he thought I might hesitate, he'd twitch his magic into my tattoo and force my hand, literally. Those results were never clean. So, I learned to delay my shaking and get the deed done, cold and quick. Clamp a hand around the jaw, stretch out the neck. One cut. Painless as possible.

This time, I almost refused.

The yacht's hold was all cream leather, polished wood, and electronics blinking with LED sensors. It stood at odds with the medieval brutality of Gwydian's ritual—the gleaming silver bowls; the ancient tome lying open on the rocking floor; the naked, senseless girl. And me, standing there ready to open her throat.

Tonight, my victim was one of the sex-trade captives Gwydian had hijacked from a boat off the keys. Her description could have been mine: around eighteen, thick hair caught between brown and blonde, too little curve to soften her sinewy muscles. She lay stretched across the table in the hold of Gwydian's yacht, drugged into oblivion.

He'd probably chosen her precisely because she looked like me and forced me to hold the knife for the same reason. Magic wasn't the only thing he used to control us.

I swallowed, shifted my sweaty grip on the knife's handle, and tracked Gwydian's movements. He knelt on the floor, chalk in his elegant hands, drawing the glyphs within the outer ring of a mandala. I'd seen members of the Sorcerers' Guild cast spells with other drawn forms, but the mandala was the way most people favored. The biggest difference was that the Guild never spilled blood for power. In fact, it clearly went against whatever law underlay the hidden world of magic, because they wanted nothing more than to turn my master into a heap of charred viscera.

I was right there with them.

Our master was young, in his early thirties, and his gentle Scottish brogue didn't scream "gang leader" to the average person. That was how he got you—a business deal and a joke about golf or kilts or haggis. Next thing you knew, you'd have a pair of new tattoos and a dead Cuban teenager at your feet. And Gwydian, with blood dripping from his suit cuffs, his veins glowing and flush with the power of someone else's blood...if you were lucky enough not to be the sacrifice.

The tattooed mandala on my shoulder prickled—a twitch of power from my master, priming it for use. I had one on each shoulder, though they were very different, and served different purposes. One gave the man before me power over my body, and the other...

...the other was complicated. And it itched as if the Celtic hounds circling the inner ring bristled and growled with the crash of conflicting emotions.

I didn't want to kill this girl. If tonight's plan worked, I would never have to kill again. If I could only stall a little while, maybe I wouldn't have to kill her either. Maybe I could save her.

My mother flicked her gaze from my hand to my face, and I looked up to meet it. She stood at the girl's feet, there to brace her legs against the death flails. Mom was blonde, square-jawed, full of angles and lean planes, and she'd have looked delicate without the dark-ening bruise across her cheek.

I tamped down a flash of anger, remembering the dull impact as Gwydian backhanded her a few hours earlier. As if he'd known what we were planning, he'd commanded Mom, me, and my cousin Morgan to accompany him alone. We'd expected half the pack's help subduing him, so the order was a wrench in the gears, but we had to go with it. We didn't have a choice.

Mom couldn't speak now, not with Gwydian crouching a few strides away, but her jaw tightened. She gave me a slight shake of her head, as if she knew I had rebellion on the brain.

One last time, her eyes said. *Do it one last time, Helena, or Gwydian will suspect we have a plan.*

That look banked the rebellion kindling in my chest. Mom had already lost so much to our master's magic—her brother, her husband, fifteen years of her life. If anyone deserved to get out, it was her.

Somewhere out there, in the brackish black of Miami bay, the Sorcerers' Guild waited in the waves. We should have been on deck, ready to help them aboard, but that wasn't happening without the rest of the pack.

I call us "pack" partly because I can't bear to refer to us as a gang, not when most of us have been coerced by threats and blood magic. The rest of it was because of that second tattoo.

Gwydian stood with a grunt, stretching out his arm and dropping the little column of chalk into an ashtray. He turned his hand without lowering his arm and gestured at my mother.

"Lola, darling," he said. "Come here a moment."

Mom tensed, gave me a quick glance, and walked stiffly around the outline of the mandala. From my side of the table I only saw a piece of it, and the open spell book was tilted away. It only took me a glance to memorize them—I was one of *those* people—but I couldn't guess which one it was this time. Plenty of spells had a similar set on the outer ring. Most were nasty.

I tried not to think about this as Gwydian stretched his arm around Mom's back and drew her in front of him, facing the circle. An electric zing shot down my arms, prepping my muscles to tear that man to shreds. The sight of his hands on her elbows sent a rush of disgust through me.

"Do you know what that spell is?" he asked, his chin dipping toward her ear. "Think. You've seen it before."

Mom's throat flexed. She shook her head, but from the tension creeping into her expression, I knew she at least had a guess. Gwydian caught up one of the silver bowls beside him.

"Take this to Helena," he said, nodding in my direction. Mom's nostrils flared, and I watched her arm twitch, then go still. Gwydian clenched her shoulder. "Lola," his voice was a croon, and it fluttered the curls around her ears. She shuddered, but did not give in.

We were too much alike. I wanted to yell at her for doing the same damn thing she'd told me not to, but part of me was also proud at her resistance. We Martin women didn't take well to playing slave.

Mom's shoulder flared magenta. She gasped and an instant later, her arm shot up. She took the bowl and turned to Gwydian, stiff as a toy soldier. His smile was a little sad as he ran a finger down the bruise on her cheek. His finger dimpled her flesh, pressing too hard on the discolored skin.

She didn't blink. Right now, she couldn't.

"Mom," I said, my voice sharp and a little shaky. I stretched out my free hand for the bowl, keeping the other gripped tight around the knife.

The waves slapped against the hull, disturbing the otherwise perfect silence as Mom marched around the table. When she reached me, I grabbed her hand, holding it tight around the bowl.

"Stop," I hissed. "Stop fighting him. Please."

Her eyes were hard edged sapphires, but they softened at my words, and that was exactly why Gwydian wanted both of us. I was her weakness, and she was mine. At last, she blinked. Her throat flexed and her muscles relaxed, and she stepped back, squeezing my wrist before returning to her end of the table.

Gwydian was watching me. His expression mild, arms loosely crossed. Outwardly, he looked so clean-cut, so normal. But beneath those sleeves, every inch of him was tattooed with mandalas and ancient glyphs, at least half of them primed and ready to go.

Drawing spells took too long in a fight, but we humans excel at retooling skills for war. Permanent spell circles got chiseled in stone, etched in metal, tattooed on skin. Provided the order of drawing was correct, all the mandalas needed was power.

He nodded at me, crystalline eyes glossy with the melting-kindness that had fooled so many people into trusting him. A shiver of revulsion worked up my back.

He licked his lip like a snake tasting the air and touched an intercom button on the wall. Without breaking eye contact, he said, "Morgan? Come down." He released the button and nodded at the girl below me. "Shall we begin?"

It wasn't a question.

I drew in a short breath and redirected my gaze to the girl. Abrasions across her body mapped out her struggle for freedom. She'd fought, and though she'd lost, I was proud of those bruises. I only wish the Guild had gotten here fast enough to spare her.

I fixed her face in my mind like I did all of them, then pulled the blade in a clean, powerful arc from ear to ear. She jerked and gurgled, choking on the blood filling her airway as Mom wrestled with her ankles. I dropped the knife and pressed her shoulder into the table. The flesh was hot under my fingers.

A sheet of blood sluiced down her neck, soaking into her hair before it spilled over the side of the table. It spattered my boots and slicked my fingers as I shoved the silver bowl under it. The vessel filled fast at first, pulses of bright arterial blood growing thinner, then slowing as the heart failed. Finally, only residual pressure pushed the remaining blood from her cooling body.

She was sweating. Dead, but still sweating. I gripped the table's edge, hoping to disguise the tremors skittering up my arms. My hands shook, but I kept my mind rigidly blank.

I didn't look at Mom, though I felt her eyes on me.

The door in the hatch above clanged open, and I heard Morgan's footsteps a moment before his boots came into view.

Unlike Gwydian, my cousin looked like the kind of man who controlled a human trafficking crime syndicate with blood sorcery. He was a modern day Viking—long hair the same wild white-blond as Mom's, and eyes that matched the hunting knife strapped to his thigh. His features were impassive, tanned from days on boats and bikes, killing whoever needed it to make Gwydian's point. He thrummed with the vicious power that stopped conversations when he entered a room, though every iota of that brutality focused on our master.

Morgan ducked beneath the lintel, sparing a glance for me as he sidestepped the table. His eyes were expressionless as usual, but he glanced at the girl and back at me with a quick nod. I'd done a good job. He never spared me the truth when it was nasty.

He continued around the table in a few long strides, passing Mom without a glance. Gwydian's gentle gaze looked almost proud.

"How's the bay tonight?" Gwydian asked.

Morgan waited a beat. "Quiet," he said. "The harbor lights are dark, as you ordered."

Gwydian was nodding, already redirecting his attention to Mom. He beckoned again, and I tensed. Unease zipped down my spine—I didn't like that expression. It was too close to triumph. Very little gave him that much pleasure.

Mom's jaw tightened, but she approached him.

"And Helena," he said.

I wanted to drop the bowl. Actually, I wanted to fling it in Gwydian's face, grab dad's gun, and fire a couple bullets into his skull. But I would never get that far. He'd take control of me before I even lifted the gun. I didn't want to think about whose blood he would make me drain instead.

I didn't look up until I stood right in front of him. My work boots put us at eye-level. His, hazel and deep with fondness. Mine, amber-gray and, no doubt, burning with hatred.

He reached up and tweaked my chin. "Cheers, love."

I didn't say, "You're welcome." He wasn't.

The bowl lightened in my grasp as Gwydian hefted it. I sprang away, the hair on my neck standing, lip curled as if I were about to growl. Mom's fingers closed around my arm, tugging me against her side. She was strong—shorter than me, which I still wasn't used to, but what mass she had was honed from years of desperate fighting. She tilted her head to whisper at me.

"What spell is it?"

I tensed, keeping my eyes on Gwydian as he dipped his fingertips into the dark liquid. I waited for the veins in his hand to light up, glow traveling up his arm to his shoulder, and across his breast to his heart. Soon enough, it would pump through his whole body. He wouldn't notice me.

I glanced beside me at the mandala on the floor, getting my first good look at the intricate spell circle.

Fear jolted down my spine. It took a second for my brain to regurgitate the memory of that spell circle, and where I'd seen it before.

"Mom..." my voice shook. Her fingers tightened around my arm.

"Run, baby." In an instant, she shoved me toward the stairs and went for dad's gun. My heart leapt into my throat, and I lunged for the table where I'd left the dead girl, and the knife. Before I got my hand around it, a powerful arm lashed around my neck and hauled me backwards. Morgan held Mom in one arm, me in the other.

The tattoo on my shoulder flared. It was like every limb filled with lead. I couldn't move my legs, couldn't strike out at Morgan or even wipe my bloody hand on my shorts. I was a marionette in Gwydian's control, just like Morgan. Like all of us.

Gwydian *tsked*. Morgan released me, walking with Mom to Gwydian's side. I, however, stepped right into the center of the spell circle. Fear shuddered up through me, images and sounds replaying in my head with picture clarity. Dad, writhing in pain, his muscles growing, splitting open his skin until it hung in rags. Mom, scream-ing. Blood and magic, everywhere.

Mom moaned, and Gwydian released enough control for that moan to form words. "No, no, please—not her." Her eyes glittered. I watched, almost as horrified by the sight of her tears at the thought that, in minutes, I would be like Dad. Twisted into something horri-ble, and forced to kill until my body gave out.

Gwydian extended a hand, and those glowing veins seemed to extend from his fingers, shooting into the edge of the mandala. Violet spilled first around the outer edge, then spreading like fire to each progressive ring. I willed my legs to move. The muscles strained and pulled and I gritted my teeth against the resistance. We had been so close.

Gwydian chuckled, wagging a finger at Mom. "How long has it been since I had your husband on a mandala just like this? Four years? It doesn't seem like that long ago, but I suppose Helena was shorter." He combed Mom's hair behind her ear, streaking it with red. "You're a clever woman, Lola. I'd have thought you clever enough not to test me again. Didn't I warn you?"

He waited, as if she might respond. I sensed the surge of energy an instant before his face shifted. He backhanded her. Mom crashed into the wall. Hatred flashed through me, sharp and hot.

He seized her hair and all trace of kindness vanished as he tilted her head back. "Didn't I!?"

A choked whimper flooded up my throat. My foot moved another centimeter. I wanted to pin him down and use that knife to carve out his heart.

He stroked the tears from her bruised cheek, leaving smears of orangey blood on her face. "You should have known it would end up like this. What's that?"

He must have relaxed his hold on her enough to hear her speak.

"M-me," she said. A shaking hand took Gwydian's. "Me. Please...."

"Take you instead?" He tilted his head toward me. "Oh, poor Lola. The parent, sacrificing all for the child—so noble, yet so cliché. I suppose it's a cliché because it happens. Still, that goes against my purpose, which is teaching you what you failed to learn last time. There will be no defying me, no helping the Guild hunt me down and put a bullet in my head. You think I don't have ears in the Guild? I do. And they listen."

"Well, that's good to know. I'll bet it's Anderson," said a new voice.

Gwydian's head snapped toward it just as something heavy slammed into my back.

CHAPTER TWO

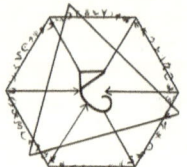

We landed hard, and wiry arms closed around my body, hauling me into a roll that brought us under the table. Gwydian gave an angry shout, and the next second Morgan's boots thundered past us. Bright spell flashes painted the underside of the table, even as I realized Gwydian had dropped the threads of power connected to my tattoo. He'd focus all his magic on a shield mandala —one of his many tattoos.

I twisted around, panic thrumming through me. Mom—was she safe? Where was she?

"Stay still!" Strong, spidery hands shoved me to the floor. I looked up, a growl on my lips, and found the Guild Sorcerer over me. He was tall and narrow, worn down to the sinews by magic. Studs pierced his eyebrows and lips and burned bright as constellations with amber power.

Fingers scrabbled at my shirt, tugging the tank top straps aside. I grabbed his wrist and twisted it.

"Ow, fuck!" the Sorcerer hissed. "Which one is it, then?"

Tattoo—he was after my slave tattoo. That was right. With the sweeping anger and fear, I had almost forgotten the plan. I jerked my chin at my right shoulder.

"It took you guys long enough!" I snapped.

"Your plans changed, so ours had to change too," he said. "We were expecting a little more-"

Morgan slammed into the table next to us, buffeted back by another spell. The dead girl slid off the tabletop and dropped beside us in a thick slump of limbs. Her open eyes stared straight at me.

"...help," the Sorcerer finished.

Morgan shoved off the table's edge, even as the Sorcerer's fingers found my shoulder. An electric pulse of magic shot into the circular design, and the glyphs lit up like fire. Then the glowing magic wheel lifted from my shoulder, a sparkling twin of the ink still embedded in my skin.

Gwydian's power burned violet and angry, arcs of energy branching between mandala and skin. The Sorcerer's hand shook. Amber power pushed back purple and, one at a time, the enslavement spell's tethers snapped away.

I craned my neck to see what was going on. Morgan was on one knee, hunting knife in hand. A second Sorcerer stood with one foot on the stairs, her opposite arm extended, power gleaming and crackling over the handle of a matte black Walther PPK.

She was just as emaciated and pierced and tatted up as the Sorcerer above me. All the metal on her flashed like LEDs, and the tracing of power in her veins made lightning patterns down her arms as she pushed magic into a shield mandala.

Morgan lunged, testing the shield with his knife. A clash of light, and he staggered back with a growl of pain, shoulders hunching.

That was when I heard dad's Baretta fire off a shot. Above me, the Sorcerer ducked. My pulse punched at the inside of my throat. I couldn't see Mom.

With a grunt of frustration, I grabbed the Sorcerer's jacket, locked a leg around his hip, and heaved his weight sideways. A holster dug into my thigh as I rolled on top.

And there was Mom. Her face was blank as she aimed and fired, aimed and fired. The bullets spanged off the Sorcereress's second mandala. Why hadn't she fired?

In an instant, I saw the answer—Mom and Morgan stood between the Sorceress and Gwydian, Human barriers to the Guild Enforcers' magic-laced bullets. There was no telling how many bullets it would take to drop Mom and Morgan. She didn't have a clear shot at Gwydian.

But I did.

The Sorcerer below me fought for dominance of my slave spell. My spirit felt unstable, whipped around like a flag in rough wind. I ignored it. I reached down and wrestled with the holster at his hip.

"What the-" he muttered, glancing under his arm at my hand as I freed the gun and twisted it into my grip.

It settled solid and heavy in my hand. I pulled it between us and dragged back the slide, chambering a bullet with a satisfying metallic ratchet. I wasn't as good a shot with my left hand, but Gwydian was mere yards away. I couldn't miss.

I lined up my sights and conjured three picture-perfect memories: the dead girl's face; my father's writhing, screaming form; and tears coursing over Mom's livid bruise.

This would be my last kill, and the only one I would lose zero sleep over.

My tattoo burned, and the Sorcerer grunted. For an instant, I thought it was the death throes of the enslavement tattoo breaking up under his power. Then my arm grew heavy.

No.

My hand lifted, turning that matte black barrel away from Gwydian. I resisted, hand trembling. Adrenaline-spiked blood thudded in my ears and, for a second, the gun pointed at the floor beside the Sorcerer's head. To his credit, those brown eyes didn't shift from my tattoo.

Pain throbbed in my head, a hot spike of violet. My arm gave out. The mandala-etched barrel shoved cold under my chin. My pulse throbbed against it, hard and desperate, as if it could defy fate. My finger tightened.

At least it was over.

A gut-wrenching tug jerked deep in my core. The enslavement spell flared, searing an amber ring into my eyes before going dark. A blown bulb, fading in my brain.

I barely had time to register what that meant. Warmth spread in my chest. A plume of turquoise fire filled my mind, ignited my veins like my blood was pure ethanol. I was blind with it.

Spidery fingers snatched my wrist. The Sorcerer twisted the gun from my grip and fired. The clap rang in my ears, and before I reacted, he spilled me sideways off of him. My elbow hit something soft, slick. The girl's body. I recoiled.

The Sorcerer fired again. Bright amber and blue flashed through the turquoise in my vision, clashing with the violet of Gwydian's magic.

I recoiled, willing my eyes to focus, to see anything but light. It was like breaking that enslavement spell had broken something else inside me, something that had been holding back this dense, pulsing flame. I squeezed my eyes shut, forced back the ringing thrum of electricity.

Focus, eyes. Focus, focus, *focus.*

I opened them and met the sight of the polished hardwood floor, an intricate mandala ruined by bloody boot-prints, and splintered fiberglass. Splintered real glass, too, because the whisky decanter and glasses had slid from the bar.

Gwydian stood against the door to the rear cabin, his grimoire clutched under one arm. A phalanx of mandalas surrounded him, flaming out from the tattoos on his wrists. He was flush with the dead girl's blood. It was enough power to turn me into a monster, or protect himself from a pair of Guild Sorcerers for a long while. But not both.

Luckily, he had turned me into a different monster long before the threat of this ruined mandala.

I concentrated on the tattoo on my left shoulder—the one with the trio of Celtic hounds chasing each other around the inner ring. I recalled the sight of the Irish wolfhound lying next to me six years ago, its blood and mine mixing on the mandala beneath us. Its spirit entering me, twining around my bones. Becoming us.

It was the power Gwydian had given my pack. The power the Sorcerers' Guild wanted, and which my mother had offered in trade for our freedom. A spell in that book.

The tattoo on my shoulder flared, not violet, but that searing aquamarine like the water around the Keys. I blinked, thinking for a moment that the vertigo had returned.

It didn't matter—I could see, and I didn't have time to think. The middle circle of the tattoo prickled and energy flowed toward the design, draining my chest and my limbs. I waited for the tipping point, my body growing weaker as the tattoo brimmed with power. Then, just when I thought the sound and shake of the fight would fade into oblivion, it happened.

Magic spilled from the mandala, racing backwards through my veins as it burned through the iron in my blood, searing straight into my heart.

My face ached. My bones went hot and malleable as forge-glowing iron. I felt the shift and bend of my jaw, the lengthening of my teeth, the shift of organs in their visceral cavities. Hair grew like pins and needles from my skin.

I willed the change to happen faster. My hearing was getting better, and Mom's voice still sounded in pained cries.

She was the most vulnerable person here. I had to protect her.

My nails hardened and hooked down into claws, and I stopped trembling with change. My body was no longer that of a seventeen-year-old girl, but an Irish Wolfhound of the same mass. As a human, I was just a rougher, taller cut of my mother with Dad's tawny hair and ski-jump nose, but as a hound I was battle-ready and vicious.

And prepared to take out Gwydian's throat.

I pawed off my jeans and shirt. Then my nails dug into the wood and I lunged from beneath the table. I tore across the ruined mandala, dodging around the streak of a spell from the Sorcereress still on the stairwell. I followed its glimmering trail, straight for Gwydian.

My teeth latched onto the edge of his protective shield mandala, which crackled around my teeth like a sparkler. Shapeshifting was a handy skill, but this was the real reason we were so valuable to Gwydian, and so dangerous to the Guild.

The mandala pulsed, and burst. Violet light sent constellations across my vision, but I still made out Gwydian's silhouette. The muscles in my legs coiled. My lips curled back, exposing teeth that longed for the crunch of something more solid than magic.

I exploded forward. Gwydian's livid blue eyes flashed, and he swung the book, but I was ready. My jaws closed around salty leather, my weight ripping it from his hands. I knew an instant of triumph before a rough grip caught me by the throat.

Morgan hurled me backwards. I crashed into the table, releasing the book with a bark of pain. The Guild Enforcer lunged, a shield springing from the tattoo on his hand even as Mom fired. Bullets clinked to the floor in tiny blossoms of metal.

The Sorcerer scooped up the book and dashed for the stairs.

Mom fired off two more. I'd lost count of how many bullets she had, but it wouldn't be enough. The Sorcerer ducked around his partner's shield, which spat mom's shots back into the wood paneling. He sprinted up the stairs, Morgan on his heels.

I was the only one not being controlled, spelled, or shot at. With the chaos distracting Gwydian, this could be my only chance to kill him. I clambered to all fours and slunk around the table.

Gwydian heaved a spell at the Sorcereress's shield. The two forces crackled together, twin circuits of energy battling. They cracked and spiraled out in a pinwheel of lightning. Through the wash of light, the Sorcereress fired her gun. The bullet struck Gwydian's shield and hissed. Molten metal dripped to the floor, smoking.

I tensed, ready to spring, but Gwydian's skin lit up with a clutch of tattoos. I scrambled back—in the years I'd been part of magic battles, I'd never seen someone prime so many spells at once.

He fired them all. Across the planks, the Sorcereress hurled herself to the floor.

Gwydian's spells struck in a flurry of light and fire and chaos. Glass shattered, speakers and books toppled from shelves, and chunks of wood and fiberglass flurried in the air.

The explosion settled. I looked up from my hiding place. Gwydian hunched against the wall, breath heaving. By the stairs, the Sorcereress struggled to remove the magazine from her gun. Shrapnel littered her body and her arm hemorrhaged around a curving fragment of decanter.

I saw the moment Gwydian noticed her wound. His blue eyes sharpened, and a smile curled onto his handsome face.

He extended his hand. I lunged.

My teeth sank into flesh, the taste of blood and linen filled my mouth. The bone cracked in my jaws.

His scream raked my ears. He staggered but I held on, shoving the full weight of my canine form into him. I pinned him in place and willed the Sorcereress to fire now, while he focused on me. While I had him-

A gunshot, followed by a thudding impact in my shoulder. I was down before I registered the pain. For a moment, I lay there on my side, staring at the petite, blonde woman with the barrel of her gun still aimed at the place I'd been. Her face was twisted, teeth bared in a grimace.

I heard her guttural scream through the haze of shock.

It was just my shoulder. The long bone of my scapula curving over my ribcage, protecting my heart. She could have shot me in the skull. She had probably aimed for it, fought it. Hit lower instead.

I tried to call out and tell her I was okay. It came out a whine. That's right. Paws, tail, muzzle. I was a dog right now.

I didn't think about transforming back, I just did it. Somehow, it was easy. Then I was curled naked at Gwydian's feet, my shoulder a mess of blood where the bullet had torn through the remaining ink of my enslavement tattoo.

A second gunshot rang out at the exact moment the TV over Gwydian's head let out a shower of sparks. The Sorcereress collapsed onto her bleeding elbow, her black gun shaking at the end of her reach.

I relaxed, knowing the next seconds would bring freedom, at last.

Small, rugged boots staggered into me. Mom's legs knocked me aside. I looked up to see Gwydian's uninjured arm around her neck, holding her in front of him.

I reached for her, missed. Panic jolted through the haze of shock, and I swung my gaze to the Sorcereress.

"Wait," I said, but it was like a nightmare—the words came out mangled and watery. "Wait, wait!"

The Sorcereress blinked as if batting away my words with her eyelashes. I watched the moment she decided to pull the trigger anyway.

My whole world balanced on the sharp tip of an instant and then, with a sharp *crack*, changed forever.

CHAPTER THREE

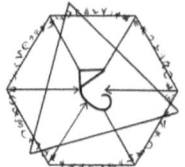

I felt the jerk of Mom's legs, saw her knees buckle, but she didn't fall. Then the sound of a second shot. And a third.

Gwydian cried out, and for the second time that night, the body of a woman dropped next to me, dead eyes staring. Flat green, dead as emerald. And there was a hole the size of a thumbtack underneath her eye. I stared at it, fingers moving without my permission, as if I could brush it away.

Something grabbed my hair, hauling me up with shocking force and pain. Gwydian's bloody arm slid trembling around my neck.

Or it tried to.

I'm not sure what came over me then—I should have been a rag doll of horror, but I grabbed Gwydian's arm, heaved my weight forward, and hurled him over my shoulder at the Sorceress.

Magic-use made him light and adrenaline strengthened my throw. He hit the edge of his own mandala and tumbled into the Sorceress. I dropped to my knees, grabbed mom's face in my hands. Her skin was still warm. A moan strangled off in my throat —I had seen this happen too much to hold onto hope. I had to move.

I grabbed dad's Baretta from her cold fingers and bolted up the stairs.

Hot salt air struck my face as I shoved through the door onto the deck. An orange moon hung full over the ocean, spilling just enough light to illuminate the two figures hunkered at the bow. One was enormous, long blond ponytail ripped forward by the wind, the other slender and glimmering with the barest hint of amber power.

I staggered onto the upper deck and let the hatch fall closed behind me, breath sharp in my throat. Part of me wanted to shove something over it or lock it in case Gwydian defeated the Sorcereress and came up after me. But my brain kept stalling out, my gaze flicking from Morgan and the Guild Enforcer, to the piles of rope and sailing paraphernalia scattered on deck, unable to form a plan.

Morgan hadn't moved. I stepped toward him, and the Sorcerer's gun swung toward me. He scanned my naked body, blinking hard. He'd have seen us transform before, but I didn't fit the scarred ex-mercenary profile. I guess I couldn't blame him. At last, his eyes fixed on the bullet wound leaking blood down my shoulder.

"Is he dead?" the Sorcerer demanded.

I shook my head. The Sorcerer cursed. He held a bag in one hand —one of the waterproof bags the gang members used to bring clothes and guns with us when we swam from boat to shore. It bulged, the thick corner of Gwydian's grimoire pressing out against the nylon.

I stared at the barrel of his gun, remembering when he'd wrestled it from my hand and shot at Gwydian. Dad's Beretta warmed in my hand.

The other Guild Enforcer shot Mom. Downstairs. She'd shot her.

Through the dizzy haze, it occurred to me that this shouldn't have happened. The Guild should have helped us go free. We'd known there was risk in trying to kill Gwydian, but we banked on the Sorcers' help.

Part of me hadn't trusted the Guild, but I hadn't realized how much I was using cynicism as a mask for hope. Hope that now grew cold in the hold below.

"You...you shot her," I said. The Sorcerer's pierced brow pinched. "You—I mean, her. Your friend. She shot her—Mom. She shot my Mom." The words came out jumbled and disorganized. My vision blurred. I glanced over the starboard gunwale. The Miami skyline made a serrated jag of concrete and neon against the sky.

A flicker of turquoise brightened my vision, pulsing with my heartbeat. The pain in my shoulder spiked, but my mind cleared.

Though the Sorcerer still leveled the gun at me, he seemed hesitant to shoot. I stared back and shook my head, mouth parted as if I could express the rising tide of horror. Strands of hair whipped my cheeks.

"We had an agreement," I whispered, even as dread and certainty hardened in my chest.

He shifted his grip on the gun. "Your mom was still under his control," he said. "She knew the risk."

I lifted dad's Beretta. The Enforcer's dark eyes widened, and his gun wavered. If he'd noticed the gun, he hadn't expected me to turn on him.

"She shot her in the face," I growled. "Twice more in the chest, because Gwydian was using her as a shield. Maybe if she'd actually hit him...." But no. Even that wouldn't have mattered. The Sorceress had dismissed Mom as a slab of meat barring her from Gwydian. I shook my head again. "You were the good guys. We thought you'd help us. This is what I'd expect from Gwydian."

Morgan stepped forward. My momentary relief shattered as he approached the Sorcerer, tattoo glowing. Not with Gwydian's violet power, but with the same amber fire I'd felt when the Sorcerer had freed me. I stiffened.

"Morgan...." But my throat closed on the plea when my cousin stepped between me and the Sorcerer. If he'd put his back to me, it wouldn't have been shocking. He'd be facing off my enemy, protecting me, like he always had. Instead he faced me, grip tight on his hunting knife.

My throat throbbed. A quick rush of panic and anger flooded into my head, bringing with it a haze of turquoise that haloed everything.

"Sorry, kid," the Sorcerer said. "None of you were supposed to make it off this ship."

I swallowed, staring into my cousin's steely eyes as if it were him talking, and not the Sorcerer behind him. Of course they wouldn't let us go. How naïve to think we could trust them.

Though it pointed at Morgan, I held Dad's gun surprisingly steady and fought the brightness inside me. I buried the fear of what might burn in my veins.

"We may have done a thousand terrible things," I said. "But none of it was our choice. Mom was a biologist. Do you think she wanted to spend the last fifteen years of her life sewing up bullet holes and watching her daughter slit throats?"

"Doesn't matter what any of you wanted," he said. "You don't rehabilitate pit bulls once they've learned to fight. Can't trust them not to fight. It's possible for you—you're young. You have power. But not the others."

"Morgan's only five years older," I said.

"This guy? Not a chance. You know how many Sorcerers he's killed?"

"Morgan has killed no one Gwydian didn't-"

"Sixteen, last count. Sixteen Guild Sorcerers with full training. Four of them were Enforcers. No, he can't stay on the board."

Now the gun was shaking in my grip, each thud of my heart against my sternum sending a swell of light behind my eyes. It pulsed like a headache, like the blinking numbers on an alarm clock.

"What did you do to me?" I said. "This light. What spell is this? What's happening to me?"

The Sorcerer hesitated. I heard the splinter and thud of the continued fight in the hold.

"You really don't know?" he said. The next moment, he leaned around Morgan, gun preceding him as he stepped to the side. I shifted my gun with him, but he didn't seem to care. He scanned me, and then his mouth twitched into a disbelieving half smile. There was only exhaustion in it. "You've got magic, kid. Trapped under that slave tattoo, tethered to him. He was sipping off you this whole time, like a cute little energy drink."

I stepped back, as if to dodge the information before it reached me. It found me anyway. Mom's death, my freedom from Gwydian, the Guild's betrayal. Now this. The facts sat sharp and heavy in my head.

Turquoise light threaded through me, pulsing at the edges of my vision. Magic. I had magic. Just like the Guild Sorcerers. Just like Gwydian. Heat rushed to my face.

"They might make an exception for you," the Sorcerer said. "You could train as a Guild Sorcerer. With your skills, you'd make a good Enforcer someday. You could help–"

"And the others?" I demanded. "My pack? Will you make exceptions for them?"

His expression darkened, and the ship rocked on a hard swell. Or maybe that was realization making me lightheaded. "If you've hurt them, I swear...." My finger moved to the trigger.

Lightning fast, Morgan's free hand knocked my arm up. I fired, heard the bullet clang off the gunwale as he bore me to the ground and shoved his hunting knife up under my throat. I shrieked, pain arcing through me from my injured shoulder. Morgan's hand shook, the knife drawing back just enough to keep from cutting into the skin. His face reddened, a vein throbbing over his temple. Blond hair swung down and dragged through the blood on my shoulder.

I remembered Gwydian's fingers, carding red streaks through Mom's curls.

A scream worked its way up from the ocean floor, building inside my chest like a tidal wave. It surged through my veins, spilling across my tattoos and rushing from my body in a single, furious crash. For an instant, a mandala burned in my brain. It drew itself in perfect precision, following the exact pattern I had watched Gwydian tattoo onto his own skin.

The deck exploded into turquoise fire. It knocked the Sorcerer backwards and sheeted across the deck. Everything lit up—the seats, metal rails, steering cabin. Glass shattered, and turquoise fire leapt, spreading to rope and canvas.

I curled in on myself as the heat flared against my skin. The blade at my throat disappeared, and Morgan was over me, big arms crushing me into his chest as he blocked me from the fire.

He was free, which meant....

I shoved Morgan with my good arm. "Get off," I said, adrenaline spiking through me. He relinquished his hold, rolling to his feet as I leapt forward to where the Guild Enforcer lay, a mandala seared into the flesh of his narrow chest. I smelled his cooking skin and choked back the need to gag. Reaching down, I snagged the waterproof bag from his hand.

"Aunt Lola," Morgan said, his voice uncharacteristically thin. "She's—"

"Dead." I said, refusing to feel the brutality of my own harsh word. Morgan made for the hold.

"Morgan, no! Gwydian was still alive when I left."

"We should make sure he doesn't stay that way."

I couldn't disagree. But, fierce as he looked standing stark and angry before the Miami silhouette, I still didn't want him going down there. He was my only remaining family. If he went down there, Gwydian could enslave him again. There had to be another way.

My eyes landed on the steering console. An idea leapt into my head.

"We need to raise anchor," I said, staggering beneath the canopy that covered the helm. Morgan went to work on the anchor and I started up the engine.

More waterproof bags lounged against the benches. I snagged the one with my clothes in it and, with agonized cursing, pulled a sports bra over my damaged shoulder. Shorts came next. I released the magazine from dad's gun and ejected the chambered round. It pinged off the floor and rolled toward the stern as I shoved the gun and magazine into the bag with the rest of my clothes.

My injured shoulder throbbed, though not as much as it should have. I shuddered, glancing toward the still-closed hatch. It had gone quiet, but I didn't trust that silence. With the motor now rumbling through the fiberglass beneath me, I used my good arm to steer us toward the harbor.

A forest of masts rose from sailboats, and the windows of other motor yachts gleamed silent and serene as Miami bay's inky water rippled around their hulls. I steered us a notch to starboard, where the harbor's docks vanished, shifting into concrete and rock that buttressed the land against the attentions of the changeable Atlantic.

Morgan made his way over while I checked the fuel gauge and retrieved a rifle from under the bench. He followed my gaze to the barrier. Comprehension dawned with a furrowed brow.

"Can you swim right now?" he asked. His fingers hovered over my shoulder.

"I hope so," I said. "Since I'm about to send this piece of shit up in flames." I peered farther along the coast, where a craggy finger of uneven stones jutted out into the water, breaking up the black bay. Beyond the tangle of low, marshy trees was an access road we'd used many times climbing out of this bay.

I aimed the yacht's bow toward the concrete barrier and sent the engines burbling with sudden power. I opened the throttle. We picked up speed, wind tearing at our hair and clothes as I grabbed the rifle and jammed it through the wheel to keep the boat on course.

Morgan took my bag and the one containing Gwydian's grimoire. We took off toward the rear of the boat.

The boat thudded over waves, over a hundred feet of fiberglass, metal, and electronics careening toward shore. Morgan hesitated, one boot up on the rail, watching as if to make certain I jumped. Below, our wake churned the water into snarls of white and reflected neon lights, like magic swirling out of control. Like it would swallow us up.

We were two hundred meters from shore—too close. We had to

jump, now. I tucked my injured arm against my chest and called up the image of my mother's face.

I'm sorry, Mom, I thought, before leaping into the air and, a heartbeat later, crashing into the bay. The water rushed over me, filling my nose and raking cool fingers against my scalp. It jammed its claws into my shoulder, my ribs, but slid cradling arms to hold me safe.

I don't know how long I hung there, my hair floating around my face like seaweed. Then the concussion hit—a shudder in the ocean, and a blossom of orange flaming through the water. A silhouette reached me, and then a hand snagged my elbow, hauling me to the surface as a second eruption shuddered through the air.

The yacht was a diesel-fed inferno, and with it burned the bodies of my master, my mother, and the Guild Sorcerers, who never intended to set us free.

It was time to warn my pack. Time to run.

CHAPTER FOUR

W e flew through traffic; the party night gridlock in Miami was passable on a motorcycle if you weren't scared to nip down alleys and battle drunks for sidewalk space. I refused to think. Not about the burning yacht, or the bullet in my shoulder, or the new brightness of turquoise fire in my chest. Not about my mother's body, which was ash in the bay by now.

My hastily donned shirt snapped against wet skin, and my boots skidded against asphalt as Morgan laid the bike down on almost every turn. We doubled back in a frantic heat-run as if Gwydian's ghost could follow us. When the bike growled to a halt at the warehouse, I slung my legs off. My muscles were like jelly, and the instant I slid to the ground, my knees gave out. I caught at the seat for balance, and Morgan steadied the bike until I found enough strength to stand.

Morgan raised his eyebrows, and I nodded to show I was fine. I had to be.

I scanned the area, skipping off familiar industrial warehouses and loading cranes, stacked cargo pods and heavy rolls of industrial steel wire. Nothing stood out, but I couldn't shake the caution nipping at my neck. The hair on my arms prickled, and it wasn't just wind on wet-skin.

"Back way," I whispered. Morgan, grave and long-faced as a wolf, drew his remaining hunting knife. I took the lead, moving from shadow to shadow.

We didn't live at this warehouse anymore, but we had once, three years ago. The Guild no longer watched it, so it had been the ideal spot to meet after the fight. We'd planned to leave from here and head north, use our fake IDs and passports to get into Canada. All last week, we'd packed and moved necessities, stashing them in this place that had once been our home, so we could escape and find a new one.

I ducked from an alley and slipped under a tarp lashed over the back door. My brain fizzed with exhaustion, and I was so hungry I could barely see. Soon, I would be in the relative safety of my pack, and I could take care of my body's needs. Injuries. Food. Rest would come later. I knocked once, waited a beat, then knocked three more times before opening the door.

I stepped into the darkness and day-ripened heat of a metal room. The quiet pressed in, and I couldn't tell if I was hearing the hushed sound of many quieted breaths, or the soft rustle of wind.

"It's us," I said. My voice vanished into the shadows. "Eamon?" But my Godfather didn't respond.

Something hardened in my throat, and I stepped forward, tensed and ready to dive to the floor. I paced forward until my outstretched hand caught the cool slip of a ball-chain and pulled it.

Light expanded onto dusty concrete, revealing a circle of boot and paw prints. Above, the naked bulb sung from an orange electrical wire. On each swing, it picked out the warehouse's empty corners and the broken pallets left behind by past tenants.

I gazed at a cracked panel in the wall, and beside it, something shiny on the floor.

"They must have seen the explosion and gone," Morgan said. I wanted to agree, but couldn't. The Enforcer had been clear about killing my pack. Morgan crouched to examine the footprints.

I headed for the broken panel. Up close, the shiny object proved to be a small key—the kind used for lockers at train stations or gyms. I snatched it up, not daring to let the stirrings of relief quite reach my heart.

"Eamon left us a key," I said.

Morgan pushed to his feet. "That's the signal. Is it North or South station?" he asked, crossing the space between us.

"North." Mom and Eamon had chosen several potential rendezvous points, but had planned not to decide which to use until the last moment. All I knew, all anyone knew, was South meant we were to head to South America and North meant we should run for Canada.

Morgan took the key and held it as though it might change in his hands. "So, Canada. Which is stupid. We're closer to Cuba or Mexico."

"That's a lot more expected." I crouched by the broken panel, lifting aside the sheet of tin to reach into the dark space. Three backpacks awaited us—another good sign.

I dragged Mom's from the space last. It was a dark, worn blue, still stamped with the name of her university. I spread my fingers against the front pocket and clenched my jaw. This twenty pound backpack of clothes and coins and makeup were all I had left of her. The bag of things my dead mother couldn't live without.

The contents of my backpack seemed pointless in comparison, but I shuffled over clothing, rolling them up tight beside my mom's things in the bottom of the bag. I took my sketchbook, my fake passport and IDs, and the piece of sea-glass Dad had given me. And a picture, in a cheap plastic frame.

The photograph's uneven bars of pigment did poor justice to its occupants. Mom and Dad sat together in the back of a car, leaning in as someone captured what must have been a happy moment, before Gwydian ruined them. Before I was around to worry about. It was the only picture of them I'd ever seen; ours wasn't a life much worth documenting.

I left everything else. I dug the book from its waterproof bag and wedged it in on top.

"You're taking that thing?"

I glanced up at Morgan, startled. "I didn't drag it with us for thrills."

Brow furrowed, he rifled through the contents of his own bag, taking the time to collect his words. He set aside a plastic baggie with a burner phone, another with a roll of cash, four knives, and a tangle of holsters and straps.

"What?" I demanded.

At my hard tone, he gave a little jerk of his head then paused, holding a box of power bars. At last he said, "We don't need them chasing us."

I lifted a hand toward the door. "Dude. They're already chasing us."

"So we should leave that book. You—I know right now you're-"

"I'm what? Pissed off? Murderous? Ready to fucking kill any Sorcerer I see? Because I am all those things. And I'm also not willing to give my mother's murderers what they want."

My vision twisted as I glared into Morgan's gray eyes. I needed food and rest. I needed this wound on my shoulder seen to.

"Even with Gwydian gone, they can just prime our tattoos and and re-enslave us. That one on the deck did it to you. We've gotta destroy the design so the spell won't work and tell the others to do it too."

The adrenaline was fading, and something new burned in my chest. The Sorcereress's gun, pointed at my mother. Three shots. She hadn't even hesitated.

"If we don't want that to happen, we need to escape. The book makes the perfect distraction. Just leave it and run," Morgan said. "They can't catch us if we run—not all of us."

"I'm counting on them catching me." My hands clenched in my mother's backpack.

"You want to fight them?"

"They shot her! *In the face.*"

The words came out strangled, but in the following silence, I heard them echo in my head. In my mind, it was a scream. They shot her. They shot her. They shot Mom.

Morgan closed his eyes for a beat. His pulse jumped in his neck.

I felt the simultaneous smallness and bigness of the warehouse, the stifling air, the darkness around our puddle of light. Those walls were such thin metal—I'd seen ones like them peppered with bullet-holes until they looked like giant drain-covers. The Sorcerers were out there now. I was the only reason this wasn't a death-chamber.

I stood up, Mom's bag hanging from my hand. "They're just a different gang pretending to be the good guys. I'm not giving the book to them." I swallowed and closed my eyes, dreading what I needed to say next.

Because Morgan was right. Without the book, the Guild might give us up for lost—they'd leave us alone. But they wanted these spells more than anything else, and if they realized I'd escaped with the book, they'd never give up hunting us.

Which meant I had to choose. Give Mom's murderers what they wanted, or protect my pack by staying away from them.

Morgan stood, blocking out the light with his shoulders. I stared at a little aberration of thread on his black shirt instead of at his eyes.

"You have to warn them," I said. "Eamon, and the others. Tell them what happened, and that the Guild broke their word, and they have to destroy their tattoos. Tell them Mom's... that she's gone. And I won't let them have the spells. I-"

"You're not going off alone."

"They can't have these!" I shook the bag with its dangerous contents. "Do you know what's in here? It's not just the spell that made us! It's the enslavement spell. It's the *Hellhound* spell. No one should have that!"

I ignored the look piercing my cheek. I had to stay mad. It kept me moving.

Morgan shouldered his bag. "I'll go with you."

That made me look up. His hair had dried, cleaned of blood during his swim to shore. His long, solemn expression held mine. I swallowed.

"One person's harder to track."

"We can split up," he said. "Give me the book."

I shouldn't consider the offer, but it would be nice not to be alone. Was I willing to risk his life? I looked up at those cold eyes, the ones that had gone dead so he could live with all he'd done. He deserved to leave this life. Maybe more than anyone. I couldn't let him come.

"I'll be fine," I said. "The pack needs you. More than I do. Traveling as a group is more dangerous."

He didn't argue, just stayed standing before me as I fished out my burner phone and zipped the front pouch. Then he extended his hand, proffering a solid steel butterfly knife and a thin roll of hundred dollar bills.

"I won't need them as much as you."

My lungs stopped working a moment, but his hand stayed outstretched until I took the knife and the cash. Between the money my mother had saved, what Eamon had stashed in my backpack, and Morgan's offering, I'd have two thousand dollars. I had a feeling it would go faster than expected.

"Take the Beretta," I said, shoving the second of the waterproof bags toward him.

It killed me to give up dad's gun, but I wouldn't leave Morgan without one. Not after the Enforcer had talked about him like a rabid dog.

"There's only one magazine, though. You'll have to find more ammo somewhere." I shifted my bag, wincing as my shoulder burned. "You're a better shot anyway."

I slid the knife between my sock and boot and the small roll of hundreds into my bra. Morgan's fingers found my shoulder, probing at the edge of the wound.

"When did they heal you?" he asked.

Startled, I glanced down, looking where he'd pulled up the sleeve of my shirt. I'd imagined a fresh bullet wound, but instead, there was a dark scab over a messy matrix of bright pink tissue. It looked several days old.

I tensed, shaking my head even as my brain reeled back through the past few hours, grasping for explanation. "I don't know, I..." He looked down at me, eyes cool as ever.

"You have magic too," he said. "It might've been instinct."

I shuddered, wishing he hadn't reminded me of the unpleasant fact that, in some ways, I was like the Guild.

I needed to move. If they knew about the yacht, they'd come to take control of the pack soon. I touched my wounded shoulder. At least the bullet destroyed the tattoo. They could never control me now.

I accepted a black windbreaker, slung my mom's backpack over my good shoulder, and walked to one of the warehouse's two doors. Morgan strode to the other.

Then we slipped from the warehouse, into cooling sea wind, and vanished into the night.

CHAPTER FIVE

I leaned the bike into a hard swerve. A streak of crimson slashed past my boots, blistering the asphalt to the left with a molten red mandala. An instant later, and that would have been my tires.

I forced out a breath and burned past the pothole, shifting my weight left and right. The bike growled and jerked beneath me, raging against my exhaustion. When the Guild Sorcerer said they wouldn't let us go, I'd thought they'd just enslave us again. But they didn't seem interested in taking prisoners.

They did, however, want the book intact. That was the only thing keeping me safe from a body shot or a spelled bullet.

An acid green mandala slammed the asphalt ahead of me and burst, sending a shower of sparks into my face. I ducked behind my arm, felt angry cinders sear my crown and knuckles. Panic lifted in my gut, but I forced it down. It was just pain. Just collateral sparks. They needed a direct hit to do real damage.

Think, Helena. The spell had come from above, which meant they were on top of the warehouses. A perimeter. That might work in my favor—they wouldn't be fast. I could lose them. It also meant they'd be ready to intercept my scattering pack, who didn't have a priceless book on their backs and 989 CCs of angry crotch rocket growling beneath them.

I locked down that worry. Now was the time to focus. If they'd set up a perimeter, they'd set up someone to—

Headlights flicked on ahead, followed by the low, juddering start of high-horsepower engines. I roared past, just as the driver slammed his foot on the pedal and launched the vehicle out of the alley.

A fresh wave of electricity crackled up my spine and I ducked low behind the windscreen. High beams cut past me, throwing my shadow out ahead. I felt the roar of a pursuing vehicle—a truck or a hummer, there wasn't time to study it. It was gunning forward, a tiger on my heels.

The time for maneuvering was over. I opened the throttle.

The warehouses sat low and long, broken up by the occasional side roads or streetlamp. I had to get back to populated areas, where their own code of secrecy would force the Sorcerers to stop firing spells. I needed to go west. West and north, to the suburbs.

Someone shouted behind me. A quick glance in my mirror revealed shadows, leaning out beyond the glare of headlights. I zipped right, clawing for a strategy. I couldn't lay this thing down like Morgan, and I was going way too fast to turn in such a narrow chute.

That was it. I clenched my teeth and moved to the right, swerving like I had before, losing speed. The vehicle—a shiny black Hummer rendered inconspicuous in this party-mad city—moved up next to me, revealing a man with a heavy black gun, training on my head.

I dropped off the throttle. The hummer raged past me, and I didn't stop to see how long it would take them to slow down, realize they couldn't turn around. I pulled a dangerously fast U-turn, scraping my knee on the road, and took off back the way I'd come. The crack of a gunshot followed, then the spark of a ricochet off a steel post.

In seconds, I was out of gun range, hurtling back toward the perimeter. A side road opened on my right, and I skidded into it. I zipped through the night, ears open for the hummer, cutting west every few streets and doubling back until I was certain the Sorcerers were off my tail.

Warehouses transitioned to gas-stations, motels, and surf shops. Crumbling asphalt shifted to something better maintained, though still radiating tarry fumes of absorbed heat. Industry gave way to low-slung suburbia, where moonlight glowed off sandy yards and turned every clump of pampas grass into a treacherous silhouette. When I emerged onto NW 37th St., I opened her up, heedless of speed limits and lack of helmet.

When at last the tracks appeared ahead, I let my muscles relax their iron grip on my spine. The glowing sign of Miami Amtrak shone like a beacon ahead.

In the parking lot, I climbed off the bike with heavy, shaken limbs, and gave the hot console a pat of gratitude. It was a nimble escape vehicle, but it wouldn't keep me anonymous. The Guild would have the plates. I could take those off or switch them, but it wouldn't take long for the police to stop me, especially once I crossed state lines.

I considered the tracks. Mom and I had planned to continue down them on foot, hop the scheduled freight train north. Fog threatened at the corners of my brain and my body ached, pains both dull and sharp prodding at every limb.

I gave the station entrance a long look. It would be such a relief to sit, to let the train's sway and the clack of the rails lull me to sleep. I had money—enough for a sleeper.

I swallowed, took a step toward the doors. A train headed to Fort Lauderdale in twenty minutes. One glance at the timetables posted online had been enough for me to memorize the schedules. I didn't have that kind of memory for everything, but patterns and pictures stuck with me. Dad had been the same way, and it proved itself damn useful in situations like this. Mom did the talking, I memorized the details.

I deserved rest and privacy. A chance to process all this shit. My hand fell on the ticketing office door, but I paused, the black memory of Mom's face, with its dark little bullet hole, rose in my mind.

Even with fake IDs, the Guild will track us. They'll see the bike. They'll be at every station.

The words echoed in her voice. Even burned to bones, sinking in the wreck of a yacht in Miami bay, she was still helping me.

I drew a shaky breath and, keeping my face turned down, glanced at the ceiling on my right and found the security camera.

"Shit." My voice sounded surprising over the groan of traffic in the distance—too human in this night-world of asphalt and machines. I drew my hand from the door handle, checked the time on my phone, then squinted at the jumble of tracks in the distance. That train to Ft. Lauderdale would board in twenty minutes.

Weeks of researching escape plans had turned up an interesting discovery: Amtrak's rails were mostly owned by freight companies, which rented out their use to passenger trains. We chose this spot because it was the easiest way to find the right track, but I hadn't considered its usefulness in misdirection. An idea gathered in my head, and before it fully formed, I pulled open the station door.

Thirty minutes later, I collapsed under the roaring overpass of highway 924, a ticket to Rhode Island going sweaty in my palm. I'd jogged perhaps a mile down the tracks, passing the loading yard of the freight company that owned this stretch of rail. It was a convenient hiding spot—far enough from the Amtrak station that I didn't think the Sorcerers' Guild would look for me, yet close enough to the freight station that any trains pulling out would still be slow, navigating the track's joins and splits.

I shredded the ticket in shaking fingers. With any luck, the Guild would spread out down the route to Rhode Island, waiting to pounce at every stop.

I leaned back on the scummy concrete and shivered, though the darkened air was still in the seventies. I wished I could get a glimpse of the stars, but I shut down that possibility. They'd only remind me of Dad, and then of Mom. I'd been channeling my feelings into fighting, into running. I couldn't let myself give into them yet.

A cool tide was working its way into my core, waves of numbness creeping ever higher. I still didn't feel it. Images of Mom flashed behind my eyes every time I blinked, but I didn't feel the life-cracking horror you should feel when your parents died. Now, it was just a low-grade nausea. Hadn't I loved her? Why wasn't I screaming and raging and sobbing like the world was ending?

I stared at my hands. Dirty fingers intertwined, they looked like foreign things—they looked like they belonged to someone else. I pulled the backpack up into my lap and shoved aside the book, still in its waterproof bag. I dug out my burner phone and tapped out a text to Morgan and Eamon, hoping it would get through to both: SAFE.

I was shaking. I should eat and drink a bottle of water. My pulse was invading my skull.

I crammed donuts in my mouth whole, chewing and swallowing until I inhaled powdered sugar and forced myself to slow down. After surviving fourteen years as a slave to Gwydian, choking on a powdered donut would be a stupid fucking way to die.

When I'd eaten most of the bag, my two-way radio crackled and emitted a string of train-yard lingo. These past two weeks, I'd done my homework, sneaking around the freight yard in the evenings, finding out which hobos and yard workers would drop information, learning to beware the rolling cars. I didn't know most of the coded terms, but I recognized enough. The train was coming.

I crumpled the bag around the remaining donuts and shoved them back in my backpack. A headlight broke through the palms. It was a straight line down the tracks—not much curve to account for, except the distortion of distance. It was big. I hadn't thought about how big it would be until just now—thousands of tons of steel and inertia. I stepped back into the fronds of an elephant-ear plant.

It closed in. Arteries in my neck throbbing, I dug in my toes and prepped to run.

The engine thundered past. I squinted into the wind, looking down the line for a likely car.

We'd practiced this. Mom's hand pushing me forward, up to speed. *Grab on and don't let go—pick up your feet.*

I saw the inverted rhombus of a grainer car and broke from my hiding spot. I ran. Fear quickened my veins, sharpened my vision. I saw the porch-like grate, the handle, the step. I lurched toward it and grabbed hold. A few paces more and I pushed off the ground. My injured shoulder screamed. I sensed the ground rushing below me, the train's deadly forward motion. With a last burst of effort, I drew my knees up and got a foot on the step.

I hauled myself to safety, collapsing on the cross-hatched metal stoop just as the northbound freight picked up speed. I tucked myself into the car's yawning chute, stowing the backpack inside.

Moments later, the tracks broke free of the trees and snaked into a jungle of concrete and metal. It all flew past me: sprawling stucco neighborhoods, the shimmer of residual heat rising off the asphalt, the smell of cocoa butter, cigarettes, and tar.

I'd have sworn I hated Miami. It hadn't been a kind home, or a safe one. But it was what I knew—all beach and crumbled asphalt, palms and snakes and everglades, and the smell of trash heating in the oven of summer. I didn't know if I'd miss the oiled bodies and oiled guns, but at least I knew how to stay on the right side of them.

This train hauled me toward places I'd never seen. My future was unclear as the light-polluted sky. I took a breath, memorized the teeth of Miami's skyline. My mother's resting place.

Maybe someday I'd tell them both a proper goodbye.

CHAPTER SIX

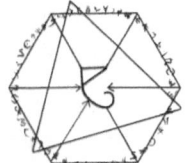

I changed trains in Manassas, and the second freight took me all the way to Chicago, where I discovered that northern autumns don't fuck around. The wind froze the metal grainer car, so I shed my clothing and transformed into a hound. My shaggy fur made for welcome insulation in the frigid Illinois dawn.

We flashed through suburbs until skyscrapers pushed above the low-slung shops, highlighted by the rising sun. Buildings grew larger and more uniform, corporate blocks of concrete and glass dripping with condensation. I spotted few glyphs among the graffiti tags. Maybe the Guild's Chicago branch wasn't as organized as Miami's. I could only hope.

The train pulled into an enormous freight yard. I wrestled the zipper on my backpack shut and leapt onto the tracks with the top handle in my mouth. If any yard workers saw me, they didn't pursue.

The rail-side gravel was cold and sharp on the pads of my feet. The tracks rode low on the city's landscape, bordered by a river on one side and a large embankment on the other. The built-up roads atop the embankment rumbled with the pulse of city life. It was weird to see a city on so many levels—I was so used to Miami's flatness. Before now, a city with an underground infrastructure had only existed in theory.

I found a parking deck with a lower level that butted up against the gravel. It was empty but for service vehicles, so I hopped the concrete barrier, ducked behind a white security van, and transformed. Goosebumps crept down my arms. Crouching on damp concrete, I hauled on clothes, but they were worthless in the morning chill.

I needed to get above ground, find a place to buy food and warmer gear.

As I shoved the book deeper into my backpack, my hand knocked against the burner phone. I clicked it on. Eamon had responded! Relief rushed through me as I walked to the parking lot's elevator.

RDVZ at Lola's hometown. Will send message on arrival.

I stepped into the elevator and hit the button for ground level, my eyes burning. If Eamon was okay, the rest of my pack probably was. The Sorcerers hadn't caught them.

And the rendezvous point made sense. Mom had grown up in a small college town in Minnesota, where her grandparents had raised her and her twin brother—Morgan's dad—until they moved to Florida for University. As far as I knew, those great grandparents were dead.

At least the Guild wouldn't trace connections or have anyone's wellbeing to hold over my head, but that was small comfort.

I strode from the parking garage onto a busy thoroughfare. It was still a mile or two from the larger skyscrapers, but South Canal Street clearly serviced a good number of families. Everywhere I looked, people strolled in fast-paced herds, hunched against the wind while carrying Whole Foods bags and chatting on cell phones at the crosswalk. Children too small to be in school waddled along in bright parkas and bobble hats, clinging to their parents' hands.

I pulled out my prepaid phone again. Eamon hadn't skimped on the model—this one was a Samsung that could piggy-back off any nearby WiFi connection. Most of the pack's burner phones weren't this nice. Eamon had probably given me this one to up my chances of survival. With the freight yard so close, there would be an Amtrak station nearby. I didn't think the Guild would look at train stations this far West, and with a scarf, hat, and jacket, I could fool a security camera.

A quick search confirmed Union Station, less than a mile away, with a train for Minnesota leaving at two.

An hour and $400 worth of cold-weather gear later, I slipped into a family bathroom at Union Station and threw the lock. The backpack slid from my shoulders, and I heaved the shiny gray duffel bag onto the sink. It still had its tags, and the insides bulged with clothes that smelled like store.

I was just about to unzip it when I caught sight of my reflection and recoiled.

My hair was stiff with sweat and dried saltwater, and so oily the whisky-gold color had gone dull brown. Grime streaked my face, and I suspected the funny looks I'd gotten from cashiers had been more about the livid red cut on my cheek than my cagey behavior.

But that wasn't what startled me. Once, the girlhood softness of my cheeks had rounded off those features Mom passed down, and though I knew we had passing family resemblance, I never thought I looked like her. Only now, with stress and grief melting away the last of my childishness, did I see my mother's face in mine.

Then the thing I'd been pushing down welled up, rising from the depths like a body cut loose from its weighted block.

Mom was dead, and it couldn't be taken back.

Heat rushed into my cheeks. I watched my eyes shimmer and overflow, tears carving through the grime on my face. They made dark splotches on the shiny gray bag.

My legs gave. I caught my good shoulder against the wall and rolled my back to the tile. My lungs clenched, stomach hiccuping so hard I couldn't breathe. This was like panic, only worse.

Mom was gone, and all I wanted right now was for her to hold me, to make me feel safe the way she always had. Until this moment, I'd operated under the delusion it somehow wasn't real. But in my mind I saw the image of that tiny hole in her cheekbone, felt her heat escaping beneath my hands. It was real. Relentless and cruel and real.

Part of me wanted to blame her, or myself. We had counted on change—fought for the possibility that our lives could be different. And in the worst possible way, we'd won.

I don't know how long I cried—long enough for two people to knock, wait, and give up on the family restroom. Some subconscious part of my brain forced me to get up, to wash my face and hair in the sink. I stuck my head under the hand-dryer until my hair puffed out like a lion's mane, then tamed the unruly waves into a braid down my back. I didn't look in the mirror again.

The most valuable things went into the backpack—my mom's jewelry, the photograph of my parents, the money I hadn't shoved either into my boot or sports-bra—but my hand paused on the book.

I could just shove it in a locker here in Union Station. Leave it for time to forget. No one would find it, not for a long time, and the likelihood it would fall into the Sorcerers' Guild's hands....

I clenched my fingers around the cover, rejecting that idea. There were more spells in here than just the one that created spellhounds. The enslavement mandala was in here too, along with the spell that bastardized our canine forms, twisted us into those horrible, demonic creatures.

I'd never give the Sorcerers' Guild that spell, no matter how they insisted they'd never create what they themselves had dubbed Hellhounds. They'd proven themselves to be liars of the first degree.

Still, there was useful knowledge in here. From it, I'd seen Gwydian draw mandalas that crossed magic from all over the world, hybrid spells that intertwined glyphs from Celtic and Indian, Asian and African, Mayan and Greek traditions. Futhorc runes flowed into Sanskrit, which transitioned into Arabic, then twisted into languages I'd never found again, though I never forgot the shapes.

Heat pulsed in my chest, and I tightened my fingers on the book.

Magic was in my blood, flickering hot and turquoise over my heart. I didn't know how to use it, but I could learn. Maybe then I could protect my pack from the Sorcerers' Guild, and we could stop running. Maybe then, we could be free.

I pushed the book into my backpack and rushed out to catch the train.

CHAPTER SEVEN

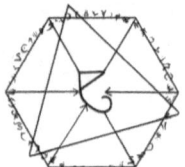

The Greeks believed Hades was cold. The pits of Tartarus, beyond the river Styx and the Elysian Fields, were frigid places of darkness and ice. By the fourth hour outside Chicago, I thought Homer or Hippocrates or whoever had started that rumor must have taken a long-distance train ride.

It hadn't started out so bad—I had an aisle seat, and the old woman next to me seemed uninterested in removing her nose from her novel. I'd lived in close quarters, so the human noises didn't bother me. Coughing, laughing, crying, and conversations half-lost in the low thrum of steel on rails—all that I could handle. The cold was another matter.

At first, my new clothes were enough to keep me comfortable. Three hours into the journey, however, I noticed my fingers and nose going numb.

The terrain outside the window was a shock—vast, flat fields interrupted by mountains. The sky looked like the same hot blue I saw in Miami, but every lake we passed was trimmed in a lace of frost.

By seven, the sun vanished and the old lady had bundled herself into a hot pink snuggie and fallen asleep. A kid walked up and down the aisle, holding a plastic dinosaur, but no one else moved in the car. I pulled my backpack into my lap. I hadn't wanted to look at the book with other people around; not only would it look weird to those who didn't know magic was a thing, I still thought anyone—the old lady next to me, the girl with neon orange hair, the kid with the dinosaur— could be a Sorcerer.

But I'd been on this train for five hours, my fingers ached, and it was too dark to study Wisconsin's alien landscape. My bladder insisted on attention.

Since my incident that morning, I'd been avoiding bathrooms, but my body was at its limit. Still, I didn't want to leave the book behind, in case the kid with the dinosaur turned out to be a Sorcerer.

I stood, balancing on the rocking train like I might a surfboard, and made my way down the aisle. The kid with the dinosaur stomped past me, and I had to lift the heavy tome over my head and spin to keep the corner from stabbing him in the eye.

"Jesus," I whispered. The pair sitting at the front of the car looked up. The orange haired girl looked like a roller-derby queen with her spiked pixie cut, multiple piercings, and powerful frame. As I twisted past the dinosaur-kid, her blue eyes popped wide.

"Ten of ten from the American judge!" she announced, and golf clapped.

"Kim Yuna would have done it with a smile," her companion offered. "Korea says nine."

I glanced. Asian. Black hair close trimmed on the sides, long on top. Thick-framed glasses. Metrosexual art nerd? Maybe an edgy business student.

"Come on, Jay," the girl said. "You gave porn-stache guy an eight."

"Eight-point-nine, then. For disappointing lack of creepy facial hair."

I shut the bathroom door on the girl's sound of disgust and locked myself in. When I emerged a few minutes later, they were discussing scores for the suited man lumbering back down the aisle.

"He gets an extra half point for the tie alone," the guy said. As I passed, his gaze flicked up. He had masculine features—strong nose, angular jaw, overlarge canines—though with the smooth beauty I associated with the Asian models of Miami's club scene. There was a small tattoo behind his ear.

"I was kidding," he said. "Korea totally gives you nine-point-eight."

The orange-haired girl thwacked him in the chest. "I am so sorry," she said. "He's had, like, three hours' sleep and he thinks you're hot."

"Bitch, so do you!" the guy said, rubbing at his chest where she'd hit him, but he didn't look back up at me.

How the hell was I supposed to respond to that?

"It's fine," I mumbled. I shuffled the book under my arm and gave a weird shrug before escaping back down the aisle.

I slumped back into my seat, resolving to trip the stupid dinosaur kid if he came back this way. He wasn't all *that* young.

The aisles were empty, the train dark as people huddled in their coats, sleeping or peering at electronics.

I pulled down the tray on the seat ahead and set the book atop it. It sat, heavy with importance. I flipped open the cover, looking down at the complex form of the first mandala. Old spellbooks didn't mess around with introductions.

Over the years, I've memorized the effect certain combinations have when cast in mandalas, and I recognized most elements of this one. What I didn't know was the most important part, and the reason having a book was necessary at all: the order of the drawing.

Mandalas are finicky things. It matters what direction you draw the circle, what order you write the glyphs and characters, because that determines the power's flow. I'd seen them drawn in the wrong order, and depending on the spell, the backlash could be deadly.

The next page showed the first few steps, scribing the outer circle counter-clockwise from three, then filling in the first row with glyphs, starting with the Chinese character for fire. Each subsequent page detailed more steps, including a central ring inscribed clockwise from nine, more glyphs in Arabic and Hebrew, until the mandala was complete.

I chewed on the inside of my lip, tracing my finger over the steps in sequence several times, then attempting to repeat the pattern on the finished mandala. I did this until I could close my eyes and picture the completed spell-circle, drawing it with a mental stylus.

After an hour, I almost missed the dinosaur kid. My brain was used to making pictures, but this was a different technique. It might have been bearable if I were drawing it in my sketchbook. Exhausted, I tucked the book between my leg and the armrest, leaned back my chair, and dozed. The rocking train almost felt like a boat. And when we pulled into a station around 10 pm, the old lady next to me tapped me on the shoulder.

"I gotta get by, shug," she said.

"Yeah, sure." Groggy, I raised my seat and let her by. Outside, passengers had gathered on the platform to smoke. I spotted the orange haired girl and her friend. She sucked on a vaporizer, puffing out a laugh as he flashed his teeth and scrubbed a hand through his black undercut.

I peered at them, unable to help the envy that welled up in my throat at the easy friendship they seemed to have. I also envied her bright pink mittens. I'd left my gloves in the checked duffel bag and my fingers stung.

The train hissed and settled, and the passengers crowded back on, refilling the empty spots in the car. Thankfully, the old lady didn't return—I had three more hours to fill before my stop, but at least the whole row was mine.

I set my backpack where the old lady had been and demolished a pack of cheese crackers. I flexed my fingers and pressed the backs to my cheek.

Ice. And my nose was running. I needed coffee.

I grabbed my backpack and levered myself into the aisle. The train rocked as I made my way forward, and the main lights had dimmed to little more than runway illumination between the seats.

Most passengers were asleep, or trying to be, and I noticed no Sorcerer-like levels of jewelry.

The dining car, which was little more than a concessions counter and a couple booths, smelled like burned coffee and popcorn. At the counter, a woman in a black dress accepted a plastic cup of wine, leaning into a man I assumed was either her coworker or her corporate boyfriend. Behind them, the girl with bright orange hair and her very *tall* Asian friend.

I considered ducking into the bathroom again, just to wait for them to leave. The only barrier between us was a middle-aged man in a baseball jersey. They were just the type to strike up conversations with strangers, and if there was one thing I felt uncomfortable doing right at this moment, it was talking to anyone.

The girl conferred with her friend, then stretched out of line and tossed her jacket into an empty booth. I swallowed a groan. They weren't going anywhere fast.

I stepped in line behind the baseball fan, resolving to drink my coffee in the accordion-walled space between cars. Part of me wanted to dig out the burner phone, just to have something to do, but it was nearing the end of its battery life, and the seat had nowhere to plug in a charger.

"Where you goin', honey?"

It took a moment for me to realize 'honey' meant me. I glanced up and found the baseball fan eying me. His eyes were glassy. I smelled beer on him.

The last of my energy seemed to drain away. I just wanted to get my coffee and go back to my seat—curl up, figure out my next step. I didn't have the energy to deal with this guy. What about me right now said: open and inviting? The crossed arms? The cut on my face?

Mom would have given a guarded answer. But Mom wasn't here. That was the problem. Answering would've been polite, but I wasn't about to encourage a conversation I didn't want to have. I let my eyebrows flex and looked to the window. All I could see against the darkened landscape was the dining car's reflection. The orange-haired girl stepped forward to order.

"I asked where you were goin'," the jersey said. "Hey." He tapped me on the arm with three thick fingers.

Several defenses flashed through my mind at once—I could twist his hand, bend him forward into my knee; I could step in, bring up a knee and put him on the floor; and if all else failed, I had Morgan's knife in my boot.

But those things were for the streets, for hardened men with guns in their belts and blood on their minds. This was nothing more than a drunk guy, feeling entitled to a conversation on a train.

"I didn't want to answer." I jerked my arm from his reach, still watching our reflections in the window. He had no visible piercings, and besides a wedding band on his left hand, he wasn't wearing any other metal. Not a Sorcerer.

"Fine," he said. "What's your name?"

I sighed, hooking my thumbs in the straps of my backpack. In the window, I saw the orange-haired girl glance around her friend toward me, frowning. The woman in the black dress gave us a look and moved to the back of the car, clearly annoyed that we were disrupting her peace.

"I don't feel like talking," I said. Even to my own ears, it sounded tired.

"Weird name," he slurred, leaning my way, as if that had been a fantastic joke. "Were your parents hippies? How 'bout I buy you a drink. Will you tell me your name then?"

His sleeve brushed my arm. I leaned away, maintaining silence. And that was the end of his limited patience.

"Why is it so fucking hard to talk to you Millennial chicks?" His voice rang in the car. The orange-haired girl jumped and the Asian guy, who had just reached for the cup from the cashier, turned his head.

"You got some feminist bullshit stick up your asses. Think you don't owe a man basic politeness?" He stepped in toward me, close enough to feel his breath on my face. I braced, refusing to back away from him. "I just wanted to buy you a fucking drink and you can't even tell me your name. It's ridiculous. Someone needs to send y'all back to your mommas to learn how to act like goddamned ladies."

Spikes of pain shot through my chest. At my side, my fists clenched. Suddenly, I wasn't tired anymore. I was furious.

"My mom taught me something slightly different." I drew back a boot.

Then the Asian guy turned from the concession bar, gave a spectacular stagger, and upended his coffee down the white and blue jersey's back.

"Ohh shit," he said. The train swayed, and metro Asian lurched into irate baseball fan, shoving him into the wall. "I am SO sorry!"

If I hadn't been so taken aback, I would have laughed at how staged it was. The tall guy had total control of where his weight moved the baseball fan, who spluttered in an apoplectic fury. I ducked around them, backing toward the concession bar. Strong fingers grabbed my arm, and the orange-haired girl propelled me behind her, toward the counter. "Go, go, go," she whispered, her voice ripe with contained laughter.

I went. The man behind the bar gaped at the spectacle. I glanced back at the paper cup rolling gently back and forth on the train floor.

"Two coffees," I said.

CHAPTER EIGHT

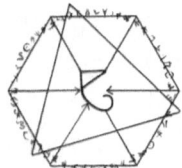

"Y ou're shitting me." The orange-haired girl looked at me with horror in her bright blue eyes. "You rode the train all the way from Miami? Why didn't you fly?"

I hadn't meant to sit with them. I'd intended to hand over the replacement coffee, pass along my appreciation that they'd kept me from shanking a fellow passenger, and flee back to my seat. Intentions crumbled, however, when I'd noticed there was a perforated heating duct running along the baseboard. Even with two coffees in my hand, I'd still been shivering.

So I'd introduced myself to orange-haired Krista and mispronounced my first two tries at Jaesung's name. Fifteen minutes into our acquaintance, my coffee still burned my palm through the cup, but I didn't mind. It was a thousand times better than the fridge that was the passenger car.

Unfortunately, warmth also came with questions.

"I'm not a fan of airplanes," I said, taking a cautious sip. Coffee scalded my tongue. I didn't know if I liked airplanes or not. Security was too tight to pit against the quality of my fake IDs.

Jaesung, who was busy stacking tiny cream containers, snorted. "Amen to that," he said. "I hate planes."

"Planes, but not heights," Krista said. She rolled her eyes at me and went back to her phone, glittery blue thumbnails tapping at top speed. "He's weird."

"*I'm* not flying the damn plane." Jaesung gestured with the hand that wasn't clutching his own coffee. He had sprawled in the seat across from Krista and me, one foot on the cushion beside him. There was something energetic about even this relaxed pose, though he didn't quite seem restless. More like an idling engine, or a human example of potential energy. It reminded me unfavorably of a Sorcerer. I couldn't look at him for longer than a few seconds without going tense.

Krista looked up from her phone, incredulous. "You're weird because you think planes are dangerous but you spent the whole fucking summer at the top of cell towers!" She turned to me, her mouth curving into a smirk that invited me to join her teasing. "It's one of the most dangerous jobs in America and Jae was just like—no, it's fine. I have a harness."

"I *do*." He lifted his orange backpack from the floor beneath the table and dropped it again with an audible clank. The movement upset his creamer tower. "And it's mostly just dangerous when you're not paying attention." He glanced at the ceiling, head cocked, and after a beat, he shrugged. "Or when there's lightning."

"Fzzt," Krista said. "Korean barbecue."

I surprised myself with a chuckle. I hadn't realized I had the energy for humor. I hadn't realized laughing was a thing I still did.

Jaesung cut his gaze to Krista. Behind his thick-framed glasses, his eyes glinted in amusement, but he gave her an arch look as he swung his legs back under the table and slapped a hand on the formica.

"You're up to a dollar twenty-five in the racist jar."

"So?" Krista's tone was saccharine. "You're up to three-fifty in the homophobia fund."

I raised my eyebrows. Jaesung seemed to notice the change in expression.

"We're roommates," he said, pointing between himself and Krista. "That's how we know each other. The jars are...uhh...." He looked at Krista for help.

"I get the jars," I said.

"Tell you what," said Krista. "Just give me two twenty-five."

Jaesung met her eyes with a bland expression, then turned his full attention on me. "So, Miami? Why the hell are you going to Minnesota?"

"In winter," Krista added, tacking with the conversation. I leaned back, the force of their combined attention like two eager search lights.

I took another sip and gathered the threads of my cover story. Luckily, we only had another two hours or so to the stop.

"Moving," I said. "My mom's from Henard, so everyone's meeting there."

"You're moving to Henard?" Krista slapped the table in excitement. "Oh my God, that's awesome!"

A frisson of worry crossed my skin. I looked from Krista's excited face to the sudden appearance of Jaesung's grin. He had slightly over-large canines. I looked back at Krista. "You guys...live in Henard?" My gut sank. Jaesung and Krista wore expressions of impish glee.

"We're students at U.M.H."

"If we seem excited, it's because fresh meat is so rare. We can smell it a mile away."

"Like sharks."

I faked a smile behind my cup and avoided another question by asking one. "What are you guys studying?"

I steeled myself for jealousy, no matter what they answered. My self-study high school ended at fifteen, and the stolen hours I'd spent buried in textbooks had been a glorious escape from life as Gwydian's slave. I'd have killed—probably literally—to go to college.

Jaesung, wiping his eyes underneath his glasses, answered dismissively. "Sociology."

"No one cares about sociology," Krista said. "*I'm* in veterinary school."

Jaesung rested his jaw on his hand, hair falling into his glasses. "Because being shoulder-deep in cow vagina is *so* interesting compared to the effects of cross-cultural media in Asia."

"I'm hands-on."

I snorted, lowering my coffee. The banter had the easy confidence that came after years of friendship, and regret rang in the emptiness of my chest. I dropped my hand to my sternum as if to stop the echo. I would be with my pack soon. New friends were not in the plans—I needed to stay safe, and to do that, I needed to keep anonymous.

Jaesung's eyes were on me. He'd caught the movement, and his full eyebrows were making an upward migration. Between his fingers, the tattoo looked like a series of small stars. A constellation? I couldn't see enough to figure out which.

"What's it like?" I asked.

"Being shoulder-deep in cow vagina?" Krista said. "In two words, uncomfortably warm. In more words, worth it when-"

"I think she means in general," Jaesung interrupted.

Krista poked her tongue out at him, but we had achieved segue.

"I like it," she said. "I'm only in class two days a week, and the rest of the time I'm doing clinical work at his cousin's dog rescue." She nodded at Jaesung.

"A *dog rescue?*" I hadn't meant to sound so incredulous. Krista's smile faltered.

"You no like puppies?" she said, and I could already see her bottom lip threatening to poke out. She was a strange one—punked out head-to-toe, tall and strapping, and apparently as soft-hearted as they came. I set down my coffee to keep from clenching my hands around it too hard.

"I like dogs," I said, leaning into my backpack as Jaesung smirked at me from across the table. "It's just a coincidence."

"You...work at a dog rescue too?" Krista ventured.

I hadn't meant to turn the conversation back to me. I fumbled for something that wouldn't sound like a lie. "No. I—we—my family, I mean. It's not a dog rescue; we've just rescued a lot of dogs."

It wasn't a lie if most people in Gwydian's gang could become hounds.

Krista reached across the table and swatted Jaesung's hand. "See!" she said. "I told you she was a dog person!"

If she only knew.

After that, I kept the conversation steered toward them. Interrupted by an increasing frequency of yawns, I listened to the exploits of their long weekend in Chicago, where Jaesung's mother lived with his aunt and uncle. At Krista's prompting, he talked about scaling cell towers, swinging high above the ground with the smell of lightning on the wind, and the particular challenges of bodily functions while suspended 300 feet in the air.

Krista regaled us with enthusiastic stories from the farm where she'd done her first year of veterinary clinicals, and we both sniggered at Jaesung's grimaces. Judging by the amount of product in his hair and the crisp cuff of his shirt under the bomber jacket's sleeve, he was either a clean-freak or very metro. Or both. I'd have guessed gay if I hadn't noticed his eyes straying when it got warm enough to take off my woolcoat.

All the while, I traced mandalas on my leg, reviewing steps and sequences, trying to commit them to muscle memory. After three cups of coffee, my fingers shook on the finer glyphs, but I thought I was remembering them correctly.

We rolled into Henard at 1:17 am, all three sleepy and caffeine-buzzed. Jaesung and Krista had carry-ons, but seemed content to trail behind me, chattering as I collected my duffel bag from the luggage car.

There was a cold snarl on the wind, carrying the smell of wood-fires and water, and by the time my duffel had been unloaded, I was shivering all over again. Leggings, even thermal ones, weren't enough to block the cold. Who knew? As if to make things worse, my body finally demanded attention to its injuries. I shouldered the gray bag with a wince.

"You got that?" Krista asked. She either didn't hear or didn't believe my yes, because she grabbed one handle and helped me haul it to a bench nearby. "Your family's meeting you here?" Worry tinted her friendly tone.

"Yeah." I scanned the platform and parking lot, my breath making chilled puffs. The only vehicles in the lot were an old Volkswagen, a red Prius, and a battered pickup. I dug into my coat for the burner phone and made a show of tapping out a message to Eamon.

At RDVZ. ETA?

"They're coming from out of town," I said. "They should be here soon." I stowed my phone, but when I looked up again, I caught Krista and Jaesung exchanging a look. I gave them my best reassuring smile. It didn't feel like a good fit on my face.

"Is there somewhere I can drive you?" Jaesung asked. He was tapping the toe of one clean white sneaker behind him, nervous maybe, or impatient. It was hard to tell. "Henard isn't the most dangerous place in the world, but it has a thriving population of—"

Krista elbowed him.

"Snow sharks?" I guessed.

Jaesung rolled his eyes. "It's not cold enough for snow."

I gaped. If this wasn't cold enough for snow, what was I going to do in Canada?

Jaesung persisted. "Whatever. There are weirdos. Are you guys staying in a hotel? We can give you a lift."

Something inside me twisted. I'd known normal people were like this—concerned for practical strangers—but I'd never believed it.

That casual concern had never extended to me. I was glad to push it away.

"I'm fine. They'll be here soon."

Jaesung looked at Krista, brows drawn. "We can wait with you," she offered.

The sharp feeling was back in my chest now. I looked down at my backpack, at my fingers curling into a seam, and forced back the desire to just tell them to get out of my face, or something equally rude. I wanted to drive them away, but for whatever reason, I didn't want them to dislike me.

Ridiculous. I shouldn't care. But I did.

"I'm fine," I repeated, stronger than before. "Don't worry. I know Kung Fu."

Krista grinned, but Jaesung didn't react. He stood at the end of the bench, foot meeting the concrete in a steady rhythm. Despite his slenderness, he was at least as tall as Morgan. Six-two, maybe six-three. I hadn't realized Asians came in that size. I hadn't realized I'd internalized that stereotype in the first place until being surprised by a living, breathing counter-example. He was unlike Morgan in every other way, but that single commonality was enough to make me wish I'd let my cousin come.

I glanced at the trees swallowing up the track, searching for potential hiding spots to distract myself from the pang of that mental association. The mulch between the platform and the parking lot was empty, as was the well-lit waiting area. A single graffiti tag stood out on an outdoor trashcan, but the place was otherwise clean and deserted.

Jaesung's toe-tapping stopped. "I still don't feel right leaving you out here by yourself," he said. "This isn't a great area."

"This is nothing," I said. "I'm from Miami."

He leaned forward with a half-smirk. "I'm from *Chicago*. And you haven't seen the other side of the tracks." He nodded at the train, which hissed and lurched, creaking as it prepared to leave the station.

He had me there. The passenger train didn't have convenient

openings between cars. I mentally kicked myself for not paying better attention when I was still on the train. I usually cased my surroundings far better, but I'd had images of cows and cranes and storm clouds over cell towers filling up my brain.

Krista plucked my phone from my hand. "Tell you what—here's my number. If they haven't showed up in, like, an hour, call me. You can crash on our couch."

I bit back the protest. Maybe if I agreed, they would go. It wasn't as if I had to call them. I forced my lips to bend upward and accepted my phone back from Krista.

"I will," I lied. Jaesung's eyebrows twitched up, like he didn't believe me, but he hefted his jingling backpack and gave Krista an expectant look.

"Let us know if you're in the area for a while," she said.

"Yeah, we'll hang out," I said, because that's what people say. I don't know what hanging out entails, but I think it involves video games, malls, and fro-yo.

"Take care, Miami," Jaesung said, lifting a hand in a wave. "Waterproofing spray is your friend."

Krista's grin reappeared, though her eyes were a little too bright. "Stay warm."

I watched them walk to the parking lot and climb into the pickup. A roar of engine, flash of headlights, and wave through windows later, they were gone. Behind me, the train had crept forward.

Alone. Again. It's what I'd wanted. Or maybe just what I required, and that was close enough to count as wanting. Still, the night felt heavy now, like all the emptiness had turned solid and pressed down on my shoulders.

The final car rolled past. Florescent beams spilled across the tracks and lapped at my duffel bag and backpack. I felt the phone in my hand, hard corners and inorganic smoothness reminding me that I had a lifeline. My breath puffed in front of me, freezing and sinking.

The light from the platform across the tracks shifted.

I looked up, senses surging to alertness. A man stood on the far side, backlit by headlights from the other parking lot. The hairs on my nape stood on end. All I could make out was his silhouette, but it didn't matter—I sensed what I couldn't see.

I don't know how they'd done it, or if they'd just made a lucky guess, but it didn't matter. As the man stepped forward, he triggered a floodlight, and I saw him.

Skeletal, covered in ink and piercings. The lighting shadowed his eyes into skull-like pools, but I knew the instant his gaze landed on me. We both froze, me with my hand on the backpack with the book in it. Him holding a cell-phone to his ear with one hand, and in the other, a gun.

A Sorcerer stood before me, seeming as shocked to see me standing across the tracks as I was to see him. I didn't think, I ran.

CHAPTER NINE

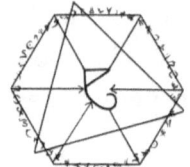

Banging into the station's lit interior, I darted out the opposite door into the parking lot.

Shit. Shit shit shit shit. My mind went too fast to isolate any single question. I dove for the nearest cover—the red Prius—and pressed myself into the wheel, listening. Nothing but night sounds greeted me, and I held my breath, grappling to control my racing thoughts.

It didn't matter how he'd found me, not just yet. Right now what mattered was getting away. I clutched my backpack to my chest, felt the book solid and heavy inside.

One Sorcerer. I had to get away before more arrived, which meant I had to make sure this guy didn't follow me. I swallowed and let myself exhale. Transforming would be too hard.

I pulled Morgan's knife from my boot, the handle was warm in my palm from where it had rested against my skin. It wasn't my preferred weapon, but it was better than bare hands. Reaching behind me, I checked the Prius's door. Locked. The Volkswagen lurked by the trees at the edge of the parking lot, battered and promising. I peeked through the windows toward the station, but it sat bright and inviting, bearing no sign of the Sorcerer. Either he was still looking for me inside, or he'd stopped to tear apart my gray duffel in search of the book.

I sprinted to the Volkswagen and hurled myself behind it, scrabbling for the back door. The handle gave a solid clunk under my hands and the door swung open, light flaring to reveal a filthy backseat filled with fast food bags, library books, and dirty coffee mugs. I scrambled for the light and turned it off, then buried the backpack in a heap of Burger King bags.

I eased the door shut and leaned around the car, peering over the hood toward the station. This time, I didn't trust my luck in the open parking lot. I ducked into the woods and crept close to the platform. My gray duffel had been torn open. A station attendant stood over it, speaking into his radio. I clenched my jaw, scanning the opposite platform. Whether the Sorcerer was searching the station or had left my bag there as a trap, I didn't know.

I waited until the attendant was looking the opposite way down the tracks and crouch-ran to the side of the building, pressing myself against the bricks. Though my nose and ears stung with cold, my palm had gone sweaty on the knife.

I heard a door open in the station, followed by a voice.

"Hey, yeah—that's mine, sorry," a man said, his voice high pitched and rough, like a smoker. "Girlfriend's inside. Just got off the train."

The station attendant said something reprimanding and official, and from the grunts and zipping sound, I could only imagine that they were picking up my stuff. I peeked around the corner. The Sorcerer was average height, but I could see from here that his buzzed hair was a sheen of red-gold over his scalp. He shouldered my bag with a grunt and retrieved his phone from a pocket. The station attendant stumped back inside.

"She's not inside. No." A pause. "I didn't see her out front. Well, who the hell's bag did I just go through, then?"

I forced my breaths to remain steady. His footsteps paced toward me, scraping across the concrete.

"No. No, this is the last one for fifty miles. She's not still on the train—I saw her on the platform. Well, that's why they pay me the big bucks."

I braced myself as his feet came closer, shifting my grip on the knife. Surprise was the only advantage I would have in this, since there might be a dead body when I finished.

His footsteps scraped the concrete just around the corner from my hiding spot, and stopped. He sighed, and I watched the plume of breath waft out, white against the dark forest.

That's when my phone rang.

I started, thrown off my strategy, and an instant later, I attacked, swinging around the corner with the knife coming up low, aiming under his guard. It was an instant too late. He dropped his phone, and my knife plunged into the shiny gray duffel bag. He reeled, cursing, and stumbled backwards as I came in again, undeterred, and swung my left fist.

It cracked across his cheek. Pain exploded in my knuckles, jarring down my arm to my elbow, but I didn't care. It was familiar. It felt good.

Sorcerers, on the whole, are not physical creatures. What they are is tactical, and I'd given him enough time to think. He hurled my bag at me, forcing me to duck to the side, and reached for a ring.

I wasn't the best fighter in my pack by a long shot, but I'd been fortunate enough to learn from them. The kick was muscle memory— a pivot and lash that struck the Sorcerer's hand, knocking his spell astray. I didn't see what it was. Momentum brought me back around and I slammed an elbow across the Sorcerer's temple. It sent him to the concrete, where he stayed, groaning. If I'd had Dad's Beretta, I would have shot him out of sheer reflex. Instead, I snatched up my duffel and ran.

I made it to the Volkswagen before the pain caught up with me. My left hand throbbed, and my elbow felt like someone had taken a hammer to it. Fighting was never painless, but this had taken more from me than I'd had to give. I dug through the Burger

King bags, tempted to just crawl inside and cover myself with trash.

But I couldn't risk that. This Sorcerer had found me somehow, and if he'd tracked me with magic, staying close would just make it easier for him. I pulled my backpack out, wishing I knew how to jump a car, when my phone chirped.

I swung my backpack on and hefted the duffel, heading for the street before I checked the message. It was a voicemail from Eamon, but when I put it to my ear, it was not Eamon's voice that came through. It was Morgan's.

"Hel," he said, and I could hear the sharpness of his breath, a rush of language around him like he was hurrying through a public place. "They got Eamon. Where are you? You can reach me on this phone."

I stopped at the curb, those three words replaying in my head. They got Eamon. The fact dropped into my brain without a ripple, settling at the bottom of my consciousness with all the other things that were too big to feel. I stood there on the sidewalk, just outside the glow of a streetlamp, and stared at a darkened thrift shop across the street.

I lowered the phone. The duffle bag slid off my shoulder, then the backpack. A car turned onto the road, but I didn't care. I sat on the curb, boots in the leaf-filled gutter, and bent my forehead to my knees.

This was useless. Why had I ever thought I would be strong enough to face up to the Guild? I couldn't keep running like this forever. Should I have just given them what they wanted? If I did, would they let Eamon go?

The rumbling vehicle slowed down as it neared me, and I lifted my head to wave the good Samaritan on when a head of orange hair emerged from the passenger's seat.

"I have a capture pole and I'm not afraid to use it!" Krista yelled, extending a length of narrow pipe with a loop at the end. "We already made up the couch. I promise Jae doesn't have fleas."

I blinked up at her, barely comprehending. She pushed the door open and reached for my duffel bag, hefting it into the truck bed with a grunt. "Come on," she said, extending both hands. A second later, she glanced behind me and the hair on my nape stood on end. I twisted around to see the Sorcerer, holding his phone to a swelling face. He stopped in the street, gaze flicking from me to Krista to the truck, and I saw his mouth flatten.

Something clicked in my mind. I put my hands in Krista's and, ignoring the pain in my knuckles, let her pull me to my feet. I shoved my backpack into the truck and climbed in. Jaesung gave me a smirk as I settled in beside him and fumbled to unearth the seatbelt from between seats. Krista settled into place and slammed the door, then redirected her vent so a blast of hot air hit me right in the chest.

I sat stiffly, watching the Sorcerer watch me, both aware of what I'd only just realized: as long as I was with civilians, he wouldn't attack me. As far as Jaesung and Krista knew, magic didn't exist, and it was his job to keep them ignorant. I could use the Guild's own laws against them—as long as I was with these two normal, unthreatening people, I was safe. I almost wanted to laugh.

Jaesung executed a three-point-turn and Krista gave the glaring Sorcerer a wave as we drove back the way they'd come.

"What's his damage?" she said.

Jaesung glanced in the rearview mirror and yawned. "Told you there were weirdos."

I kept from looking behind us the whole ten minute drive to Jaesung and Krista's. Despite the lack of headlights reflecting in the rearview mirror, it was a matter of time before the Sorcerer figured out a way to follow me. This was the exact reason I hated license plates—so easy to look up when you knew the right people.

I was surprised to find us driving into town. With all the amber waves of grain we'd passed on the train, I'd assumed the dog rescue would be on a farm at the edges of Henard. Instead, Jaesung drove us down an idyllic Main Street with drugstores, boutiques, and barber shops, then turned left on Erickson Street. We pulled up in front of a three-story brick firehouse.

A pair of enormous garage doors dominated the lower half of the building's facade, with two stories of bay window jutting out over the sidewalk. A smaller door peeked from under an arched lintel on the left, bearing a plaque that read: Ruff Patch Dog Rescue.

"Vintage firehouse. Sweet, right?" Krista said, correctly interpreting my appraising stare.

"Does it still have the pole?" I asked.

"Everyone wants to know about the damn pole," Jaesung said. He flicked off the headlights and killed the truck engine. "No pole. My cousin wanted to keep it, but the fiancée thought it invited disaster."

"She's not wrong," Krista said. "I'd ask all sorts of people to come polish it."

Jaesung laughed through a yawn. Krista pushed open the door, letting in a flood of frigid air. My skin shrank into goosebumps, but I followed her out, shifting my backpack onto my shoulder. I winced as it scraped over my hand, grateful it was too dark to see the bruises forming on my knuckles. This time I didn't protest when Jaesung snatched my bag from the truck bed and, holding both handles in one hand, slung it behind his shoulder.

That is, until I noticed the knife still protruding from the fabric, flopping near his shoulder with each step.

I flashed back to the fight, when the Sorcerer had blocked my stab with the bag. He'd twisted the knife from my hands with it, and I'd lost track of the blade after that. But there it was, still tangled in the shreds of gray nylon. Even I hadn't noticed it.

God, how was I supposed to explain if they saw it? If they found out about the fight, they'd do what most civilians did: call the police. That would be a whole lot of attention I didn't need, especially if the local force had any Sorcerers on roster. What excuse would I have to own a knife? Most girls carried pepper spray, not razor-sharp tungsten steel.

As Krista unlocked the door, I shuffled back, pretending to admire the architecture, and moved in behind Jaesung.

"How old is the building?" I asked. Krista grumbled at her keys.

Jaesung gave a sniff, as if his nose was running from the cold. "1913? 1903? More than a hundred years old. There's a plaque somewhere."

I nodded, extending my fingers until they curled around the handle. Jaesung was squinting at Krista through his glasses. His shoulder was level with my eyes, which put the knife at convenient grabbing-level.

"Did it take a long time to remodel the building?"

"Jesus, yes," Jaesung said, and as he expounded, I squinted at the knife. The guard had gotten tangled in frays of nylon, so I made the twists as slowly as my sleepy, shaky hands could manage. "They'd already been at it for ten months when I moved to Henard, and they didn't finish until I was nearly done with my Freshman year."

"They?"

"Dude, can you shine your cell phone over here?" Krista asked. Before I could react, Jaesung stepped forward, and the knife jerked at the bag and sprang free. Unfortunately, it also tugged at the duffel, which tugged at Jaesung, who had to twist around or fall off balance.

I whipped the knife behind me, fluttering it closed and shoving it into the side pocket of my backpack, behind a map of Union Station. Jaesung blinked at me, and I held my breath. Had he seen it? His pinched eyebrows told me he'd seen something, but I might have been fast enough. Expectation is everything when tricking the senses. Who would have expected to see a knife?

He opened his mouth, but a soft sigh of parting fabric cut him off as the duffel bag regurgitated its contents onto the dog rescue's front stoop.

"What-" he twisted, slinging the bag so the last of my clothing and toiletries scattered across his shoes. Krista turned around and squeaked, which alerted the rescue's occupants of our arrival. A single bark sounded, like the first drop of rain, and was followed by a hurricane of howls and excited yips.

"There was a tear!" I said, sinking to my knees to stop a bottle of shampoo from rolling back toward the street. "Sorry, I'd only just noticed and I was trying to hold it closed-"

"Fuckballs!" Jaesung crouched. The deluge of doggie greetings crescendoed as Krista swung the door open and ducked inside. "Sorry —I didn't notice there was a tear," Jaesung said. "It was probably something in my truck. Shit."

I wanted to protest, because he had a frantic look in his dark eyes. It took me a moment to recognize it as guilt. I gave a one-shouldered shrug, making use of a few pairs of underwear to smuggle the knife from the backpack's side pocket to the top. It dropped in, settling behind the book, and I shoved socks and tee shirts on top of it.

"It could have been something on the train too," I said. "Don't worry about it."

"No, I feel bad. We can replace it-"

"It's fine."

Jaesung winced, his hands grabbing anything and everything, including underwear, jeans, a box of tampons, and stacking them back into the bag's flaccid remains. Krista reappeared with an enormous dog bed.

"Pile that shit on here," she said, flopping it on the threshold. Hands on hips, she surveyed my things, then frowned.

"I am disappointed in the lack of sex toy." I rolled my eyes at her.

"You're always disappointed in the lack of sex toy," Jaesung said, scooping up the majority of the mess. "Though she did hide something in her backpack."

I squinted at him. "You are terrible at secrets."

He smirked. "I promise you, I am very, very good at secrets."

His eyes went dark when he said it, intense like the stare of a predator, and for a moment my pulse thrummed in my throat. Had he seen the knife after all? Or did he know another, worse secret?

How *had* that Sorcerer find me anyway? I gave him what I hoped was an arch look.

"Maybe it *was* a sex toy," I said.

He smirked, eyebrows lifting.

Krista gathered the dog bed into her arms and stood. "If you're done with the grand tour of the front step, can we go inside?"

The dog rescue's front room had a wide counter and racks of collars, leashes, treats, toys, and other pet paraphernalia. A computer blinked from a desk behind the counter, its scrolling screensaver proclaiming, "Ruff Patch Dog Rescue - Man's Best Friend's Best Friend".

A door stood on the righthand wall, into what had once been the fire station's garage. Now it looked more like a cross between a science lab, a kennel, and an industrial kitchen, with polished concrete floors and incandescent track lighting. The back wall was lined with built-in kennels housing a dozen dogs, all attached to very excitable tails. The shelves were stacked with labeled tubs and bottles, and the center of the room had three jumbo-sized sinks with shower heads. A large examination table dominated the back wall. The place's smell was part dog, part bleach, and part evergreen sap.

Krista dropped the laden pet bed on the examination table with a grunt, then pivoted around to face me, arms out like a dolphin trainer.

Krista grinned. "This is it! My Queendom. And those are my babies."

I was already moving toward the cages.

Jaesung yawned, leaning against a sink. "Wouldn't they be your subjects if this is your Queendom?" Krista ignored him.

I paused in front of a kennel where a skinny German Shepherd mix sniffed my bruised hand. A pink tongue curled out, warm and damp, and stroked my injured knuckles. I crouched, seeing not the dog before me, but Morgan's hound form, starved and timid, with patches of missing fur giving evidence to long mistreatment. Torture. Like the Sorcerers were probably torturing Eamon now.

My eyes burned, and I swallowed at the ache in my throat,

fighting the weakness that seemed to follow me no matter how far I ran. I trailed my fingers over the German Shepherd's furry face and silken, upright ears. Krista crouched next to me and stuck a hand through the bars. If she noticed my glassy eyes, she said nothing.

"This is Poo-stank," she said. "We actually named him Radar because of the ears, but he smelled so bad for so many days after we caught him that Jae just kept referring to him as Poo-stank, and then the rest of us couldn't remember anything else."

I heard Jaesung's footsteps behind me, his shadow falling against the cage bars just before he squatted on my other side, hands clasped behind his back. Poo-stank wagged his tail and whined, greeting the new arrival with desperate energy.

"Poo-stank! Poo-stank!" Jaesung said, in that cartoonish voice people only use when they're trying to rile up a dog. "How's my Poo-stank?" The German Shepherd's whine turned into a bark and he shoved his nose between the bars. Claws scrabbled the concrete.

"Oh my God, Jae. Give him whatever you have before he wets himself."

Jaesung snickered, then brought a nubbly chew toy from behind his back. Poo-stank grabbed it, chewing even as Jaesung used both hands to scratch and ruffle his ears. "Were you a good boy for Gene? Did you poop on his shoe? You did? Good boy!" Poo-stank dropped the chew toy as Jaesung talked to him, that pink tongue reappearing to bathe his favorite person's face. "Not the glasses! Not the —gah, blegh."

Krista rolled her eyes. "I told you to keep your mouth shut," she said.

The exchange had given me enough time to banish the weakness. I stood, turning away from the licking, wagging reunion, and let Krista introduce me to the other dogs. There were eleven, some who had been almost fully rehabilitated from their separate ordeals.

I met the eyes of a skinny boxer and though he raised his hackles, there was a tiredness in his eyes I thought I recognized. Maybe, if he could learn to be happy here.... No. This was a pit-stop. A one-night respite from running. No matter how good the Ruff Patch Dog Rescue team was, I doubted they could fix my problems in one night. Or ever.

"My loyal subjects," Krista said. "I am their Queen."

"Some of them like me better!" Jae called from the cage of a one-eyed teacup poodle.

Krista didn't look at him, but her face twitched theatrically. "Some of them like Jae better because all he's qualified for are walkies and play time. Sanadzi and I do all the medicating and examining and poking."

She led me back to the exam table, and as I slung my backpack over my shoulder, she hefted the dog bed and nodded toward the stairs beside the garage doors.

"Sanadzi is...Jae's cousin?"

"She's the vet—engaged to Jae's cousin, who owns the building. She works at a regular vet downtown, but the rescue is her labor of love, I guess. You'll meet her tomorrow."

"And you two work here?"

I resituated my backpack, which dug into my trapezius muscles with insistence. I imagined the book inside as an imp crouching on my back, sharp little fingers digging into my shoulders.

"Sort of?" she said. "We're technically volunteers, but we're both poor students, and Jae's family, so—" she shrugged. "We're 24-hour live-in volunteers. The whole upstairs is a boss-ass finished apartment. I'll never be able to afford something like this on my own."

We climbed up the staircase, which curved alongside a cutout that must have once encircled the fireman's pole. Now it held a thick pane of plexiglass.

Krista lumbered through the door with her armload of dog-bed. I followed behind her into the smell of coffee, pine, and lemony cleaning solution. The light up here was warmer, reflecting off cognac-colored hardwood. The whole floor was open but for two brick columns.

Had it been well-decorated, it would have been the kind of place where rich people have gallery openings or parties with wine and things served on toothpicks. It was not well-decorated. At least, it didn't look like the fancy sort of places Gwydian had used to swindle clients. They had furnished the place with overstuffed bachelor-pad castoffs and the flimsy particle board fare of back-to-school sales. Bottles of liquor made a little cityscape on the fridge, and they'd utilized every horizontal surface as a repository for books, loose change, and discarded outerwear.

I halted on the welcome mat. This wasn't some drug lord's living room, all cold marble and sleek leather, the air tinged with bleach and cologne. Nor was it warehouse lighting and mattresses parked on concrete. It was so normal, so nice. I wasn't used to normal. I certainly wasn't used to nice.

I did not belong here.

Krista marched around the huge brown sofa and dropped the dog bed onto a coffee table, displacing a stack of magazines. She ignored the glossy-paged deluge and pointed to the blankets folded on the arm of the sofa. "You. Here. Sit."

My brain stuttered, unable to step into the strange, warm, normal-person home. Would it be weird to insist on sleeping with the dogs?

Krista trundled into the kitchen and opened a cabinet, oblivious to my internal struggle. Footsteps clanged on the stairs. I had deliberated long enough. I scampered to the couch, the hairs on my arms prickling as Jaesung sprang, graceful as a deer, up the last three steps. He really had great body control—quick feet, and a boxer's tight, explosive power. All that disappeared under his jacket.

Once again, I scanned his ears and fingers for jewelry, but the only metal he wore was a heavy silver watch. He had narrow wrists, which gave me pause until I noted the thick veins standing out over his knuckle, and threading down the back of his hand. The paranoid part of me demanded wariness, but Jaesung was too athletic to be a Sorcerer. I'd never seen one who could eat enough to put on muscle, not when so much of their protein-consumption went toward spellwork.

He pulled a large FedEx package from under one arm and slapped it onto the counter.

"Why is my mom sending you packages, Kris?" He gave the package a shove, sending it sliding toward the edge. Krista abandoned her cereal box and dove for the package, but it hit the hardwood with a slap.

"Asshole!" She said, straightening with the package in her hands.

"What did she send you?"

"Nudes."

"So, the bridesmaid's dress?"

Krista scowled and marched around the counter to a long fold-out table beside the bay window, snatching up scissors. Jaesung smirked and picked up the abandoned cereal box, pouring out three bowls.

I sank onto the leather couch, which gave a squeaky protest at my bodyweight. The leather had scars and no few stains, which I imagined was why it had stayed here and not left along with Jaesung's cousin. I let the backpack slide between my feet, flexing knuckles that still stung from their impact with the Sorcerer's jaw.

Krista pulled something blue and filmy from the package, shuffling for a moment before holding up a strapless dress. I couldn't remember the style's name, but the skirt started just below the boobs and hung in layers of sparkly, sheer blue. The top was a band of shiny blue slightly darker than the skirt.

It was pretty, but all three of us could fit into it at the same time. And maybe Poo-stank.

Krista's face had gone scarlet, clashing with her orange hair. "Your mom knows I'm not 500 pounds, right?" she asked, one dark-drawn eyebrow lifted. "I mean, I'm thick, but...."

Jaesung grimaced. "Maybe she thought we measured in inches?" he offered. "I should have told her it was in centimeters—I just assume she knows I change everything into metric for her." He walked over with two bowls and held one out like an apology.

Krista shook her head and tossed the dress over a chair, blinking fast. "Whatever. I'll have to get it fitted." She trudged into the kitchen and dumped the last bowl of cereal back into the bag.

"Krista!" Jaesung admonished. "Come on, you know you're not fat."

"Whatever you say." She rinsed out the cereal bowl and shoved it back into the cabinet with a clatter. "Clearly I'm Korean fat."

"*I'm* Korean fat. Anyone who's driven past a McDonalds is Korean fat. Most of South Korea is Korean fat."

Then he glanced at me. His expression was a clear plea for help, those dark eyebrows lifted and pinched together, mouth set in a grimace. I wanted to shake my head. You can't spit in downtown Miami without hitting someone who's counted calories or carbs or steps, but it always seemed like such a pointless thing to worry about. There were way worse things a person could be than fat.

Jaesung jerked his head toward Krista, clearly thinking that, as a fellow girl, I might have something comforting to say. But I was an athlete. A half-starved one. I doubted she'd find anything I said comforting. "Or, if you don't alter it, you could smuggle in two or three dogs."

Jaesung's expression spasmed. Before I could decide what that meant, Krista let out a sound that was something between a squawk and a honk. She disappeared behind the counter, crouching and clinging to the edge so that just her sparkly-blue fingernails were visible.

Jaesung and I froze, both waiting to see whether her helpless wheezing was laughter or despair. The high-pitched keen made me think despair, and I leaped up, an apology getting tangled on its way past my tongue. Jaesung, however, relaxed. A laugh bubbling up from somewhere in his chest.

The next shriek from behind the counter was slightly more distinguishable as a laugh. Jaesung set the bowls on the counter and danced around it, leaning over the spot where Krista still crouched. A moment later, he had pulled her upright, and she leaned onto the breakfast bar, still making helpless sounds.

My comment hadn't been that funny, but laughing was clearly an emotional release for Krista in a way it never had been for me.

"B-B-" she stuttered, struggling over the word. Jaesung's grin was a white streak, crinkling his cheeks and eyes as he caught the giggle bug. Krista managed a gulp of air and said: "B-bridesmutts!"

It wasn't that funny. I could have sworn it wasn't that funny. But as she slapped her hand on the counter and doubled over in renewed shrieks, I found myself jolted into bewildered laughter.

It took a few minutes for us to stop giggling into our cereal bowls, and I found my stomach ached like I'd just finished a few hundred crunches. It was a good ache, though—a better ache than any of the others I could name. I kept my sleeve shifted over my bruised hand, even as I loaded my bowl into the dishwasher and bid my temporary roommates good night.

Their rooms were up a set of stairs to the left of the TV, in perfect line of sight to my borrowed couch. Krista clambered up, calling down her wishes of sweet dreams, but Jaesung stopped with his hand on the light-switch.

He half turned and glanced at me, a question flitting through his eyes, but it wasn't a question I was meant to answer. It was the sort of question people ask themselves before leaving a complete stranger alone in their living room.

"Night," I said, hoping to hurry his exit. The laughter had been a nice respite, but now I wanted to call Morgan, to find out what was going on and where my pack was.

Jaesung's gaze darted down to my hand, and his lips pursed for just an instant before relaxing back to fullness. He smiled then, and though he looked tired, the suspicion I'd seen had vanished so completely I might have imagined it.

"There's a bathroom at the top of the stairs," he said. "Door straight ahead."

I gave a tight-lipped smile and nodded, breaking eye contact and going for my bag, hoping he'd get the hint and go upstairs to bed. A moment later, the lights went out with a click—all but the light over the kitchen stove, which spilled past my shoulders and limned Jaesung's forearms and glasses in amber.

For a moment, he was featureless as a shadow, and just as unknowable. Then my eyes adjusted and I made out the relaxed balance of his weight shifted to one leg, and the darkness of his eyes beyond the reflection of the lenses.

"Night, Miami," he said. His voice sounded much lower in the dark.

I clenched my teeth, listening to each footfall on the stairs, noting which ones squeaked under his weight. I didn't move until his door opened and closed again.

Then my phone was against my ear, ringing as I held my breath, prepared for my cousin's voice. One ring, two, three...but Morgan didn't answer.

I called again, left a whispered voicemail, and ignored the swoop in my gut. It was late. He was probably sleeping or tucked away somewhere with his ringer silent—that was the sensible way to think about this. A traitorous voice whispered that my cousin didn't know how to sleep soundly. Even something as innocuous as the change in lighting from a brightened screen would have roused him.

I forced myself to set the phone down, stretch out on the battered leather sofa, and tuck my forehead against the back of the couch. I couldn't help Morgan now. All I could do was get some rest and try to learn as many mandalas as I could before the Guild caught up with me.

A wall clock ticked somewhere in the room, measuring out my heartbeats as I traced the magic circles in my mind. My fingers twitched against the soft leather, drawing the way power would flow to the four anchors, then through each concentric ring of glyphs, twisting and shaping until it leapt from the mandala as a fully-formed spell. Fire and water, earth and air—these seemed simple, their effects obvious. But there were hundreds of markings in each one. Too many ways it could all go wrong. If I was going to learn these spells, I would have to learn them flawlessly or risk blowing a crater in the nearest solid object. Or myself.

Despite the pressure, my phone's presence tugged at my brain. It was like the connection to Morgan created a magnetic pull, dragging me back to the phone with inexorable gravity. With Mom gone, he was the only blood family I had left. Still, I refused to turn back over, squeezing my eyes shut so blurred stars bloomed behind my eyelids, the sky through my cousin's binoculars.

For a moment, I imagined the smell of the sea. I was thirteen and lying on the dock at our harbor hideout, tears blurring and clearing the crystalline lights above before they slid back into my ears. My father was gone, and I didn't think I'd ever feel safe again. A silhouette appeared at my side and Morgan held his binoculars to my eyes. He let me cry, pretending he didn't see as I twisted the focus dials, trying and failing to make the sights behave like a telescope.

"What's the one right there?" he'd asked. "The W."

"Cassiopeia." That night, I'd taught Morgan the constellations Dad taught me. Later that week, he'd shown me how to clean and shoot a gun, and where to hide a knife on my body. That was the only way we knew how to grieve. And love.

He would call.

CHAPTER TEN

I'm not sure when I fell asleep, but I woke to the baying of a low-voiced dog downstairs and the deep, earthy smell of ground coffee. My brain throbbed, and I sat up with the overwhelming sense that my whole head was wrapped in packing foam. My eyes felt swollen, pulsing where they pushed back into the sockets, and every muscle in my back seemed to have shortened overnight.

I'd been running for days. I couldn't quite put my finger on how many it had been—two? Three? How many days since the Sorcerers snapped the enslavement spell? How many since Mom died?

I opened my eyes, knowing I was alone before I even glanced around the sun-striped floor. Good. I hated to think what pitiful animal I resembled, nested in the living room of two near-strangers. The dizzy, punch-drunk exhaustion of last night was gone, and I no longer thought I'd be able to talk to Krista or Jaesung like a normal person. Not that I'd managed much of that last night.

Despite my awkwardness, the muffled voices that rose from downstairs sent a swirl of comfort into my chest, like the beckoning steam of a hot drink. It felt good to wake up knowing there were other living beings so nearby. Too good. I was dangerously close to wanting to stay on this cognac-colored couch and steal a few more hours of sleep.

I massaged my forehead and raked the heavy bramble of dirty blonde hair back from my face. It had come out of its braid in the night, smelling of sweat and train and car exhaust. There was no lingering scent of ocean or blood—just the tacky feeling of salt water gone dry, refusing to let my fingers pass through.

That's when I noticed my phone, and the little message bubble.

I snatched up the phone, clicking into the message and racing through it. Within a few words, however, the unspooling tension tightened right back up.

Hey, I ninja'd your number while you were drooling on our couch!
If you're in town for a few more days, you should hang out with us.
Poo-stank would love someone to throw things for him while I'm
not home.
Anyway. Don't leave without saying bye! J.

I stared at the phone—my lifeline to my pack and the bearer of brutal truths—and this incongruous message stared back. I had brief, military-style texts from Eamon, that terrible voicemail from Morgan, and now this. There were little icons in the messages—a laughing face, a cartoon dog, a waving hand. I wanted to delete it.

My brain prickled. It felt like anger, but warped, and it pushed out the brief sense of comfort from not being alone. He'd taken my phone and put his number in it. Called or texted himself. He hadn't even asked. What if Morgan had texted me something important and he'd seen?

Part of me wanted to give him the benefit of the doubt. Maybe this was commonplace in normal-people society. Maybe he was flirting with me. I didn't get honest flirtation that much, not from guys who were my age or anything near as clean as Jaesung. I should probably be happy he didn't think I was a crack whore, not mad he'd committed a minor invasion of privacy.

But the rest of me remembered the restrained power of his movements, the way he picked up bags and vaulted stairs and steered unwelcome train passengers like he had total command of every muscle—like he had training. The rest of me had read threat from him last night, when he'd met my eyes and spoken about secrets. And now he'd gone into my phone. What if he'd been looking for something other than a way to get in contact with me?

And, sweet hell, what if he'd just tagged me like a shark? I couldn't give up the phone—it was the only way to contact my pack— so if he was working with the Sorcerers, he'd be able to call me any time he wanted. I wasn't sure how phone traces worked, but I imagined having a cell number helped.

Which meant he could have Morgan's number now. He could track him too. I felt sick. The likelihood of Jaesung being a Sorcerer wasn't overwhelming, but there was no text or missed call from Morgan to displace the anxiety.

"Good morning!" Krista's singsong greeting sent me halfway off the sofa. With the barking carrying on downstairs, I hadn't heard her feet on the stairs.

I whipped around to see her standing in the doorway in a pair of khaki cargo pants and a tee shirt stained with a streak of yellow gunk. A flush colored her cheeks, and her blue eyes were bright beneath orange-penciled brows. What caught my attention, though, was the enormous tattoo down her left arm. It was a riot of colors, and though I couldn't see the entire thing, it looked something like a rock star from the 80s surrounded by freaky creatures in gray and green.

"Morning," I replied. I lowered my phone from where I'd clutched it against my pulsing chest.

She grinned and headed for the kitchen. "You sleep like the dead, babe," she said, knocking the handle of the sink so the water turned on. "Have you eaten anything yet?"

"No, I just woke up," I said. I slid my phone into my pocket as I stood up, but Krista's gaze followed it.

"Did your people call?" she asked, soaping up to her elbow. I shook my head and made my way over to the breakfast bar, sliding onto the stool across from her.

"No, they're taking their fucking time."

Krista flashed a grin up at me as she dried her hands. "That just means you'll get roped into helping out here. After lunch. Well, I guess it's breakfast for you."

She tossed aside her towel and snagged an empty mug from the counter, wiggling it in my direction. I gave her a thumbs up. She slid it into one of those single cup pod-coffee machines and, after some arcane ritual of button-pressing and lever-pulling, had the device gurgling.

"So, I was telling Sanadzi about you working with dogs in Miami and she said you could help out today, if that's cool with you."

I shrugged—until I knew what was going on with Morgan and the pack, I didn't want to leave the rendezvous behind. Local Sorcerer or not, this was the safest place I'd found, and it didn't cut into my bankroll. I could study the book, but I could only memorize so many mandalas before my brain overheated.

"Sa-NA-jee," I said, sounding out the name. "She's the one getting married? The vet?"

"Yeah. Oh my God!" Krista grinned, rocking back against the fridge and clapping her hands. "I told her about the dress and she fucking died. Sooyoung—that's Jae's mom—did the same thing for the other two bridesmaids and we all have to get our dresses taken in. She's really embarrassed she made them too big, but there's plenty of time for alterations, so Sanadzi wasn't upset."

I nodded, though I had a hard time faking interest. Wedding prep drama just seemed so...domestic. I might have craved a normal life, but the thought of getting caught up in such pointless worries almost made me thankful for the perspective of growing up enslaved to a blood magic gang lord. Almost.

Krista grabbed my coffee, and as she slid onto the stool beside me, I wondered what it would be like to be her, where my chief concerns were college, bridesmaids dresses, and weight. Was that privileged life easier, or did it feel just as hard?

This time, I heard the footsteps on the stairs. Rapid, measured steps that hit every stair on the way up—not Jaesung. Not anyone I knew. Krista turned on her stool in time to intercept a tall, out-of-breath woman with two laden plastic bags.

She was unique enough to draw anyone's eye. Her facial structure suggested at least one of her parents was black, but her tight curls were blonde and her skin was a freckle-dusted fawn that still held a tinge of pink from her flight up the stairs. She had a long, curvy body adorned in green corduroy overalls, orange paisley shirt, and a grin that could have dimmed a lighthouse.

I blinked, certain this was the first time I'd seen overalls in real life. Or corduroy.

"You've gotta be the waif!" she announced, and headed for me like a missile. I saw the spreading arms and tensed. She was about to hug me. Why would she do that? We hadn't even met! I leaned back in shock, stopped by the bartop pressing into my spine.

Then Sanadzi wrapped thin, strong arms around me, and I found my chin jammed over her shoulder. Her hands pressed into my back. Multiple chunky necklaces clicked against my cheek. It wasn't so much politeness that kept me in place as surprise, like I'd found a mythical beast of legend: the Hugger.

I patted her elbow, thankful when the hug didn't last more than two heartbeats. She pulled back, both of her hands on my upper arms, squeezing like even her fingers had to hug me.

"Oh, she's no waif," Sanadzi said. She grinned and looked over her shoulder at Krista. "She's one of those *solid* skinny people like Baby Jae."

Krista rolled her eyes. "That figures."

With one last squeeze of my biceps, Sanadzi let go. Her eyes flicked back to me, a striking amber-green. "I heard you're a dog person?"

At last, I found my voice. "Yes!" I said, snatching my coffee cup and holding it in front of me to ward off any future hugs. Luckily, Sanadzi seemed satisfied with the first one and joined Krista in doling out huge plates of Chinese take out.

We ate, they talked, and I avoided questions with well-timed bites of lo mein, glad when discussion turned to Sanadzi's upcoming wedding. I took a second helping of sweet and sour chicken, packing away energy while I had the chance.

After lunch, we descended to the dog rescue. As Sanadzi opened the office, Krista and I rolled up the two enormous garage doors to display a day as cool and clear as glass. I hadn't looked at the seasonal changes around me since Virginia, and the nipping cold at my cheeks and nose warned me before I blinked the day into focus.

Miami skies were the kind of blue that made a person squint, burning hot into your irises whenever you looked too long, but up here, over a line of fiery maple leaves, the sky seemed to ache with color, like there was too much blue to hold. Across the street, a small park entrance lay behind a wrought iron fence, which stretched between two buildings in a more contemporary brick than the fire house.

I sniffed the air, which had a tinge of spicy smoke to it.

"Is something burning?" I asked, and took a deeper breath to make sure. It reminded me of patchouli, or men's cologne.

"Leaves, probably," Krista said, then pointed across the street. "Yup, in the park. They're raking today."

I spotted the piles of leaves, amber and brown and gold on grass still green despite the chill. For a minute, I just stared, taking in the trees and the sky and the chill air nipping at my cheeks, taking the colors and scents of fall. This was October. The word finally connected with an image.

For the next four hours, I worked with Krista and Sanadzi, clipping leashes to harnesses and jogging up and down the street with the dogs that could run. I cleaned out soiled newspaper from the kennels and helped reapply foul-smelling paste to Poo-stank's patchy fur.

It was almost four-thirty when my phone rang. I was sweating, lifting a limp, one-eyed mutt onto the examination table for Sanadzi to look at. He was in bad shape, and didn't even twitch at the buzz of my phone against his spine. Krista met my eyes, then looked at Sanadzi.

"We got it," the older woman said. "This booboo's not going anywhere, poor thing."

I jogged to the stairs and snatched up my phone on the fifth ring, my breath short as I reached the top of the stairs.

"Hello?"

"Are you safe?" Morgan's voice sent a rush of relief through me, so strong that I had to lean against the door for a moment, dizzy with it.

"Yeah," I said.

I heard him let out a breath, as if he'd been holding it too. Something creaked, like a chair, and I imagined him sitting at some motel-room desk, tattoo crawling out from the collar of his shirt, his riot of white-blond hair restrained in a hasty ponytail.

"Where are you?" he asked. His voice was so tired, so raw that I almost answered.

"I'm in—I'm at the rendezvous."

He grunted. "I don't know where the rendezvous is. Eamon didn't tell us. He just told us which places to go next. Had us up and down the East coast, breaking off into groups. The Guild sniffed our asses the whole way."

I swallowed. "Are you okay?"

"I'm not hurt."

The clock on the wall ticked softly and I flexed my fingers, as if punishing myself for my safety with the sting of raw knuckles. "Me either."

I pushed off the door and headed to the dog bed that still held the remnants of my shredded bag. "Where are you? Eamon didn't want me to say anything about the rendezvous, but I can come to you."

"No." The word stopped me at the edge of the coffee table. I moved the phone away from my ear a second, as if the speaker had delivered a sting. Morgan's voice was farther away when he said, "I'm being watched."

I gave a humorless laugh. "Who isn't? They were waiting for me at the rendezvous, though I don't think they know that's what it is."

Morgan breathed a curse and, his tone agitated, growled out, "I thought you said you were safe."

"Compared to what?" I picked at the seam in my jeans. "I got away. Some good Samaritans I met on the train adopted me and the Guild backed off. They don't want to involve mundanes."

He was silent for several breaths. I sank onto the arm of the couch, staring at the bottles of shampoo and conditioner peeking from beneath a pair of jeans.

"Do you still have the book?"

"Yeah." I nudged my backpack with a boot.

"And you're sure they won't mess with the mundanes?"

I couldn't keep the bitterness from my voice as I replied. "Kinda their whole schtick, isn't it? Protect the ignorant from magic. Kill the blood Sorcerers and anyone who works for them. Even if they have no choice."

"Stay put," Morgan said. "I'll contact you when I've lost the tail."

He cut the call. I stood for a moment, staring at my pile of stuff, processing the command. What the hell was I going to do until he got here? Krista and Jaesung might let me stay, but I didn't know how long it would take Morgan to lose his Guild pursuers. The longer I was here, the more chance I gave the Guild to get me good and surrounded.

I shoved my phone back into my hoodie pocket then trudged back down the stairs. It was like walking into a brick wall, the atmosphere was so different. I paused on the stairs, taking in the scene. Krista stroked the face of the limp mutt with gentle fingers, her orange head bent near its ear. Sanadzi's hand lay across the dog's prominent ribs and the light of her smile had gone out.

Then I saw Jaesung. He leaned against the pillar beside the examination table in a black hoodie, red sweatpants, and the same pristine white shoes he'd worn yesterday.

He'd shoved both hands in his pockets, and eyes dull behind his glasses. Unlike Krista and Sanadzi, he noticed my movement on the stairs and glanced up. A small shake of the head confirmed my assumption. The one-eyed dog was dying.

I eased down the stairs, positioning myself on the unoccupied side of the examination table. Fat tears rolled down Krista's nose as she stroked the hair along the dog's muzzle. I listened to the labored breathing, glancing at Sanadzi's drawn face.

"We can't save them all, baby," the vet said to Krista. "Sometimes they wanna go."

I closed my eyes, gripping the side of the examination table as my mother's face flashed behind my eyelids. Fine-boned and hard-eyed. The blood on my hands, in her hair. The little hole that didn't seem big enough to change anything.

There had been so much death in the past few days. I wasn't sure I could watch more.

The presence loomed on my right an instant before I felt the light touch on my elbow. I opened my eyes and inhaled, trying to calm shaking hands as I glanced up at Jaesung. My nose was level with his collarbone, and he smelled like sweat and cold air, a hint of burning leaves. Up close, his eyes weren't as dark as I'd first thought.

I followed the tacit instruction. Together, we climbed the stairs and left Krista and Sanadzi to their grief.

He pulled the door shut behind us and dumped his backpack. I struggled with the silence, sure there was something I should say. But Jaesung just headed for the kitchen. He ejected a pod from the coffee machine and selected a green-labeled one from the carousel. I slid onto a barstool, an uncomfortable witness.

The machine gurgled. Jaesung slid his fingers under his glasses to rub at his eyes.

"Sorry you had to be here for this," he said, voice muffled by his hands. "We don't lose dogs often, but it really sucks when we do."

My heart jolted. He and Krista and Sanadzi were the ones in pain. Why was he apologizing to me?

"No, it... I mean, it happens," I said. I paused a moment, wondering what Mom would say. Normal people said something at times like these. "If you had to rescue them, they were already in bad situations."

Jaesung leaned his elbows on the bar across from me, looking down at his hands, but he seemed to be listening, accustomed to the dance of normal human interaction. Playing his part. I licked my lips and went on.

"Everyone loves the stories about people and animals bouncing back from hell, but most of the time it doesn't work like that. Most of the time they just drag that hell along behind them. It wouldn't be inspiring, I guess, if everyone beat the odds."

I glanced up to find Jaesung watching me, his chin cupped in both hands, fingers curled in like he might bite his nails. It wasn't a look I could read, and it lasted a second too long. At last, he looked away.

"I never know what to say to them," he said. "I mean, I'm sad, but Krista and Sanadzi get invested, you know? We've had Lulu a week and she was touch-and-go from the start. I just... I guess I don't let myself attach the way they do."

I nodded, relieved to hear a sentiment I could recognize. "Yeah. I'm like that too," I said. "Like you, I mean. It takes me a long time."

Jaesung sucked in his lip and spread his hands out in front of him. The veins were prominent today, and I traced his knuckles in my head, sketching the length of his fingers and the muscle of his thumb, the shell-like gradient of his fingernails. He had draw-able hands. I glanced up at him, considering his full mouth and the little scar on his chin. He had draw-able everything, really, and there was something malleable about his movements now, like his muscles were warm and ready to work.

What had he been up to besides class? I glanced at the backpack he'd dropped by the door, then back at the pile of my things on the coffee table, thinking of my sketchbook. It had been a long time since I'd sketched a person. One who wasn't dead.

"Did you hear from your family yet?"

I twisted back to him, fumbling for a lie that wasn't a lie. "Yeah, my cousin got ahold of me. They ran into some delays, so it'll take them a few days to get here."

"That sucks," Jaesung said. "I mean, not that I'm, like, super eager for you to go or anything, but it's no fun to have everything up in the air."

I lifted my eyebrows and nodded.

Jaesung went back to the coffee machine and took his drink. "Do you want one?" he asked. "Tea, I mean. Or coffee, I don't know."

I looked at the steam rising from the mug. "You're one of those?"

"One of what?"

"You drink tea hot."

Jaesung lowered his cup and gave me a challenging look. "Yes. I drink it hot. Like it's been drunk for thousands of years before white people chucked ice at it."

"If you lived in the South, you'd chuck ice at it too."

He shrugged. "To be fair, we drink cold tea in Korea sometimes. We don't put sugar in it, though. Ever."

I cocked my head. "You're actually from Korea?"

He nodded, circumventing the bar and walking past me to the stool next to the wall. He collapsed onto it and leaned into the brick. "Yep, born in Seoul. Came to the U.S. when I was nine."

I leaned back. Miami had a diverse population, and I was decent at detecting non-native accents, but nothing about the way Jaesung talked suggested he wasn't a native speaker. He had a better vocabulary than I did.

I glanced at the top of the fridge, where a pair of jars sat half-filled with quarters and bills, and decided to end that line of questioning.

Jaesung chuckled, having seen me look. "She learns."

A clatter came on the stairs and a moment later, Krista burst through, an orange blur making a bee-line for the stairs to the third floor. Jaesung tensed, leaning forward as if to stand up.

"Shit," he said. We made our way to the stairs, but just as I took a step down, I heard a voice that was not Sanadzi's.

"...not sure what kind of dogs you have. I'm looking for something big. Great Dane or Irish Wolf Hound."

Sanadzi sounded tired. "No, sorry. we've got a German Shepherd mix and a lab, but nothing that size. I'm sorry, now isn't a great time—if you'd give me your contact information...."

Jaesung tapped me on the shoulder. "What?"

I turned around and shoved past him back up the stairs. "I should check on Krista," I said.

"Okay...?"

But I knew that voice. I'd heard it last night, in a one-sided conversation with the people who had killed my mother—that tenor with its smoker's rasp.

I pulled the door shut and crouched next to the circle of plexiglass, my pulse shuddering behind the notch in my collarbone. Jaesung made it to the bottom of the stairs and disappeared into the garage. All I heard were murmurs, but after a moment, the light below squeezed off with the rumble of shutting garage doors, and I knew he was gone.

It was no comfort. I also knew he would be back, and next time I wasn't sure he would be alone.

CHAPTER ELEVEN

I slept on the couch another night, memorizing two more mandalas before I fell asleep. The next morning, I rose at the respectable hour of 8AM and put in a full nine hours of scrubbing and medicating, feeding and organizing, and making myself familiar to the dogs at Ruff Patch. Maybe they could smell the hound in me, but even the ones Krista insisted were timid sniffed at my hands and let me stroke their ears.

Though both Sanadzi and Jaesung were gone most of the day—Sanadzi to her actual vet office and Jaesung to class and "practice"—Krista kept up a constant stream of chatter that kept me from panicking about the Sorcerer.

The Guild must have traced the plates on Jaesung's truck. That would explain how he'd found me, unless he'd used a magical tracker. Or Jaesung really was a Guild spy. With any luck, the Sorcerer would have assumed I moved on after last night, but just in case he was keeping eyes on the place, I avoided any task that took me out the open garage doors.

"Poor, cold Miami girl," Krista teased. She'd recovered from her shock the night before and, considering I'd made good on my words to

Jaesung and checked on her, seemed to consider me "good people".
She'd said as much to Eugene when he called.

It was still hard not to think about Morgan, about the Sorcerers
trailing him and the fact that, unlike me, he didn't have a book to use
as collateral. The thoughts made working a relief. Even if it wasn't
what I wanted to be doing, at least it was progress, and that kept me
from driving myself crazy. By the time Sanadzi arrived that evening,
I'd polished every bit of stainless steel, swept every inch of concrete,
and sanitized all the unidentifiable veterinary instruments.

"Girl, you're staying," she said, approaching where I sat in a
folding chair next to the kennels, tugging at a jumble of leashes. "I like
a clean-freak."

"I'm not really a clean freak-"

"Na-ah-ah!" She held up a hand. "Don't tell me that when I'm
about to offer you a job."

I set down the leash. "A job? I'm not—I mean, my family—they're
coming."

Sanadzi squatted in front of me, picking at the knot for a second
before dropping it again. "Yeah, Jae told me about your people this
morning, but it's not a paycheck and 401k kind of job. It's volunteer
work, with housing benefits. You could work afternoon and night
with Jaesung, or keep working days with Kris. Just till your family
makes it into town. Or longer, if you guys are planning to stay."

I tugged at a knot in the leashes, wondering if I could stand the
normalcy for a few more days. I was sure the Guild wouldn't hurt
them, even if they knew where I was. It was a better offer than I could
have imagined.

I glanced up at Sanadzi, whose face had softened from her
blinding smile to something more like how she looked at the dogs.
She was rescuing another stray. "Thanks."

Krista insisted we go out to one of the local pubs to celebrate the
new-hire. Though my brain fizzed with warnings, it was hard to deny
people who just wanted to be nice.

I took a long shower, and changed into jeans and a warm top. I'd bought it for the length—which hung almost past my butt and concealed the butterfly knife in my pocket—but the white fabric was kitten-soft and I liked the thin red stripes.

By the time we'd made the mile walk through town, I thought I'd never stop shivering. A pool of light spilled across the wet asphalt in front of Rinkenburger's Pub, where patrons smoked in fleece-lined jackets and college sweatshirts. I was glad to see the pub, but only for the instant it took to recognize it as a tactical disaster.

A bouncer guarded the door. Windows opaque with steam suggested both a crowded room and a lack of ventilation. That meant exits were sparse.

Krista and Jaesung rushed up to the heavy door, lifting their ID's to the red-coated man. The door guard wore a beanie, gloves, and an earring, but unlike the bouncers in Miami, he looked somewhat pleasant. Krista was waved through, and they gave Jaesung a large black X over the back of his hand.

I hesitated. I didn't want to go into a bar when I didn't know the layout—not when it was so busy, and not when I'd have to show my fake ID to someone who could be watching for me. But Krista turned around to look for me, Jaesung was already disappearing into the crowd, and there was a divine smell coming from inside.

My stomach growled, betraying logic for the promise of meat. I extended my hand and the bouncer drew an X.

Jaesung had stopped around the middle of the room to squint at the TV mounted above the bar. I peered over just in time to see the Packers leading the Saints.

Sound hit me like a punch. The crowd around the bar boiled up from their seats. Before I thought about it, I jumped back. If there'd been room, I would have crouched, ready to spring either toward the threat or away from it. Instead, I plowed backwards into a table. The outer ring of my tattoo burned.

I heard a yelp, then the sound of cracking glass. Beer splashed down my calf and something tangled around my foot. The table toppled beneath me.

I had an impression of graying beard and baseball cap as an older man tried to save both me and his beer at the same time. Two women in boots and puffy vests pulled me to my feet. They looked like mother and daughter—the older thin and tan, the younger athletic and blond—and their grip on my arms was firm. I repressed the instinct to fight. They were helping me. Not restraining.

All the same, when I regained my balance, I twisted from their grasp and stepped back, hands up.

They were a nice midwestern family. Jeans and leggings and college sweatshirts—the man's hat had a fly-fishing logo on it. There was something impossibly wholesome about them, as if they got up every morning to a rooster's crow and dressed up on Sundays. They probably had a dog, and a tractor. I bet they cut their own Christmas trees.

I felt sick.

The parents were righting the table as the girl, who was about Krista's age, asked me if I was okay. She'd knelt to pick up the contents of the purse, but seemed more concerned with my welfare than the state of her scattered makeup.

My heart punched my sternum—a desperate animal battering its cage. These were nice people. A nice family. A father and a mother and a daughter enjoying a night out, like it was the most expected thing in the world. Like it was so. Fucking. Easy.

I wasn't certain if the feeling rising in me now was adrenaline or rage, but it swelled, pushing my lungs aside and leaving no room for air. Static seemed to fill my brain, occluding everything that wasn't fight, run, escape. I had to get out of here.

A man's arm hooked around my shoulders from behind, crossing over my collarbone. I grabbed his sleeve and reached back, prepared to throw him right into that nice midwestern family's nicely righted table.

"Go Saints!" Jaesung's voice at my ear halted me.

It was his forearm pressing against my collarbone, his hand death-gripping my shoulder, his jacket pressing into my shoulder blades. He shifted his weight to the side, and I realized his free hand had anchored itself at my belt. It wasn't the perfect counter Morgan had taught me for Judo-like throws, but given how unyielding that arm was around me, it might have worked.

Worse, it told me he'd known what I was about to do.

But, apparently, his sports exclamation was all the little Henard family needed to excuse my behavior. They cheered too, concern dissolving into relieved laughter.

There was static building up in my body, a feeling like imminent lightning. The charge seemed to crackle across my skin.

A waitress appeared with replacement beers, followed by another with a dustpan to sweep up the glass. Together, they erased the evidence of what I'd done, and the ebb and flow of the crowd around us went back to normal, as if nothing had ever happened. As if I'd never walked in, or never existed.

My heart still hammered against Jaesung's forearm, cheeks prickling. I let go of his sleeve and pushed myself away, half expecting sparks to crackle over his wool jacket.

He smiled, but his eyes were serious when he said, "You good, Miami?"

I clenched my jaw and nodded. My Spellhound tattoo itched, as if the hound's spirit trapped inside me wanted to run, escape the encroaching lightning. But I would make myself look more abnormal by running now, and I couldn't do that if I wanted to stay.

'Wanted' maybe wasn't the right word. I didn't *want* to stay with these people, who in a handful of hours had kicked the struts from my belief that even normal people weren't all that good.

Krista appeared at my other side. "I found them!" she called, pointing to a raised area in the back corner. Beyond a waist-high barrier, three standing tables lorded above the rest. I would have picked the corner one, protected on two sides, but Sanadzi had chosen one in the middle. I didn't like it—it would have a good view, but if I could see her, it wouldn't take long for a Guild toady to spot me either.

Sanadzi stood next to a big man in a red button up and leather jacket. From the arm draped over her shoulders, I knew it had to be Eugene. He was not at all what I'd expected. His brown hair was both shorter and neater than Jaesung's, and though closer inspection revealed eyes and cheekbones that must have come from the Korean side of his family, the rest fell somewhere between linebacker and lumberjack.

We climbed up to meet them, and though electricity still prickled through my veins, I forced an apology for the scene.

"It's okay, baby!" Sanadzi shouted over the noise. "Folks here get rowdy when we play the Packers. I should have remembered you didn't like crowds!"

I winced, wondering what Krista had told her about my behavior on the train, and slipped in next to her. The humidity of the room was sinking in, and as Krista and Jaesung worked at the toggles of their wool coats, I unfastened my beer-streaked jacket. I moved in, turning my back to the wall. The cool wood felt good, solid and dependable, covering me from at least one direction.

Krista started to take the spot next to me, but her phone flashed. She shook it at us, pushed back past Jaesung, and plowed through the crowd with a finger in one ear and the phone in the other. Jaesung installed himself next to me, cutting off both my view of the front door and hope of easily extracting myself from the table. My arms buzzed with the growing charge, and I felt it prickle the hairs on my neck.

Who was he? What sport or martial art did he do that taught him to move like that? Why did I feel like he'd sketched his own ideas over the gaps in my story, and that some were scarily accurate? It bothered me almost as much as my inability to get a good read on him. One minute he was sharp-eyed and shadowed, the next he was a city-slick geek with a labrador's haphazard energy. Was I inventing half of it from paranoia?

As Jaesung passed his coat to Sanadzi, I scanned the room. The kitchen was to our left, along with a restroom sign and double doors that opened onto a beer garden. A few groups cradled steaming drinks beneath the glow of antique bulbs. Krista stood near the fence, her shoulders hunched against the chill. She didn't look happy with her phone call.

"How do you like Minnesota weather, Helena?"

I dragged my gaze from Krista. Eugene grinned at me in a way that suggested he knew how miserably cold it was. I tried to cut through the static in my brain for something to say.

"I assume we'll be hitching the dogs to a sled soon."

"Now there's an idea!" Sanadzi poked Eugene's arm. "I want a dog sled for my wedding present." Eugene gave her a doubtful look.

"You'd make *me* pull it before you hitched up a dog."

"What's your point?"

Eugene shielded his face from Sanadzi's view and mouthed "She's crazy!" at me behind his fingers. "So," he said, returning to an audible level of partial-shouting. "Why's your family moving from Miami?"

I should have been prepared for the question—had been prepared with appropriate deflections and redirections when the others had asked—but the tension still building from earlier had pushed all cleverness aside. For a second, all I could do was stare at him, my brain glitching over the thought. Why had we left Miami? Why. Why. Why.

"It's..." I sucked at the air. "It's complicated. Family stuff."

He gave a sideways nod, as if to grant my right to vagueness. I twisted my fingers together beneath the table, resisting the desire to scribe the glyphs popping into my head, the ones that might help release this building charge burning away my paper-thin calm.

"You looking at going to school up here?"

Breathe, Helena.

"I don't know. I mean, I'd like to, but I don't really know if we'll be sticking around."

Eugene nodded, lifted his beer, and Sanadzi tilted her head, looking at me over the horn-rimmed glasses she'd donned to read the menu. "Speaking of school, isn't mid-semester a weird time to move? You're, what, a senior?"

The questions were friendly enough and, to anyone else, innocuous. But here I was, having never set foot inside a normal classroom, trying to figure out something to tell them that would stop the questions and give me a chance to calm down. No thoughts came, and I found the truth spilling from my mouth before the pause went on too long.

"I'm d-done with High School." It came out as a stammer. "I finished when I was fifteen."

Sanadzi tapped my arm with the back of her hand. "Oh, we got a smartypants!"

I laughed, and there was a strange warble of panic to it. "More like bored and homeschooled. I didn't take summers off."

New questions brewed around Eugene and Sanadzi, gathering like a storm cloud. Jaesung had been quiet during the interrogation, and I caught him looking at me over a menu. He looked down, his chin giving a little jerk, as if to shake his head in denial of spying.

The waitress came for our orders before they came up with any more questions, and by the time she had left again, Krista was pushing her way through the crowd.

She mounted the stairs, her face pinched at the brow. She held her features tense, and the smile she gave the waitress seemed ready to cave in as she tacked on her order. Sanadzi drew her chin back when Krista ordered four tequila shots.

"Everything okay?" Eugene asked.

Krista gave an exaggerated sigh and slapped her phone on the table. "That's what I still want to know."

When she realized everyone was looking at her, she smiled and waved a hand in front of her, as if trying to disperse the concern. "Stop—I don't want to think about it right now. I just want to have fun, okay?"

She turned to me, her smile desperate, as though I were a fun-producing fairy godmother.

"Helena! We should play a game! One of those team-building things people do on office retreats."

Eugene grimaced. "You want to play a cheesy college ice breaker?"

"Jae and I *are* in college, kay thanks."

Jaesung balanced an arm over Krista's shoulders, visibly siding with her against his cousin. "I *like* cheesy college ice breakers."

"As long as it's not spin the bottle."

In mock offense, Jaesung clapped a hand to his chest. "You don't want to kiss me, cuz?"

"I don't give a shit about kissing you. I don't want your dirty little mouth anywhere near Sanadzi. Or yours!" He pointed at Krista. "And Hel, I don't know what way you swing, but my fiancée is not on the college ice-breaker menu."

Sanadzi gave him an amused eyebrow quirk as the waitress returned with their drinks. Four shot glasses of tequila and a plate of lime wedges appeared in front of Krista, who opened a sugar packet with a grin.

Eugene frowned. "Those had better be unrelated to the college ice breaker."

"Bitch, back off my shots." Krista picked up a glass in one hand and a sugared lime wedge in the other, making short work of both. She dropped the lime peel into the empty shot glass and shuddered. "Let's play never-have-I-ever."

She raised a hand in front of her in a "stop" motion. Sanadzi laughed and copied her, followed by Jaesung. Eugene rolled his eyes, but held up a hand.

I copied, hoping to catch onto the rules as we went but there must have been a neon sign on my forehead flashing "WTF?"

Sanadzi leaned over. "You say something you've never done, and anyone who's done it has to put down a finger. Last one with fingers up wins."

"I'll start," Krista said. "Never have I ever been admitted to a hospital."

Jaesung and Sanadzi each lowered a finger. It took a moment to remember whether I should put down a finger or keep one up. Despite some serious injuries, I'd never been to a hospital. It was why my left pinkie finger didn't move well, why there was a lump on my collarbone where a crowbar had snapped it two years ago.

"Okay," Jaesung rocked back on his feet, four fingers in the air. "Never have I ever...been to Disney World." His gaze flicked to me, a fledgling smirk on his lips.

I kept five resolute fingers up.

"Oh, come on!" He said. "But you lived in Florida!"

"Disney's, like..." My brain vomited up a map. "200 miles from Miami."

"That's closer than here."

"We just never went. It wasn't a thing for me."

"But it's Disney!"

I shrugged. I only ever saw snatches of cartoons in dark, tinfoil-scattered living rooms. Maybe it was the stained carpets I sat on, but the stories never seemed like fun. Cat and mouse, coyote and roadrunner, hunter and rabbit—they were always about characters chasing one another, trying to kill one another. I couldn't laugh at it, just sat, waiting for the bird, the mouse, the rabbit to make its fatal mistake. Even as a child, I'd been too fatalistic to think it would last.

Jaesung was still shaking his head at me when Sanadzi nudged my elbow. "Your turn."

"Never have I ever seen snow."

A collective sigh went up around the table. They'd expected it. Sanadzi went next, and I put down a finger. Then it was Eugene's turn, then back to Krista. She was down to three fingers and one tequila shot, and wore a mellowed expression.

"Never have I ever...um...fuck...."

"You've done that," Jaesung said. She elbowed him.

"Been in a fist-fight!" she said, triumphant. She downed her last shot, wobbling.

Everyone but Sanadzi put down a finger. Eugene grinned across the table at me. "I've got to hear that story."

That story. Like it was one time. I gave another nervous laugh. "That's a little beyond college ice-breaker-level," I said.

Jaesung glanced between me and Krista, like he wasn't sure which of us to keep under surveillance. "Never have I ever spilled an entire bottle of nail polish remover on my roommate's three-hundred-dollar textbook."

"That was targeted!" Krista whined. She was down to a single finger, and gave me a pleading look across the table. "Nothing about snow!"

"Get her, Hel," Sanadzi said, sparkling with competitive glee.

But something was wrong. Krista's eyes said she needed to play—needed to keep laughing and distracting herself from whatever she'd heard on the other end of that phone call.

"Never have I ever been out of the country." *Legally*, I added in my head.

"You suck," Jaesung said, but he didn't look unhappy as he put down his third finger. He glanced at Krista, who grinned at me with the tip of her tongue poking between her teeth.

Sanadzi was first out, followed rather inevitably by Krista. Eugene knocked Jaesung out with something about a costume involving tights, which had everyone but me laughing in fond memory.

Then it was just us—me and this near stranger. I could have said something targeted and easy, something about kissing Sanadzi, or buying a house. Instead, I stared at his brown beard, his broad shoulders, his arm around Sanadzi, and found myself thinking of the picture of my parents. They'd smiled like that, touched easily. Seeing these two now was a cruel smudge of reminder. Those people were gone.

"Never have I ever been to a funeral." I said it almost dreamily.

The pressure in my forehead dimmed my thoughts. Eugene hadn't dropped his finger, but the corners of his lips lowered. He glanced at Jaesung so fast I'd have missed it if I wasn't staring. My pulse throbbed behind my ears.

Eugene's eyes narrowed. "Never have I ever run away from home."

That was it—the twinge of suspicion, explained. Jaesung's shrewd expression, the glances between him and Eugene. The worst part was the knowledge that he was right. I had run away.

My mother's face appeared, overwhelming my vision as she stared at me like a ghost, a thin ribbon of blood trickling from the hole in her cheek. Her hair blew in the sea wind and crackled with static, static that echoed the buzz on my skin.

I'd felt like this on the boat, right before I'd lost control of my power. That turquoise flash, the shattering glass and spreading flame. It had loosened something inside me, some door I no longer knew how to close.

My body was a storm cloud, and magic raced through it like particles building a charge. My veins prickled, making pathways for that unrestrained bolt of power.

It was going to happen again.

I backed away from the table. I heard nothing, felt nothing but the rolling mass of humanity around me, no longer individuals. A hand grabbed my arm as I reached the stairs—a feminine voice speaking—but I wrenched away.

Out. The closest exit was the beer garden. I charged through the press of wool and body heat, hunting light, hunting open.

If they caught me, they would contact someone. Report the missing minor. Then the Guild would claim me and it would all be over.

I shoved my way into the beer garden, frigid air sheathing my body. My throat opened. Magic flashed on the wings of my scream, bright turquoise.

I had the split-second relief of knowing only I could see that flash, before every lightbulb overhead exploded.

CHAPTER TWELVE

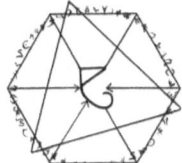

I'm not sure how I got out front. One moment I was on my hands and knees, staring at the sparkling frost of broken glass on the beer garden slate, the drain of magic sucking the light from my vision. The next, I registered the front patio of Rinkenburger's and the sour smell of bile.

Flashes illuminated wood paneling in quick, colored succession. Red-blue-red-blue. For a second I struggled with the familiarity of that pattern. Magic? Police cars.

I staggered backwards, halted by something solid behind me. Someone. I stepped forward again, trying to turn, and found gentle hands on my arms.

"It's okay, baby. We've got you."

Sanadzi, her voice gentle. Memory caught up with me, anchoring me to where I was, and what I'd done. I looked up, finding her face in the flickering police lights. Her expression was tense, despite the comforting smile that curved her lips. A piece of glass sparkled in her dense curls.

Behind her, Krista was holding onto the fence surrounding Rinkenburger's patio, vomiting into the bushes. That was the bile-smell. Other people stood in clumps, arms crossed, breath making little ghosts in front of their faces as they spoke to dark-clad officers. Eugene was one of them. When he saw me looking, he tapped the officer's arm and started toward us.

A flash of reflection at the front of the pub drew my eyes away from Eugene's approach. The door—now webbed with cracks— swung out, and Jaesung exited, coats folded over his arms.

He and Eugene converged where Sanadzi and I stood, Eugene looking serious and worried, Jaesung smiling with forced, false calm.

"So," he said, grinning around at the three of us. "Tuesday. Major success."

Sanadzi made an attempt at a laugh and extracted Krista's bright green coat from his arms. The warmth of her disappeared from my side. I hadn't even realized she'd been standing so close. I shuddered, stared at the bundle of coats, knowing I should put one on.

"Sanadzi and I should take the girls home," Jaesung said to Eugene, handing over his cousin's leather jacket. He glanced back at the officer, then to me. "Unless you want to talk to the police?"

I should have shaken my head. I tried to shake it, but nothing moved. My jaw wouldn't open, bones shuddering with either cold or utter exhaustion.

This felt like post-transformation. I hadn't been this tired after my first magical overload—I'd been able to swim, to run, to fight. Maybe I'd had more magic in me then, more energy. After two trans- formations and so many days of travel and stress, maybe I didn't have the energy to spare like I had back on the boat.

I didn't remember Jaesung had asked me a question until he stepped into my space. He swung my coat around me, not bothering with the sleeves as he tugged it closed, then braced both hands on my arms as if holding me up. Maybe he was.

"I don't think they should leave the scene," Eugene said. "The police might want statements."

"Uhh, one of them is catatonic and the other is barfing into the junipers," Jaesung said. "I don't think they'll be much help."

"Helena was out there when it happened. She probably saw something."

Jaesung's hands tightened on my arms, though whether from protectiveness or something else, I didn't know. He rubbed my biceps up and down, and I realized I was shuddering.

"Come on, Gene. She doesn't want to talk to them." His voice was lower now. I could feel it vibrating in his chest, right in front of my face. He lifted a hand to my hair, half covering my ear, as if it would keep me from hearing his next low comment. "We don't know what happened."

He wasn't talking about the explosion. He was talking about why I ran away. I ducked backward—the first movement I'd been able to make since coming to awareness. His hands offered no resistance.

Eugene sighed, but looked back at the officer, who listened to a bartender's account. "Yeah," he grunted. "Okay. Go on."

Though I was too tired to feel guilty, it was a relief to turn away from the pub's fissured windows and dead lights. Krista made a sinusoidal track ahead, her focus returned to the cell phone on her hand. Jaesung and Sanadzi walked on either side of me and discussed the wisdom of letting Krista drunk-text.

"Last time she drunk-texted Alina, the shrink put her on phone probation," Jaesung said.

"We can't babysit their relationship," Sanadzi said back.

"Friends don't let friends text drunk?"

"I don't think that's how it goes."

I focused on Krista's bright orange hair bobbing in front of me like a single tail-light, showing me the way. The desire to sit down on the concrete, cold as it was, dragged at my every step. Twice, Sanadzi stopped to pull me along with her. The third time, she didn't let go, keeping an arm around my shoulders as she steered me along beside her.

They had to support me up the stairs. At the top, I found my head lolling into Jaesung's arm as Sanadzi unlocked the apartment. The rest of me threatened to continue the sideways tilt, and I thought the landing seemed a comfortable enough place to sleep. Jaesung shifted his arm from my shoulders to my waist, pulling me up against him to stop my floor-ward motion. My cheek met wool, and I inhaled the lingering smell of pub on his coat, threatening to sleep right there with him holding me vertical. I didn't even care that he was a stranger, or that I looked like a freak to them all now. I just wanted to sleep.

My coat had fallen to the floor, and his hand was growing warm on my back. I thought of Morgan, who was tall and solid like this, and darkness reached up for my consciousness, threatening to steal it away.

The tumbler turned over in the lock, and I heard the squeak of the door open. My eyes didn't want to open, but Jaesung's knee jostled my leg. I lifted my head enough to see a slice of tan jaw as he turned me toward the door and walked me over to the breakfast bar.

None of us had eaten, and at least half of my dizziness was probably because of post-magic hunger. Sanadzi and Jaesung worked with restaurant efficiency, and by the time Eugene joined us, there were five stacks of pancakes. I'd been working my way through a tray of bacon, practically absorbing the salt and protein through my fingertips, feeling more alert with every slice. The butter-drenched pancakes gave my blood-sugar the spike it needed to restore my senses.

I stared at the pattern of syrup left on my plate, pushing the crumbs around with my fork until they resembled Pleiades. It would be a miracle if Sanadzi didn't rescind her job-offer or call the police. After all, didn't most people try to reunite runaways with their erstwhile families?

Sanadzi shepherded Krista up to bed, and my muscles tensed at the silence as Eugene and Jaesung waited for her return. I knew what was coming. I just hoped I could convince them to let me leave without alerting the police. When Sanadzi clomped back down the stairs, she sank into an armchair with a gusty sigh.

"Hel, come on over here," she said, pointing to the couch.

My body resisted the movements, and walking across the room felt like trying to walk through water. I sank onto the opposite side of the couch from Jaesung.

Sanadzi pressed her hands to her knees, looking at them for a moment as she considered her words. When she looked up again, her amber eyes settled on me.

"I want you to know," she said, "that whatever is going on, you're safe here. We won't send you home."

I fought to process her words. "But.... Aren't—I mean—isn't it what you're supposed to do?"

One corner of Sanadzi's mouth turned up, though it wasn't a happy smile. "Baby-girl, anyone who spent five minutes with you can tell you shouldn't go back where you came from."

My fingers convulsed into fists. I'd known they thought me different, but not how plainly I wore the violence I'd grown up with. What could I say to that? I had not prepared for acceptance.

"Look, we're in the business of rescue," Eugene said. "I've worked here long enough to say we understand how sometimes the best choice is to get out."

I thought of some of the cowering and growling dogs caged below, and the loving ones who'd once been so untrusting. The normal thing right now would be to say thank you, but something stopped me. Pride? I swallowed. Nodded.

Jaesung shifted his weight, and I glanced to the side to see him massaging a hand. He inhaled sharply, but the breath halted in his lungs. He held it. Both Sanadzi and Eugene had transferred their gazes to him, and there was something in the look they gave him— some discomfort or anxiety.

I remembered the way he'd caught me in the pub, how he'd stopped me first from bolting, then from throwing him off. How he'd reminded Eugene that they didn't know why I'd run away.

Sanadzi interrupted the discomfort. "Look, you don't have to tell us anything about why you left just yet. I'm sure the power surge freaked you out enough as it is."

I glanced at her, panic prickling across my cheekbones. No, no—she meant an electrical power surge. That would be how they explained the bulbs shattering.

It didn't explain the cracked windows, but people accepted all sorts of things when they didn't want to believe in magic.

"The people who are coming," Eugene said. "Your family, if that's who they are. Will you be safe with them?"

"Yes," I said. My voice came out raw, scraped by screams and magic. "My cousin. He's—he's safe."

They relaxed a little, but whether it was because I'd finally said something or because they knew who was coming for me, I didn't know. Maybe it was some of both.

Eugene gathered up his coat, and Sanadzi gave me another one of her hugs before they left. It was gentler this time. She rubbed my shoulder blade. "You can talk to them," she said.

"Jaesung and Krista, or the dogs?" I said. She chuckled.

"Both. Either. Any of them will understand at least a little."

They left, and it was just Jaesung and me sitting on the couch, not looking at each other. He had switched which hand he was rubbing, and one foot sat on the coffee table next to my dog-bed full of things.

He toed my sketchbook, which had half-slid from my backpack. "You draw?"

It was a graceless change in subject, but relief washed through me all the same.

"Yeah," I said. "It's pretty much the only thing I'm good at."

His serious expression eased, lips quirking. "Can I look?"

I thought of the mandalas, which were the only things I'd drawn besides a few quick sketches of passengers on the train to loosen up my hand.

Part of me wanted to be paranoid enough to still suspect him of being a Sorcerer—it would mean I hadn't dropped my guard. But the barrage of contrary evidence had weathered away my suspicion. Jaesung wasn't a Sorcerer and wasn't working for one. All those

surreptitious glances, the moments of seriousness, the cryptic statements—he'd been the one to realize I'd run away. He'd been trying to
let me know.

He sucked at subtlety.

"Yeah, if you want," I said. "It's mostly just mandalas right now."

"Like Buddhist mandalas?" He teased the sketchbook from my
bag, flipping it open before I could answer. "Whoa." I saw his eyes
spring wide behind his glasses, flicking this way and that as he
scanned over the page. I watched, still afraid he would follow the flow
of magic in its specific pattern. He didn't.

"Damn. That's some detail. Oh—that one's 'hwa'," he said,
pointing to one of the Chinese characters. "Fire." He flipped through,
picking out several others. "How long do these take you?"

I shrugged. "Most of them are copied from other stuff, but I can
do them pretty fast, I guess. I remember patterns."

He'd stopped on a sketch of a train passenger, blowing out a long
breath. "You should be an art student. These already look
professional."

Heat flashed across my face, startling me for a moment before I
realized it wasn't magic, or illness, or something else sinister. I was
just doing something I wasn't sure I'd done in years: blushing.

While he flipped through the next few mandalas, I searched for
something to say to distract myself from the unaccustomed reaction.

"What—I mean, do you..." He looked up when I spoke and I tried
again. "Is it boxing? Martial arts?"

He was silent a moment, just looking at me. Then he set down
my sketchbook, stood, and went to the bookshelf. A moment later,
he'd set a jangling jar down on the coffee table in front of me. It read
"racist" in bloody letters.

"I said boxing first! I didn't say martial arts because-"

He was grinning. "Nope. You owe the jar a quarter. And now I'm
making you guess what it is."

"Soccer? Basketball? Football?"

He was shaking his head, laughing.

"Come on! Is it yoga?"

He rolled his eyes. "I do some yoga, but that's not my '*martial art*', so to speak."

"Is it a martial art?"

"It's not. I did some *tae kwon do* as a kid, but only because my best friend did it. It's not what I do now."

I lifted both hands in surrender. "Track?"

He laughed, tapping the back of the couch twice before he headed for the stairs. "Keep guessing, Miami." Then he was climbing, weight creaking every step.

In the vacuum of his absence, unwanted thoughts moved to the forefront of my mind. I'd made a mistake tonight, letting my magic explode like that. It was lucky there hadn't been any Sorcerers nearby. If one had been trailing us, he'd stayed back from the chaos.

Which made no sense. If I'd had a vulnerable moment, it was in that beer garden.

It was possible no Sorcerers had trailed me, though that was as unlikely as the thought of being truly safe with a bunch of mundanes. Even if they hadn't followed, they'd hear about the ruckus tonight. Did they feel magical explosions? Did they have some way to tell when people nearby used magic? I couldn't fathom any other way they could find the rogue Sorcerers they so despised.

Which meant that, if they hadn't known where I was before, they would have a general idea now.

I swallowed, glancing at the open sketchbook sitting next to the racist jar. Why was it so hard to control my magic now when I'd done it for my entire life?

A horrible thought crystalized, and I reached up to cover the destroyed mandala on my shoulder.

That spell had done more than just tether my body to Gwydian's will. He had known about my magic and kept it under lock. I couldn't control it now because he'd been using it all along.

Food threatened to rush back up my esophagus, but I clamped it down as I dug in my backpack for the book, flipping through the pages until I found the enslavement spell mandala. It only took an instant to recognize it as the one that had been on my mother, Morgan, and Eamon.

I clamped my eyes shut, drawing up my father in my mind. I hadn't seen his tattoo as often as my mother's—he'd already had them on his shoulders, so Gwydian had put his enslavement tattoo directly over his heart.

Something had always been a little off about dad's, the same way something had always been a little off about mine. I'd never been sure why, or if it even mattered, but now the truth arrived in my mind, sharp and certain: our tattoos had been different because *we* were both different. I hadn't been the only one in my family with magic. My father had had it too. Gwydian had used us both as batteries.

So why had he turned my father into a Hellhound? Why had he let one of his main sources of leeched magic die?

My fingers trembled on the pages of the book. I flipped through, glancing at the different mandalas, guessing at their effects where not specified. An unformed emotion was expanding inside me, too mercurial yet to risk naming.

I traced a mandala with my finger.

I had enough power that Gwydian had wanted to keep me alive, to siphon it off of me like a vampire. Maybe that meant I had enough power to keep the Guild away and protect my pack.

Despite my exhaustion, I took a long time to fall asleep, and when I did, it was with my sketchbook beside me, filled with the weapons I would use to wage my war.

CHAPTER THIRTEEN

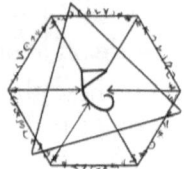

Two weeks disappeared into the dog rescue, and all the while the weather got colder. It hadn't snowed yet, but frozen puddles cracked under my boots when I walked the dogs. I'd never been so cold in my life.

I'd also never been so content. It wasn't happiness—I wasn't certain my body still produced that feeling—but I had food and companionship, I was starting to sleep through the night, and I'd seen no sign of the Guild.

Still, doubt gnawed at my thoughts. It all seemed too good to last. I couldn't help waiting for the axe to fall. I kept my eyes sharp on those walks, and every night I bundled up with sketchpad and book and worked through several mandalas.

The sketchbook was two distinct stripes of color—the gray pages, thickened with graphite and abuse, and the flat white layer of crisp, neat pages waiting to be filled. I liked the discrepancy. Knowing more pages waited meant I had more left to do.

By Halloween, I'd memorized the flow of all thirty-seven mandalas in the book. They were all complicated—far more than the

Guild's combat mandalas—but I mentally scrolled through them each night, one by one, until I had each detail perfect.

I saw little of Sanadzi, who came three evenings a week and half of Saturday. I walked the dogs in the morning while Krista bathed and treated them, and Jaesung went to class. He left on foot and jogged until he rounded the corner. By the time he returned in the afternoons, Krista was on the front register doing work for one of her online classes and I finished the easy grooming and cleaning.

I was just clipping Poo-stank's back claws as he distracted himself with a rubber chew when Jaesung returned, smelling of sweat and cold air.

"Hey Stanky," he said. "And my favorite dog."

"Hilarious." I checked the angle of the file on the ragged edge of Poo-stank's claw. "You know, these dogs have better nails than I do. Lacrosse?"

"Wrong," he said, crouching next to me and poking his hand through the bars for a cone-bedecked Pomeranian to lick. "About the lacrosse, not the nails. Your cuticles are atrocious."

I sighed, crossing another sport off the list. He didn't play soccer, basketball, tennis, baseball, water polo, football, or rugby, and he didn't do boxing, swimming, rowing, running, racquetball, cross-country skiing, downhill skiing, or any extreme sport. I was out of guesses. Almost.

"Curling."

He laughed. "I'm only good with a broom because Sanadzi's a neat freak."

I stood up, shoved the clippers in my pocket, and dusted my hands on my jeans. I'd left my knife in my bag while I worked in the rescue—I bent and squatted so much there was every chance it would fall out. Though, I wasn't certain the others would be surprised.

"So question," I said. "Is there a place to hike nearby?" A plan was forming in my head, but I needed to be several miles from civilization.

Jaesung frowned, casting his gaze ceiling-ward as he thought. "Uhh, I'm sure there is, but I don't do the outdoors."

"Somehow I sensed that about you."

"I mean, I do outdoors if it's climbing three-hundred foot steel towers, but not if it involves trees and dirt and bugs."

"So no?"

He typed something into his phone. "Why would you want to be outdoors? You're always complaining about the cold."

I shrugged. "Just feeling cooped up. I'm pretty much always at the dog rescue."

"I'm sure we can find something. Do you have a driver's license?"

"Yeah," I said, and didn't mention it was fake.

Half an hour later, I tossed my backpack into Jaesung's battered truck and started the ignition. Part of me wondered why he trusted me with it. If it were me, I'd be afraid the runaway girl would do just that—run away. With my car. But two weeks was apparently long enough for Jaesung to trust me. While he took over the evening shift at the rescue and Krista retreated upstairs for dinner, I drove.

The little wooded parking lot was empty, and there was enough undergrowth creeping out over the trail that I was fairly certain I wouldn't meet anyone on my hike. It was cold, but by the time I had hiked to the first campsite clearing, I steamed inside my coat. I shucked my outer layer. Sweat dampened my shirt where the backpack pressed it to my skin. For once, I enjoyed the punishing cold and approached the little fire ring. Someone had left a pile of firewood between two trees, but, if everything went well, I wouldn't need it.

I unzipped my backpack, feeling almost reverent as I slid the book out into my arms. The embossed "Master and Commander" had lost most of its foil, and the corners of the hardback were mashed in and dirty. It looked like such a well-loved novel. I opened the front cover, just to remind myself that it wasn't a book I was about to burn, but the spells that had enslaved my pack for decades. The spell that turned my father into a monster. I flipped to that page and stared at it, letting the anger and hate and grief consume me.

For several long moments, I burned as hot as the fire I planned to set. Gwydian was dead, and this was the only instruction for that mandala. He'd made certain of it. There would never be another Hellhound.

I swallowed, then set the book among the stirred ashes in the fire ring. I knew the spell, though not from the book itself. I remembered it, flashing bright in my memory every time we fought the Guild.

I knelt, the edges of the stones biting into my knees as I took a deep breath and searched for the bright turquoise light inside me, found it waiting deep in my chest, as if it hid there between my lungs and my throbbing heart. I imagined it buzzing in my arteries, shunting down my arms with each pulse of blood, carried to the capillaries in my fingertips.

My hands moved almost of their own accord, drawing the mandala in the same order I'd watched Guild Sorcerers do it; I pushed energy out of my fingertips, imagining them like the open-tipped syringes Sanadzi used, bleeding out magic like ink in the air.

I gasped when the first mark of turquoise appeared in the air. Concentration broken, it disappeared almost at once. Then my hands were shaking.

It wasn't that I hadn't expected it to work, so much as that I hadn't been ready to see my magic in that form. I'd known that I would draw a mandala in the air like a Sorcerer—inscribing it as if on a pane of glass, watching it light up like a neon sculpture. But it was different to actually do it. To face the truth of what I was.

I breathed deeply, centering myself in my body as I fought to reclaim the feeling of power in my fingertips. This time, I didn't let myself falter. I drew the outer circle, the inner circle, the four directions. The spiral of glyphs followed, directing power through the spell's circuitry.

Then it was done. I lifted my hand, staring for a moment at my creation. I felt what I needed to do next—the mandala pulled at me— it asked for energy, sucked at the thin threads of connection between myself and it. Little crackles of energy reached back to my hands like tiny lightning bolts, drawing at the power still buzzing in my fingertips.

I peered through the mandala at the lit pages of the book, at the Hellhound spell staring me in the face, and opened myself to the pull.

For a moment the draw felt like putting my fingers over an open bathtub drain, the light tickle of whirling water sucking at my hand. I watched the brightness sparkle across the mandala, illuminating the turquoise with an extra layer of crackling static. It wasn't until the added power reached the center of the mandala that the draw went from drain to riptide.

The center glyph erupted. Arcs of energy leapt from the four anchor points and a jet of fire shot straight down. I watched the first page catch fire. A bright line of amber ate through its center until the page ripped loose.

It soared up on super-heated air, burning and blackening as it went. A page of slavery. A piece of my past I could never forget. I memorized the way it looked against the sky, crumbling black edges against the blushing blue and peach of sunset.

The flames licked and curled the book's thick cover, eating down into the thick-packed center pages. I had won.

I let out a shaky breath and pulled my hands back. Or, tried to. The current of power jerked them forward again, sending me so off balance I toppled toward the fire circle. I jerked back again. The heat of the real fire radiated against my thighs, far too hot and far too big. Still the mandala sucked at my power, insatiable.

My face prickled. I'd only ever wondered how to put magic into the mandala. I didn't think of learning to stop the draw. Panic brightened my senses. The mandala sucked at the turquoise fire inside me, the real fire swelling. It drew and drew, and I felt the core of magic in my chest lose its radiance.

Magical fire took its energy from the caster and, like real fire, it would keep going as long as there was fuel. Until I was totally empty.

God, I'd been such an idiot not to figure out tying off spells. I hadn't realized I needed to know it. What a stupid time to die, just when I'd shrugged off this last chain.

Flame licked at the inner rim of the campfire circle, sending thick black smoke into my face. I coughed, thrashing against the magic as I might an undertow.

...except I wouldn't thrash against an undertow. I'd learned better than that. To escape a riptide, you swam across the current, not against it. The same logic might not apply to magic, but direct fighting wasn't working. My thighs stung with heat, even through my jeans.

How the hell was I supposed to send my magic sideways? I squeezed my eyes shut and clamped my jaw, trying to picture what the Sorcerers did to launch their mandalas. Was it a sideways movement?

The memory of Gwydian blossomed into my mind—his kind blue eyes on my father even as he inscribed the complicated spell that would twist him into a monster. It had been a shock of magenta, palms flat to the mandala. Then a fist, a cut of the hand sideways, as if declaring a runner safe on home base.

I dispelled the memory, forced my fingers to curl into fists. Then, focusing every ounce of will, I slammed my arms sideways.

The draw cut. I toppled onto my flaccid backpack. The mandala vanished in a column of fire, jetting straight up, and didn't even pretend to look natural.

I stared, detachedly wondering what I would say if hikers came by. Or a park ranger. It wasn't a great idea to stick around and find out. Without me to feed it more and more power, the fire's white center faded to yellow-orange, then dark amber. Finally, it was little more than a smoldering outline of mandala in the fire-circle, pale gray ash already blowing into the air.

It almost didn't seem real, that pile of ash. Like I could reach out and dust it aside and the book would be there, staring back at me with all the spells I'd sought to erase. But it wasn't, and with it vanished any hope the Sorcerers had of retrieving those spells. Even if they got ahold of my sketchbook, the order of drawing was lost. It existed only in my memory.

They could kill me now, and still they wouldn't get it. No one would suffer under spelled slavery again, not under that mandala's power. My mother's death, while not even avenged, at least felt less meaningless now that the Hellhound spell had gone to its grave with her.

I stood. I felt... good. There was weariness and hunger, but not the marrow-draining exhaustion of transformation or panic-blasts. When I turned my focus inward, the magic hub glowed dully, as if someone had turned a dimmer switch down a few notches. In fact, I still had a large percent of what I'd started with.

It didn't seem like a lot, considering how many spells the Guild's Sorcerers cast at us, but they had the aid of metal, amplifying the currents.

Maybe I needed a piercing....

I shoved that idea aside the instant it occurred. There was no way I wanted to look like them. No piercings. No more tattoos. I would eat my bodyweight in food, even if I had to use the stash of money Morgan left me to supplement what I ate at Ruff Patch.

Because now that I'd started, now that I knew how to cast, nothing stopped me from using magic to fight back.

This thought kept my steps light on the hike back to the truck. When I accepted my drive-through burgers, I might have smiled at the girl in the window. I felt fierce, suddenly, even with the windows up and hot air blasting and ketchup sliding down my chin. The hound stirred in me, ready to howl at the moon.

I wasn't quite happy; I was high. The thrill of accomplishment and rush of knowing I could do *magic* jumbled in with memories of Mom and imaginings of what she would say if she could see me. If she could know what I'd done.

I arrived on Erickson St. with an empty takeout bag, the last centimeter of a melted strawberry shake, and an empty backpack.

When I pulled up to the rescue, Jaesung and Krista were shoving

gear into her SUV. The engine idled and the red taillights illuminated a long catch pole and a medical bag. Jaesung heaved his heavy
orange backpack onto a seat. Why did they need climbing harnesses?

I parked across the street. Uneasiness tamped down my mood as I
hopped out. I knew that alertness—the tension and efficiency of rapid
movements and little talking. It was how my pack looked when we
were about to unload people from a boat, and do it fast, before anyone
with a badge noticed.

"What's going on?" I asked. The plume of my breath joined
Krista's.

"We got a call," she said. "Night rescue. There's a dog out on the
ice in Verena Lake."

I stared at her, a collision of thoughts hitting me too fast to separate out.

"You don't have to come," she went on. "But it would be awesome
if you did. They think the dog has a collar."

The first coherent question staggered off my tongue. "There's *ice*
on the lake?"

Krista fixed me with a look of frustration. "Where do you think
you are?"

"To be fair, it's not totally frozen," Jaesung said, coming around
the SUV with a large steel-wire cage.

"Which just means it's even *more* dangerous for the puppy, so
can we *go*?" Krista said.

Jaesung glanced at me. "Good hike?" I nodded. "You coming?"

I thought of all the dog rescue had done for me and knew I could
not refuse.

"Let's go save a dog."

CHAPTER FOURTEEN

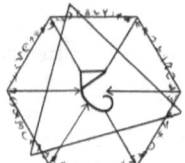

"The hell?" Krista said. I crouched in the back of the SUV, the toe of my boot jammed into the socket where the rear seat had once been. At her words, I leaned between the front seats, peering out the windshield. Trees flashed by, tall pines crowding close and straight as soldiers, and beyond them, a full sheet of solid white.

A field? No, the way the ground sloped down to it along the sides was wrong, and it was mirror-flat.

"That can't be right," Jaesung said. "The lake shouldn't be in full freeze till mid-month. I Googled it before we left."

Something in my gut lurched as we skirted the lake. Under the grin of the moon, all that ice glowed blue-white. It looked too peaceful to my Miami eyes.

We swung around the jut of trees and the major part of the lake opened before us, wide and featureless except for the center. A dog's silhouette moved there, back lit by a slash of headlights from the far bank. I spotted a weird tinge of color, like someone had thrown glow sticks onto the ice.

We pulled into a dirt parking lot and right down the concrete boat ramp. Krista stopped inches from the ice and I toppled against the center console, gasping.

"Up and out, people," she said. I pushed myself back and clambered into the cold. Jaesung stepped down onto the ice, extracted a small pair of binoculars, and pressed them to his glasses. I climbed the angled concrete to where Krista was unloading the trunk.

"Is one of us going out there?"

"Not sure yet." She handed me a cage. "The ice is probably too thin. We didn't even think it was frozen yet."

The hair on my neck stood on end. I set the cage on the ground and accepted the heavy backpack full of climbing gear, unsure whether it was instinct or cold shivering across my skin. I heaved the gear onto my shoulder and returned to Jaesung.

"What's the deal?"

He grunted and handed over the binoculars. "It's acting weird— keeps backing in either direction like it's stuck, but I can't see anything. People on the other bank are trying to call him."

I held the binoculars to my eyes and scanned. A black and tan border collie bounced on its front paws, rushing forward and backing down. I refocused the lenses, trying to get a better look at the ice near its back paws. I gasped. Four tiny mandalas, which I had mistaken for glow sticks, created a circuit around the dog, keeping it in place.

"What?" Jaesung said. I pushed the binoculars back into his hands.

"It's paw's stuck." Forgetting I stood on ice, I turned. My foot slipped sideways, and I snatched at Jaesung for balance, catching myself on his forearms. His feet slid out just slightly, bracing. The backpack of climbing gear clanked to the concrete as he caught my elbows.

"Shit," I whispered. "I wasn't expecting that."

"Clearly," he said, holding me steady as I got my feet back under me. I glanced up, squinting at him.

"Figure skating?"

Air puffed from his mouth in a chuckle. "Nope."

"Your nose is too intact for hockey."

"Not hockey."

Krista skidded down the concrete incline, the capture pole in one hand. "The fire department's on its way, but it's taking care of something at Drury farm—some sort of crop fire."

"In this wet?" Jaesung said.

"Where's that?" I asked, suspicion mounting. Even without the mandalas on the ice, it was too warm for a frozen lake, too wet for a crop fire, and too conveniently bad for us. This was not a job meant for the fire department. It was meant to draw me out, and it had.

Krista winced. "Not close enough—they've only got three engines and they're all there."

Jaesung was peering through the binoculars again, his mouth set in the grimace people sometimes do when they're squinting. He tensed.

"No," he said. "No, no, you idiot." Then he lowered the binoculars and waved a hand. "Go back!" he shouted. "Don't go out—fuck!"

Krista and I followed his line of vision to see a figure on the far bank step out onto the ice. The boy in the red jacket inched toward the dog.

Jaesung snatched up the bag of gear, pulling out lengths of cord, a clanking harness, and a half dozen carabiners. He handed me the cord and nodded to the SUV's grill. "Can you tie knots?"

Without responding, I made my way around the front of the car, careful not to slip. The hood was hot and smelled like oil and exhaust, but I suffered it and secured the line with a quick anchoring hitch.

Krista hunched over a first aid kit, her phone cradled between shoulder and ear. "Yes, there's a boy on the ice at Verena Lake. I don't know. Yes, we're on the far bank. Uhuh. Ruff-Patch Dog Rescue. Kristina Howell."

I made my way back to Jaesung, sorting out the straps of the harness with his feet still braced wide. He'd taken off his right glove, and it dangled from his teeth. I took it and shoved it in his coat pocket.

"I should have done this in the car," he said. "Damn." He looked to the lake, where the boy had almost reached the collie.

Then a sound like a gunshot bounced off the ring of trees. I ducked, but Jaesung went still. It took only a second to realize it hadn't been a gunshot. A crackle followed, and the boy on the ice froze. The mandala at the edge of his shoe flared.

The collie barked and the boy's arms pinwheeled. Then, with a desperate flail, he shot beneath the ice.

Krista screamed, and on the far bank, people shouted.

The harness clinked next to me as Jaesung slung it on, ignoring the loops meant for his legs. He clipped it across his chest.

"Jae, no!" Krista said, skidding down and grabbing the harness. "Rescue workers are coming."

He turned, breaking her grip, and his eyes flashed hot behind his lenses. "He went under! Probably inhaled water from cold shock— he'll drown before they get here."

My gut plummeted. This was my fault—Guild machinations, trying to draw me out. They probably hadn't intended for a civilian to get hurt, but if he did, that was on me too.

Krista grabbed Jaesung's jacket. "Don't let your rescue complex get rid of your common sense. You can't swim!"

I looked at the end of the rope in my hand. "I can."

Before they could react, I dashed out across the ice. My feet slid, and it took two spills onto my hands before I stayed there, crawling like I was in hound form.

Krista shouted behind me, and the people across the bank shouted too, but I didn't look at them. It had already been half a minute. Accident or not, I wouldn't let someone else die because the Guild was after me.

I got to the near edge of the collie's mandala-created cage. The dog was ballistic, barking at the opening in the ice after his master. There was no sign of him bobbing up from the slushy hole.

I pulled myself to the edge. It was sturdy and thick, even where the cracks had formed. Plenty thick to hold that boy's weight, if I were to guess. The chunks in the water, however, had gone to slush faster than it took a cube of ice to melt in Miami. That spelled out events well enough.

The ice had been frozen by magic, the break intentional and meant for me. Or one of my friends. The call to Ruff Patch had to have been one of the Guild Sorcerers baiting the hook. Maybe civilians weren't so safe from them.

I tugged off my boots and jacket. Cold air cut through my sweater and my jeans were already damp from sliding across the ice. I looped the cord and tied it, reeling in slack until it tugged tight against its anchor on the SUV.

Hesitation only wasted time. I took a deep breath, held my nose, and slid feet first into the water.

Before, I hadn't known what Jaesung meant by cold shock. Now I found out. I caught myself halfway in, keeping my head above water as my body seized up. Every organ stopped its work and shrank from the cold. All except my lungs, which expanded in shallow bursts, my stomach jumping in time, completely out of my control.

Dizziness overcame me. I clung to the ice's edge. The cold burned worse than my mandala fire. I wanted to climb out. I wanted to make it stop. But someone on shore was screaming. I glanced up. A girl a little younger than me clutched her jacket against her chest, looking sick. His girlfriend? Sister? Friend?

I thought of Morgan, possibly twisted and dead, and dived.

Cold filled my ears, my nose, shuddered again at my lungs, but my eyes were the worst. They stung at the chill water, closing involuntarily. I forced them open in a squint, shuddering deep in my body as I spun, looking for a bobbing shape.

There, fifteen feet away, a dark silhouette drifted against the ice.

I heaved myself into motion, though my limbs came over stiff and uncooperative. The cold had set in faster than I'd thought. I kicked harder, moving through eddies of painful chill until he was in reach. I stretched out numb fingers.

The line pulled up short under my arms, jerking me back.

No. No, no, no—I was right there! I struggled at the end of the line, which drew back hard, reeling me toward the hole. Air bubbled from my nose and lips, but I got one arm through the loop, then the other. I twisted, feeling the scrape of it over my forehead as it sprang loose and slithered away.

It took only a few more seconds to swim back, toss an arm around the boy's chest. My lungs pulsed, begging for air. I could hold my breath for far longer, but something about the cold and the urgency.... I found the bright hole in the ice and headed for it.

When I broke the surface of the water, a metal ladder stretched above me. I tossed my free hand toward it but slipped off and plunged back under. With all my strength, I kicked, bursting through the slush. I cast my arm blindly. An elbow hooked around the rung, and I halted, holding onto the boy's jacket, thoughts fracturing like frost.

My ears rang with shouts; crystals hardened on my lashes. How the fuck did it get so cold so fast?

"Th-the rope," I managed, but it was barely a whisper. I couldn't get the breath to shout. I gulped in air and tried again. "I've g-got him! Give me the rope!"

Something slapped the slush next to me—the line! I had to release the ladder to get it around the boy. I fumbled. My legs felt like they'd been shot up with Novocain, and my legs refused to kick as hard or fast as before. At last, I tugged his arm through the loop. "Pull!"

The rope went taut. I did my best to help boost him over the lip of the ice. He slid out, making a shiny trail of wet behind him. I grasped the ladder and clung, finally aware of the collie still barking next to me.

"It's okay," I wheezed, reaching for the mandala. It zapped at me, but the magic arced away, forking down to the ice instead. "Fuck you too," I said to the unseen Sorcerer. Then I closed my eyes, reached for the magic in my trembling chest, and drew it out, shoving power into the mandala the way the Enforcer had done with my enslavement tattoo.

Anger fueled me, and it was only a second before the mandala glowed turquoise. I dragged numb fingers into a fist, cut sideways. The mandala flared, leaving a carved shape behind. I reached out, drew a line across the mandala with my own power, and interrupted the circuit.

It shattered, spraying sparks into the air.

The collie bounded forward to the ladder and barked at me. I reached for its collar, but let go as the weight of my body almost drew it over the edge. There wasn't enough traction for a dog of that size to pull me out.

"Go on," I managed, waving a hand at the dog. It turned and, with one last bark, bounded after the shining trail left behind by its master.

"Stay where you are," a voice commanded. I looked down the ladder. The man holding the end had sharp cheekbones and a strong, square jaw, but his face was hollowed out, no flesh between skin and bone. A trio of eyebrow rings caught the light, and when he grinned, a set of silver grills flashed back at me—each tooth a tiny headstone in his mouth.

Sorcerer. He had to be, but something was off about him. The shape of the mandalas on the backs of his hands were all wrong. He had the piercings, the tattoos, the emaciated frame, but not that self-righteous spit-shine most Guild members had.

That meant one of two things: he was either a bounty hunter hired to bring me in or a rogue sanguimancer, capitalizing on a potential power-source.

He pulled the ladder, sliding me half up onto the ice. A ring on his finger glowed, and even with my blurred vision, I knew it was a spell meant for me. I let go of the ladder and slid back into the frigid water.

CHAPTER FIFTEEN

The water was over me before I could grab the edge. I kicked, but my legs were sapped. I barely moved in the water.

An arm shot down, snagging first on my hair and pulling me toward the surface. Then the hand snagged the back of my sweater and another plunged in to grab my arm. I twisted, trying to get out of the Sorcerer's hold, but his hands were strong—much stronger than my numb, weakening body.

I crashed through the surface of the water and he heaved me half onto the ice. I wrenched sideways, trying to roll away.

"Hel, stop fighting me!"

It took a second to place the voice, but I stopped resisting. Frigid strands of hair covered my face, sticking to my mouth as I gasped for air. They blocked my vision, but the arms that had pulled me up dragged painfully under my arms. Something clicked behind me, and I felt my weight supported by a strap around my back.

"Kick, girl, kick!" Jaesung shouted. I tried, but my legs were too heavy, and I only managed a few weak thrashes at the water.

It seemed like enough. The strap around my back pulled me forward and with Jaesung's help, I struggled over the edge. Then he was dragging me. No, not him—the strap was dragging me, dragging both of us in short jerks. He'd clipped the lanyard around my back to a D ring on his harness and now, on his side, was using one hand to help maneuver us across the ice.

Back at the SUV, people pulled the line, and in the glowing light of flares, I saw paramedics bending over a slice of red jacket.

"Is h-he a-l-l-live?" I choked it out, and Jaesung waved at the line-pullers. Apparently, it was far enough in that he seemed confident in the integrity of the ice. Without answering, he dragged me to my knees, hands strong even through the numbness. He shook me. He wasn't gentle. It jerked the lanyard between us tight. I wanted to twist away, but couldn't manage it.

"Are you insane or just *completely* fucking stupid? You don't just run out onto the ice! You don't just jump in the water with no gear and—and wearing freaking wool and-"

"You were going to!"

"Helena, I have a harness! And I wouldn't have gone in the water —I'm not that stupid!" On the last word, he shook me again. Only once, but hard enough to piss me off.

"Stop it!" I snapped. I thrust my hands up between us, catching his chest and shoving against it. He let go, but the lanyard caught us, conspiring to hold me near him. I was shuddering now, the cold air eating through my wet clothes and into my flesh. His chest was soaked, cold water pressing out onto my fingers as I held myself at the end of the lanyard.

"I got that kid out," I managed, though my teeth chattered. "He'd drifted too far from the hole. I couldn't let him—I just—I can swim, okay? The water was cold, but I'm really, *really* good at swimming. And I had a line."

"Which you took off."

"I couldn't reach him!"

Jaesung's face was hard, and the look he gave me seemed to bore into me like fire. I was used to anger. I was used to abuse. I was used to being scared. But I was not used to *this* kind of anger, the kind that was on my behalf. My throat tightened as I looked up at him, stripped to a half-drenched gray hoodie, harness covering his chest and looking almost like a tactical vest.

His glasses rested askew on his nose, and there was a rapid pulse throbbing in his neck. I watched his irises flick this way and that as he scanned my face. Then his hands found my shoulders, lightly this time, and he bent his head forward with a sigh.

"Look. The cardinal rule of rescue? Don't make yourself a second victim."

I sucked in my lips, glancing back over his shoulder toward the hole and the Sorcerer. The ladder lay abandoned on the ice.

"Where'd he go?" I asked.

Jaesung's skin had seized into goosebumps across his neck. "The ladder guy?" he asked. "I don't know. I stopped paying attention to him when you went under."

Jaesung reached between us and, fingers clumsy, unclipped the lanyard. He shoved himself up and offered me a hand, and though anger still crackled around his head like a storm, that hand looked like a peace offering. I took it. My legs did not want to work, and my bare feet were little more than blocks of ice themselves. I grabbed onto Jaesung's harness, my weight jerking down against it. His hands found my waist, fingers threading through my belt loops.

"Steady, Miami." A slow, warm tone blunted the edge in his voice, and he no longer sounded angry. This was more like the voice he used with frightened dogs—that low, smooth sound that made my sternum vibrate. I took a few breaths, wind cutting across us and stinging my ears. He stepped forward, cutting off the breeze with his shoulders.

It was too cold to think. All my concentration went into staying vertical. Jaesung put an arm low around my back and half dragged me to the edge of the lake.

Five EMS workers lifted the boy onto a backboard. They'd cut open his clothes, and the pads of an AED stuck to his pale chest. A woman stood at his head, holding a breathing mask to his face. His border collie sat at the doors of the EMS van and was only prevented from hopping in by a technician. I was glad to see the comforting scratch she gave the dog in consolation.

One officer was busy interviewing the hysterical teens that had been on the far bank, and the other was with Krista, who shot us a look of patent worry.

As we reached the SUV, Jaesung hugged me against his side, turning his face into my wet hair. For a second, I was stunned, thinking it an affectionate gesture. Then he spoke.

"Do you have a medical record?" he asked, breath hot across my forehead.

I tensed. "Not really."

He nodded, then took a breath for a second question. I felt him shivering under his harness and hoodie, and my fingers tightened on the dry fabric at the small of his back.

"Do you think your parents have reported you missing?"

"My parents are dead."

I said it immediately, and simply. The truth of it sank deep and cold into my bones. It was true. Both of them were gone now, not just Dad. I guess I qualified as an orphan.

Jaesung's breath hitched. His body went rigid. You'd have thought I stuck a knife in his gut. A beat of silence hung between us, populated only by the puffs of our exhales. Then, at last, he pulled me around the dark side of the SUV. The flashing lights of the emergency vehicles patterned the trees, glimmering through the windows of the car now blocking us from sight.

Then, weirdly, Jaesung started to undress me. I was stunned for a second, barely able to react because, of everyone I had ever expected to take advantage of my state, he was on the list only slightly ahead of Poo-stank. I was so shocked, in fact, that I let him get my sweater and shirt hiked halfway up my abdomen before I asked, "What are you doing?"

"These clothes'll freeze right to you," he said.

I let him pull off my sweater, and the shirt under. I probably would have let him go on, but he grabbed a towel from the back seat. Apparently, my sports bra and jeans were a line he wasn't willing to cross.

"I d-don't usually strip on the f-first rescue," I said. He glanced up, and I knew by the annoyed look he gave me that he must be blushing. I dried off my arms, my stomach, my chest. Frost clung to the ends of Jaesung's hair. He shrugged out of his own hoodie.

He turned away slightly when he pulled off his shirt, which was odd because he was... actually better-formed than I'd realized. His chest had mass to it, and though he didn't have the perfectly defined abdominals of a model, there was a pronounced furrow down his midline. His arms were bulkier than I'd thought, too, given such narrow wrists. His mass simply stretched out down long bones, which made him look thinner than he actually was.

And yet even with the hints his physique offered, I still couldn't guess his sport. Something that worked everything, apparently.

I shimmied out of my jeans, keeping the towel around my waist, and Jaesung, shirtless, reached past me into the van for more towels. That was when I saw his back, and the reason he'd turned away.

A network of small scars webbed the left side, most of them stretching across his shoulder blade. Some went lower, cutting across the big muscle along his spine. They were too irregular for knife wounds and too deep to have been something like welts from a belt. It looked like the scars one gets in a car accident, or being thrown through a window.

Jaesung came back up with two scruffy wool blankets and handed one to me, wrapping himself in the other. He opened the driver's door, stepped up into the SUV, and turned the keys in the ignition. I struggled into the back seat. The whole place smelled dank and familiar, like the kennels. I laid down on the stack of old blankets kept for the dogs, nesting into them.

My hair crunched, pressing cold against my head where strands had frozen. I closed my eyes. My whole body trembled. Probably a good sign. I felt the vehicle move as Jaesung climbed up into the back with me. I kept my eyes shut, but I knew it was him—his teeth were chattering.

Something thick and heavy spread over me, and I smelled that combination of night air, burning leaves, and sweat he always brought home with him. His presence moved away again and the back door shut. Then the driver's door opened and closed. I cracked my eyes enough to see him fussing with his watch, alternately holding his hands and it up to the vents.

The charcoal wool up near my face was his coat.

The air in the car got warmer, and I must have drifted to sleep, because it seemed like only seconds later when Krista climbed in the passenger's seat.

"One of his friends is taking the dog."

"What did they say?"

"They're not sure how long he was without air. No telling if there'll be any brain damage. The news crews are here."

Jaesung grunted. "Did they ask about Hel?"

"Yeah. They want to talk to her."

"She's out. And I doubt she wants to talk to them any more now than she did at the pub."

Krista shrugged. "It's police. What are we supposed to say?"

He didn't have an answer for that.

They brought an officer around to the SUV. Neither Jaesung nor Krista said anything when I told them my name was Mildred Johnson. I'd seen the girl's ID at the grocery store a few days before, when she'd handed it over to the clerk that rang up her cider. I gave him her home address, to increasingly bunched eyebrows from my companions. I let the officer have my cell number in case of follow-up calls.

The news crew stood nearby, casting bright lights across the churned up ground as I gave my statement behind the shelter of the SUV. It was lucky I still shuddered with cold, because the officer let me off the hook with a lecture about leaving the rescue to the rescue crew.

Once he left, Krista slammed the driver's side door and wrenched the car into reverse. "You know, if Hel were a dude, they would have been calling you a hero, but you're a girl, so instead they're going all...all...."

"Patriarchy?" Jaesung offered.

"God, it makes me so mad! I mean, you're a moron, but you saved that kid's life."

"Emphasis on the moron part," Jaesung added. "Kris, I think we might need to get a moron jar."

"Honeypots, we'd have that shit filled in no time."

"Because I'm the only one with common sense?"

"I hate to break it to you, bruh, but you climb cell towers. You qualify as a moron."

As they discussed the relative merits and drawbacks of a moron jar, I huddled back into the pile of blankets and pulled Jaesung's coat up to half cover my face. The whole ride home, I sat up only once, to satisfy myself that we were alone on the streets.

I managed the stairs only because Krista was in front of me, holding my hands on her shoulders. Then came the most excruciating bath of my life. It felt like boiling water, though Krista assured me it was room temperature. My skin went a bright, livid red.

Finally, I climbed into dry clothes and the now-familiar comfort of my couch. Krista brought down the hair-dryer and went to work on my hair while Jaesung, now in fuzzy-looking batman pajama bottoms and several layers of long-sleeved shirt, made us all enormous cups of tea.

It wasn't until the third cup that I noticed my sketchbook on the coffee table and remembered what I'd done that afternoon. I smiled into my mug, inhaling the grassy-smelling steam of green tea.

Even if the Guild or some rogue Sorcerer had found me, I could fight back. I *had* fought back. If they caught me, the only thing they'd get out of it was my death. Not my pack. Not the book.

Part of me wanted to call Morgan and tell him the good news, but a thin thread of uneasiness kept me from reaching for my phone. In his last text, Morgan had told me not to contact him unless it was an emergency.

Krista had settled into the chair across from me and, after drying his own hair, Jaesung sank onto the couch, so close he practically sat on my throbbing feet.

"Sorry if I scared you," he said.

I looked up, uncertain when he meant. Grabbing me from the water? Yelling? Taking off my shirt? He seemed to note my confusion.

"When I shook you," he said. "I'm—that wasn't... I'm-" he wiped a hand across his mouth, as if punishing it for not knowing what to say.

"It's okay," I said, shrugging it off.

"It's not."

"It didn't scare me."

"Still. It's not right for me to be aggressive like that." He looked up at me, brows furrowed. "If it didn't bother you, it should have."

I shrugged, and he glanced at Krista. She shook her head.

After another beat of silence, I gave Jaesung a nudge with my foot. "I'm sorry for scaring you too."

"Um, and me?" Krista said. "Because I'm pretty sure you both left me on the bank, wondering whether I'd still have roommates tomorrow."

"Sorry," we said in unison. Jaesung and I glanced at each other, and I saw the smile that threatened at the edges of his mouth.

"I mean, the dog's fine," Krista went on. "So, like, mission accomplished. But damn."

Jaesung laughed. "The damn dog came out better than any of us!" He reached out then, settling a hand on my shoulder. I wasn't certain what the gesture signified—forgiveness, or affection, or relief—but when he pulled away, I leaned after the touch.

"Kay," Krista said, setting her empty mug on the coffee table and heaving herself from the chair. "I need to go check on the babies. You-" she pointed to me "-stay warm. Get rest. And you-" she trained her finger on Jaesung, who halted halfway off the couch "-are unnecessary this evening. Go to bed."

She disappeared down the stairs, the door falling shut behind her.

For a moment, I thought Jaesung would sit back down, but he didn't. Instead, he picked up Krista's empty mug, then his own, then mine, and took them to the dishwasher. I listened to him open it and load them in, leaning my head against the back of the couch.

I didn't realize my eyes had closed until a light touch on my wrist startled them open. Jae stood above me, dark hair sketching a jagged edge across his forehead. I wasn't used to seeing it not spiked back away from his face. He looked younger this way. I actually believed he was nineteen.

"I just wanted to tell you that... the reason it's not okay. What I did."

I bit back a groan and blinked up at him, wondering if I should push myself up straighter, if only to look more attentive than I felt. It was such a small thing for me, that moment of anger he'd had. Before a few weeks ago, I'd have been lucky to escape an entire day without the threat of much worse. I didn't care to assuage his privileged sense of guilt.

But his face was troubled, and he had just pulled me from a frozen lake. I sat up.

He knelt by the arm of the couch, one long forearm propped alongside mine, wrist to elbow.

Despite the flannel pajamas I had on, and the down comforter, and the quilt, Jaesung looked unfairly warm. Something about the way his body looked in dark colors, kneeling there next to me. Or maybe it was the warm gold of his skin, reminding me of hot beach sand or baked terra-cotta tiles. I caught myself leaning toward him.

Luckily, he wasn't looking. Instead, he studied our forearms—the light blue of my sleeve against the black of his, like two different skies —and plucked at a wrinkle near my elbow.

"I told you I was born in Korea, in Seoul," he said. I nodded. My hair swept onto the arm of the couch, across the back of his hand. His fingers twitched. "Mom and I moved here when I was ten. We had to move in with her sister. She'd married an American guy—her ESL, teacher, actually. Gene's Dad."

I didn't know what ESL was, but I didn't interrupt to ask. It seemed like a tough thing for him to talk about, his past in Korea, though he'd only ever spoken of the country like he missed it. Maybe he didn't miss all of it, or maybe, like my feelings on Miami, his past complicated his feelings about the place.

"There's a stereotype about Korean men hitting their wives but it doesn't happen that much anymore. Probably about the same as America. The difference is in how difficult it is, socially, to get a divorce. Most women don't leave, and when they do, a lot of times their whole family gets upset at them. It's just not done."

I moved my hand then, fingers crawling up onto his forearm. It wasn't a natural gesture, but it felt like the right response. His opposite hand lifted, covered mine. His thumb swept over the back of it a few times before it settled.

"Anyway, Mom—she put up with it for years, I guess. Dad was a boxer back in the late eighties, a really good one. When the craze died down, he opened a gym and trained other people. Then he got in an accident, a few years after I was born, and..." Jaesung shrugged. "Couldn't fight anymore. Even train. It got to him, I guess. He probably needed therapy, but that's another no-no in Korean culture. He'd flip his shit if someone suggested it to him. Anyway, he took it out on Mom."

My teeth clenched. This was not an unusual story, but it was weird to hear it from someone like Jaesung. He wasn't from a drug-torn family, or a gang, or any of the people I was used to hearing that story from. He was middle class. And in college. He was clean, and smart, and...nice.

"Did he ever take it out on you?" I asked.

Jaesung's lips twitched and he glanced up. "Once. That's when we left. I saw him shove Mom, so I jumped on his back. He flipped me into a coffee table. Broke my arm. I went to the hospital and two days later we were on a plane to Chicago. I was so doped up on pain killers. God, that flight sucked."

I swallowed, moved my hand to his back. "Is that how you got those?"

He winced, pulling back, and I worried that I'd invaded too much. But then he sighed. "It was a glass coffee table. It broke too."

This time I winced. "Was he...I mean. He was sorry." I said this with confidence. Jaesung gave a soft laugh.

"He was definitely scared. Mom went nuts, started throwing shit at him. He left pretty quick. She called her brother, and he came and got us. I guess Dad's sorry. At this point I sort of don't care. Sorry excuses nothing. Anyway." He shrugged again. "That's why I wanted to acknowledge that I shouldn't have shaken you. I promised I would never touch a girl when I'm mad, and today I did. And even if it's not a big deal to you, it is to me."

"I get it," I said, and then, because magical ice seemed to have shattered my usual defenses, more words tumbled out. "It's got to be harder, when you're being hurt by the people who are supposed to protect you. My parents couldn't always protect me, but they never hurt me themselves."

He looked up, and the hand that had covered mine went to my shoulder. "What about these? You're not eighteen yet."

My tattoos. He would have seen them when he stripped me from my wet clothes, and the scar now forming over the slave tattoo. And here the truth had to end.

"They're just decoration," I said.

Some of the openness in his face closed off. "They look like those mandalas you draw."

"They are."

He nodded, then drew his arm out from under my hand and stood. "Get some sleep, Hel."

"Thanks for telling me," I said. The words had come without my permission. Not because I'd really wanted to say them, but because I wanted him to stop walking toward the stairs.

He did. He glanced back at me, mouth making a smile that was neither happy nor exactly faked.

"Yeah. It's hard to talk about. Embarrassing, I guess. Don't worry. I get it."

But he didn't get it. It wasn't embarrassment that kept me from talking about what happened to me. It was that, even if I told them, they wouldn't believe me.

And I found, to my horror, that I wanted them to believe me. To like me. This place was starting to feel like home, and that was ten times scarier than the Guild.

CHAPTER SIXTEEN

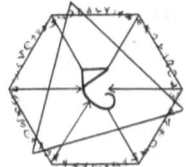

I stayed on alert after that. It wasn't so much that I confined myself to the rescue, but it manifested as a constant tingling on my neck. Halloween was a blur of dog costumes and parading children, and the first days of November stole the last hopes of warmth. With it came turkey, furious wedding preparations, and my eighteenth birthday. And no messages from Morgan.

Part of me wondered if I should tell them. Morgan's absence would look suspicious by now and I was sure they'd be annoyed if I didn't mention my birthday, but I couldn't think of a way to bring up either. The idea of going to another pub or being the central focus of a song or having people feel obligated to get me presents sent a pang of nausea into my gut.

My eighteenth birthday arrived without fanfare sixteen days into November. At least, I thought there would be no fanfare. The world seemed to have different plans.

It was still dark when Jaesung shook me awake. He was still in t-rex pajama pants and a sweater, clutching a cup of coffee and wearing a sly grin. A dim stove light shone from the kitchen. For a second, my groggy brain was sure he'd guessed. I sat up, startled.

"Come over here," he whispered, then grabbed me up, comforter and all, and backed me into the middle of the room. When he let me go, I reached for his coffee, which he relinquished. He turned me to face the bay window.

White fluttered past the panes, thick and fast. Somehow, even though everything in my vision was white, the world outside the window still had depth. I made out the brick buildings across the street and, between them, the distant darkness of trees in the park. Everything bent under a thick layer of snow.

I gasped, mind boggling over just how fast it fell. I'd imagined snow to be slow and fluffy, like dandelion flocks. It wasn't. It raced down like rain, only thicker and brighter. Though still under a darkened sky, the world glowed like morning.

"I thought it might be worth waking up for," Jaesung said. He let go of my shoulders and made a second cup of coffee as I settled on the cushion in the window with his first. He liked it sweet, with milk, and even though I preferred mine without sugar, it was still strong and hot.

I don't know how long I watched the snow, hypnotized by the pattern of it falling. Jaesung sat with me for a while, sipping his new cup, then disappeared upstairs. I finished my coffee, set the mug in his empty spot, and pressed ceramic-warmed hands to the glass.

Little rings of fog grew on the pane around my fingers. I leaned forward, letting my breath do the same and drew a snowman in the condensation.

I made another coffee and, just as it finished, Jaesung descended the stairs from the third floor, dressed in thick boots and a dark green jacket with a fur-lined hood.

"Where are you going so early?" I asked, whispering because the clock on the stove said it was five thirty, and Krista was even less of a morning person than me.

"Martial arts," he said with a wink, and stole my coffee on the way out the door.

I smirked, wondering if he could drink it without sugar.

Then I was alone, with hours before anyone else would be awake. Just me and the snow. I traced more figures on the windowpane before retrieving my sketchbook. I flipped past the pages of mandalas and set my pencil on the page.

It had been a long time since I'd drawn for pleasure. I let myself fall into the feeling of pencil dragging over paper. I drew each point on the wrought iron fence, each icicle forming on the eave of the law office across the street. Even as I sketched the scene below me, I imagined people and creatures to populate it. Children peeking from behind trees. A pair of lovers walking down the path, Poo-stank and Leeloo gamboling in the snow.

When my hand cramped, I set down the sketchbook, looking at the picture critically. The lovers were almost definitely my parents. The children crouching behind the trees, snowballs in hands, could have been Krista and Jaesung as kids.

I saw a spot in front of the fence where I could draw a girl looking back into the park. The lovers would be walking away from her; the kids wouldn't see her; the dogs would be too busy to care.

I closed the sketchbook and put it away, dressed in a thick pair of tights, jeans, and tall socks, topped with a thermal shirt and long, loose gray sweater. I had to loosen my boot laces just to fit the layers.

Krista joined me not long after eight, and together we fed all the dogs and opened the garage doors, kicked back the snow that had piled up against them.

"This is my favorite time of year to work at the rescue," she said, cheeks pink from cold. "Know why?"

"Because the cold keeps the dogs from smelling like-"

"Dog sweaters!" she interrupted, unable to wait for me to finish talking. It startled a laugh from me.

"*Dog* sweaters? Like...?"

"Sweaters! For dogs!" She pointed back toward the kennel. "You know how Stroodle, Piper, and Mayhem have so much fur gone?"

I grimaced, but nodded. Those three had all been here before me, and most of them had skin conditions weeks in the healing. Their fur was growing back, but it was still sparse and patchy. "You put sweaters on them to make up for the missing fur. It's adorable."

It was, sort of. Stroodle the pug wore his little fair-isle wool proudly on his barrel chest, tongue lolling out of his flat black muzzle. The corgi Piper seemed less happy about his own red-cabled ensemble, but stopped shivering after a moment, and Mayhem, a skinny beagle-boxer mix, rolled in his fuzzy yellow sweater vest, barking at motes of snow that whirled inside.

"I'm going to start on meds," Krista said. "You want to take those drooligans out for business?" She lifted her eyebrows at me almost suggestively. "Play in the snooow?"

I couldn't help it. I grinned at her, excitement building in my stomach like a shaken-up coke bottle, waiting to explode.

"Whoa," she said, leaning back. "You're *smiling*. I'll take that as a yes! Grab Stanky too. He's gnawing at the bars."

I bundled up and trotted the dogs across the street. Poo-stank was the biggest but by far the best-behaved. He heeled, even as Stroodle and Mayhem strained ahead. Piper could only move his short legs so fast through the inches of snow.

I listened to the squeak of it under my boots, grinned when Stroodle plowed ahead into the fresh crust as high as his chest and stopped to lick snow from his flat nose. Poo-stank lifted a leg at a nearby tree, and I tried not to snort at the steaming hole he left in the snow at its base. The sun was up, glowing through a sky now white as the earth, and the entire park looked like something from another world.

I let Mayhem lead us around a frozen duck pond, where he snuffled at the trails of small, fuzzy creatures. Piper yapped, bouncing on his front feet, nipping at the falling snow.

This went on for ten minutes before I noticed the quiet. It wasn't the silence I'd sensed fall over the world when the snow had first come down, but a different kind. The dogs had gone silent and tugged at their leashes. Tails still wagged, but not as vigorously as before, and Poo-stank's tall ears kept swiveling backwards.

Were we being followed?

I could have cursed, realizing that—in my excitement about the snow, I hadn't been paying much attention to what was behind me. I slowed, pulling the dogs to a stop, which they didn't seem happy about. Four heads turned back to look at me, mouths open, steam drifting from their panting mouths. I bent down as if to check my shoes and glanced down the path behind.

The man didn't step behind his tree fast enough. I caught a glimpse, and it was enough to tell me what I needed to know. The left side of his jacket hung lower, carrying the weight of a pistol. His gaunt face was young beneath red hair buzzed on both sides. In the patched black bomber and studded belt, anyone would think him some tatted subculture punk. And maybe he was, but that didn't matter. What mattered was the necklace on his chest: a silver double spiral. The Guild insignia. This was not the guy I'd seen at the lake, and I couldn't recall the guy at the train station's face enough to say if it was him.

I righted myself, looked down at the dogs. If I let them go, would they run back to the rescue, or would they stay here with me, loyal little idiots? I swallowed, making my decision, and let the leashes drop. With any luck, that would make them easier to catch if they didn't make it back to the rescue, or if something happened to me.

Mayhem scampered off at once, startling Piper and Stroodle into following. But Poo-stank stayed, whined at me. He nosed my hand.

"I know you're back there," I called. "You can either come out here and talk or fuck off."

The man stepped out, the slice of a smirk across his face. He kept one hand deep in his gun pocket. The other held a cigarette still smoldering at the tip. As he approached, I noticed the lip ring and gauged ears filled with mandala-etched silver plugs. He had tattoos up his neck, all the way to his ear, and more down the backs of his hands and fingers.

If he hadn't been so skinny, it would have given him an appealing air of rebellion. More so if I hadn't known already that he followed rules as closely as any secret agent. No question—this guy was Guild.

Heavy boots crunched through the snow, erasing paw-prints.

"You got something I need, doll face," he said, and took a drag of his cigarette. He was in his mid-twenties and his vivid green eyes were direct.

"It's a bad day for you, jackass, cause I've got nothing to give you." I said. My jaw was tense. It took a lot of effort to make it work.

He chuckled, smoke puffing out his nostrils. "Yeah, you've been making it hard for my guys ever since Miami."

"You mean, since you shot my mother in the head?"

He responded with a slow blink. My hands fisted, and my triceps twitched. I wanted to deck this guy, gun or not. I wanted to punch him right across the jaw hard enough to break my own knuckles. Then I wanted to keep hitting him until he was pulp on the snow. Until blood spread around us like it had spread around my mother's head.

"Where's the book, sweetheart?"

"I don't have it anymore."

"Is that all you've come up with in a month, that you don't have it? Look, babe, we know you've-"

"Don't infantilize me with nicknames," I shot back. Krista would be proud. "I burned it in a campsite at Abbie Ridge. Get some of your *guys* to dig through the ashes if you don't believe me. It's gone."

I watched the shift of his face, subtle though it was. He had decent control over his expression, but the little things I'd learned to watch for tipped me off—the tensing of his under-eye muscles, the slight clench of jaw and flare of nostril as he processed the stick I'd thrown in his bicycle spokes.

"Why the fuck would you burn it?" He sounded honestly shocked.

"Why the fuck do you *want* it?"

The surrounding chill was complete and the snow only seemed to isolate us further. I watched him consider me, consider the fight I could put up now that neither of us had the element of surprise. Part of me wanted him to go for the gun, because seeing a member of the Guild again made my muscles itch with the desire to hurt something. I just needed an excuse.

The potential of happiness had gnawed at me for weeks, sweet and torturous. If Mom had survived, would she have had it too? Would we be in Canada already, starting a new life?

Poo-stank growled, sensing my anger.

The Sorcerer glanced at the dog. "You." For a moment or two, he added nothing, too baffled or too angry to string words together. "Y'know that book was the only leverage you had to get our help, right?"

"I've seen what your 'help' looks like."

His face twitched into that thin-lipped smirk again. "Just thought you'd be more interested in some backup, now old Master Fuckface's got his hunters out on you."

I shook my head, staring at those glass-green eyes like they might translate his words into something else. A small laugh escaped my chest. "What the hell are you talking about?"

He stepped toward me. Poo-stank gave a low warning growl. I grabbed his collar, dragging him back behind me. He pressed into my leg.

"We caught a rogue that was tailing your friend over in Iowa—a sanguimancer. Known bounty hunter. Sorry to say, but he told us the price on your pretty little head, doll, and you ain't pretty enough to talk your way out of it." He flicked his cigarette into the snow, where it hissed. "He wants that book back bad. How d'you think he'll feel about you burning it?"

I shook my head, frost creeping up my spine as I scrambled through his words. "You're fucking with me," I said, like saying it would make it true. "No. I saw the boat explode. He's dead. Gwydian is dead."

Friend in Iowa. Was he talking about Morgan? I backed up another step, my heart thudding in my throat. Had Morgan mistaken the Sorcerer that captured Eamon as a Guild member when he was actually a rogue? A sanguimancer. Which meant....

I envisioned Eamon, hanging from a rope around his ankles, bleeding from a cut throat like an animal in a butchery. The pulse of turquoise in my chest started up, a surge of lightning threatening to spill up my throat. My control slipped.

The man lunged forward, grabbing me by the jacket. In the same instant, Poo-stank launched himself at the Sorcerer's arm and latched on. I kicked, connecting with the Sorcerer's shin, and he cursed, but kept ahold of me, acid green power sending cables around my body and battering back the surge of turquoise power.

"Ground, you stupid bitch! Don't you know how to fucking— Jesus, get this mutt off me before I shoot it!"

"Let go!" I shoved at him.

He released me, and I grabbed Poo-stank's collar, tugging him back behind me, though he snarled and barked at the Sorcerer loud enough to ring in the snow-insulated trees. The man's jacket was ripped, and blood leaked from his arm.

"Good boy," I murmured, rubbing Poo-stank's prickling ruff.

The man grimaced at me. "You need to ground your fucking magic before you turn this park into Chernobyl."

"Funny enough, no one ever told me how to do that. See, I was getting the life force sucked out of me by a sanguimancer for the last seven or so years, so-"

"It ain't life-force, doll-face. It's *iron*. In your blood. Conducting magic, which he sapped from your little magic umbilical cord-" I winced at the imagery. "-and dumped into his own spells. And grounding's just what it sounds like. You take that magic and you send it—guess where?"

I kept my jaw shut.

"Into the fucking ground, like a lightning bolt. Fantastic. You're welcome. Don't blow yourself up."

"Why would you care if I did?"

He was already turning away, more concerned with the state of his arm than confronting me. Which was worrying because he hadn't really done anything threatening yet. Probably had to regroup, figure out what his bosses wanted to do with me now that I no longer had the book. Or maybe they really would go check the ashes in Abbie Ridge.

"You got a lot of power, Martin. Your little stunt at Rinkenburgers proved that. The Guild is interested in what you could do if you actually learned."

"If they think I'm going to do *anything* for them-"

"Whatever. We'll see what you say when the hunters catch you."

"Fuck off."

He lifted a hand, waving blood-stained fingers back over his shoulder as he walked away, leaving both me and Poo-stank tense and shivering by the duck pond.

Gwydian was alive? No, that couldn't be true. The Guild was lying, trying to get me to cooperate with them so they could get the book, or recruit me, or whatever it was they really wanted. If I complied, no doubt they would come up with a story of my ex-master's defeat in some remote, unverifiable location.

Hands shaking, I found Poo-stank's leash and dragged him down the path, where we located the other three dogs huddling near a clump of some thick, evergreen bushes. I gathered their leashes, and they were much subdued on our walk back to the rescue.

CHAPTER SEVENTEEN

The dogs didn't hide their jumpiness. Stroodle bit Krista when she went to remove his sweater. We joked that it was because he was fond of fashion, but Krista kept glancing over at me, giving me a startled smile whenever I caught her. But she didn't ask if anything happened, and I offered nothing.

The moment Sanadzi relieved me I dashed upstairs. I pulled my phone from the couch cushions and checked for a response from Morgan. I'd texted him at lunch, but he either hadn't had time to respond, or hadn't been able to.

I clamped my mind shut against the barrage of imagined tortures. Directionless energy soaked into my arms and legs. I wanted to change the situation, whether by hunting down Gwydian—if he was even still alive—or bashing in some Sorcerer faces.

I shivered, partly from the cold, and partly because of how much my way of doing things had changed since that night on the boat. My life had always required a run-first, fight if necessary strategy, but watching mom gunned down apparently changed my tactics.

Feet sounded on the stairs—Krista's, judging by the timing. Not in any mood to talk, I hustled up to the third floor shower. The tile was cold, though the steam that filled the air curled in against my skin in warm eddies. I made it a long shower, scrubbing as if I could wash away the anxiety.

When I emerged in a cloud of steam, three voices bounced around downstairs. Even if I was grumpy, at least now I was clean and somewhat calmer. On my way downstairs, I caught the end of Sanadzi's remark.

"... don't think another bar is where we should—hey, baby!"

At the sight of me, Sanadzi's face lit up and Krista, looking slightly panicked, twisted around on her barstool.

"Maybe Hel should choose," Jaesung said. He sprawled in the window seat where I'd been that morning, looking sly and smirky. I didn't want to be glad to see him, but if anyone would read my mood and adjust for it, it was Jae. Peacemaker, my Mom called it. Once, I might have said pushover. Now, I understood what Mom meant.

"Choose what?" I said, stepping off the last stair and sinking onto the arm of a chair.

Sanadzi shot Jaesung a dirty look. "It was supposed to be a surprise."

I crinkled my brow. "For...."

Another dirty look. Jaesung held up his hands in defense. "I'm just saying, maybe she'd like to have a say, considering."

Considering? Considering what? They seemed too happy to be booting me into the cold.

Sanadzi leaned against the bar. "Your birthday. We were trying to decide if you'd rather go out somewhere to eat or celebrate here, just us and Gene."

"You want to go out, right?" Krista said. "You've barely been anywhere since you got here, except Rinkenburger's, and that wasn't a typical example of Henard's nightlife."

"Henard doesn't *have* a nightlife," Jaesung said.

"Shut up, city-boy."

I realized my jaw was loose. "But... how did you even *know*?"

"Baby girl, you handed me your driver's license when you agreed to volunteer. I know I ain't old and white enough to be Miss Marple, but I can figure out your birthday."

I decided not to tell her I had no idea who Miss Marple was. Instead, I winced. I'd handed over the only of my five licenses with my real name on it. It was old—one I'd gotten at fifteen because I'd needed it to take the SAT and finish school. And the only one that was legal.

"Don't you dare tell me you're one of those abominations who hates birthdays?" Krista whined. "You like them starting now, right?"

My wince deepened to a grimace. "Just don't sing," I said. "Or get me anything."

Sanadzi put a fist on her hip. "There's a cake on the way and we're not taking it back. In this house, we birthday."

I groaned and pressed my palms to my burning face. I didn't want to seem ungrateful, but shocks of guilt and helplessness coursed down my back. How was I supposed to celebrate when everyone I loved was captured, running, or dead?

Krista laughed and came over. She tried to pry my hands from my face.

"You're so red. Oh my God, fine, we won't sing to you. Sanadzi, look."

"Well I want to sing, so I guess we could sing to one of the dogs."

"Sully's not getting any younger," Jaesung suggested. "And I bet she'd love to wear a hat and get sung to. Especially if she got cake."

They took pity. Eugene showed up with a cake, and Krista led an aged Giant Schnauzer up the stairs. The bearded canine accepted a party hat and barked along to her birthday song, wagging her stump of a tail. The slice of carrot cake shut her up.

"Now that the scary singing is over," Sanadzi teased, wiggling her fingers at me. "You can't get out of presents. They won't work for Sully."

I swallowed a too-big bite of cake, so my response came out a little strangled.

"I... didn't—"

"We know, we know," Eugene said, tossing an arm around my shoulders. "We shouldn't have. But, silly us, we did!"

Sanadzi and Eugene had gotten me a beautiful fair-isle sweater and Krista, a hardback sketchbook and pack of charcoal pencils. I was bright red and already overwhelmed when two hands slapped the counter in front of me.

I jumped and looked up. Jaesung stood on the other side of the breakfast bar, leaning in.

"My present isn't a thing," he said. "It's..." he glanced at Krista for help. "An experience?"

Krista snorted. "The Jaesung Park Experience."

He rolled his eyes. "We'll have to wait a few hours, though."

I quirked an eyebrow, baffled but grateful that he hadn't gotten me anything. I liked the sweater and the sketchbook. A lot, actually. But it felt weird to accept presents from people I'd met only a month ago, and who I'd leave any day, especially when they were all stretched so thin by the approaching wedding.

We played board games until Eugene and Sanadzi could no longer restrain their yawns. They left with hugs for everyone—Sanadzi hugged me twice—and Krista dashed upstairs to grab coats.

We piled into the truck, which heated fast with us all in ski jackets, and drove through an alien terrain of black and white. The sky had cleared since the storm that morning, gauzy clouds lingering over a partial moon, but leaving the rest of the sky deep and dark. Not that I could see much of it beyond the trees and buildings in Henard, but it wasn't long before we broke from the trees and into a full sheet of white-iced farmland.

I leaned forward in the middle seat. Moonlight glowed on the snow and dark streaks of asphalt peeked through the packed road, making sketchy lines ahead of us. Twenty minutes outside town, we turned down a service road between two fields, which looked so much like every other field that I wondered how Jaesung remembered the right one.

We bumped slowly along and halfway down the lane he killed the headlights.

"This is creepy," Krista whispered. She sounded happy about it.

Jaesung leaned forward, squinting down the road ahead. As far as I could tell, it ended just past the field, where a grain elevator stood flanked by a pair of silos. Just as we passed it, Jaesung slowed, put the car in reverse, and backed right up next to the metal scaffold beside the grain elevator.

"What are we doing?" I asked. "Is this some weird midwestern ritual? Are we cow-tipping?"

Krista and Jaesung both laughed. "We'd need cows for that," Krista said. "But I'll let you tip me, if it'll help."

I shook my head, but Jaesung had already turned off the engine and hopped out. He put one foot on the back tire and swung himself into the truck bed. "Come on!" he hissed.

Krista winked at me and got out. I followed and eased the door shut. The silo was at least four stories high and covered in scaffolding. The ladder beside us went straight up to what looked like a crow's nest far above. I had an inkling why Jaesung had backed up to it.

I pulled myself into the bed, where three backpacks awaited us. Jaesung retrieved his tower-climbing gear from one. He glanced up at the top of the silo, where the grain elevator's main set of scaffolding stretched across.

"Okay, so, this isn't exactly legal," he said. "But...I know the guy who owns the farm and I've been up this ladder a few times before, so I know it's at least safe-ish."

"Ish," Krista said.

"Ish. Which is why I brought this." He held out the harness to Krista. "I'm going up first to make sure it's not icy."

With that, he performed some sort of wizardry with a pair of lanyards until they made a makeshift harness around his chest, and hauled himself up the ladder like freaking Spiderman. Krista made a face at me and strapped herself into the harness. I followed behind with lanyards of my own.

It was slow going, clipping and unclipping myself every few feet, and the metal rungs were frigid, even through my gloves. I pulled myself onto the black metal catwalk with a grunt, over-warm and breathing fast. The catwalk stretched out above the silos, ending at the huge concrete tower of the grain elevator itself. Another ladder led up there, but that wasn't our destination. Krista had unrolled a sleeping bag next to the concrete wall.

Jaesung glanced up from his gear.

"Take a look." He nodded toward a spot behind me. I turned, then grabbed a rail as the vertigo of extreme height drew me off balance. From up here... God. I could see everything. The fields stretched out in endless rolls of white, etched with the sparse lines of dark road and trees. The moonlight glowed off pristine snow, and a chill wind blew the remaining clouds into streamers across the sky, as if Sanadzi had called them up too, demanding decoration.

While Jaesung unfastened the clips at my waist, I gazed out over miles of snow-covered land.

"The snow was a lucky bonus," Jaesung said. "I was afraid the clouds would ruin it."

"Ruin what?"

He snagged his bag and nodded back toward Krista. "Come see."

The backpack I'd carried up also contained a sleeping bag, along with a large quantity of fancy cookies and two thermoses of 'special' hot chocolate.

We settled on one sleeping bag, Jae situating himself in the middle and holding up the second sleeping bag like a cape. He draped his arms, and the blanket, around our shoulders, and pulled us both back against the concrete wall.

"Okay, they should be here soon. Over that way," he pointed east with the arm that was around my shoulder. The movement tugged me closer under his arm, which was... not uncomfortable.

I gazed up at the stars, found Orion at once, then Taurus and the Pleiades. My gaze wandered then, just out of a strange sense of irony, to Canis Major. I found the brightest star in the pattern, Sirius, the Dog Star, and gave it a little mental salute.

"You'll have to tell me what constellations those are," Jaesung said, breaking the silence. "All I know is Orion."

"Yeah. And is that really a sword belt?" Krista added. "It looks like Orion Jr." Everyone giggled, and I pointed a cookie just above the top star of Orion's bow.

"Look up from him," I said. "See the sort of skewed W?"

"Uhuh."

"That's Cassiopeia, mother of Andromeda. Andromeda's below her on the right but it's hard to describe. Anyway, the five stars above Cassiopeia? The ones that make a house kind of shape? That's Cephus, and right next to him is Polaris—the north star."

"Dude, I thought that was a satellite," Jaesung said.

Krista gave a soft laugh. "I believe you now, Jae."

Smirking, he took his arm from around her to reach for a thermos.

A small part of me was glad he had let go of her instead of me. It was hard to accept physical contact from people outside my pack, and though Jaesung wasn't an exception, he held himself in a way that was friendly and undemanding. So undemanding, maybe, that I wanted to lean in. I accepted the canister of spiked hot chocolate instead.

On my third sip, a small streak, flashed across the sky, light as a pencil stroke. Jaesung's whole body tensed. Krista slapped at his leg.

"Did you see it, did you-"

I straightened up so fast it knocked Jaesung's arm off my shoulders. It settled lower down my back.

"The Leonids!" I said. "What? I used to watch them with...." I trailed off, shaking my head as if it could erase the memory of a different birthday.

I turned thirteen on my dad's boat, way down in the Keys, where November was still windbreaker-weather. I hadn't expected presents or cake—sailing without twenty desperate, frightened illegals packed in the hold was gift enough. I could work the boat with Dad, worry about nothing but the scrutiny of the men Gwydian had watching us.

Near midnight, hours after we'd dropped anchor in a sandy cove, Dad had stretched out with me on the deck. We'd squinted past rigging and furled sails, me watching where Dad pointed, until the first of the meteor shower started.

It had felt like a stolen moment, even then. I'd wanted to preserve it, a little snow-globe of wonder and happiness. But Dad never made it to another birthday, and I'd forgotten about the Leonids.

The mix of disbelief and excitement sent a rush of heat to my chest. I twisted around to look at Jaesung. He grinned. In the bluish moonlight, his features stood out in contrast—everything black against everything tan, like he was drawn in bold, expert brush strokes.

"How did you even...."

"You said you knew a bunch of constellations," he said, shrugging. "I figured you liked stars so I looked up the next meteor shower and, well, the timing was good."

Krista held out a cookie. "Lay back, sweetie. You're missing it."

I did, and this time I let myself lean, my bent knees tilting slightly against Jaesung's extended thighs. We watched the sky come to life above us. Little needles of light rained toward the southern horizon, toward Miami and all the heartache I'd left behind.

Maybe it was the memory—that perfect little globe of peace, which I never thought I'd feel again—but I caught myself memorizing. It would be something for the next snow-globe. Instead of a boat, there would be a grain elevator. Instead of Dad, there would be Jaesung and Krista.

The burgeoning warmth in my chest begged me to come to harbor, drop anchor, reef the sails. It whispered of a safe place to wait out the storm.

Don't make yourself too at home, I thought, hearing my mother's voice, as if she still coached me. *You're leaving as soon as Morgan gets in touch.*

But my fingers curled tighter around the thermos, and when Jaesung's wrist settled across my shoulder, I leaned a little more. Maybe, if she'd met them, Mom would understand.

~

The meteor shower was still in full force when we called it a night. Krista, dancing with the need to pee, strapped on the harness and started down. Jaesung gestured for me to go next, but I hesitated. He couldn't have known about my dad's desire to share the meteor shower with me, or the serenity of that moment. But still, I wanted to thank him for dusting off that memory, and for giving me a new one.

The rest of me wanted to let the moment pass. In a few days, Morgan would come and I'd be gone and it wouldn't matter. But it seemed wrong to be so grateful then leave as if it meant nothing.

"I'm... not good at saying thank you," I managed.

A meteor flashed, reflecting off his glasses. He glanced away from me and shrugged. "Nah," he said. "It's cool—I get that."

"No, what I mean is..." My gaze flicked to the grain elevator, to the sky behind him, to his shoulder. I wanted to give him something in return. The truth seemed like the only thing heavy enough. "I just... it's hard right now. A lot of things are hard, and I don't want you guys to think I'm not grateful—"

"We get it, Hel."

"No. I mean, I'm sure you do, kind of but...." I struggled to dredge up the words that would ease me into the truth, blunt its sharpness for human consumption, but found none. "Right before I met you guys—days before—my Mom died. She... " my lungs squeezed. "She was shot."

That was all I said—more than I should have. I couldn't look up at Jaesung's face. Getting shot wasn't something that happened to normal mothers.

At last, he released a breath, the fog of it creeping into the space between us. "God..." he murmured.

"So, anyway," I said. "It's still hard to feel the good things." A finger touched my elbow. I tensed, but didn't shrug it off.

"Yeah, of course," he said. "God, I had no idea... none of us did."

"I didn't want you to. It just provokes more questions. Could you not tell Sanadzi and Kris?"

"Yeah," he said, and his hand slid up my arm. I could tell he wanted to hug me, and I leaned away. "Sure. I mean, if you need... If you're in more trouble—how do I say this?"

"I'm good. Better than I'd hoped."

I heard his jacket shift as he nodded. "Thanks," he said. I looked up. "For trusting me. Telling me that wasn't easy for you."

I shrugged, trying to displace the weird, tingling discomfort those words caused. "You trusted me first, so..."

"Well, you know." Another pause. "Talk if you need to."

"Yeah."

Neither of us looked at each other, and his hand dropped from my arm. After a moment of fiddling with my lanyards, I gestured to the ladder and started my climb down. Despite the lingering awkwardness, there was a warm, thick sensation in my chest, like the brightness of my magic had turned from turquoise to amber, from flame to something slower and softer that responded to my heartbeat.

I should have left that alone. It was new, weird. Attached to the dog rescue, and Krista, and Sanadzi, and probably more than anything to Jaesung. Something about him made me want to feel it, and whether that was the scars on his back, his arm around my shoulders, or the way his voice vibrated in my chest, I had no way of knowing. The warmth should have frightened me more.

I jumped off the ladder just as Krista extricated herself from the harness and chucked it in the back of the truck.

"My God, I have to pee so hard it could cut metal."

A smile forced its way onto my face as she made a show of holding herself and waddled around the side of the silo. She let out a great cry of relief as I tossed my backpack into the bed of the truck, prompting a snort from the ladder above.

"Pee shivers?" Jaesung yelled, leaping down.

"Fuck yeah!" Krista called back.

I pulled myself into the truck bed. "Are we over being quiet?"

He shrugged and climbed in after me. "The owners aren't actually home."

I shoved the backpacks up next to the cab and, sweating now from the climb down and the extra insulation, I shrugged off the down jacket. A rush of frigid air hit me, but it was like walking into an air-conditioned building after hours in the Miami heat. Actual licks of steam curled off Jaesung's back.

"Whew, that's brisk," he said, and dropped his jacket onto mine.

I glanced around for Krista and found her leaning against the grain elevator, her phone against her face. I'd left mine inside the truck cab—Morgan had been silent for over a week, so there'd been no reason to take it with me.

"Who's she even calling at three in the morning?" I asked. Jaesung leaned back, following where I was looking.

"Alina probably."

"Who's Alina?"

He started, meeting my eyes. "She hasn't told you about Alina?"

I shrugged. "Guess not."

He licked his lips and winced. "She probably forgot you didn't know." He leaned against the cab, plucking off his gloves. "Alina is Krista's girlfriend. She's been in a psych ward for a few months, under suicide watch." He stopped flexing his fingers, cocked his head, then nodded. "Pretty much because her ex husband is a dick. And there's a kid involved, which makes everything worse."

I glanced at Krista again, at the way she cradled her phone against her cheek. At Rinkenburger's, she'd taken a phone call that had upset her and gotten drunk. That had been Alina too.

I winced. My first night at the dog rescue, I'd assumed that the biggest worry in Krista's life had been the size of a bridesmaid's dress.

It wasn't running for her life or dealing with the murder of her mother and a lifetime of fear and slavery, but it wasn't the superficial, petty problems I'd assumed, either. A thread of guilt tightened around my gut.

"Hey," Jaesung bumped my shoulder with the back of his hand. "You're not allowed to stress on your birthday."

"It's three hours past my birthday."

"We haven't slept yet, so it still counts."

Krista had settled against the silo, looking for all the world like she'd forgotten we existed.

The chill was getting to me, but I found I didn't want to put my jacket back on. It was bulky and constricted my movements too much, and my muscles were still too warm for its insulated heat. I sat on the truck's back gate.

Jaesung glanced back at Krista. "She'll be awhile. So..." he pulled out his phone, and for a second I thought he was just going to stand there, browsing the internet while I waited without entertainment. "It occurs to me you'll probably be around for Gene and Sanadzi's wedding." Seeing my confusion, he elaborated. "It's in about a month."

I nodded, but the only reason I'd still be here was if Morgan hadn't gotten in touch. I didn't want to think about that. Then again, I also didn't want to think about leaving. It made the warm place in my chest go tight and painful.

"I guess," I said.

He seemed too wrapped up to notice my moment of hesitation. Or maybe it just looked normal for me.

"Anyway, there's... well. They had everyone in the wedding party and local guests go to this workshop because of a reception video they want to film."

I lifted my eyebrows. "A workshop?"

"Yeah." He squinted, unhappy with his explanation. "Anyway. You taught me some constellations, so, I'm showing you what we learned so you won't look like a loser." He hit a button on his phone, and music leaked out. It was slow, a decades-old song. He held out a hand.

I lifted my gaze from his hand to his eyes. It hadn't hurt me yet to trust Jaesung Park.

I took his hand. Some of the tension released from his shoulders and he tugged me to the middle of the truck bed. It was still slick with refrozen snow. His other hand found mine, directed it to his shoulder, and he took my waist.

The instant I realized what this posture meant, I laughed. "Are you teaching me to *dance*?"

"I'm gonna do my best."

"I've never danced once in my entire life."

"Neither had some at the workshop. You'll be in good company. Step back on your right foot. Step." He pushed against my hand, grip on my waist tightening. I stepped back, and his foot followed mine. "Bring your left foot back and shift your weight to it." I shifted. "And shift back to your right. Step forward on your left. Keep tension in your arms—I can steer you that way. Step. Shift-shift, step. Shift-shift, step."

I watched my feet and his, overcome by the absurdity of learning how to dance in a truck-bed, in the middle of a snowy field, when there were Sorcerers after me and a meteor shower still streaking by above. Also, a little, because his hand was on my waist and his shoulder was firm and steady. I had a weird urge to laugh and pull away.

"Stop looking at your feet," he said. "You've got it."

I looked at his turtleneck, too afraid to look at his face when we stood so close. He steered me easily—shift-shift step, shift-shift step—until the rhythm of it sank in. Then he pushed against my hand and pulled my waist, turning me under his arm. I fumbled, but he caught my side and pushed me backward into step, chuckling. "Nice."

"So is this it?" I asked. "Your martial art?"

"Ballroom? No. I learned a little, but that's not it. Turn."

This time it was more graceful, and I remembered to step backwards at the end.

Krista laughed. I twisted my head, thinking it was at us, but she wasn't looking our way. Unfortunately, I forgot to step forward when Jaesung stepped back. His feet slid on the ice in the truck bed, and he pitched forward. He grabbed my shoulder for balance. I caught him around the ribs but wasn't braced for the sudden weight. We staggered.

"Damn ice," Jaesung said, catching his footing. He drew back and a sharp pain jerked at my head.

"Ow!" I grabbed his wrist.

"Shit, sorry! My watch. Your hair's caught." His hand slid around to my back, pulling me forward. Then both arms circled my shoulders, and he plucked at the hair that had tangled itself in the strap. It brought me almost against him. My fingers pressed into his ribs, which radiated heat right through my knitted gloves. His chin hovered against my temple.

It would have been easier for me to turn around but neither of us suggested it. He untangled his watch and set his hands on my shoulders. Enough of my heat had been leached away by the air or displaced by the unsteady flicker in my chest that I was shivering again.

I wanted to lean in, to see what it felt like to press my forehead into his neck and have his arms tighten around me. They would. He wasn't hiding his attention. If I was honest, I knew what he wanted. What I couldn't decide was why I wanted it back. Because of that warmth in my chest? Or did I just crave the comfort of arms around me, someone to insulate me from the world—anyone?

I stepped away. His fingers dropped from my shoulders, the moment broken.

Luckily, Krista returned soon after, because Jaesung and I had run out of things to say. We piled into the cab, wrangling coats and seatbelts. Krista tilted sideways and grabbed my phone out from under her.

"Looks like you got some love, birthday-girl," she said, and tossed the phone into my lap.

The screen showed two missed calls and a text, all from an unknown number. My stomach fluttered. Morgan must have chucked his phone and gotten a new one. That would explain why he hadn't responded. Was it his idiotic idea of a birthday surprise to tell me he was okay?

As the truck trundled back between the fields, I pulled off my glove and swiped the lock screen, hunching so my coat obscured it from line of sight. A single word, no punctuation, sat stark in the message field.

Answer

Uneasiness pressed in around my lungs. Nothing about the message was off; it was just the kind of stark, utilitarian text Morgan might send. But a shudder built in my spine.

A photo attachment hovered beneath it. I curled my fingers into a fist, rubbing my thumb along my knuckle. Somehow, without seeing it, I knew that picture would end the fantasy of peace.

My thigh pressed warm against Jaesung's and, as I stared down at the attachment, Krista scanned through the radio. The truck pulled onto the main road just as she stopped on some loud, bass filled dance music. Above, the darkness of the sky was shot through with meteors. This was the life I might've had if things were different.

But things were not different. I needed to stop kidding myself.

I un-clenched my fist and tapped the attachment. The picture swam up onto the screen: dark room, dirty concrete floor; the Hell-hound mandala sketched out in blood. Beside it lay a familiar shape, his brindled fur matted and torn—Eamon.

It was like falling back into ice water. Every inch of me seized up. Thoughts crashed against each other and I fought with my lungs, trying to batter myself back into control. I thought the *Guild* had caught Eamon, but they didn't have the Hellhound mandala. I'd destroyed the only copy of the spell. The one other person who might have had it memorized was dead.

Should have been dead. I'd watched him die.

The truck shuddered into a pothole, knocking me into Krista. The text had told me to answer. That could only mean Gwydian was alive. He had Eamon.

He was coming for me.

CHAPTER EIGHTEEN

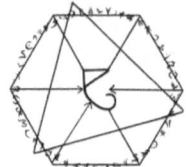

If Krista or Jaesung noticed anything was wrong, they didn't acknowledge it. As they dragged the gear upstairs, I edged around the exam tables to the kennel, trying to look busy while I begged my phone not to ring. Not until I figured out what to do.

The weight of Eamon's broken, bleeding form dragged my brain into blackness. How had I been almost happy an hour ago? How had I let myself forget the danger my pack still faced?

My phone burned like a coal in my pocket. What would happen if I threw it away? If I gave up on Eamon, gave up on Morgan ever finding me, and concentrated on staying alive? It was the likeliest way to survive. I could hunker down here. I might not be invisible to the Guild, but they would never let Gwydian continue unmolested. They would take care of my problem for me.

Only, if Gwydian had Eamon, it was likely he had more of my pack, and the Guild had always seen them as acceptable sacrifices. Especially if they were under an enslavement spell.

An enslavement spell that Gwydian would use if the others hadn't mutilated their tattoos. Not that he couldn't just make another tattoo.

Then there was the rogue Sorcerer on the ice. If my Guild harasser was right, Gwydian had several on my tail. And if one bounty hunter found me, more would do the same, and they wouldn't have any code against hurting Krista or Jaesung or Sanadzi.

Poo-stank pawed at his cage and gave a low woof for my attention. I patted his neck and forced myself to breathe. Upstairs, Krista and Jaesung's footsteps traced paths across the kitchen and living room. Their voices were low, muffled.

I let my head bang into the bars of Poo-stank's cage and closed my eyes. What if we'd been attacked at that farm, stuck on top of a grain elevator with no way to run? God, I'd put them in so much danger tonight.

My phone vibrated in my pocket. I opened my eyes. In front of me, Poo-stank's black-tipped ear flicked toward the sound.

My gut was a solid stone as I pulled the phone from my pocket. The unknown number displayed on the screen. Fear crashed over my back in a cold, bright surf. I shuddered and hunched over, holding onto the cage bar for balance.

On the other end of the line was the man whose kind eyes had haunted my nightmares since I was four. And now he had Eamon, and the spell to twist him into the same demonic beast he'd made my father.

Answer.

But would he even stop if I did?

My throat went thick and tight. I forced myself to stand, walking from the small circle of light to brace myself against a pillar. I tapped the green icon and lifted the phone.

I said nothing, just forced myself to breathe, forced myself to press the phone to my cheek.

"Helena?" The soft voice made my breath hitch, my stomach turning to poison. It was the voice I knew—the cadence and the tone, but the quality of it was wrong. Raspy, as if he'd been choked, or swallowed a hand full of glass shards.

Smoke inhalation from the explosion. He'd survived, but not unscathed. That made it worse.

"Helena, I need you to come home."

Fear at my back, unrelenting, every day. Violence, and my fingers dug into some stranger's shoulder, holding him down for torture, for blood. For magic.

"Helena, I know you're there," Gwydian rasped, his Scottish accent softening the edges of the words. "Eamon is here. Answer me, Helena. I don't want to hurt him."

"That's bullshit." Fear strangled the words.

He made a soft, disapproving grunt. "Now, that is unkind. All I want is to help you help your friends."

"The way you helped my mother into a bullet?" My chest pulsed, the turquoise fire shuddering into my veins. Anger swarmed into my brain, scribbling out the instinct to back down, to be careful and do what this man said. "Go to hell."

The voice on the other end chuckled, and the smoky rasp of it sent crackles down my legs. My power was threatening to snap. I clenched my fist, thinking of my feet as roots, imagining all that power pulsing down into the concrete floor, through the skin of the earth and into her own veins.

"Bring me the book and I'll let him die. No more spells necessary."

I felt myself shaking against the pillar. Its cold, smooth surface seemed too still, too solid. The scaffolding of the world was crumbling yet everything around me was painfully static.

"W-why do you need it? You remember the spells."

"Knowledge is more valuable when it's scarce."

I snorted. "You think I'm sharing those spells? Like I'd get out of your control just to hand my leash to the Guild. I'm not an idiot."

"That's very good to hear," he said. The dangerous softness of his accent raked down my spine. "Very good. Now. I want you to take the book, and come to me in Miami. Can you do that?"

I swallowed, ignoring the pulse in my stomach, the thrashing fury in my brain. Eamon was as good as dead, and if he had the others, I couldn't rescue them. I couldn't go toe-to-toe with Gwydian. Not yet. Maybe not ever.

Still, I had to drag the words out of me. "I'm not going back."

"No? Mm, that's not what I wanted to hear." I heard him moving on the other end of the line, shoes scuffing on concrete. He sounded so conversational, as if we were talking about something unimportant. He grunted, and another sound started up. A voice, whimpers shivering over the line—a man past the point of prideful silence. I heard the muffled sound of a gag, and then the shuddering whimpers rose in volume, in urgency. A smothered cry of panic, the sound of heels jittering on the floor. Then a scream.

My knees shook from under me, buckling at the force of that sound. I slid down the pillar, a hand clapped over my mouth, because I knew that voice. Knew the way that scream sounded. And I was close to screaming back.

Morgan.

My entire being rejected it. I dropped the phone. It clattered to the concrete, a bright rectangle of light. The scream faded. A whisper replaced it, tinny with the distance from the speaker.

"What happens next is up to you," Gwydian said. "Come home, or I can send them to fetch you."

My diaphragm was spasming. The desperate air wheezed past my sinuses, creating a high, uneven hiss in my nasal cavity.

Poo-stank whined in his cage. One of the smaller dogs gave a growl, followed by a yap.

"Helena," Gwydian's soft, raspy voice said. "Answer me, Helena."

I couldn't listen anymore. It was over. It was all over—he had caught everyone I cared about. Everyone that mattered. And he would kill them. Or turn them all into monsters, like my father, and send them after me.

I clenched my eyes shut. Morgan, twisted and bulging with fangs, lunged at me. The sight was too easy to imagine.

Poo-stank barked, and I jerked up. I muffled the scream with my fingers, nails digging into my cheeks. The bright square of phone was beneath me—a leash to Gwydian. I fumbled for it with my free hand, ending the call, and hurled it away from me.

It clattered to the concrete and spun under the bottom shelf of a sink. There it stayed, like a bomb.

My hands rattled against my face. I heard the wheezing in my throat, a sound that didn't have strength to be more.

"Hel?"

Footsteps on the stairs, the shifting shadows of someone coming down. The dogs were making a racket. I had to get up, had to scrape myself together—whatever it took to keep them from asking questions.

But what point was there? Everything was over. Everything was gone. The thoughts flitted into my brain and vanished. I had no strength to fight this.

"Hel?" Jaesung's voice was beside me. Fabric rustled as he crouched next to me.

My hands refused to leave my face. My knees trembled, breath shuddering. I'd never experienced this malignant despair. It seeped from my bones, curled through my guts and grew in hard, vicious clumps—a fast-moving cancer. It was too big for my body. I would crack open. I'd go crazy.

Hands found my shoulders. "Breathe, sweetheart. Come on."

I tried to listen, but the panic was too deep. There was no surface, no light.

One of Jaesung's hands found my fingers and slid behind them, drawing my hand from my face. It rattled in his. He pulled, and my arm stretched stiffly until my fingers pressed into his chest.

His palm found my face, and he smoothed my hair back. A moment later, a knee insinuated itself between my ankles, and he was there in front of me, leaning in so close it blocked out the sensation of light through my eyelids.

"Helena. Talk to me. Tell me what's happened."

I sucked in a gasp, clenching my teeth and pressing my tongue hard against the roof of my mouth to keep the breath held. For a second, it worked. My diaphragm spasmed again. I let out the breath, sucking in a few more sharp gasps.

Both of Jaesung's hands were on my face now, holding my head up, keeping my face tilted toward him. I forced my eyes to open. And there he was, close as he'd been earlier, when I'd thought my life had never been so good. But now?

Morgan wouldn't find me. Or Eamon. Or Rodolfo or Zenia or Cai or my mother. If they weren't dead they soon would be. All because of the Guild and Gwydian. And me. I shuddered and said the only thing I knew Jaesung would understand.

"I don't think they're coming."

Heat swelled in my eyes. I sensed the rising tide and could not hold it back.

"Shit." Jaesung pulled me up to my knees. Then, like I'd known they would, his arms closed around me. The wave inside me broke. I collapsed into him, a limp, ragged body sobbing into the warmth of his chest, sobbing like I hadn't let myself in years, like you only did in the arms of a person who had you anchored tight.

And God, he did. The harder I sobbed the harder he held, until the shuddering of my stomach barely registered against the tightness of his arms. The world fractured and crashed, and I forgot about being brave.

When I could breathe again, his arms slackened and he pulled me to my feet. We climbed the stairs, crossed the empty room, and continued up to the third floor. I didn't resist when he opened his door and pushed me inside. I stood in the darkened room, ignoring the walls and the bookshelves and the desk. All I wanted was to sink back into him. Weakness was addictive.

He stepped around me, but his fingers stayed on my arm as he drew back the dark covers on his bed. I didn't even wait for him to say it. I climbed in, scooted toward the wall, and waited for him to climb in behind.

He drew up the covers instead. I heard the creak of a chair, the thunk of first one shoe, then the other. His belt clicked and hitched from jeans. There was an unzipping hoodie, the snap and clatter of him setting his watch on his desk, and then a lighter click. Glasses, maybe.

I listened to him take off socks, shirt, jeans. Heard a drawer open, and more fabric sounds. Probably one of his multitude of patterned pajama trousers.

My head throbbed, pressure hot and thick in my sinuses. I'd forgotten how miserable it was to cry.

Jaesung's footsteps were light on the carpet. The mattress shifted as he sat. He leaned down, clicking something by the floor.

"Jae?" I managed the word, though my voice was heavy.

"Hm?" I heard him lift an alarm clock from his side-table and click through the hours.

"Can you stop being nice to me?"

The clicking ceased. "I'm not sure what you mean."

"I mean stop being nice to me. Doing things for me. Birthday stuff or tea or waking me up for snow or... Can you not do that?"

He was silent a beat, then the clicking started back up. He didn't answer again until it was set, and returned it to the side table with a clunk.

Then he stretched out over the covers, propping himself on an elbow behind me.

"Why wouldn't you want me to be nice?"

Because I didn't deserve it. Because I couldn't stay. Because I wanted to.

"Just... I can't handle it right now. It makes it harder to keep myself together."

There was a light tug at my hair, and I realized he was pulling the tie from the end of my braid.

"You don't have to keep yourself together. After what you've been through, and knowing they're not coming to get you...I mean, it would be weird if you didn't fall apart."

"I can't," I insisted, scooting toward the wall and turning my head so the loose end of my braid pulled from his hands. "I can't fall apart. I have.... There are things I can't tell you. About what happened. About what's happening. I didn't think I'd be here this long."

That's when I noticed the lines of heat radiating through the blanket. For just a moment, I thought it was a spell, and the fear halted me mid-sentence. Then the pattern of warmth wrapping me up made sense.

"Is this an electric blanket?" I asked.

"It might be."

I let out a sigh that was half despair, half resignation. "I'm in the middle of telling you not to be nice to me, when you brought me up here to be nice to me."

"I can turn it off."

"No."

He chuckled at my back, fingers returning to my hair, combing out the thick plait.

"You're being nice," I warned.

"Nah. I've got a hot girl in my bed—this is totally self-serving," he said. I let out a huff and closed my eyes again as his fingers worked their way up to my scalp.

"I guess I'm vulnerable right now," I said.

"See? I'm an asshole." He said the words softly, with his thumb sweeping along the skin behind my ear.

"Is the asshole sleeping on top of the covers? Because it's twelve degrees. I will tell Krista to make that moron jar."

"It's not twelve degrees," he said, but a moment later he had peeled back the covers. He slid into bed behind me, and the weight of him tipped me back. I resisted only slightly, holding myself still as he adjusted his long limbs on the full-sized mattress. His hand found my back beneath the covers, rubbing my spine between my shoulder blades.

"You're being-"

"Selfish," he interrupted. I wanted to protest, but speaking was getting harder and harder with his fingers working their way up my spine, rubbing away tension. I opened my eyes again and glanced at the window at the foot of his bed. It framed a navy sky and the edge of the building next door.

So little separated us from danger. Just a pane of glass, some brick, a few centimeters of sheetrock and wood. So little to keep out the things we feared.

A pinprick of light streaked over the visible patch of sky. A meteorite. It was strange to think that, no matter how my life had changed in the past hour, the world raged on, impassive and inexorable. And no matter what horrors happened to me or the people I loved, it would keep going.

In the great scheme, I didn't matter. And now that Gwydian had re-enslaved my pack, neither did much else.

Jaesung's hand on my back felt dangerous. His warmth, seducing me toward the center of the bed, was a siren song. Instinct dueling with desire. I needed to figure out my next move; I needed to do that without a warm, solid complication against my back.

His hand slid up to my elbow, fingers tracing down to my wrist until his arm rested around me. Without meaning to, I spread my fingers to accept his. Long, strong bones, short nails. He had beautiful fingers.

I leaned back, and he met me, rearranging himself against me like that was what he'd wanted all along. Body warm, solid. Then his face nestled into my hair, and his breath blew out against my scalp, and I was, for the first time, enveloped by another person.

I felt drunk. Sad and scared and drunk with the delirium of being safe. I wasn't, of course, but every beat of Jaesung's heart against my back told me that lie. The long thigh he pressed between mine knocked away the protest that he couldn't protect me. His rough chin nestled against my nape, his long arm drawing me tight, and the toes that curled up under the arch of my foot all conspired to build a fantasy where everything would be okay.

I didn't need a fantasy. I needed a plan.

But my chest ached. My heart was ragged and spent. Just for tonight, for the few hours while the Leonids were in the sky and Jaesung's weight pressed against my back, I wanted the lie. Because tomorrow I'd have a plan and it would not involve staying here.

CHAPTER NINETEEN

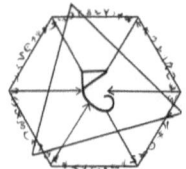

The following day passed in a haze of overly bright smiles from Krista. Sanadzi, though absent due to final wedding preparations, sent a text mostly comprised of hearts and exclamation points. It wasn't hard to guess that Jaesung had told them no one was coming for me. If anyone noticed I slept somewhere other than the couch that night, they said nothing.

I applied myself to scrubbing kennels and hefting bags of dog food, avoiding eye contact with anyone who looked like they might want to start a conversation.

Last night's despair had been a hurricane, blowing through my insides and scrubbing them raw. There was nothing left intact, just the wreckage of feelings I'd once been able to name, broken and buried half-deep in the sand. Still, the day after a hurricane was always clearer than the ones before. My heart might have been that ravaged coast, but my mind felt sharper than it had in ages. I no longer questioned what I had to do.

The wedding was coming fast. Spare time vanished into pre-addressing thank-you cards or sorting seating placards. Even I'd gotten roped into tying white and green ribbons around tiny vials of bubbles. It was the perfect distraction. Everyone would be so busy with preparations, there wouldn't be time to worry about me.

I trudged down from my post-work shower to find the furniture pushed toward the middle of the room and what looked like a large blue raft inflating in the corner. Krista had unloaded video games and DVDs from the shelf and jammed an end table between it and the raft. She'd moved the rug into the corner, as if to define a separate room.

My pulse jumped. Making a separate room was exactly what she was doing. I forced a breath in past my pulsing throat, hating the swell of gratitude threatening to complicate my trajectory. At the sound of me on the stairs, she twisted around and waved me over.

"Grab that fitted sheet," she said, gesturing to a pile of linens in one of the displaced armchairs. "So? I was talking to Sanadzi about trying to get you something more permanent bed-wise, and she offered their air-mattress. We're thinking wire shelves or something to give you a wall and some storage?" She dusted off her hands, shoving her sleeves back up her tattooed arms. "It's not as good as a room, but it would have a little more privacy...."

She trailed off, watching me with apprehension in her bright blue eyes. She was trying very hard to show me I had a place here without mentioning my family. Sadness plucked at my heart, but I sent it away, finding the barest of smiles to reassure Krista.

"Thanks," I said. "I meant to say it before, but I'm not good at that. The whole 'friends' thing is new."

The apprehension in her gaze transformed, and for a second I feared she'd throw her arms around me. True, I'd spent the night with a boy wrapped around me, but I still wasn't ready for spontaneous hugs. Luckily, Krista was not the indiscriminate hugger Sanadzi was. She took the sheet from my hands.

"It's cool. I can tell you're sort of overwhelmed by everything so don't worry about offending me. I won't be mad because you don't react like, you know...."

"A normal human being?" I offered, snagging one corner of the sheet and stretching it over the edge of the mattress.

"I hate using the word 'normal'. It assumes a standard mold everyone should fit into, and anything outside that *is* flawed. I mean it's fine for you not to react like everything is okay and you've had a happy, suburban life."

I winced, thinking of my assumptions about her, and what Jaesung had told me about her girlfriend. "Have any of us?"

Krista stretched her part of the sheet to the top corner of the mattress and glanced up at me with a grin. "Right? I mean, I fit the suburban thing, and mostly the happy thing, but I'm a five-foot-ten orange-haired lesbian with the Goblin King tattooed on one arm. Life has not been without challenges."

"I can imagine," I said, though I really couldn't. "Also, sorry. I didn't know until last night, about Alina."

Krista's grin slipped a degree, but she nodded. "Yeah—it sucks. But," the smile hitched back onto her face as she shoved the last corner over the edge of the mattress. "You'll get to meet her at the wedding! They said she was doing well enough to leave by then."

I tried to act enthusiastic, as if I really would meet the woman who had such a large part of Krista's heart. Either it was convincing or, as Krista had said, she didn't expect a normal reaction from me.

I helped her finish making the air mattress and rearranging the chairs, couch, and coffee table in the center of the room. It gave the whole second floor a studio-apartment vibe, with the bed in one corner and the living room and kitchen stretching down the length of the room.

I hated having to leave.

"We should go get you a few things," Krista said. "You need an electric blanket, and maybe some of those cloth shelf boxes to put your clothes in. And a lamp."

I considered protesting, but the shopping trip would give me a decent excuse to buy another duffel bag and pick up a few things I might need for the road.

Despite her propensity for glitter and grunge, Krista had a flair for picking out things I liked. I'd been afraid her idea of an acceptable blanket might have laddered holes with safety-pins or rainbow unicorns. Or both. Instead she found a comforter in a pale gray that wouldn't look too odd in the main room, and the bedside lamp was a stack of graduated glass globes beneath a white shade.

"So you can have a snowman all year," she teased. I rolled my eyes, but twin spikes of longing and regret pricked my chest as she tossed cardboard organizers into the basket. These things would be useful to them even without me, but I hated making them believe I'd stay.

I was jealous of the Helena Martin they thought existed, the one that would get to sleep on that air-mattress and fill these boxes with clothes and sketchbooks. The me that would turn on that lamp over the picture of my parents and feel the ache of missing them turn bittersweet. The me that would build a new life with a new family.

"Hell's bells, hello?"

I snapped back to reality, my hands resting on a pile of plastic-packaged sheet sets. Krista presented two packages, both of them holding electric blankets. One was the same cream color as the cloth boxes, and the other, a blue-gray plaid. I pointed to the plaid, which Krista added to the cart.

"So," she began, pacing toward the end of the aisle. "Tell me to mind my own business if you want, but...."

I tensed, my mind going to Jaesung's body warm and heavy against my back. She would do the thing I'd feared upon slinking downstairs that morning. I gripped the handle of the shopping cart, realizing I'd have to lie to her—not about what had happened, but how I felt about it.

"Why did you run away?" she asked.

I opened my mouth, then shut it again. I'd thought Krista would stay in the realm of superficial for a while. There was every possibility Krista knew I'd told Jaesung some of it, but I wasn't sure how much I wanted to tell her. Whatever pain she had in her past, there were no scars on her back.

"I had to leave," I said. "My parents are dead and the people in charge of me were...they didn't treat me well. Me and others."

She nodded, looking down at the silver sequined pillow she'd pulled from the shelf. "I thought it might be something like that." She picked at a bedraggled bit of wiry thread poking from the shimmering discs. "So, what happened to your people? Why aren't they coming?"

I swallowed and shook my head. "It was my cousin. He's not... he can't come."

Krista tossed the pillow into the basket. "I know it's not the same, but you have a place here. You're not stranded. Like, we're weird around here and all, and you're probably wondering what the hell I even know about you, but I'm a good judge of people, and I think you fit here. With us."

I closed my eyes, in case the sincerity in her voice reflected in her face. This was exactly what I'd been trying to avoid—the kind of moment I would ask myself about later. Whether I might have fit with them, and had a real home.

I could sense her about to say something else when her phone erupted into sound. She snatched it from her pocket. I looked around for an escape—somewhere to be besides the home-goods aisle.

"Seriously?" she said, following my turns toward the front of the store. "Yeah, no—I've got the SUV. Sure. Yeah, text me the address and we'll head over."

I glanced back, curious despite myself. She seemed to be cataloguing something. "Yeah, I think we've got it all. How bad did they say it was? Could it walk?"

A dog. I inhaled deeper, holding my breath and pushing toward a rack of hats, gloves, and bags. Another rescue, then. Or was it another setup? I clenched my teeth and reached for the handles of an army green canvas duffle, ignoring the bird stenciled along the side in favor of the bulging side pockets. Part of me wanted to beg off—to use this opportunity to return to the rescue and pack my things—but the knot of fear in the back of my throat made it impossible to ask. If this was another setup, I needed to be there to protect Krista.

We went through the checkout line, where I dropped another two-hundred of my stash on items I wouldn't get to use, and drove west under blossoming street lights and frosted buildings.

Ten minutes later, the town had morphed from well-lit brick edifices to the corrugated tin and cinderblock of non-gentrified back streets. A familiar tension hardened my limbs, sent my gaze skipping around dark corners and likely spy holes.

We pulled up next to an unused lot between two boarded-up buildings. I slid from the passenger's seat, touching my back pocket for the ridge of my knife. I saw no magic circles like I had at the lake, but that didn't mean there weren't Sorcerers, or even just the garden-variety criminal. Or maybe I was being paranoid, and this would be a normal rescue.

While Krista retrieved her supplies, I squinted into the lot. A flickering street light set the chain-link fence's silhouette across the snow, and from what I noticed through the grid of wires, the far side of the lot ran up against the back of another cinderblock building.

A clump of unrestrained bushes against that back wall provided the likeliest cover for the dog...or anyone else who might be waiting. Still, none of the graffiti on the nearby walls was familiar, and most of the junk heaped up on the side appeared to be construction refuse and litter.

A sign at the edge of the fence claimed it was a property both private and for sale, but the owner clearly cared little about cleaning up the place.

"Where did they say the dog was?" I asked.

Krista appeared at my side. "I'm not sure. Jae said someone saw the dog limp through a hole in the fence. They were supposed to wait here and watch, but..." she looked around, raising her eyebrow as the streetlight behind us flickered. "Would you?"

"Not so much."

I walked along the fence, my boots kicking up little pebbles of snow as I scanned for a bend large enough to admit a dog. I found it near the left corner, where the bottom of the chain link fence had rolled up and away from the metal post. The edges had a clean, pinched break to them. Bright and shiny, like they'd been clipped rather than rusted apart.

It would have been useful to know how recent the cut was, but my forensic skills ended there. As the street light flickered behind me again, the shadows shifted across a series of impressions in the snow, half hidden by the shadow of the lefthand building. Something dark ran alongside, streaking the snow in drips, like oil from a leaking engine.

The hair on my neck stood on end, even before I recognized it as blood. I whipped myself around, scanning the street for movement or aberrations of light. Wind keened through the trees, picked up snow and tossed it around like beach sand. I tasted the sourness of my own fear.

Krista angled a flashlight beam into the bushes. "I think I see something in there," she called.

"Yeah." My voice was a croak, and I refused to take my eyes from the street. "There are paw prints over here, and a hole in the fence."

She approached and, upon seeing the opening, gave me a skeptical look. "My ass isn't fitting through that."

"We'll have to climb over," I said. I pulled off my gloves and gazed up at the six-foot fence. I'd need to take off my jacket to avoid getting stuck on the top. "At least there's no barbed wire."

"Whoa, whoa, whoa, miss military school. We're not—we can't—that's trespassing. The rescue can't do that."

"How are we supposed to get dogs on private property?" I gestured to the sign at the other end of the lot. "You want me to wait while you call those guys?"

"No, we lure it out with these." She held up a bag of dog treats. "Nitrate free and meaty."

"What if it's too hurt to move? That's blood."

She sucked in her bottom lip, gaze tracking along the spattered paw-prints. I unzipped my jacket. "If they cared, they'd fix the fence."

Shucking the coat, I tossed it into the bags on the floor of the passenger's seat. That afforded me the opportunity for a second look down the street. Nothing moved that should have been still, and nothing was still that should have been moving. All was as it should be.

So why was my neck still prickling?

I shivered, chafed my bare hands, and sprang up onto the frigid chain link fence.

I may not have been good at many helpful things for the Dog Rescue, but I'd smoke every one of them at trespassing. In a matter of seconds, I was on the other side, breath clouding in my face, hands stinging where the thin metal wire dug into my palms. Krista passed the treats and flashlight through the opening.

"Just let me know if anyone's coming," I said.

I ghosted into the shadows of the building, following the paw-prints with my eyes until they disappeared into the bushes. Edging forward, I dropped into a crouch and peered in through the thick branches.

At first, I saw nothing. The shadows were deep, shifting in the light of the flickering street lamp. I opened the treat bag, letting the scent waft into the chilly air. A mound I'd taken for a twist of roots gave a shuddering sigh.

So there was a dog. I sighed in relief, but on my next inhale, I caught the scent of treats and the richer, teeth-clenching odor of blood.

I twisted the flashlight beam toward the dog, shoving the barrel in a little deeper. Every leaf on the bush tinkled with ice.

There, in a patch of stained, melted snow, lay a large dog. From where I crouched, it was hard to tell exactly what breed, but the barrel chest and long limbs pointed at some breed of sight hound. Steam curled up from one flank, which was a mess of charred skin.

Revulsion clogged in my throat, deepening as I edged in and got a better look at the scraps of fur left on the beast's flank. Long haired and gray, like my own hound form.

Something was wrong, though I wasn't sure quite what it was. I tossed a treat toward the wretched thing. The dog didn't move. It was too pained, too exhausted. Probably too scared.

If I crawled in there and grabbed it, it might attack, forcing me to hurt it more to subdue it. I had to keep it calm.

"Kris!" I whisper-hissed to her. "Throw me a blanket or a towel or something."

As she ducked back to the van, I closed my eyes, blocking out the image of the creature. Dogs saw on a spectrum only humans gifted with magic could. Every glimmer of power was visible to them, including the spirit-forms we spellhounds cast forward.

The outer ring of my spellhound tattoo prickled with magic, and a moment later, I found the second heartbeat that seemed to exist alongside my own. The wolfhound who'd given me her shape and now gave me the form of her spirit. I filled it with my thoughts, with the turquoise fire that seemed to have become brighter and brighter over the past weeks, and stepped out of my own body.

When I opened my eyes again, it was to a different world—one that shone back in strange, colorblind shades. I glanced back, through my own shaggy, translucent form, and saw my own body crouching there at the edge of the bushes, flashlight in hand.

My paws made no sound on the snow, no movement among the leaves as I paced forward on four paws. The injured dog cracked open amber eyes, nostrils flaring as it strained to smell me. I bent my head, though I couldn't catch scents in this incorporeal form. What I could do was see, and far more than my human eyes allowed.

Dogs see magic better than humans, which I suspected was a good part of the reason they'd been chosen as the animal form for the spell. What I'd failed to detect as a human now lay before me, plain and sickening.

Magical residue clung to the burns on the hound's side—a deep, curdled yellow I associated with the way these eyes saw blood.

Which meant this was not the ordinary magical residue I was used to—the gummy remains of spells that stuck like bandage adhesive, but did no further damage. This was the residue of blood magic.

That was when it clicked—the reason this dog looked so familiar. It looked like me. Like my hound form.

The Rogue Sorcerers must have seen it and thought it was me, showered it with spells before realizing it was nothing but a normal dog.

If my spirit form had had a voice, I would have growled. Instead, I ducked forward, teeth snapping at those charged remains. They crackled in my jaws, snapping and sizzling, struggling against the pure magical energy of this form. The destruction was faster than usual, my form brighter with all the extra magic pouring from me now that Gwydian no longer drained my energy.

The Guild recruiter hadn't been lying. There were bounty hunters after me, and judging by the poor animal beneath me, they didn't seem to care much whether they brought me back half dead.

The last blood magic residue fizzled away in my jaws. Saving the dog now would be in Sanadzi and Krista's hands. I glanced back, past my own inert, crouching form. Where was Krista with the towel?

But it wasn't Krista who stood on the other side of the chain-link fence, hunting knives in hand, jacket zipped against the frigid breeze.

It was Morgan.

CHAPTER TWENTY

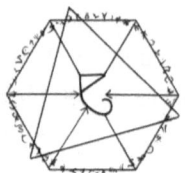

The sight of him struck me so off guard that for a moment I couldn't do anything but look at him. He was the same as ever —long blond hair and rigid features, holsters and sheaths strapped tight beneath his jacket—a modern day viking. I looked for signs of the torture Gwydian had made me listen to, but if there had been any, it was where I couldn't see.

Shock overcame my better senses. I stepped forward on silent paws, drawing up next to my unmoving human body before remembering my cousin couldn't see this form. Morgan had no magic beyond what the tattoos gave him.

...which was why the sight of a spell crackling around his knife halted me in my tracks. It was just a glimmer, just a slight, unusual sheen along the blade, and I almost missed it. He shifted his grip, gaze riveted on the human body I'd left behind.

I watched him watch me, gray eyes taking in the stillness of my human form, so vulnerable and still in that abandoned lot.

This wasn't Morgan. The understanding slipped in without mercy. He stood there on the other side of that chain-link fence, a realized example of what I'd been hoping for the last seven weeks. Except everything was wrong. Morgan hadn't come of his own volition, but because Gwydian had commanded it. Which meant he had a new tattoo on him somewhere, a newly minted leash back to our old master.

Gwydian must have known I wouldn't fight hard enough to hurt Morgan.

He would bring me in, and then Gwydian would have me. Would find out I didn't have the book. Then my old master would have nothing to lose. I backed up toward my body, ready to dive back into it.

Morgan hauled himself onto the chain-link fence, quiet for a man of over six feet. A muffled thump sounded from the other side of the SUV, and I remembered Krista.

Panic felt different in spirit form. I had no aorta to throb behind the dip in my throat, no ability to sweat, no breaths to come up short. Instead, it came in a frazzled rush of energy, my spirit form crackling like a thunderhead. I dashed forward, bypassing Morgan and bounding straight through the fence. I skirted the SUV's front and pulled up short.

A man had Krista pinned against the back door, one arm across her throat, the other pointing a knife at her eye. Her hands shook on her keys, but her face was all fury.

The man was saying something to her, but I couldn't hear. My body was too far from my spirit form, and only sight carried in spirit form. Everything else came distorted and strange, mixed with what I was smelling and hearing and feeling in my physical body. I recognized the man, though, and the acid green magic that coiled around his fingers and down the length of that blade: it was the man from the ice. The rogue Sorcerer. Which meant that, unlike Morgan, he could see me.

I lunged at the knife, and though my teeth passed through the metal, they latched onto the sparkling glyphs. The rogue jerked back with a curse. Definitely not Guild—none of them would have flinched at the sight of a spirit hound. I felt magic sizzle and fight against my own and clamped harder.

The rogue swung the knife away from Krista's face, trying to hold it from the reach of spell-rending jaws. Krista shoved off the van, sending him staggering back from her. In one swift move, she brought up her keys and loosed a cloud of reddish spray into the rogue's face.

He screamed and dropped the knife, hands going to his eyes. Krista's boot connected between his legs, and the second scream reached even my inert physical body.

I wanted to cheer. Instead, I dashed straight through the SUV and across the chain-link divide. Morgan had whipped around at the sound of the screams, but that wouldn't last long. I bounded past him, unseen, and slammed into my human body. Senses exploded into cold and color. I didn't think; I pivoted and sprang, slamming the weighted flashlight head across the side of Morgan's temple.

I didn't expect one hit to drop Morgan. He crashed to his knees, the knife flipping into the snow, and groped at the injury. Dropping the knife surprised me—how many times had Morgan drilled me on holding my weapon? Then again, there had to be a part of him fighting the compulsion to take me.

My heart thundered. Common sense was taking over. I had to incapacitate him. I wouldn't kill him, even if he had a knife to my throat, and that made him dangerous. Gwydian had known that. As Morgan lowered his hand from his temple, gray eyes unfocused, I brought the flashlight down on the back of his head with an audible thunk. He grunted, slumped, and toppled into the snow.

I snatched the knife, ripping down the collar of his shirt to find the tattoo. Maybe—just maybe—I could overtake it the way the Sorcerer had overtaken mine. Then I could cut it and Morgan would be-

"HELENA!" Krista's scream shattered the frigid air.

I jerked upright just in time to see the black form barreling toward me. I staggered back. A dog the size of a small bull slammed

into the chain-link fence and sent it crashing from its metal supports. It missed me, but fell over Morgan like a metallic net.

It shook its bulging head, scraps of pelt flicking the blackened and exposed muscles on its jaw. It didn't matter that the beast was a twisted, bulging version of what it had once been. The snarling jaw had a familiar square shape.

My pulse throbbed behind my ears. I gripped the knife in one hand, the flashlight in the other, and stared down the Hellhound that had once been my godfather.

It growled, circling, waiting for me to make a move. I bent my knees, muscles coiled and ready to run. This thing wouldn't be on its own—Gwydian would have given it a handler. Probably another sanguimancer, like him.

"Krista, go!" I called, praying she would listen. I wasn't so lucky.

A loud honk sent me leaping back, and the Hellhound took that as an opportunity to leap.

I ducked, rolled over Morgan's prone and fence-covered form, and came up running. I heard the Hellhound hit the snow and skid. It would be right behind me; there was no time to get in the SUV. I could sense magic overloading the street like static buildup. Whatever happened here, I couldn't let her get caught up in it. "GO!" I shouted again, waving her on.

This time, I didn't give her a choice. I slammed into the SUV and used my rebound to change directions, sprinting off down the street. Headlights came on, and the SUV zoomed up alongside me. Krista screamed something unintelligible from the seat.

I ducked down the first side-road I found and a guttural howl followed me. Fear rippled up my back, quickened my legs. I turned again, forcing myself to have more care on the ice. The cold stabbed into my lungs, and soon I was breathing in ragged gasps, dropping the flashlight as I launched myself onto the top of a dumpster and vaulted the dividing fence.

It didn't keep the Hellhound long. I made it to the end of the alley before Eamon slammed into the barrier. Wood splintered at the force of his impact, then buckled. I swung down the road and found myself at a dead-end between buildings.

I cursed, stopping for just an instant to get my bearings. There had to be something to climb on. Some way to get out of this.

The Hellhound bounded from the alleyway, skidded on the snow as it stopped. Pinkened drool slid from between finger-length teeth, sliding in steaming ropes as it puffed out breath.

I had three directions to choose from. Left, right, or straight back?

I feinted left, then whirled around and made a dash for the rear building, where a blackened alley might give me a way out. My boot slid on the snow as I pivoted, sending me to my hands and knees. It was only a second before I was up and moving again, but it was all the time Eamon needed.

Bear-like paws slammed into my back, sending me down onto snow-covered asphalt. I hit hard, felt the scrape of knee and elbow and cheekbone. I twisted violently, bringing the knife back, hoping to hit at anything. Then the jaws closed on my shoulder, and bit.

I screamed. Teeth impaled my muscles, scratched into bone. Then the Hellhound lifted me, and I knew what would come next. He would shake me. Set claws into my flesh and tear my shoulder from my socket, rip it off like a chicken leg.

Instead, the Hellhound froze. I felt its breath against my neck, huffing hot and thick. Even the misting clouds of breath were tinged bloody pink. It was all I could smell, all I could feel sluicing down my side.

Then I remembered that Gwydian wanted me alive. Whoever had this Hellhound's magical leash would not let it kill me. Which meant I could fight back.

I heard my cry as I moved a knee, more of my weight supported by the demon-hound's jaw until I got both knees under me. The movement took everything from me. I stilled in the darkened cul-de-sac, shivering and kneeling in my own blood. The liquid steamed and melted snow around my knees. My fingers tightened around the knife, which was slick with my own blood. With a wrenching cry, I twisted my arm back, passed the knife to my right hand.

I swung the knife over my head, stabbing down behind me, and felt it hit. I felt it split muscle, dig into bone. Spinal cord? Skull? I didn't know. I stabbed again. The beast howled around my shoulder, backing up, dragging me off my knees.

Finally, it dropped me.

I shouted as its teeth ripped from my shoulder. Blood spattered the ground, but I didn't care. I was single-minded.

Eamon was gone. This thing that Gwydian had made was no longer my godfather. He'd helped raise me, taken me under his protection after Gwydian killed my father. He'd never want to live this way. I owed it to him to see that he didn't.

I rushed the Hellhound that had once been Eamon, ducking to the side just as it lunged. I threw myself on its back and held on. Headlights spilled across the cul-de-sac just as I slammed the knife sideways into its throat. Eamon jerked, tried to shake me off, but I held on. I brought my arm out and back, again and again. Each stab flung fresh blood, the thick resistance of meat growing thicker as the blade went dull and greasy.

Eamon dropped to the ground, rolling over me, trying to crush me under him. Tears streamed hot from my eyes, but I ignored them, stabbing again. Again. Again.

The knife was glowing now, purple spell bright as the headlights now slashing through the snow. Even without looking, I knew they were too low to be from an SUV. Part of me registered relief that it wasn't Krista. The rest of me was too busy acknowledging how fucked I was.

I drove the knife hard, twisted. The Hellhound spasmed. At last it slumped. Dead.

I had a hard time catching my breath then. Between the agony of my shoulder and the tears streaking into my mouth, I couldn't get a good inhale. And then there was the fact that I'd just killed my godfather, and his blood was everywhere. All over me. Soaking into my jeans and boots.

A car door slammed, then another. Through the sound of my own gasps, two sets of footsteps crunched in the snow. Above, the sky had deepened to starry black, but through the haze of my own breath lit up by headlights, I couldn't make out any constellations.

"Shit," a man said. His accent was strange, almost Australian sounding. "He said she wouldn't kill it."

"He also said it wouldn't kill her," said another voice, this one female and low-pitched. "But it looks like he was wrong about that too."

"Shit," the man repeated. Then he emerged over Eamon's corpse, a man with graying black hair and a cruel twist to his thin lips. An iron spiral dangled from a chain around his neck, but otherwise he wore none of the metal accoutrements of magic. He looked too big to be a Sorcerer, even one that used other people's blood to power his spells. Still, he leaned over me with a scowl and scribed a complicated mandala in the air over my shoulder.

I tried to move, pulling at my leg, but it was trapped beneath the dead Hellhound.

The woman leaned into view, her dark skin limned by reflected moonlight. She had beautiful features, full and carved as if from ebony. Her teeth were white and straight as she smiled down at me. Silver rings in her eyebrows stood out like stars against her skin, and both of her ears had bars through the cartilage. If the piercings had stopped there, I wouldn't have thought it unusual. But her tight-fitted jacket was unzipped to the waist, revealing two rows of safety pins spearing her chest above her tank top's collar. Tiny metal discs dangled from each pin.

She knelt beside me as the man finished scribing his mandala. I hadn't noticed him press a cloth to my wound—probably because I hardly felt it anymore—but he lifted it above the spell and squeezed. Blood dribbled onto the mandala and sizzled like water in a pan. It flared to life, first turquoise, then fading to a darker blue.

After that, he used Eamon's blood, feeding more power to the spell as it stopped my bleeding.

"Not too much," the woman said, staving off his next pass with the rag. She seemed unperturbed by the blood that streaked across her hand. "We don't want her struggling too hard. Trust me," she said, addressing me. "You'll prefer this boring."

She wrenched the knife from the Hellhound's neck and used it to slice open the front of my shirt. I tried to lift my arm, to push her away, but it was like being in a nightmare where I couldn't move. Only this was real.

She straddled my waist, one knee on either side, and I glared up at her, twisting to dislodge her. Then the man grabbed my shoulders, digging into the still-raw wound. I screamed, and he held me down.

"Your master taught me this," she purred, flipping the knife in her grip and setting the tip of it against my chest, just below the hollow of my throat. "He said it would help keep you house broken." I felt my heart hammering against it, as if trying to push the knife away. "I don't know, though—I think there are better things to make a bitch do."

The knife point dug in, then dragged an arc of fire across my chest. I bit down on the scream, my thighs twitching beneath the Hellhound as I struggled to move, to make her stop, or at least to mess up her work.

I bucked, but she was too high for my hips to reach. She carved, making the first few arcs of a mandala I knew all too well. I gasped, reaching for the turquoise fire behind my heart. But it was dim—I'd lost so much blood that the magic had no means of conduction. Fresh tears streaked down my temples, into my ears.

I couldn't go back to Gwydian. I couldn't go back to being a slave. This couldn't be the end of my freedom—no. No. No no no.

A crack split the night. Something warm and viscous splattered across my face, and the arms of the woman over me. A second later, the rogue holding my shoulders dropped sideways and crashed into the snow. The woman was on her feet, priming one of the mandala disks at her chest. Another crack and she dove sideways, rolling over her shoulder and coming up with a glowing red mandala poised like a shield. It crackled, and she brought her arms down in a cross.

The spell launched up behind me. I heard the sound of an impact, then the hiss of metal. I tilted over, twisting myself onto my good shoulder just as two quick, successive cracks sounded out. One headlight went out, and I twisted around to see the rogue dive into the driver's seat, her beautiful face twisted in rage. She touched her chest, calling forward a bevy of mandalas, and reached for something in the glove box. A second later, she smashed vials of blood across the spells, which sparked to life under her hands.

I twisted, looking back to where a single Sorcerer stood, his red hair bright in the glare of the headlights. A gun glimmered at the end of his reach, two separate mandalas hovering above him and to the side. I recognized the design of a protective shield.

He fired again, knocking out the second headlight. Again, the tire. A flare of sapphire behind me sent me turning back to see that the spell he'd fired at the tire was melting the rubber. One of the woman's mandala's flared, and the windshield shattered out, spraying glass so far I had to shrimp curl behind Eamon's corpse to avoid being hit.

And then there was fire. Fire that jetted out like a geyser, spraying across the building behind me. The redheaded Sorcerer darted forward, liquid flame sliding off his shield into the snow. Steam enveloped the entire cul-de-sac, cutting off my view of the fight. Tires squealed, but I couldn't see which direction the car was moving. I struggled against the weight of Eamon on my legs, convinced she was about to cast aside Gwydian's orders and run me down.

Then a mandala slammed down onto the asphalt beside me, and the bright sapphire of the Guild recruiter's magic leapt up around me. He knelt by me, shoving a crowbar under Eamon's corpse. He was so spindly I doubted he could lift that much weight, but leverage is a thing of beauty. He raised the body enough for me to wiggle out.

I slumped back against the inside of the shield, pain searing through every cell. Tires squealed again, farther off, and as the steam cleared, taillights flickered around the corner.

"Bitch knew she was outclassed," the Guild Sorcerer said. I closed my eyes, every limb throbbing and shaking. I wanted to curl up and disappear, hide until the world was safe again. "Hey, Martin. You can go into shock later. Take one of these." Something cool and curved pressed against the side of my face.

I opened my eyes to find a green bottle of Ferrous Sulphate supplements. I glanced up at him, feeling my expression twist in confusion.

"Iron pills," he said. "You don't know fuck-all, do you?"

I ignored the jab and opened the bottle with slippery fingers, tipping a pill into my hand.

"Two this time—you'll need it."

I grimaced at the metallic taste, but swallowed. Behind us, one warehouse was still on fire, belching gouts of black smoke into the air. Any minute now, there would be sirens. Given the bodies of the rogue Sorcerer and Hellhound growing cold in the street, I didn't want to be here when the authorities arrived.

The Guild Sorcerer met my eyes, then his gaze flicked over my injuries and his lips tightened. His pocket let out a squall of sound.

"What the hell is it now?" he said, pulling out his cell phone, which was lighting up with message after message. "This is probably backup requesting more backup because the sanguimancers have backup."

I shuddered, craving the safety of my hound form. Changing would take everything I had left, so unless the iron pills worked fast, I doubted I'd be able to get home after. Then again, I'd rather get caught as a dog than a mauled human girl. There would be fewer questions.

I closed my eyes again, relieved to find the turquoise flames I reached for brighter than they'd been when trying to fight off the sanguimancers. Either the healing had worked, or the iron pills. I didn't care which.

My good shoulder burned with the magic that infused my tattoo. I tipped into the change. It ached, my broken and bruised bones grating as my body rearranged itself, twisting my knees backward, elongating my jaw. When the shift was done, pain pulsed out across my back and ribs, making it hard to struggle out of my clothes. I was tired—perhaps not as tired as usual after changing, but tired enough that I wanted to curl up and sleep.

The shield dropped. I craned my canine head back to see the Guild Sorcerer staring into the distance, cell phone against his ear.

"Well, step on it," he said. *"Their* backup's already here."

I swung my head in the direction he was looking. The crippled car had turned the corner, mandalas blossoming out every side like a festival float. There had to be at least four sanguimancers, including the pissed off face of the woman.

He glanced down at me. "Alive. Barely. Damn thing nearly tore her arm off. She's just gonna get in my way at this point. Yeah? Then tell *her* to send an actual fucking healer to—you know what? Bugger off. I've got a fight to win."

He shoved his phone back into his pocket. "Find the girl, Isaac. Fight the sanguimancers, Isaac. Do everyone's fucking job, Isaac. I ain't paid enough for this shit." His fingers flew to the rings at his hands, priming the etched shields. "Hoof it, Martin. Paw it, whatever. I don't have time to keep you alive. And reconsider joining us. Fuck-face Number One ain't nice enough to leave your friends out of this."

A low rumble vibrated in my chest and Isaac nodded toward downtown.

The first of the sanguimancer's spells flared, shattering the asphalt a few feet away. I snapped up my ragged jeans and shirt and limped toward the alley. The cul-de-sac erupted into light and sound, and I felt the heat of the flames at my back as I limped toward the dog rescue.

What the hell was I going to tell my friends?

CHAPTER TWENTY-ONE

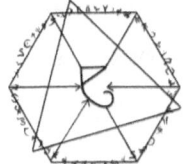

I staggered back onto Erickson Street without a plan. The iron pills had done their work on my magic if not my body; the flame in my chest was bright, gossamer tendrils unfurling through my arteries, but my legs trembled and threatened to give out with each step. Every time I stumbled, I tipped onto my injured shoulder and spent several long moments suspended in pain, unable to move or even breathe before struggling back to three paws.

Pinkish ice matted my fur. The sanguimancers had stopped the bleeding on my shoulder, but the carving on my chest still seeped into my fur, pulling apart a little with each limping step. For a long time, all I smelled was blood and smoke, and all I heard were my own ragged huffs, the sound of paws in snow, and the distant wail of sirens.

Now, I smelled home. I smelled the dogs, and Krista, and Jaesung. I smelled fear and sanitizer and dog food. It felt like a kick in the chest, stopping my heart for a moment.

Krista's SUV was parked out front, and though the lights were on upstairs, someone had drawn the curtains. I couldn't imagine what Krista was thinking, or what she'd told Jaesung, and part of me wanted to hunker down in the doorway and let them find me as a dog. They'd take care of me, and there would be no need to explain. Isaac could still find me, so I wouldn't even be putting them in danger.

Maybe the Guild would adopt me, and I could just give up.

No. I rejected that idea as soon as it surfaced. I wouldn't give up. This power play between the Guild and Gwydian had taken everything from me: my father, my mother, my godfather, and now Morgan and the rest of my pack. I whined at my paws, ducking my head in frustration as even my simplified canine emotions fought for release.

I'd destroyed the book, but it didn't matter. Gwydian had taught at least the enslavement spell to another sanguimancer and as long as they lived, they could make more unwilling soldiers. They could force my cousin to come after me again and again, and I wouldn't always be lucky enough to escape him.

Another soft whine escaped my jaws as I limped into the shelter of the doorway alcove, tail tucked low. I dropped the clothes onto the doorstep, licking the blood from my muzzle and hating that, as a dog, the taste wasn't repulsive.

I couldn't let them find me like this. They deserved to know at least some of the truth, and that meant I couldn't let them tend my injuries as a hound only to find those same injuries on my human body. I had to shift back.

The replenished magic made it faster. I was so numb that it didn't hurt like before, though it was still torture on my ravaged shoulder. One-handed, I pulled on my jeans, but my shirt was harder. Half of it was stiff with frozen blood. Pulling it on was an exercise in agony.

I wouldn't have gone to so much trouble for anyone in my pack—they'd seen me naked often enough after transformations, and I them. But the only thing I could imagine terrifying my friends more than my finding me so bloody I couldn't walk was finding me *naked* and so bloody I couldn't walk.

My keys were still in Krista's car, but I grabbed the spare from underneath a dog statue. It took several tries to get the key in the lock. When I opened the door, my legs wobbled.

It had been one thing to walk as a dog, with four legs to share the weight and keep me stable. Well, three. Even three was better than two, and one of those still stinging from being trapped beneath a 200 pound demonic canine.

My knees hit the linoleum, and I fell forward, twisting so I landed on my less-injured side. The impact jarred everything. Something in my shoulder seared, and a warm trickle slid over my arm.

The dogs barked from the other side of the lobby door, and footsteps moved above me. I wanted to get up. To at least greet them standing, so they knew I wasn't dying.

Teeth gritted, I pushed myself up onto my elbow, then twisted over my knees until I was balancing on three limbs. Just like I had been as a dog.

Wind gusted in through the open door behind me, and I lifted numb fingers to flick back the hair that fluttered into my face. The strands were gummy with blood, ends sticking together where they'd snaked through my wounds.

I recognized Poo-stank's throaty bark among the din, and Jaesung's voice hushing them. The deadbolt on the door to the garage turned, and the door flew open.

I winced as light rushed into my face, but made out two familiar silhouettes. Both were tense and armed, Krista with her pepper spray and a kitchen knife, and Jaesung with a lighter and a can I recognized from his computer table. Pressurized air.

The instant he saw me, he dropped both and lurched to the floor next to me. "Oh my God...."

Krista shrieked.

"It's not as...It's okay," I started, but my words sounded wrong, thick and slippery.

Jaesung cut me off. He grabbed my face in both hands and for a crazy second I thought he would kiss me. Instead he stared, gaze mapping my face as if he could read every lie I'd ever told. His thumb found the pulpy bruise on my cheek, then the bloody wreck of my nose and lip.

The door behind me closed. The deadbolt slid home with a comforting finality and Krista knelt beside me. She plucked at the ribbons of shirt over my shoulder, fingers shaking. "That—that *thing* bit you? Oh my God. Oh my God. I'm calling the police. Oh my God."

I shook my head, prompting Jaesung to let go of my face. "N-no police," I said.

He looked up at Krista, and I didn't like his expression—dark, either angry or protective. Both were frightening. "Kris, get the door." He turned back to me. "There's no way to do this without hurting you."

It sounded like both an accusation and an apology. I reached for his shoulder and, just like before, he grabbed my belt-loops and used them to heft me to my feet. I bit the insides of my cheeks, but a whimper squeaked out. It was such a weak sound. I twisted my fingers into Jaesung's shirt, pressing my forehead into the muscle of his shoulder.

My knees trembled and my vision went dark at the edges. A heavy throb pounded in my head. I'd gone vertical too fast, with too little blood. I felt the swoop in my sense of balance and tipped.

"Helena, don't you dare." He caught me over his arm and knelt, propping my weight against his knee. The dizziness didn't recede and my shoulder seemed to have torn open again. He lifted a reddened hand to the light, and I heard the growl in his voice when he spoke again. "For fuck's sake. Krista, move shit out of the way."

The arm I wasn't slumped over slid under my knees. I knew what was coming but there was no way to prepare myself. It would hurt like hell.

I thought he'd struggle, lifting me from the floor, but he straightened up without so much as a grunt, like I weighed no more than Poo-stank. I choked out a gasp, but pressed my lips tight against the pain. The heat of his body burned.

"Where are your shoes?" Krista hissed as we passed through the door.

"Not so important right now," Jae said.

I kept my eyes closed as he carried me up fifteen jolting steps. My cells had memorized the feeling of this place. I knew the pressure in the air, the temperature, the quality and color of light off the bricks. I knew the sound of Jaesung's feet on the hardwood floors. The muted whisper of heat. The hum of appliances. It was home.

My equilibrium swooped again as Jaesung knelt, lowering me to the air mattress Krista and I had made only hours before. Time moved strangely after that. I might have drifted off into sleep or unconsciousness, but through it all I heard them murmuring, felt the warmth of rags wiping my face, the sting of disinfectant in my wounds. A cold sheet whispered over my skin, and I realized my shirt had been cut away.

It was the return of smell that caused my eyes to flutter open. Something savory was twining through the air, alerting me to the desperate growling of my stomach. I twisted my head, blinking, and found Krista and Jaesung in the kitchen. Krista leaned on the bar, fingers clenched in her bright orange hair. Jaesung had pressed his back to the counter, arms crossed as he glared at the floor. Beside him, the microwave whirred.

I grunted and tried to sit up, good arm flailing out to push against the air mattress. I was no longer sticky with blood, but being clean almost made my wounds worse. Air hissed through my teeth, but I forced myself up on the mattress, clutching the sheet against my chest with my bad arm. I couldn't just sit here. I had something I had to do. What was it?

I couldn't remember, but there was an overwhelming sense of urgency nipping at my back. Something about Mom, and the book, and keeping my friends safe....

"No, no, no," Krista said, and I heard the heavy tread of her boots across the floor. A moment later, she was at my side. I braced for her to push me down again, but her hand found my naked back, supporting me. I blinked, noting the colorful electric blanket we'd picked out that day had been spread over me. "Jesus, Hel. Here, let me grab a shirt."

A moment later, she was rummaging through the stack of clothing. She extracted my mother's purple plaid shirt—the only button up I owned—and shook it out. Mom would have killed me if I'd come home this beaten up. She'd have nursed me back to health and then kicked my ass to Tallahassee and back.

Jaesung made himself busy in the kitchen, back turned, as Krista eased the sleeve over my bad arm. I made a token effort at buttoning the shirt, but my fingers were too stiff and swollen.

I watched her fingers fasten it, the flexing colors of the tattoos at her wrists, and the scrapes that could only have come from her fight with the Sorcerer.

It hit me then that she could have died. She could have been taken hostage. Tortured. Turned into a slave or a spellhound or worse. And she had no idea how much danger she'd been in, just by being with me.

My fingers found hers and stopped her from fixing the button just below the start of the mandala carved into my chest. Her hands were warm, or maybe mine were just frigid. Both of us were shaking.

"I'm sorry," I said. "I'm so, so sorry. I shouldn't have—I should have just l-left before...." Words were coming out too fast, tripping over the guilt clotting in my throat. "They could have hurt you, and I wouldn't have been able to stop them. It would have been my fault and I couldn't have even helped. This is why I can't stay—I have to go. I have to—" I pushed her hands from me and leaned forward, trying to get my feet under me.

"What? No, you're not going anywhere." Krista caught my arms before I could stand. "Not until you tell us what the hell is going on."

I met her eyes, already shaking my head despite my earlier decision to tell them at least part of the story.

"Hel." I looked up, finding Jaesung standing at the edge of the rug, holding a mug in one hand. The other made a fist. I swallowed.

He set the mug aside and came to stand behind Krista. I thought he would crouch, get on my level, but he seemed too fired up to confine himself to that calm a stance.

"We haven't asked you because, until today, we didn't think it was any of our business. But if you've... if you're in some kind of trouble, and you're dragging it into our lives, we have a right to know what it is."

It was almost exactly what I'd been thinking earlier, before I saw them face to face and realized that, whatever I said, it would be too much for them. I'd wanted so badly to leave them, and the reason hadn't occurred to me until this moment: I had to be the one to go, because I couldn't handle the thought of them turning me out.

Now, though, I could feel the finality in Jaesung's voice. If I didn't tell them some version of the truth, they would stop trusting me. They would call the police, the real police, and I'd be shipped back to Miami, and the DEA, and Gwydian.

I had to tell them something.

Air wheezed over my vocal cords, making a soft, creaky facsimile of my voice. "I was in a gang. My family was.... W-we didn't have a choice. I was three when we got grabbed and forced into it because of my dad's boat. They-" I choked, but forced myself to keep going now that I'd started. "They made us do things. Smuggle things. People. Drugs. Whatever you can think of. They killed Dad when I was thirteen. We've been trying to get out forever, and we figured out how right before I came here. We had help from...."

How to describe the Sorcerer's Guild.

"From the authorities. But Mom—"

I heard Jaesung inhale. He knew this part of the story. Krista drew back.

"She got caught in the crossfire. She died. About three days before I met you."

Krista's hand went to her mouth, and I sensed the horror washing over her. I saw the moment she realized that the man who'd shoved her against the SUV tonight was a gang member. I was glad she didn't know how much worse he was.

"I've been planning to leave," I said. "I was going to. Soon."

Krista lowered her hand, her voice a whisper. "Where would you go?"

"Canada."

Jaesung snorted. "With a passport that says Lola Martin?"

I shook my head. "No, that's—that's my Mom." His brows drew together, and I saw him glance at my pile of stuff. He must have gone through my things for answers. I swallowed, realizing I wasn't even angry. "Look, I didn't expect... I never thought it would take this long for my cousin to get here, but they—"

"They got him too." Jaesung stretched out a hand, proffering a shiny plastic rectangle. Dread rippled down my back at the sight of my phone. I looked up, helpless. His jaw twitched. "We tried to call you and heard it ringing downstairs."

Had he seen the picture? What messages had Gwydian left me since? I shook my head, then looked back down at my knees. "Throw it away."

He kept his hand extended. I tried to ignore it, but it stayed there, a reminder of Gwydian's power over me. Over my family. Dark rings of rust-colored blood still lingered around my nails, and I remembered the feel of that knife jamming into Eamon's neck. Eamon, whose picture was on that phone—the last I'd seen of him when he was still himself.

I grabbed the cell and hurled it at the brick wall. The motion tore at the scabbing cuts on my chest, but I didn't care. It shattered, plastic casing exploding in all directions. Then I was down, fists clenched over the back of my neck, fighting against the desire to scream or cry or just get up and run.

Krista pried my fists from my hair and pulled them down.

"You need to call the police," she said, voice quavering. "Tell them-"

"They already know!"

In a way it was true. The Sorcerers' Guild fancied themselves the magical equivalent of the police.

I heard her swallow. "Are you in witness protection?"

"Not officially. The police want me to work with them, but I can't." I sat up, meeting Krista's eyes. "I wanted to go; I was trying to leave this morning, but you...." I looked at the mattress. "I've never had a—I didn't want to let you guys in. I didn't want this place to feel like home."

Krista's chin wobbled, and I saw her eyes go shiny, calling up a similar burn in my own eyes.

"I can't work with the police," I whispered. "I can't. It's—one of them shot her. I can't—"

Jaesung bent his knees, but instead of crouching next to Krista, he sank onto the air mattress at my side, a hand finding my knee. He put his head in his other hand, fingers weaving into the longer hair on his scalp. He grimaced.

"I don't know what to do. This isn't...." He sighed, looking at the ceiling. "Mom and I ran from my dad all the way to the U.S. My aunt gave us a place to stay or we'd have been shit out of luck."

"I can find somewhere else to go," I said, wondering how I could keep Gwydian from hurting them if I did. "I'm not a stray dog."

"It would be a hell of a lot easier if you were," Krista muttered. "No. Hel, we're not kicking you out, but—and I understand why you don't want to talk to the police—but this is a lot. Too much."

"No one wants to be forced into being a criminal informant," Jaesung said.

"A C.I.?" I said. "I'm *not* a criminal! Not by choice-"

"Could they put you in jail?"

I lifted both hands and let them drop, wincing at the pain. "Maybe. If they didn't believe I was forced. They'd probably let me go if I spilled everything, but I'd be watched for the rest of my life. They'd probably drag me in whenever there was even the slightest whisper of a problem."

Krista and Jaesung were silent. Dizziness was taking over again, which only made it easier to feel the pressure of their fear, their expectations. The normalcy of their lives and how abnormal even this half-truth was to them.

"I'll talk to them," I said. "Not tonight, but I will. I'm not letting you guys get dragged into this."

I wasn't sure how I'd do it, but if the Guild was going to pin me here, I had to prepare. If his bounty hunters kept failing, Gwydian would come himself. I would have to face him. Whether I wanted it or not, Krista and Jaesung would be in danger, and I had to protect them.

Jaesung reached for the mug and handed it to me along with half a large white pill.

"Half an Oxycodone," he said. "Since we're already breaking about four laws."

I took it gratefully and found the will to drink about half the broth before I had to lie back down. Krista cleaned up the medical supplies and deposited them downstairs, but Jae stayed there on the air mattress, as if guarding me. Whether it was from protectiveness or suspicion, I didn't know. My heart wanted to believe Krista's assertion that they wouldn't kick me out, but my brain told me it would have been better for everyone involved.

Krista climbed the stairs without another word, and I heard the soft sounds from upstairs as she climbed into bed. I thought of Alina, and how she would have felt if my actions had gotten Krista killed.

She would have hated me, probably as much as I hated the Guild.

Next to me, Jaesung was still, dark eyes focused on the Target bags with all the stuff I'd bought. I sucked in my sore lip and waited for him to speak.

"Tell me something," he said, finally. "Anything, as long as it's true."

I sniffed, the steam from the mug loosening everything in my sinuses. Guilt rippled over me. He'd told me everything—the whole wretched part of his past—and I'd given him only surface truth. Even now, I hadn't been completely honest, and he was sensitive enough to know.

I swallowed. I could never give him the truth he wanted, no matter how much my heart screamed at me to be honest; I could show him the truth—force him to believe it.

But that would change his world. He didn't deserve that.

"I don't know what normal feels like," I said. It was as good a truth as any. "I don't know how to walk into a room without looking for the exits. I can field strip a nine millimeter, but I couldn't tell you a single movie that came out in the last five years. I've been too busy looking over my shoulder to enjoy two of the tamest months of my life, and I—I'm scared my life will never be anything but..." I gestured to my bruised face and shoulder. "...this. Violence. Fear. All the shit I was trying to get away from."

Jaesung sighed, bracing his forearms over his thighs.

"Do you believe that?" I couldn't tell him how much I needed him to.

Slowly, reluctantly, he nodded. "Yeah. Yeah, I mean, it's obvious you have PTSD. I could have told you that after three hours." He sighed again, finally turning to look at me. Anger still lingered around the edges of his gaze, but there was a larger sense of determination there. Seeing him looking at me like that—serious, sincere, a little unsure—sent a knot into my throat.

"This wasn't your fault," he said. "You were a kid; you didn't get a choice. I know—it's not the same as my family, but I know how hard it is to get out of a bad situation. How scared you are afterwards, how weird and fragile everything around you starts to feel. It's isolating. When I got here, I didn't even speak English. But I at least had my mom. I..." he grimaced. "This isn't coming out how I wanted it to."

I didn't care. I'd stopped listening after the first sentence. My eyes were burning and my body shook hard enough to rattle my teeth. Jaesung glanced over just as I lifted a hand to cover the welling tears.

I couldn't quite believe that it wasn't my fault, but just hearing it, just having someone believe in me? I hadn't known how much I'd needed it.

He scooted closer, and as the mattress tipped me against his side, he put his arm around my back. I was going numb with the Oxycodone, and there was only a dull ache in my shoulder as I twisted into his chest. His heart throbbed against my cheek, and all I wanted was the lie of safety in his arms.

"Stay," I croaked. His shirt trapped the heat of that word against my face. I didn't care how pitiful I sounded; I had no pride left to lose. "Please."

He leaned his head on top of mine, but he took an agonizing few moments to nod and whisper, "okay."

He stood, flipped the light switch and stepped out of his tennis shoes. I made myself slide over on the air mattress and curl onto my unhurt side. He climbed in next to me. He didn't press up close like he had before. Maybe it was uncertainty, maybe it was my injuries, or both.

My stomach twisted, and I held my breath against the desire to cry again. I'd been so afraid I would lose them over this—certain they would run at the first hint of my real past. But they hadn't. And that meant I had more to lose than ever. More I could protect by walking into the arms of my mother's murderers.

My future looked grim, no matter how I looked at it.

"What do you want to do?" I asked. "With your life, I mean."

He was quiet a moment, but then his voice vibrated along the mattress. "Like, as a job?"

"Sure. Or in general. Anything."

He seemed to know what I was thinking, or if nothing else, what I needed to hear. A hand found its way onto my arm, careful to stay below the injury. "For a long time, I wanted to... do my martial art."

I let out a humorless huff. Even now, he was so persistent.

"But I don't know. I love working at the rescue, and it made me think: I want to help people too. I think—and don't freak out—but I've been thinking of going through basic law enforcement training after graduation. I mean, I could go into law next, but..." I felt him shrug behind me.

It should have been surprising, but it wasn't. Jaesung had set me on edge from the beginning. Something about him had reminded me of the Guild, and only now that he said it did I realize it was that part of them that was similar to law enforcement. That vigilant tension, the sharp eyes and quickness to act.

With his desire to do good, he would be better than any of them.

"That works for you," I said. "The world needs more good cops."

"You mean cops who are good at their jobs or cops who are good people?"

"Good people, but I guess both."

He shifted, and a minute later, his face pressed against the back of my neck. A wave of relief shuddered down my back. I wheezed out a breath, scooting clumsily back into him as his arm wound around my ribs. "I'm sorry," he murmured. "About your mom. That's—"

"-not the kind of cop you'll be," I said. There was an awkward beat of silence before his hand squeezed my arm. His legs pressed against the backs of mine, the heat of him cradling me as my body grew heavier and heavier.

"What about you?" he murmured. "What are you going to do?"

"Get through tomorrow." My voice sounded distant. I was barely aware of my lips moving. "Then the next day. If I don't die."

The hand on my arm rubbed back and forth. "You're not going to die. Things will settle. It doesn't seem like it when you're in the middle of it, but it will."

"I'm scared of that too."

He nodded against my neck. "I know. Transition sucks. But you have us. We're not giving up on you."

I remembered the mingled pity and fear in Krista's eyes. "Kris is scared of me."

"She'll get over it."

"I don't know if she should. I should never have dragged my mess into your lives."

"It's a little too late for that."

"I could still leave. Before it hurts too much to go."

The hand stopped moving on my arm. "I hope it's too late for that too."

I shivered, goosebumps rising beneath his touch. He lay there behind me for a long moment, just breathing against my skin.

"I don't want to make it any harder," I said.

He tucked his feet up against mine, the warmth of them shocking against the cuts and cold skin. He pressed his face into my neck, and when he spoke, his lips brushed against the fine hair on my nape. "I do."

I had nothing to say to that.

CHAPTER TWENTY-TWO

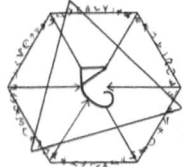

I don't remember waking up, or even when I noticed the fever. My first coherent thought was that I was alone. No Jaesung stretched out behind me, no mother pressed a cool hand on my cheek. I curled in on myself, aching with an unquenchable sense of loss.

Time jerked forward, and this time I wasn't alone. Someone propped me up, pressed a straw to my lips and told me to drink. I smelled coconut, felt the dense curls of Sanadzi's hair against my cheek. I caught my name in snatches of shouted conversation, but it was like hearing screams underwater. I willed darkness to come again.

When clarity returned, I woke to a room flooded with midmorning light. There was a dry, sunburned feeling to my face, but I had enough wherewithal to fumble for the cup beside my bed. Even that was exhausting. After drinking, I eased back down into sheets that stank of sweat and blood.

Everything was stiff and aching, and large, discolored patches of gauze clung to my shoulder and chest. The inflamed skin around the edges told me the bite was infected. It wasn't any wonder; the wound was so deep. The healing and Krista's first-aid hadn't been enough to keep it from going bad.

I thought I recognized Sanadzi's handiwork in the neat edges of gauze. If anyone would know how to deal with infected animal bites, it was a rescue vet. Maybe she wasn't a doctor for humans, but what was good enough for the dogs was good enough for me.

The water hit my stomach with a hollow, cold splash. I grimaced. How long had I been feverish, without food? I spotted a sports drink on the coffee-table and figured that was all I'd put in my stomach since the broth Jaesung had given me.

I stretched again for the cup of water but it slipped through weak fingers and splashed in a rolling arc across the rug. I groaned, draping myself over the side of the mattress to reach for it.

Someone was on the stairs and I recognized Sanadzi's footfalls before she appeared.

"Thank Jesus," she cried. "I thought we'd have to take you to the hospital." Then she was at my side, ignoring the spilled water in favor of pushing me upright again. Several pillows later, I sat up on the air mattress, fingers trembling around a cup of tomato soup as she checked the wound under the discolored gauze.

Today, she wore a long-sleeved, mustard yellow shirt under a puffy brown vest, and wooden earrings shaped like fish-bones. Green eyeshadow sparkled from her upper lids. I was overwhelmed with relief at the sight of her.

"There's someone downstairs for you," she said, peeling up the back edge. I winced and looked down. My shoulder was a mess of green and yellow and red, spots of black showing where the flesh had already been too long without circulation. I shuddered, stomach clenching. "Krista said he's come by every day to talk to you. Some officer from Miami—said he's in charge of your case."

I stiffened. She must have seen the panic in my face because she pressed the gauze back down over the wound. "We can tell him you're still sick. You don't have to talk to him yet." She reached for the electric blanket and drew it higher over my legs, as if that might stop the shivering.

Someone else was on the stairs now, someone heavier than Sanadzi. I clenched my fingers around the cup of soup, prepared to hurl it at Isaac if he'd dared shove his way upstairs. But it wasn't Isaac. It was Jaesung, sweat on his jaw, and breathing hard. He'd pulled the longish part of his hair back into a tiny stub of a ponytail, exposing wide, bright eyes.

"Jesus Christ," he breathed when he saw me. He didn't rush over, instead bracing his arms on the back of the couch, head hanging in apparent relief. "Jesus Christ," he repeated.

"I texted him," Sanadzi said. "Kris is out getting lunch, but-"

"You were out for three fucking days," Jaesung said. "Your shoulder was infected, you had a fever of one-oh-three, and there's some DEA guy downstairs who says he needs to talk to you and—Jesus Christ, Hel. You're going to kill me."

He looked up then, and I noticed something strange about his face. Of everything I could have said to him then, the four words I croaked out had zero relevance.

"Where are your glasses?"

He blinked at me. Then he looked at Sanadzi, as if hoping she would tell him I wasn't serious. When she didn't, he shook his head. "Contacts. I can't wear glasses in Martial Arts."

That's where he'd been. Why he was sweating. Probably why he'd run home. And that was not a response I deserved. But it made my chest hurt in a way that didn't involve cuts and cracked ribs.

Sanadzi stood, wiping her knee where she'd knelt in the spilled water. "I'm telling ginger to take a hike," she said.

"No."

Maybe it was the fever that made me say it, or the conflict on Jaesung's face, but I didn't want to leave this to question any longer. Somewhere in my delirium, I'd realized what I would have to do. Not for the family I'd lost, but for the family I wanted to keep.

"I'll talk to him," I said, aware that Jaesung was still watching me from the couch, but unable to look at him. "Just... give me a minute and I'll talk."

Sanadzi folded in her lips, giving me a skeptical look. "You've still got a fever, baby."

"Yeah," I said. "Better take advantage of it before I get back in my right mind."

She looked at Jaesung, who lifted one hand from the couch to divest himself of responsibility. "Okay," she said. "I'll give you a few minutes to finish your soup."

I knew that wasn't what she was giving me a few minutes for, but I didn't argue. I watched the flexing of Jaesung's throat as he swallowed.

After she left, it took him a long moment to cross the space between us. I tried to think of something to say, but my mind dragged. My heart rammed into my sternum.

One wide palm covered my forehead, frigid from the air outside. It moved to my cheek, then behind my neck. "You're still warm," he said. He lifted his other hand and laced his fingers over my nape.

"You're not," I murmured back. "For once." I sighed, the chill of his fingers against my feverish skin was a shock of relief.

"I woke up," he said. "It was maybe four A.M. and I woke up because I was too hot and you were...." He swallowed, gaze dropping to my stomach. "You wouldn't wake up. It scared the shit out of me. I got Krista, and we took your temperature and called Sanadzi and explained everything. Gene wanted to call the police and an ambulance, but she wouldn't let him. They got into it."

I clenched my eyes shut, guilt shuddering in my chest. "God, I didn't want-"

"Don't worry about it. Your buddy showed up, and that was enough for Gene. Wedding's not off or anything. Actually, they're doing the rehearsal in a few days. Which," He let go with one hand and checked his watch. "I've got to, uh.... I'm doing something for their reception that's kind of a secret and I've left the people helping me waiting, so I should probably get back. Unless," and his fingers moved back to my neck, thumb brushing along the base of my ear. "Do you want me to stay while you talk to him?"

Yes. Yes, I wanted him to stay. I could think of nothing I wanted more than a reminder of why I was giving in to the people who had shot my mother, failed to kill Gwydian as promised, and hunted me for months.

"I'll be okay," I said. He didn't believe me. This close, without glasses to obscure his face, it was easy to see things I hadn't noticed before. The freckle under his left eye, the little scar below his lip. The length of his lashes and the way his nose joined with his brow and made the corners of his eyes look so much deeper than mine. I'd always thought of them as dark, but in the light, they looked more gold than brown.

He shifted forward onto his knees and pulled me into a hug. I breathed against his collarbone, taking in the comforting scent of him as he pressed his mouth to my temple. "Be careful, okay?" I nodded. His fingers tightened on the back of my neck. I didn't quite expect the kiss. It was soft, but warm against my hairline, and over before I could appreciate it. Then he was shifting back, standing up, and rummaging in his pocket.

"Here," he said, holding out his phone. "If anything happens, call Maria. She's the—the owner of the place where I'm doing the thing."

I took the phone. "You could just tell me what your martial art is."

"You'll find out at the reception. Maria. She should be fairly recent in the contacts." The stairs creaked, and he glanced back over his shoulder. "Be careful. I mean it."

He reached the stairs just as Isaac stepped through the door. For a moment, they were face to face. Or, really, face to neck, because Jaesung was obscenely tall and Isaac closer to my height. There was something of a canine standoff in the way they glared at each other.

"May I?" Isaac said, his voice loaded with sarcasm.

Jaesung didn't make the threat someone in my pack might have. He just looked down for several more seconds, taking stock of Isaac's height, his emaciated frame, and made a soft snort. He stepped back to let Isaac through. Jaesung gave me one last look before disap-pearing down the stairs.

Isaac wasted no time kicking an ottoman from in front of the couch and guiding it to my bedside with a foot.

"Soccer?"

"Junior league."

"Must have been nice."

He snorted and dropped onto it. When he put his hand in his pocket, I tensed, ready to roll out of the way. He smirked. "Don't worry, sweetheart. I checked my gun at the door. Brought a present for you."

"A get-well card?"

"Better," he said, extracting a plastic green bottle. "Your very own magical-anaemia prevention program." He tossed them into my lap. "Now that pleasantries are over, let's get to business. What lie did you tell them? I'm not gonna blow your cover, but I have to know what to say."

"I didn't lie," I said. He snorted, his face breaking into a grin that only seemed to get wider when he realized I was serious.

"But you didn't tell them everything."

"Obviously."

He shook his head, still chuckling, as if this were the best joke he'd heard in a while. "How the hell did you swindle them into keeping you around?"

"I thought you said we were getting down to business," I growled. "If not, you can get the hell out."

He held up both hands with an unrepentant grin. "Whatever you want, Martin. I come bearing greetings from the higher-ups. Boss-lady wants you to come in."

Well, I'd asked for blunt. I swallowed, wondering what to say now that the moment had arrived. "I have conditions," I said.

"Oh, sweetheart. You don't make the-"

"Stop calling me that."

"Fine, Martin. But you don't make the conditions."

"Because your track record of forcing me to do what I don't want to is so great?"

He snorted. "We haven't been trying all that hard, kid."

"I want the people that work here kept safe. The Guild won't harm civilians, but Gwydian's hunters have already hurt one of them. Promise that, and I'll give you at least one thing you want."

His eyebrow twitched up. "What's that?"

"My copy of the spells in that book."

"Done."

I pointed at the coffee table. "The sketchbook up there."

He leaned back on the ottoman and snatched it from the table, skimming through the pages with increasingly consternated brows. "The hell," he said, looking at me. "This doesn't have the drawing order."

"You think I'd give you that? Anyway, you agreed pretty fast to protecting this place, which either means you were lying, or they're already under Guild protection and you just suck at your job."

His jaw twitched. "If you knew how many hunters we've turned away—"

"You missed a few!" I snarled. "If Krista hadn't maced that guy in the face, he could have killed her! He could have brought her to Gwydian and gotten her turned into-" I cut myself off, biting back my anger.

Isaac tossed the sketchbook to the floor beside him. "What did you expect? It's not like we have unlimited manpower and resources to devote to your merry little chase. Your parents were reasonable people—how the hell did they pop out such a difficult-"

"Parents?" I interrupted. Despite the fever, a chill slid down my spine. "What would you know about my dad?"

Isaac snorted, a laugh playing around his thin lips again. "For one, I don't remember him being this fucking hard to recruit."

Nothing moved. For several seconds, nothing existed. "My dad wasn't part of the Guild," I breathed. "He was never-"

"Well, no. Your master found out about our last plan to kill him and decided your dad wasn't worth the magic boost. After all, you were there, all young and defenseless."

Tomato soup splashed onto my stomach, warm and red as blood. Mechanically, I set the cup on the bedside table, spilling more as my hand shook with the violent emotions swelling inside me.

"Seriously?" Isaac said. "She never told you? Oh, now that's too good." He leaned back, enjoying that he'd just ripped the rug out from under me. "Yeah, your dad was gonna work with us after. That was part of the deal—big magic family, your dad. Almost all of them gone now, except you. He was a rogue before Gwydian got to him. We'd been trying to bring him in for years."

I was shaking my head, anger and hurt stoking the fire behind my sternum. "You knew it wouldn't work," I said.

"Yeah, well, we thought we'd at least get you out of it. And the book."

"You knew it wouldn't work and you let us throw ourselves into the line of fire?" My voice echoed off the brick, rising in pitch and volume. Magic surged in my veins, lighting up my vision with webbed color. "Of course you did. Because what would be better than sacrificing us to Gwydian, letting us die so you could take out your biggest threat? And on top of that, get the book? I suppose you thought I'd be happy to join you when it was over? Grateful?"

"Listen, it's-"

"I'm done listening!" I surged from the bed, sending Isaac stumbling back off the ottoman. I was in little more than a tank top and underwear, and the air rushed cold around my bare skin. I didn't care. Rage gave me strength. "Where were you when Gwydian's guys snatched Mom and me off the boat? Where were you when he put a gun to my head and forced my dad to traffic human beings? Or when he turned my best friend into a demon?"

I kicked the ottoman at his legs and he leapt out of the way, green eyes wide in shock as I staggered toward him. Frantic footsteps pounded the stairs. "I should have gone to school! I should have had a mom who taught me how to write lab reports, not conceal a gun! I should have crawled in bed with my dad because I had a nightmare, not because some fucking gang member decided he'd try to rape a nine-year-old! My dad would be alive! I'd be on my way to college! I would have had that if you had been doing your fucking job and helped us before he turned us into criminals."

"Get out!" It was Sanadzi, at the top of the stairs. She grabbed Isaac by the back of his jacket and heaved him toward the door. He was either shocked enough or light enough to let her. "You need to leave. Don't come back without a warrant and representative from local law-enforcement."

Krista was breathing hard, her fingers already typing out a message on her phone, even while she stood at Sanadzi's shoulder for backup.

"There's only so many times we ask nice, Martin!" Isaac called.

"That goes for me, too!" Sanadzi said. Her hands were in fists as she and Krista stood in the doorway, blocking him from coming back inside. He must have believed them, because a moment later, I heard him leave.

We all waited until the office door slammed downstairs.

With no target, my anger fizzled. The strength went with it. I heard my own impotent cry, felt the burn of my knees hitting the rug followed by the gentle voices and frantic hands of Krista and Sanadzi as they shepherded me back into bed. I had no tears left for this. The truth was caustic, eating holes into memories I'd long thought safe.

Sanadzi changed my bandages and forced another painkiller on me, and I looked past her to the picture of my parents in the back seat of that car. Dad, with his grin and his hazel eyes, Mom with her cloud of white-blond hair and mischievous grin, like she was getting away with something wicked by having my dad's arm around her. Had she known, when this picture was taken, what he was? Had she thought it dangerous, sexy? Or had he kept it from her the way they'd both kept it from me—until the truth caught up and it was too late to do anything about it?

Maybe I was harder to recruit than they had been, but at least in that way, I was exactly the same. What they'd done to me, I was doing to my friends now.

When Sanadzi and Krista had finished bundling me in heated blankets, I was surprised to find them unwilling to leave. Krista climbed onto the mattress next to me, tears rolling down her cheeks as she stroked my hair, while Sanadzi vanished downstairs to close the rescue for the day.

I swallowed, aware of something cool and plastic against my bare leg. Jaesung's phone. I reached for it and passed it to Krista. "Can you.... He said to text Maria if anything...."

"God," she choked out. "That's why he didn't answer my text." Her fingers flew over the buttons, and I watched her face flinching as more tears slid down it. She sniffed, wiping her eyes on a shoulder before tossing the phone to the blankets. "I'm sorry," she said, her fingers trickling through my hair, brushing it back from my forehead, which had gone damp with sweat. "All that—the things you said. I'm so sorry you had to-"

"It isn't you who should be sorry," I said. She slid an arm around my blanketed shoulders and I let myself tilt into her, head falling to her soft shoulder.

"We won't let anything bad happen," she said. I clenched my teeth against the protest and nodded. A tear dripped off her chin and trickled behind my ear. "We're your family now."

CHAPTER TWENTY-THREE

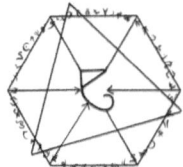

My fingers shook working the zipper up Krista's back. Despite the pain killers, my shoulder was on fire, and I clenched my teeth against the grimace that wanted to follow.

The church's dressing room wasn't meant to hold over ten people, but between Sanadzi, her five bridesmaids, family, wedding-planner, photographer, makeup artist, hair-stylist, and tiny flower girl, there was hardly enough room for me to shift onto a corner countertop and try not to pass out. Looking happy was impossible, and I was ninety percent certain my gloom had ruined at least three people's moods.

Krista exhaled as I pulled the zipper home. "I can't believe we're still doing this," she said. Hands flat over her stomach, she turned toward me and leaned against the counter. "I can't think about it without shaking."

I glanced back at Sanadzi, who sat in a chair with her white dress frothed around her, surrounded by black-smocked women wielding curling irons and makeup sponges. Her face was relaxed under their ministrations.

"It's not like they'd change the date," I murmured back. "Not when they paid for, like, ten people to fly in from Korea."

"I know." Krista's eyes went glassy. "God. It's just I still keep thinking how close it was. You could have-"

"Don't," I said. "Try not to think about it."

Krista reached past me for a tissue box. "At least everyone thinks I'm just wedding-crying."

I nodded but guilt trickled into my gut. If it hadn't been for me, Krista wouldn't have to play happy, and Sanadzi wouldn't be wrinkling her dress with clenched fists.

I scanned the room, with its single exit and its lack of windows, and chewed at the inside of my lip. Sanadzi's three sisters stood in the opposite corner, their bridesmaid's dresses catching the sheen of the lights. They were all tall and beautiful, with the same fawn skin and light hazel eyes, and had exhibited her same propensity to hug everyone they met.

I probed my shoulder beneath the silken orange scarf, almost comforted that the pain remained violent as ever. My dress—a magenta strapless castoff of Sanadzi's—had served only to bring out the purpled bruising, and I hadn't been able to get my swollen arm into any cardigans. The bright orange scarf, though clashing, at least kept the questions at a minimum.

Krista watched my movement and grimaced. "How's the shoulder?"

"I won't be doing any dancing," I said. "To be fair, if it wasn't the shoulder, it would be the fever and if it wasn't the fever, it would be the heels."

She smiled, though I had the feeling she didn't find this funny.

I had a hard time paying attention to the ceremony. Instead, I watched my friends: Krista, with her expansive tattoos, orange hair, and shimmering gown, dabbed at her eyes with a wad of tissue; Jaesung looked both polished and jittery in his tux. His hair was fantastic as ever, but I missed his glasses.

The ceremony ended, and I wobbled into the courtyard, for once relieved by the biting cold. It cleared some of the fog from my brain, and though my fever hadn't returned, the snowbanks near the spiky wrought-iron fence were tempting. I don't know why I found this cemetery more inviting than the reception hall, but I imagined sitting behind one of those massive headstones, letting the chill freeze out the pain in my shoulder.

I leaned against the rough stone wall and watched guests file across the street. All of them smiled and talked, connected by this confirmation that life as they knew it still moved forward, right on track. I couldn't imagine what my own wedding might look like. Unbalanced. All the guests would be the groom's and I'd walk down the aisle alone, with no father to escort me. No one wanted to watch that. Just as well it would never happen.

A shadow moved at the back of the cemetery, fleet enough to have been a cat or a bird. I squinted, tracing its path behind a small outbuilding. Something about that shadow had not been right.

"Sorry, excuse me?"

The soft voice startled me. I whirled around to find a woman standing a few feet away, leaning sideways as if she'd been trying to catch my eye. I felt the burn in my shoulder and grimaced.

"Sorry, sorry!" The woman's dark brown hair fluffed around a pale, freckled face. Despite being at least ten years older than me, there was something almost cute about her small mouth and huge brown eyes. "Hi, sorry, I didn't mean to interrupt. Are you Helena?"

I blinked at her, hesitant to take the mittened hand she extended. There was nothing Sorcerer-like about her, but Isaac had mentioned his boss was a woman.

She looked overstimulated. Breaths puffed from her lips in rapid intervals, and the hand that wasn't extended tapped at her deep pink trench coat. It was the pattern of cat silhouettes on her tights that finally tipped me off.

"Alina?"

"Yeah! Hi! Sorry!" She said, relief breaking over her face as I took her hand. "I was looking for you. Sorry. Kris said you might have trouble getting to the reception hall?"

Noting her trembling fingers, I doubted my injuries were the only reason Krista had sent Alina after me. She probably wanted to make sure her girlfriend had someone to talk to. I winced. Alina had been through a wedding before, as the bride. And that hadn't turned out as planned. We were two awkward peas in an uncomfortable pod.

"Yeah, thanks," I said, pushing myself off the iron fence. "I think I need to get in there and hide in a corner."

Alina nodded vehemently and took my elbow. I was grateful for the balance—these shoes, they were the worst part of all of this. I could stand the pantyhose that kept rolling down my abdomen if only I could exchange the heels for something less hazardous.

We skirted the edge of the darkened ballroom, circumventing the ghosts of tables and sheet-covered folding chairs. Alina installed me on a stool at the end of the open bar. It was almost like my favorite seat in the kitchen at Ruff Patch, a lovely corner where I could lean back against the join of the brick wall and the cool expanse of counter. I groaned in relief as I nudged my shoes off my feet.

Alina grinned at me, hopping up onto the stool next to me. "Shoe-gasm," she said, and with a little wiggle, two clunks sounded below her stool. "Oh my God. Yes. So good." She flagged the bartender. "Two bellinis, please."

The black-aproned woman turned away to make the drinks, and Alina winked at me. "I know you're, like, barely eighteen, but they're not gonna ask questions. And you look like you could use a painkiller."

I tried to smile, but it was lost on her. She fidgeted with her purse, looking this way and that, her foot jittering. The room was filling up, people finding seats and piling more and more boxes and bags on a table in the corner.

"Crap," she said, fingering a thick bit of plastic-wrapped paper in her purse. "I didn't think people would bring actual presents. I did research on Korean wedding customs and I thought we were supposed to bring an envelope of money. I even went to the bank to get new bills and kept the plastic wrapping so the envelope didn't get dirty—"

I accepted my drink from the bartender. "Nobody will be mad at an envelope full of cash," I said. The drink was cold, sweet, and bubbly.

Her eyes were huge, and she began tearing up the napkin under her drink. "Do you think? I didn't know. I mean, all Kris said is that Gene's family from Korea was flying in and I had no idea whether that meant the wedding would be traditional, but I guess Sanadzi's family wouldn't do that? Maybe I should warn her mom about the wild goose?"

"Wild-" I set down my glass. "Alina, I don't think there's a wild goose involved in any of the wedding plans."

"Right? They're probably doing the wooden one if they're doing it, which maybe they're not."

I saw the shadow on the bar and glanced up, catching Jaesung's reflection in the curve of my champagne glass.

"We're going full western on this one," he said, shrugging off his jacket. "No geese, no walnuts, no piggy-back rides. But I'm sure envelopes full of cash will be accepted." He stopped behind me, tossing the suit jacket over the bar. He was close enough to put off heat.

His presence was gravity. I leaned back and he met my weight without discussion. The metal tab of his suspenders pressed into my good shoulder, but it was worth the way he squared up to my back, one hand going to my hip.

A peppery musk cut through the general smells of crowd and clean linen. It took a second to identify it as something Jaesung was wearing. I'd gotten used to his normal smell, its hints of sweat and city and cold air. This was warmer, intentionally seductive. Good thing my back was to him. If the purpose of that scent was to make me want to bury my face in his neck, it was succeeding.

"Where's Kris?" Alina asked, and took a gulp of her bellini.

"Helping Sanadzi do something arcane to her dress, I don't know. She'll be out soon. Miss Martin? What happened to your shoes *this* time?"

"We broke up."

I felt the shake of a chuckle against my back. His hand on my hip tightened, and he tugged me around on the swiveling top of the barstool until I faced him. He pointed behind him, across the dance floor. "There's a bucket of flip-flops over there for dancing. Think you can commit?"

I set down my bellini. "Did you say flip-flops?" I pressed a hand to the tiny folds on the front of his shirt. "My kingdom for a flip-flop."

"Your kingdom?" he said, lifting his hand to cup my elbow, mimicking my mock dramatic pose. "My *God*. What will you give me for two?"

"Publicly?"

Alina giggled. Jaesung flexed his eyebrows, but there was a flush on his neck as he dropped my arm and strode purposefully across the dance floor.

"Shut *up*," Alina said, grinning over at me. "You two are adorable!"

I knew what she thought, and denying it was getting exhausting. Worse, it was starting to feel like another lie. Especially when a treacherous satisfaction snuck in at the sight of him, white shirt and suspenders and tattoo and fantastic hair, digging through a bin of sparkly flip-flops. For me.

There was a hunter in me that watched with senses wide open, taking in his solid shoulders and warm skin, tasting the scent he'd left in the air and remembering the low vibration of his voice against my back. Despite all my protests, that hunter was growling 'mine'.

Still, even Jaesung couldn't distract me completely. A niggling nervousness still prodded at my brain. I needed to figure out what that shadow in the graveyard had been. Preferably before Jaesung got back and distracted me all over again.

I downed the rest of my drink, excused myself, and made my way along the wall to the hallway. The women's restroom sported a marble-topped makeup table and one of those enormous mirrors surrounded by lightbulbs.

I wish they'd been off. I looked like shit. The dress was nice, and given the ornate caftans and floor-length velvet skirts I'd seen on Sanadzi's family, the color clash made no difference, but my skin was practically gray. Even the makeup and hair-styling failed to disguise my dark circles and the scrape across my cheek.

I sank into the curvy chair and folded my good arm across the marble. The next best thing to scouting on foot was doing it in my spirit form. I closed my eyes and I stepped out of myself.

It was nice to walk so easily. I trotted unseen through the closed door and down the hallway, passing beneath a blazing exit sign. Outside, night had taken hold, and the snow glowed blue beneath the partial moon. I loped around the building, wove between the cars in the parking lot, and scanned every dark corner for any sign of magic.

I stopped at the front of the building. A few guests smoked on the front stoop. Across the street, the cemetery drew my eye again. Something was in there. I was sure.

Across the street I went, and through the wrought iron bars. Grave markers rose before me, some of them new, some so old the words had weathered away. I hopped onto one of the big concrete tombs, translucent paws barely obscuring the carving beneath. No trace of power graced the woods, no moving shadows. Still I was convinced. Someone was here.

Pain exploded in my shoulder, and someone in the room with my body screamed.

I pivoted on four paws. Had someone snuck by me? Was my body being attacked? Had I even remembered to lock the door?

I sprinted across the street, straight through the wall. My shoulder was in agony so harsh I could barely focus. I barreled into the hallway. A clutch of raven-haired women huddled at the door of the bathroom. I breezed past them, leapt through the crouching form of a woman in a dress, only to find myself on my injured side, the chair tilted over.

I leapt into my body, shocking myself into a gasp. Control reasserted itself on my real limbs with a jerk.

"Hello, hello?" the woman above me said, her voice accented. "Hello, please?"

I forced my eyes open. The woman's slender hands fluttered around me without touching.

"Okay? Are you okay?" she said. People in the doorway were whispering in what I guessed was rapid Korean.

I made myself twist onto my good side and push to my knees, then my feet. The orange scarf had slid off my shoulder, which was once again seeping a thin line of blood. The woman crouching next to me pulled a packet of tissues from her purse, pressing them into my hands with wide eyes.

"It's okay," I said. "Thanks."

"Okay?"

"Yeah, I'm okay." Her frantic expression eased. There was something familiar in her face. Of course, she'd be related to Jaesung. Still, her fashion was sort of off. She was in her early twenties, but her lavender dress was a confection of ruffles that looked more appropriate for a twelve-year-old.

Then an older woman separated herself from the crowd. That she was Jaesung's mother would have been obvious to a complete stranger. They had the same elegant jawline, the same mouth, the same long, slender proportions. He'd even inherited her slight widow's peak, and a dimple in her bottom lip suggested the presence of largish canines. In her floor-length wine-colored dress, she looked like someone who belonged at a high-class cocktail party, or performing at an opera. She didn't look like a piano tutor.

She took both my hands in hers, her perfect eyebrows pinching as she took in my injuries.

"My son looking for you," she said, and unlike Jaesung, her English had a thick Korean accent. "I'm Sooyoung, Jaesungie's mother."

"Hi," I said, though it was through a grimace. "Sorry, I'm—still sort of...."

"You come sit down," she said. "This kind of bruise? You should not standing up so much. Come on. We take care of you, okay?"

She patted my hand, then swept up the scarf and tucked it around my shoulders. Winding my good arm around hers, Jaesung's mother pulled me to the door.

CHAPTER TWENTY-FOUR

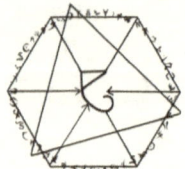

I sat with the Korean side of the family at dinner. Jaesung and Krista sat with the wedding party, and Alina seemed to have been adopted by one of Sanadzi's crystal-wearing cousins.

There had been a brief round of introductions in English at various levels of competency, and Sooyoung expounded on their relationships and hobbies. She was solicitous, refusing to let me reach for anything farther than my water glass. Through the niceness, it was hard to determine what she was like.

Was she doing this because part of her responded to a bruised-up girl? Or had Jaesung told her about my mom? My family, really. There was no way to know, and I was glad when dinner ended. I escaped to my dark corner at the bar, sparkly purple flip-flops smacking at my heels.

The lights dropped out, all but a few spotlights and the candles that flickered in centerpiece jars. The background music that had been playing surged, then dropped off as the best man stepped into the pool of light on the dance floor, microphone in hand.

"Hey," Jaesung slipped from the crowd, shrugging off his jacket and tossing it to the stool next to me. "Do me a favor?" He extended his wrist, cuffs loose and flopping.

"You want me to roll them up?"

"Yeah, flat if you can."

I took the sleeve, and he stepped in, hip bumping against my knee.

"So, you met Mom," he said.

"Yeah, she's very…. She wouldn't let me cut my meat."

He shook his head. "Sounds like her. She loves adopting people. Half my high school friends called her Mom."

I nodded, not wanting to tell him how little I wanted a replacement Mom right now. I reached for the other cuff, just as everyone laughed at something in the best man's speech.

"You're, um, maybe you can let me look at that a sec?" he said, plucking at my orange shawl. "I think you're leaking."

I glanced down, spying the dark stain blotting the silk. "Shit."

"It's on the back too," he said. "Come on."

A few minutes later, we were in the powder room. Jaesung wet a paper towel and wrung it out as I eased myself onto the counter, not trusting the spindly chair that had betrayed me before. He leaned into my knees and dabbed at the cut, head bent close to mine. His brows were drawn, and there was a measure of hesitation in the hand braced on my thigh.

It felt strange. Jaesung was here with me, like the friends we claimed to be when the truth didn't build walls between us. Even then, we were learning to care for each other through the barriers. Something in me reached for him, eager to know what we'd be without any secrets. I think he was reaching too.

"Thanks," I said. "You know there's stuff I can't tell you, but you're here anyway and, you know. Thanks."

His lips flattened into something that wasn't quite a smile, and he chucked the paper towel into the trash. I blinked, wondering where the flicker of temper came from.

"What?"

He leaned into the counter, hands braced on either side of me. His head hung, then shook. He lifted his hand in a shrug and dropped it to the counter with a slap.

"What?" I demanded again.

"I don't know, Hel." He looked back up. "I get that there's shit I can't know, and maybe I could accept that if you weren't..." He gestured to my face and shoulder. Both hands found my knees, squeezing for emphasis. "I *hate* this. Just sitting here and not knowing how to stop it from happening."

I shook my head. "It's not something you can protect me from."

"I know that!" he said, one hand going into his hair in frustration. "Trust me, I know you're a thousand times better equipped to protect yourself than me. That doesn't mean I'm just going to dick around while some asshole tries to kill you. At the moment, I can't do anything but patch the holes, and I am *not* satisfied with that."

He snagged another paper towel and drenched it, wringing it out more violently than necessary.

"You're not just patching holes." I caught his hand on the way to my shoulder. Unable to meet his eyes, I focused on the ridge of his collarbone under the dress shirt. "There's stuff that's too messed up to fix, maybe ever, but the things you guys have done are... When Mom and I first planned to run, I had no idea what to hope for. I couldn't envision the life I wanted because I couldn't imagine anything that didn't involve being scared and angry all the time. Because of you, I can. Now I know what I would want."

He set aside the paper towel. "If...?"

The bitterness in my laugh was unintentional. "If I were dumb enough to hope for it?"

"Stop." He moved some hair from my face, fingers light across my temple. I drew a slow breath, wondering why now, with him in front of me, I felt more fatalistic than ever. I couldn't help it. Everything I wanted was right there in front of me—six feet of solid, warm harbor —and I was walking away.

"Hey." His voice was softer now, the backs of his fingers warm over my ear. "You're okay."

He settled his weight against the counter, hips between my knees, and his belt pressed into my thighs. The slight pinch of it was not uncomfortable. I managed a smile.

"I can't decide if letting you under my skin was the best or worst thing I've ever done."

"Me neither."

His fingers traveled down my arm, and he caught my other hand, holding both. I turned them, nesting the backs of my hands in his palms. We were silent several moments, my injured shoulder and cheek throbbing. The weight of his gaze was so heavy I couldn't raise my eyes.

The bathroom shrank around us. That scent was getting stronger—sweat and those new, deeper notes that made me want to breathe in his skin. A tang of my blood mixed in, like a reminder of how dangerous it was to relax, even now. Even for this, whatever this was. He had no magic. He didn't even know it existed, but he was working his way past my defenses. Suddenly, I wanted to pull away—to cover my pounding heart with both hands and shield it from him. Instead, I forced myself to look up.

Our eyes met with a jolt. I watched, afraid to define the emotion in his gaze. He watched me back, dark eyes taking in my face, lingering on the scrape where I'd hit the asphalt. How many of these had he watched fade on his mother's cheek before he tried to intervene? The ache in his eyes looked old.

He curled his fingers around mine and pressed his thumbs into the hollow of my palms. Something hot pushed its way into my lungs, crystalizing sharp and ragged. The noise outside the door seemed distant, and the threat of Hellhounds and bounty hunters and Guild bullets fell away.

"I think it might be the worst," I whispered.

"Probably is."

Electric certainty sank into my bones. There was a static-filled instant when we both knew we would kiss. He drew my hands forward, tucking them around his waist, and I had just enough time to feel the thrill up my spine. He leaned his forehead against mine and our chests drew so close I felt his heart beating strong.

I didn't wait for him, just tilted my head and leaned, the bright tingle in my body intensifying as my mouth caressed his.

At first, our lips barely brushed. He exhaled. We were testing, daring each other to be the first to commit. My pulse poured into my ears, head heavy and dizzy as we breathed each other in. The scant friction of lips was terrifying—there was nothing left to disguise, no plausible denial. I could not stop myself from wanting Jaesung Park.

I moved my tongue against his parted lips, and his back tensed under my hands. Then he ducked his head and met my mouth full on. His arms surrounded me and I pulled him close, fists clenched into the shirt at his lower back.

His mouth was hot, and over the next few moments, the caress of his tongue carelessly dismantled every thought before I finished it. The rush and retreat of pleasure flushed through me, my muscles going warm and slack even as my senses opened.

I pushed the suspenders from his shoulders and heard the hitch in his breath. My hands fisted in his shirt and dragged it from his waistband. I knew where I wanted this to go, and the realization seemed to trip through him in stages. He fumbled an arm out, tipping the lock on the powder room door, then grabbed me behind the knees and hauled me hard into him.

I gasped, and for several blissful seconds, lust crowded out everything else. I let that sweet ache course out to the tips of my fingers. I wanted this. Needed it, maybe. An anchor to everything that was good and real and worth living for.

Jaesung's hands slid up the length of my thighs beneath the dress, and it became necessary to get rid of that bowtie.

We ignored the clatter of my knife on the counter behind me. I didn't want to think about that right now. I didn't want to focus on anything but the way it felt to crash into someone else, using my body to give and receive something that was the opposite of pain.

His fingers curled over the waistband of my tights and tugged. I stopped caring about his shirt. One hand fisted in his hair, holding on as he dragged tights and underwear down to my knees. I went for his belt, felt the hitch in his breath.

That was when I noticed the faint buzzing. It had been going on for a while, but only now, with my hand so close to his pocket, did I realize how long his phone had been ringing.

"Do you want to-"

"Not even slightly." He proceeded to convince me for several more seconds that anything but his mouth and hands were irrelevant. I fumbled open the suit slacks, his teeth a sharp counterpoint to the firm heat of his hands.

His phone was still going. It probably would have kept going if someone hadn't chosen that moment to try opening the door.

We jumped, snapping back to a reality significantly colder and more immediate than the last few frantic minutes.

"Must be occupied," said a loud voice on the other side of the door. One of Sanadzi's sisters.

We leaned back just enough to look at each other. I watched him weigh several things in his mind and, though my body was screaming demands, I tipped my head against his chest. His heart was beating like mad.

Jaesung lifted a hand to the back of my head, holding me to him as he caught his breath.

"Unless you have anything," I started.

"Yeah, nope. I was not even-"

"Me neither."

"Kay. We should—this is a bad time."

"Your phone."

He let go, hauling his pants back up by the belt and fastening them before pulling out his phone. "Fuck," he whispered. "Fuck,

fuck, fuck, fuck. Okay. I'm—I have to—Martial Arts. I was supposed to be there five minutes ago but-"

"You had your hands up my dress."

"Yes. Sort of distracted."

"I give you permission to use the truth as an excu-"

I didn't get to finish. His hands had gone into my hair, and he was kissing me, hard and warm. There was a humid feeling to his chest against mine, sweat and heat and truncated desire. He pulled back, located his bowtie, and shrugged on his suspenders.

"I guess this will have to be part of the look," he said.

I slid off the counter, tugging up my laddered hose and under-wear. "At least your cuffs are rolled up."

"Small miracles." He caught my jaw in one hand and walked into me, pressing me back into the wall with his full frame. I ducked away from another kiss and pushed him with my good hand.

"Get a move on, Park."

He flashed me a sheepish grin and unlocked the door, then ducked out.

I sank against the wall, pressing chill fingers to a face that felt feverish again. I wanted to be smart enough to regret what had just happened, and what had almost happened, and what I could not resist making happen at the earliest opportunity.

It took a few minutes to finish cleaning the blood from my shoul-der. I gave the shawl a cursory wash, but the stain had dried. I hung it over a stall and ducked back out to the bar, nabbing Jaesung's suit jacket from where he'd left it over the stool. The lining felt gentle on my injuries and wrapped his scent around my shoulders.

Everyone was sitting at their tables once again, watching as a mob of girls rushed to catch Sanadzi's enormous bouquet. Dizzy, still a little high on desire, I laughed as Krista nearly took out Sanadzi's sister in a dive to catch the flowers. Sanadzi bent double laughing as the two girls missed, leaving the bouquet to the tender mercy of the flower girl.

The best man emerged from behind a large projector screen,

clutching his stomach as if it hurt. "N-next!" he said. He was laughing. "Next we have a special performance from the talented and s-slightly tardy cousin of the groom, and his lovely partner Maria Graczkowski."

I covered a snort when Jaesung walked out, his hair mussed. The girl who walked out next to him was elegant, with brown hair and the long, willowy limbs of... definitely not a martial artist.

The lights dimmed, and just as the speakers let out a strain of slow string music, the girl blossomed into movement. I don't know what I'd expected, but it had not been ballet.

She was elegant, swift and light as a cat. Every muscle, from fingertip to ankle was a study in controlled beauty. Behind her, the screen showed a picture of Sanadzi as a young woman, her travels to Africa and Prague, her university years.

Then it shifted to an image—a selfie of Sanadzi and Eugene together on a boat—and Jaesung stepped in. He lifted her like she was part of the air, lowered her with grace and control, and when they danced together, it was in perfect synch.

I could see the art of those leaps, the beauty of each tiny movement, but it was the power of it that struck me more than anything. All that conditioning, all those explosive movements, it was no wonder I'd mistaken him for a fighter. This just fit so much better.

"Told you we'd stop askin' nice," a voice said behind me. Then a sapphire mandala flared in my face, and everything went black.

CHAPTER TWENTY-FIVE

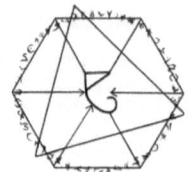

Fog pressed around my brain, cut by the sharp smell of gasoline. I clawed my way from the gooey traction of magic-induced unconsciousness over the space of several heartbeats. My brain pulsed. My legs felt cold and heavy, and when I tried to adjust my feet, I found them immobile. A thin plastic strap dug into my wrists.

Memory rolled in slow and heavy. Wedding vows. Jaesung dancing. *Kissing* Jaesung. I wanted to linger on that, but memory was intractable, and moved on. A blue flash of mandala.

I winced, keeping my eyes shut to the orange flicker I could see behind my eyelids.

"I think she's waking up," said a woman at my knee. Something thin and damp pressed against my wounded shoulder. I smelled permanent ink and braced for pain. It didn't come.

I opened my eyes. I was in a chair. Zip ties secured my limbs to the metal frame tight enough to bruise. Dim light revealed the chalk glyphs radiating out from my bare feet. I followed them to the graduated circles of a large mandala drawn on the floor. Those clean lines didn't hide the splattered pattern of oil stains.

Isaac had brought me to an auto garage of some sort, or the basement of one judging by the rectangle of open ceiling. I glanced around, hunting for potential weapons. Hydraulic risers, metal tool benches, and aging posters. There had to be something in here I could use.

A woman knelt beside me, drawing on my shoulder. An IV trailed from my opposite forearm. the thin red tube led to a half-empty bag hanging from a cord at shoulder height. The wide white label bore the name of a hospital, and someone had written 'O, Rh+' in the gap. How long had I been unconscious?

"Welcome back, sweetheart," Isaac said.

I twisted, trying to see him, but the IV catheter tugged at my arm. "Where the hell am I?"

"The interrogation room. Henard doesn't have its own Guild headquarters, so we're improvising."

The woman before me quirked an eyebrow, but continued drawing on my shoulder. She wore a coverall unzipped and tied about her waist, baring muscular, freckled shoulders covered in sharpie-drawn mandalas. Though several colors of marker stained her fingers, there were rings of grease around her nails, suggesting the garage was hers.

I glanced at my shoulder. Smudges of color lingered beneath the bold dark blue she used now, and under those ghosts of past mandalas, the ravaged skin was a jumble of healed scars. I tensed.

"Why are you healing me?"

Isaac chuckled, but I kept my eyes on the woman. Was she the boss Isaac talked about? She seemed young. She touched the mandala on my shoulder. A second later it flared bright gold, and the cells around my joint went white hot.

The woman made a slashing motion, and the burning stopped. She sat back on her heels and scrubbed a marker-covered forearm across her brow.

"That's all I've got in me," she said.

"Why heal me?" I asked again. She gave a humorless chuckle.

"We can't question an unconscious rogue. And anyway, that—"

she pointed to my chest, where the sanguimancers' carved attempt at a mandala still made a thin white scar "—is on us."

"I'm not a rogue," I said.

"You've used magic. And you haven't pledged to follow the Guild's laws. That's kinda the definition, hun." She pressed her hands to her knees and pushed herself up. "Anyway, you were about to bleed out in Ike's rental, and *someone* opted for the leather seats."

"Oh, here we go," Isaac muttered.

"I—how did I...." I looked at the IV, then down at my dress. The light had been dim enough I didn't notice before, but the right side of my dark purple dress was stiff with dried blood.

There was no way I could return it to Sanadzi now. My gut dipped at the thought. It sent a sympathetic swell of anger into my throat.

Turning my arm to accommodate the IV, I twisted to glare at Isaac. He leaned in the doorway of a small office, chewing at a thumbnail.

"It had to be the wedding." I growled. "You couldn't have waited until I was wearing pants?"

"At least I waited until your boyfriend had his up."

Heat flashed across my face, memories crowding in to be ruined by this new information. Jaesung's hair in my hands, his mouth on my throat. Had Isaac been watching us? Hearing us talk, kiss? Had he stood there, concealed and waiting as I pushed off Jaesung's suspenders?

Would he have kept watching, had we not been interrupted?

Disgust washed through me. It must have been evident on my face, too, because he grinned and spat a shard of fingernail.

"I mean, respect, though," he went on. "I see how you convinced the muggles to keep you around."

My heart gave a violent squeeze. Rage pulsed into the hollow of my throat and I went dizzy with it. I jerked forward. Zip ties tightened, and the IV bag swung.

Then a new voice issued from the office behind Isaac.

"That is enough, Mr. McOwen," said the melodic, accented alto. A shadow moved past lowered office room blinds and Isaac straightened up.

A small Indian woman stepped past him. Light bent toward her, glowing off deep brown skin and golden earrings. She appeared to be in her thirties and though she was slender as any Sorcerer, there was an elegance to her that Guild Hunters like Isaac lacked. She wore all the metal he did, but her pierced nose and stacked bangles seemed more cultural than magical in design.

The woman stopped in front of me, lips quirking into a polite smile. Her black waves had a hint of premature silver and over her slacks and silken blouse, she'd donned a white lab coat that pronounced her: Deepti Iyengar, MD. That explained the IV.

"Miss Martin," she said. "It is unfortunate we had to meet under these circumstances. I had hoped for a more willing exchange of ideas."

I wanted to laugh, to spit the same venom at this woman, but something about her serene smile made that response feel childish.

"That might have worked if you'd given me more reason to trust you," I said. "So far, that hasn't happened."

She nodded, fingers going to a clip along the IV tube and fiddling with it. "Isaac stopped the sanguimancers from taking you. Is that not a sign of good faith?"

"No." I shook back my hair, trying to keep my eyes on her. "That's you protecting your interests. So's healing me, and keeping Gwydian's bounty hunters off my ass. Cutting these zip ties is a sign of good faith."

Deepti's tawny eyes flicked to me. I watched her scan my face, taking my measure with something like new, calculated interest. She clipped off the IV tube.

"I could say you have failed to show your own good faith," she said, drawing a pair of blue latex gloves from her coat pocket. "But I do not undervalue your suffering. Given your past, a certain level of self-protection is natural." She reached for the IV catheter in my arm, drawing it out and pressing a gauze pad over the site.

"But?" I could sense it coming.

Deepti tilted her head in acknowledgement, but didn't answer until she'd taped down the gauze and tossed the catheter in a plastic trash bin.

"But you do not seem to understand what your parents offered. I believe if you knew-"

"That Dad said he'd join you? That Mom tossed in my coopera-tion to sweeten the deal this time? I know."

"You do not!" For the first time, Deepti's tone had gone hard. "What happened in Miami was terrible on all sides—you lost your mother, we lost four of our best Hunters, and still we failed to kill Gwydian. But it was not considered a loss. Do you know why?"

"I still had the book," I said.

Deepti tossed a hand in the air. "The book," she snapped. "Per-haps that was important before we knew for certain what you were. No, Helena Martin—we did not count that night in Miami as a loss because *you* survived."

I stared up at her, incredulity twisting my face. "What I *am*? Look, every single time you people have tried to grab me, all you've talked about is that fucking book, so don't turn it around now, saying I'm some magical special snowfla-"

"You *are* special, Helena." Deepti was insistent. She bent over, her hands falling to my shoulders, still bare in the dress. One rested over my spellhound tattoo, the other on my ravaged shoulder and the scar-crossed ruin of the enslavement mandala.

"There is a reason Gwydian wanted your father under his power."

I sighed, letting my head fall back, certain I didn't want to know whatever Deepti was about to tell me. "Am I the last unicorn?"

The blonde healer snorted, smothering the laugh with a multi-hued hand. Isaac's smirk was a slash across his face.

"Told you she thought she was funny, boss."

Deepti was unmoved. "Deflection is a common sign of fear. You're suffering post-traumatic stress."

I lifted my head, prepared to disagree on principle, but the warning in those golden eyes stayed me.

"You are important," Deepti said. "But not because you are powerful."

"So why am I tied to a chair?"

Her lips curved, but she otherwise ignored my question. "Your father was a Rogue. We tried for years to draw him into the Guild, but he refused. We did not know who he was then, or we may have understood that reluctance.

"Magic developed across the world at different times, you see. Much like writing, or agriculture, or science. Also like those things, it developed with variation. Certain areas learned to channel magic to different effects—the Chinese had a knack for predicting the shape of magic. In the British Isles, people carved their infinite knots into stone, creating circuits in which to store power. But it was not until the people of India tamed that power for themselves that we discovered the perfect method of casting."

I shifted in my chair. I hadn't known the story went so far back. "Is there a reason for the history lesson?"

"Yes," Deepti said. "It will also explain why we have you sat in the center of a mandala."

I lifted an eyebrow. "Fine, I'll bite."

"After the fall of the Roman Empire-"

"Jesus."

"Alexander, actually. In Constantinople, the forebears of modern sorcery gathered, exchanging their glyphs and circuits the way merchants traded silk and language and religion. Sorcerers borrowed each other's ideas and studied the effects of them together. The Silk Road changed magic as much as it changed the rest of the world. That confluence of culture started everything you see here."

She waved her hand at the chalk mandala at my feet. I scanned the glyphs sketched in concentric rings, unsure of their meaning. It

was a complicated mandala. Far more so than most of the ones I'd
seen the Guild Hunters use.

"What does this have to do with my dad?" I asked.

"That depends. Did he ever tell you his real name?"

I refused to let the surprise show on my face. Still, my teeth
clenched around the words. "I guess not."

Deepti released a long sigh and straightened up. Her hands slid
from my shoulders and she paced to one of the tool chests and selected a
boxcutter from the top drawer. My scalp prickled, but I gritted my teeth
and remained mostly empty as she sliced the zip ties from my ankles.

"I cannot release your hands, but for now, I will trust you to
remain civil." I watched where she dropped the boxcutter. Without
thinking, I shifted to confirm my knife at the small of my back.

Only it wasn't there. The sound of it clattering to the vanity
countertop came back, tangled up with the visceral memory of
Jaesung's hands on me. Perfect. Now, even if I could get my arms
free, I'd be battling three Sorcerers to get to that boxcutter first.

Deepti wet her lips. "This requires more history, I'm afraid."

I slumped back in the chair, feeling petulant as I scanned the
chalked glyphs around me for hints of the spell's purpose. "You have
a captive audience. Monologue away."

Deepti made a motion at Isaac who, to my surprise, ducked into
the office to retrieve a cheap-looking office chair, which he rolled into
place behind the petite Sorceress. "It took centuries of experimen-
tation to come to the magic circles we use now, and even so there
were rifts among the Sorcerers. Different philosophies, some of them
theoretical, others which remain contested today."

"Blood magic versus regular sorcery."

"That term is troublesome," Deepti said, settling into the chair
with crossed legs. "All magic is fueled by blood, by the inherent
magical energy in the iron. While Sanguimancy translates to blood
magic, it is the accepted word for *victimized* blood sorcery. But you
are otherwise correct: the deepest rift formed between those whose

magical philosophies included the blood of an outsider, and those that did not."

The blond healer had disappeared upstairs, and the ceiling rumble of someone rolling on a mechanic's creeper made me think she'd gone back to work in the garage proper.

"It would be too broad a brush to paint all Sanguimancy as evil. In the British Isles, for example, there was a strong culture of apprenticeship, where one who wished to learn magic would volunteer his blood for use by a more skilled Sorcerer, until he achieved a certain level of proficiency. And there were the druids."

Her golden gaze flicked to my spellhound tattoo. "They believed the power of bound spirits could bend human flesh, but the spell itself required-"

"The animal to die." I didn't need to hear this part. I had the memory: the Irish wolfhound lying next to me in the mandala, its blood sticky beneath me, brightening the grooves in the concrete.

"Yes," she said. "At one time, it was thought the most difficult spell in existence. You might have been the right hand of a queen, if not a queen yourself, among the people of Medieval England."

I narrowed my eyes, sensing the shift of the story. "So what changed?"

Deepti tipped her hand so her golden bangles chimed. "Everything. Nothing. Human nature reared its head as it always does."

"Someone got greedy?" I guessed. Deepti nodded.

"It took decades of influential Sorcerers in French salons for the great minds of the magical community to condemn all forms of Sanguimancy."

Isaac, lurking somewhere behind me, chuckled. "Bureaucracy's a bitch no matter who's barking." He paced close to my back, and the hairs on my neck stood on end. I had a strong desire to tip the chair backwards and kick him.

Instead, I trained my gaze on Deepti. "Maybe it's because magical history wasn't on my gang-member home school curriculum, but I don't see what any of this has to do with me or Dad being super special."

Deepti sighed, stretching her delicate, hennaed fingers. "I'm afraid it will not be a piece of information you find palatable. A single family had managed, beyond all odds, to remain influential for nearly fifteen hundred years. They came into prominence just as my Hindu forbears began using Chinese and Arabic glyphs within our own mandalas—an Armenian merchant and his daughter, Heghineh."

Her name sounded like mine, but with a sound not quite like an "l". I narrowed my eyes.

"From your expression, you already know what I am about to say."

"I'm guessing she's a relative."

"She is."

"So? I'm the lost descendent of an Armenian merchant Sorcerer-ess. Why does that-"

"Few women traveled the Silk Road. Do you not think it odd that a man would bring along his young daughter on such a dangerous trip?"

I shrugged. "Couldn't get a babysitter?"

Deepti shook her head. "No, he left his business in Armenia because of Heghineh. She was young, and ripe with magic. And she had a unique gift, one I suspect you have as well."

"A unique gift?" I sifted through my brain, but came up with nothing.

"You have a gift for memorizing pictures, do you not? Pictures and patterns?"

"My photographic memory? But that's not a magic thing."

"Not directly, but it gives you an ability. Like your father, like Heghineh, you can cast a mandala from your mind."

I looked at her, the pinch between my eyebrows now bordering on a headache. "I don't think—I mean, that's not how magic works, right? It has to be drawn, in order."

Deepti shook her head. "Most Sorcerers must draw it. The

human brain is complex, but we cannot hold a perfect image of a mandala in our minds. Most people, when pressed, can only conjure the vaguest ideas of their closest friend's faces: the ability to hold such an elaborate collection of symbols *and* the order of flow through the mandala is unthinkable to anyone without your combination of gifts. The likelihood that a person who has an eidetic memory also has magic is approaching zero. You are exceptionally rare."

With a sudden chill, I recalled the violent burst of turquoise magic that had killed the Enforcer on Gwydian's yacht. Had that been instinct? Had I done it again that night at Rinkenburger's, terrified as I was of the thought of being followed?

I wanted to press my hands over my ears, to drown out the sounds of Isaac and Deepti breathing, waiting for me to say something, but my wrists remained bound.

That was when the truth of it hit me.

"My dad didn't want to be a part of the Guild," I said. "He didn't want his gift to be discovered. You said you didn't know who he was?"

"We didn't," Deepti confirmed. "The Armenian surname disappeared with Heghineh's marriage. The line cropped up again in France and stayed there, benefitting both monetarily and magically from the abundance of silver in the mines. They took the town's name—d'Argent. The family gained respect, influence, and enemies.

Numbered among them was a sept of Neo-druids in the Scottish highlands. They resented the d'Argent's enforcement of the anti-Sanguimancy pact. The Lochlys created the spell you wear on your shoulder. Its outlawing left them without the strongest and most sacred of their magics."

My skin went cold. Deepti's hand spasmed, as if she wanted to reach out.

"Through much of the late Nineteenth century, the Lochly family hunted and killed most of the d'Argent family. The last two cousins went into hiding. Both boys disappeared fifteen years later, on the Western Front."

World War One. I shifted in my chair. One of those vanished boys had to be my great or twice great grandfather. Given that Deepti had their descendent zip-tied to a chair in the basement of an auto shop, she spoke of them with more respect than I'd have imagined.

"Dad changed his name. Why? To run from the Lochlys?"

Deepti shook her head. "It isn't certain. Do you know what the name Martin means?" she asked.

I shivered. When had the garage become so cold? "Dad said it was a common French last name."

"Certain old magics allied the planets with precious metals. Silver for the moon, gold for the sun, copper for Venus. And for Mars-"

"Iron."

"Yes. The sanguimancer's metal. Your ancestors changed their name from Silver to Iron. Perhaps to throw off the Lochlys. Perhaps because they considered themselves now at war."

So Gwydian wanted me as more than just a power source. He wanted to complete an ancient family grudge. I clenched my fists, tucking away the disturbing information for later, when I wasn't in a cold basement with a trio of Guild Sorcerers.

"So it's this mandala-less casting power that's got you desperate to recruit me," I said.

"You are the last of the d'Argent line."

I quirked an eyebrow. "That a hint to go make some magic babies?"

Isaac sniggered. "Drop a litter. We'll put 'em in a box at HQ."

"Children would not be the most terrible idea," Deepti said. She patted my knee. "There will be time for everything once we neutralize the Lochly threat."

Because there was any chance I'd let them near my children, if I ever had them. I concentrated on the question she still hadn't answered.

"Dad agreed to join because it would get me and Mom away from

Gwydian. I'm the opposite of a Guild fan now, so why should I join you?"

"Because we are doing the right thing."

"If sanguimancy is so important to their clan identity, I bet the Lochly sept thinks it's fighting for religious freedom. Who are you to decide what's right?"

Isaac slouched into view. "You'll notice those fucktards are into killing people, or turning them into uncontrollable hell beasts."

I leaned forward in the chair. "Remember that time a Guild Sorcerer shot my Mom in the head?"

Deepti raised a hand.

"I know we are not an appealing option, but all that history should have at least convinced you of the need for magical regulation. The safety of people like your friends depends upon it. We cannot allow someone of your gifts to remain unchecked."

I fought the desire to say something snarky. "How—what sort of checks are you thinking?"

"There is a small marking," Deepti said, rolling back her own sleeve. "A safety measure to monitor location."

"That seems easy to throw off," I said. "Especially for a Sorcerer."

"There are precautions to eliminate the chance of removal."

I didn't like the sound of that. "A magic microchip. I can't imagine you'd leave me alone."

"That is not something we can do. Regardless of intention, you cannot tell me the right leverage would not sway you to do ill. We have seen it too often."

"And if I don't want to be tagged like a shark?"

Deepti's lips tightened. She looked down at her knees, and I noticed her twist a gold band around her finger.

"I hope that is not the choice you make," she said, then looked at me again. "You are valuable to the Guild, but that same value also makes you a threat. If you cannot agree to live within the parameters of safety, I fear we cannot allow you to live at all."

My heart shuddered. Despite the cold, sweat blossomed on my neck and bare shoulders.

"You-you're going to kill me?" My voice betrayed me, shaking as disbelief and fear assaulted my throat.

Sympathy shone in Deepti's golden eyes, but she set her jaw. "We do not yet know how your gifts will translate into sanguimancy, and if our intelligence is correct, the Lochly sept has wanted to claim it for themselves since before their feud with the d'Argents."

Isaac picked at a scab on his wrist. "If he thought you were d'Argent, I'm surprised he didn't make you his baby mama."

The heat that flushed across my face made it impossible to articulate my anger without succumbing to frustrated tears. I refused to cry in front of them.

"Our protection has confirmed any suspicions," Deepti said. "This is not the path I would want for you, but it is the only way I can guarantee your gift does not fall into the hands of a terrorist."

My chest heaved, fury kicking my lungs into short gasps. "So I have to—let you c-control me, or you'll kill me. But only because you think Gwydian will force me to have a mind-casting sanguimancer baby?" Deepti swallowed. "And that's worth my life to you? You do fucking realize that none of this is my fault, and that, so far, every choice I've made has been to get the fuck away from all of you?"

"I'm sorry, Helena," Deepti said. "I despise-"

"Not sorry enough to let me live."

The head of the Northern Sorcerers' Guild pursed her lips. "No," she confirmed. "Were he to turn you against us, the loss of innocent life would be more than I could justify, even for a d'Argent. It is simple weights and measures."

"Instead of preempting that fate by killing the victim, you could, you know, kill him first!"

"Do you not think we have been trying?" Deepti said, at last cracking into anger. "For the past three months, the North and Eastern American Guilds have focused on little else. We have lost good men and women to his network, not to mention the utter cock-up of that night in Miami." Her lips curled, and I understood the unspoken animosity between Deepti and the Eastern Guild.

"You're just tripping over all that red tape, aren't you, Doc?" I said. "Sanguimancers don't need iron pills and a glock to kill a Guild Sorcerer."

Her jaw tightened. "We only need him to be stupid once," she said. I nodded.

"And killing me is the failsafe. Takes my dangerous lady-parts from the equation. Even if I hadn't had my share of unwanted dicks shoved in my direction—none of which made it close—I could promise you there would be no chance I'd let myself be some captive incubator."

She winced.

"You know what you're doing is wrong," I said.

"I do not see why it is so difficult for you to agree to our laws."

"Because I don't want a fucking magical kill-switch on my body?" I snapped, jerking my chin toward the ruined shoulder. "I've had enough of being tagged. See? You didn't even deny that's what it is—a way to kill me if I go off the grid. No idea why I don't trust you."

Just as Deepti opened her mouth, a solid whump hit the floor above us. We all looked up, peering at the opening in the ceiling, where mechanics would work on a car's undercarriage.

"Mia?" Isaac called, leaning to glimpse her in the garage above. "You alright?"

Deepti's perfect brows furrowed. "Your wards are intact?"

"I'da said something if they weren't," he said, crossing to the narrow staircase. "Mia?"

Deepti's hand was on her phone, the other reaching for the mostly empty bag of blood.

Tires screeched outside. A car crashed into the garage above, shoving a sparking, crumpled aluminum door across the opening above us. The front tires dropped through the opening. I gasped, tipping back. For a horrible second, I thought the car would plunge through, crush me and Deepti.

The grates held, but sparks and explosions of mandala-light crackled above. Oil spilled onto my hair, even as I rocked over backwards and rolled. One zip-tie broke on impact.

Cursing, Isaac ducked back down the stairs and primed a full set of rings. I scrambled into a crouch, still attached by one wrist to the chair, and snatched the boxcutter.

I freed myself in a second. Unsteady I slammed into the toolbox and overturned it. Grease and oil and my bare footprints scuffed out the neat mandala lines on the floor.

"How did they get past Marshal?" Deepti managed. She shouted an order into her phone, even as Isaac dashed up the stairs. I followed.

A shock-wave shuddered the stairs, hurling me against the wall. I clung to the railing, hauling myself back to my feet. Thank God that Mia girl healed me. Hopefully she wasn't dead.

Ahead, Isaac hurled off spells. Smoke poured into the stairs, choked the room above so the only visible part of our enemies were the flashes of mandala.

We gained the upper garage. The concrete was hot on my feet, and pebbles of shattered windshield pressed into my soles. Isaac stepped around an outstretched arm, bloody and lolling from beneath the fallen hood of a car. I smelled the cooking flesh before Deepti, behind me, shouted again into her phone.

"Mia's dead. Send Cam to the perimeter." Her fingers seized my arm. "We're sending her out!"

I jerked my arm away, but she didn't seem to care. "Go!" she said, pointing through the smoke. She twisted about and slid one golden bangle from her wrist. It lit up white at her touch, and a collection of mandalas appeared before her. She worked fast, tossing up a shield to supplement Isaac's, then launching an attack that caused all the smoke in the room to suck back out through the ruined doorway.

The bounty hunters' spells came from too many directions. I counted at least eight before a crack in the concrete below me fissured out. Isaac drew his gun, prepared to fire.

"No!" Deepti said. "Isaac, there's too much grease."

I darted toward the back exit, already planning my next move. There would be sanguimancers, and maybe Guild members now waiting for me out there. If I didn't need to draw mandalas, what better time to give that possibility a try?

Gripping tighter to the boxcutter, I called up an image of a mandala in my head—a cutting spell I'd just seen Isaac carve into the air. I willed magic to my fingers, to the image in my head, and shoved open the door.

Strong, dark arms reached for me. I kicked, and the mow hawked woman staggered back, doubling over. She shot out a hand, her tattooed palm some intricate, evil looking mandala. I swung the box cutter, forgetting the spell as reflexes kicked in.

The blade sliced through her tattoo, but not before she sent off the spell. I jerked to the side to avoid it and she seized the opportunity. She kicked my legs out and, in a second, she was on me, sliced hand on my face, knees pinning my arms.

In her free hand, a switchblade appeared, and the tip angled beneath my eye.

"We got business, bitch," she growled. "And the boss didn't say you had to come home pretty." I wasn't bleeding out this time and twisting sent her off balance. I earned only a slice beneath the eye for my struggles. It burned, but I didn't care. Her blood was making my face slick.

Blood. Iron. Mars. Martin. My grandparent, or theirs, or theirs had changed our name from silver to iron. Maybe the name wasn't the only thing that changed when they disappeared.

Deepti had said they didn't know how my gifts would translate into Sanguimancy. There was power here, all over my face. However evil the Guild thought using someone else's blood was, it seemed stupid not to. Especially since the bitch now threatening to lobotomize me through the eyeball wouldn't expect it.

I called up the mandala in my mind, imagined tethers of lightning from the slice in her hand, the same tethers I'd felt when Gwydian had used my power to cast.

The woman squeezed my face, pressed the knife in until I felt it breaking skin under my eye.

"I'm carving you up pretty," she said. "For Matt."

"Not if I carve you first," I growled, and let the spell fly.

At first, all I saw was turquoise mandala, shot through with veins of red. Then slashes of light opened out like a fan and the Sorcereress rocketed back in a mist of dark liquid. She landed hard and didn't rise.

I rolled to my knees. The boxcutter in my hand was slick. I didn't want to go over to the woman, but I forced myself to do it anyway. Her face was no longer a face. Magic had slashed her open in a tight web, crisscrossing her face and chest. I'd cut her throat, right across the carotid artery. Bright blood still pulsed from the wound.

I'd seen it a thousand times before. I'd done it with a knife in my hands. This was different. This time, it wasn't an innocent. This time, I'd done it with my mind.

I rooted through her jacket and found a cell phone, shakily pressed her finger to the unlock ID, and staggered toward the nearby cars. Deepti had been right. I could cast magic without even drawing a mandala.

And that meant I couldn't let her have me. Or Gwydian. Or anyone. I had to run.

CHAPTER TWENTY-SIX

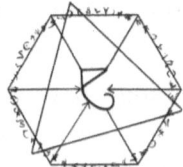

The last time I'd been this cold, I'd been in a frozen-over lake. Now, wind streaked past the cracked window of my battered, stolen Toyota as I peeled down unfamiliar roads packed high with snow.

The headlights behind me had vanished, but I didn't trust it. The moon was high and bright, and I couldn't hear anything past the judder of wind through the windows. They could still be behind me, headlights cut.

The auto repair shop had been out of town, and now I'd escaped, who knew where the hell I was. The bounty hunter's GPS got no signal, and there was nothing but straight, long, unlabeled roads. All I could do was hope it was the right way.

I risked a glance in the rearview, saw nothing but snow caked two feet high.

The gas gauge pointed toward the red. Who the car belonged to, I didn't know. In the clash of Sorcerers and bounty hunters, I'd grabbed the first thing I thought I could hot wire. Thirty-five minutes later, I was in the middle of flat nowhere with only the broken stalks of harvested corn to offer me protection.

I could feel the bounty hunters. The grip of sixth sense on my nape told me to keep going, no matter what. I wasn't safe now. I wouldn't be safe until I could get away from the hunters. The Sorcerers. Everything. With the Guild after me for my power, Gwydian after me for my bloodline and eidetic memory, I might never be safe again.

The engine gave an ominous clunk. All at once, the steering column seized up, and the break grew resistant to the pressure of my bare foot.

"Shit," I hissed, wrenching on the wheel. But without power steering, it was me against the weight of the entire car. The old Toyota fishtailed, hit a pothole, and careened into the field.

Stalks smashed across the windshield, coughing up snow. My head jerked forward, and a split second later the seatbelt hurled me back into my seat.

The engine hissed. The surrounding metal creaked and shuddered. Every light on the dashboard was a brilliant glyph of vehicular death.

I shoved open my door, crushing yet more stalks, and stepped out into the snow-packed field. A few kicking steps and I gained the road.

I stared at the car, arms wrapped around myself. Of all the cars at the shop, I had to choose the one twenty miles of farmland away from throwing a rod.

I shifted from foot to foot, unable to keep either on the snow for long. Part of me wanted to get back in the car, just to conserve warmth. I already knew I wouldn't, though. If I would die, I'd rather it be from exposure than at the hands of Guild or bounty hunters.

There had to be magic for this. The only heat spell I knew was straight up fire, though, and if my experience burning the book was any sign, that flaming column would shoot into the sky, alerting every Sorcerer, bounty hunter, and concerned citizen five miles in any direction.

My shivers were fading. I swallowed, a thrill of fear shooting up my spine as I realized what that meant—my body was conserving energy. Hypothermia was setting in, and soon everything cold would feel hot.

I crouched, rubbing my calves with hands that felt like half-thawed meat.

Maybe alerting the Sorcerers would be worth it if I could just get warm again.

Above, stars hung like chips of ice. If only I knew what direction I needed to go, I could navigate. Polaris was right above me, bright as the ring on Sanadzi's finger. The last time I'd seen the sky this clear, it had been my birthday. Jaesung and Krista had been with me, wrapped up in sleeping bags and sipping spiked hot chocolate.

I started. Without the snow, this farm land looked like where we'd driven. I turned in a circle. At the far reaches of my vision stood a farm house, flanked by two silos and a grain elevator. I'd passed others, miles back, but maybe....

My first steps were painful and grew more so as I skulked over slush and into banks of snow. I could barely walk but I did it anyway, headed for the dark juts of silo in the distance. If nothing else, I could at least hot-wire another vehicle. Maybe a truck. I put a hand to my chest, confirmed the box-cutter and phone making hard shapes in the tight bodice of my borrowed dress.

I might have been sweating. My ears were throbbing, breath coming sharp in my lungs, when I noticed the headlights. I didn't even bother to look, just pitched myself sideways into the field. Sharp stalks sliced my feet and legs as I fell to my knees, but I ignored the pain, prostrating myself behind the chaotic fringe of vegetation. Snow crunched cold and glasslike under me.

The car crept down the road. I squinted as it passed. Now that headlights didn't blind me to the passengers, it was clear who they were—hunters. I recognized the one Krista had maced, and three more, glaring out into the frosted night. They couldn't have been going this speed the whole time—they had to have slowed down after finding the car. Or maybe they had a way of tracking their friend's phone.

It was several minutes of shivering on the ground before I could no longer see the tail lights. Even then, my arms didn't want to push me up. I wouldn't make it past the farm house. I needed to get warm. I needed to call-

God. I hadn't even thought about Jaesung. And Krista and Sanadzi and all the others. I closed my eyes, tempted to sit down again. I'd wanted so much not to let my angst interrupt Sanadzi and Eugene's wedding. Now, I imagined them, sitting on the couch at Ruff Patch, surrounded by luggage, talking to police officers while the Hawaii-bound plane took off without them.

Or maybe, and I knew the hope was thin, but still—maybe Jaesung and Krista had concealed my absence from the newlyweds, sent them off to white sand and indigo seas none the wiser.

I forced myself to walk. No lights glowed in the farmhouse ahead, but it was past midnight. The owners could just be asleep. I could knock on the door. Find out where I was and maybe warm up enough to call Jaesung and let him know I was okay.

Which would be a lie. My skin burned with cold, and it felt like a few more breaths might freeze the moisture in my mouth.

It wasn't a familiar farmhouse. That would have been too much of a coincidence, but I passed a ramshackle mailbox that claimed it to be number eighty-four. I opened the box, and my spirits falling as I saw the stack of unopened letters. No one was home. I'd have to break in.

I snagged what looked like a credit card offer and memorized the address. It wasn't familiar, and it wasn't in Henard, but the zip-code was only two digits off.

I knew I should search the perimeter—make sure that car wasn't parked somewhere around the back, or under the grain elevator, but I was too cold to care. I pulled out the box-cutter, clicked out the blade, and jimmied it under one of the front door's windowpanes. My hands shook.

I didn't know I was slumping toward the door until my forehead struck wood. Sucking in a breath, I grimaced and righted myself. The boxcutter dropped from the pane, which still sat connected in its frame.

Cursing, I crouched and grabbed the tool.

A second later, the porch exploded under me. I was in the air, soaring backwards. I tucked, but I'd break something no matter how I landed. Before I hit ground, I got my legs under me. Heels first, I tried to make the impact gradual, but I was going too fast. I rolled backwards, protecting my head until I skidded to a halt, face-down on the frigid earth, dress scraped up to my waist.

I took several seconds too many to process the pain. Scraped thighs, arms, hip. No telling what else. I choked, just the twitch of a finger sending a rage of pain through me.

Footsteps crunched through the snow, heading straight for me. There were at least three. I closed my eyes, playing dead. Somehow, the boxcutter had stayed in my hand, but I was too broken to hope for fighting them physically. How much injury had they taken at Isaac and Deepti's hands?

Rough, gloved fingers gripped my arms and hauled me onto my knees. Under the pretext of pulling down the hem of my dress, I shoved the boxcutter down the tight shreds of my panty-hose.

"Bitch thought you got lucky, didn't you?" said a gruff voice. The back of a fist cracked into me, popping sparks behind my eyes. Blood welled into my mouth. I choked, felt it bubble over my lip. "Think you got away?"

Fuck. I cracked my eyes open, shocked at how much of an effort it took. The man gripping my arms was behind me. The talker—the one who'd hit me—stood in front. He was a rangy beast, bared teeth gleaming in the moonlight, hair shaggy and lank. He wore wool from head to toe, but tattoos marked the left side of his jaw.

I thought of Jaesung's constellation, remembered the taste of the skin below his ear. Stupid. This was not the time to think about that.

"Ain't no Guild to help you now," said Rangy. He grinned, but it looked forced. Like he wanted me to think he was happier about having me here than he was.

Blood filled my mouth, and I kept my lips shut. I could use that.

He hit me again, another backhand that ripped the already loosened tooth free of its roots. It clicked around in my mouth, sharp on my tongue. Gasping, I choked on the blood. The tooth lodged in my throat. Everything left me in a rush—hot bile and blood streaming onto the frost. It burned my toes.

The Sorcerer cursed. "Get her to the car," he said, seizing one of my arms.

I let them drag me, all pain and mad thoughts—the car would have heat blasting. Morgan might be at the end of this ride. Or, maybe, I could fire a spell into the engine block and blow us up. Deepti wouldn't have to worry then.

Fuck her. Fuck them all.

My feet dragged, ragged bricks of flesh across the ground. I kept one eye squinted, watching the outline of the battered Honda until I could see through the windows. A fair-haired woman sat in the driver's seat, clenching and unclenching her fingers on the steering wheel. In the back, the guy Krista had maced slumped against the window, asleep or unconscious.

At the sight of us, the woman got out of the car and limped around it. A roll of duct tape glinted in her fingers.

That did it. A memory washed up in me, vivid with the curse of my eidetic memory. Mom, her wrists bound in duct tape, suspended from the boom of my Dad's sailboat. Her toes dragged the deck. Her flower-print bikini was spattered with blood, and she'd twisted the tape into crinkled ropes.

And me. Tiny and harmless, tucked in Gwydian's arms. I clung to him, not out of trust, but because he'd threatened to drop me off the back, drag me behind on a rope until I drowned.

And Dad. The bullet-hole in his shoulder. His blood on the deck. Held between a pair of Russians too big to be Sorcerers. He'd walked into that magic circle and surrendered his freedom. Gwydian—who could barely have been older than I was now—stroked my salt-stiff hair.

Like everything else in me now, rage was cold. No one would use me. Not Gwydian. Not the Guild.

I shoved my tongue into the open gap where my tooth had been, probed it. More blood. I opened up my magic, the turquoise flame leaping into my brain, catching up the image I held in my head.

The ripping sound of duct tape being pulled off the roll split the air. I opened my eyes, met the fair-haired woman's narrowed ones, and launched the fire spell into the Honda's engine block.

The front end of the car exploded. The shock wave knocked the fair-haired Sorcerer into me and blasted aside the men holding my arms. We hit ground, the woman twitching in that way only nerve damage made a person. I went to shove her off and felt hot blood. Shrapnel. Twisted plastic had cut straight into her spine. I locked down the horror. I'd killed before. I'd killed worse, just an hour ago.

I shoved the blond woman aside and rolled to my knees. The slicing spell glowed in my mind. Rangy gave a horrible gurgle and jerked back.

The rack of a pistol slide registered just in time. I threw myself onto the dead Sorcereress. The bullet caught my hair as it shot overhead. A hand found my calf. The Sorcerer clutched at my ankle, trying to immobilize me. I kicked backwards, heel meeting flesh. Then he was on me, pinning me over the dying woman, and shoving a gun against my head.

"I don't give a fuck what Gwydian-"

He never finished his sentence because there was a boxcutter in his throat. I knocked the gun aside with my elbow and slung my leg around his hip, forcing him off me even as he pawed at the weapon in his windpipe.

I staggered up. That was all of them. I snagged shoes off the dead woman's feet and a brown wool coat from Rangy's stiffening body.

There was a phone in it. A wide, shiny Samsung, now with a cracked casing. I shoved rigid feet into boots burning with body warmth, hating that the fire at my back felt so good.

Boxcutter wheezed, gurgled over the crackling flames. Black

smoke wafted against my back, replacing the smell of blood with gasoline and burning plastic. It caught up my hair, pushing it forward across my sticky face.

For a flash, I thought of what I must look like—a battered girl in a blood-soaked dress, surrounded by smoke and flame and dead Sorcerers. Around me, an idyllic farmhouse and snowy fields. Destruction. Complete and utter destruction. I'd blown up a car, killed four people. It had barely taken me a full minute.

Worse, was the burn of power through my veins, the thrum of blood and adrenaline, and the strange desire to laugh.

I was a valkyrie. A goddess of death. Mars, driving in on a chariot of carnage.

For just a moment, I breathed it in, let the blood magic run its course in me, easing the pain in my body and the bone deep chill of hypothermia. Then I swallowed, tasted iron, and began to shake.

Maybe Deepti was right. This power was too dangerous to be unchecked—like a nuke in some distant, secret warehouse. If I could destroy so much so easily, did I really have the right to be free?

Fuck, it was too much to answer. First, I needed to get my bearings. Get home.

I paused with my hand on the phone. Home. I pulled up the GPS and pointed myself toward Henard.

The last sanguimancer was dead, his hand stretched toward the glock. I shambled past the fallen gun and did not pick it up. I wouldn't need it.

CHAPTER TWENTY-SEVEN

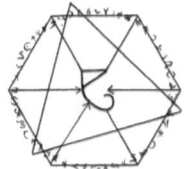

Henard was fifteen miles down the long dirt road. I made it three before spotting a familiar triangulation of evergreens, farmhouse, and grain elevator. I couldn't be certain it was the right place, but I didn't care anymore. The boots and coat did only so much, and I could feel bones grinding in my ribs each time I took too deep a breath.

Fire trucks and police cars tore past at intervals, all heading back the way I'd come. Each time, I hunkered down among the plowed rows, pulling the brown woolen coat over my head. If anyone saw me, they didn't stop. There was an ominous glow in the distance that suggested the fire still burned. Had it caught the house? There was too much snow for that. Too much distance between the house and the burning car. No, more likely the flames were persistent, magic-induced as they'd been.

Would water even work?

I turned down the driveway, feet dragging, and dialed the Ruff Patch number for the third time. No answer.

I hated that I didn't know Jaesung or Krista's phone numbers. They'd both entered them into my phone themselves, and I'd never thought to glance at the actual digits. Now my phone was so many pieces in the bottom of a trash can. Saliva stuck in my cold throat. I could feel my face swelling around the missing tooth—my gums already crowded out my tongue on that side, but I was too cold to pack snow against my cheek.

Alert bars popped up at the top of the screen. Facebook messages from someone named Reece wanting to know whether Joel was on his way back to Atlanta. I winced.

I didn't like thinking of the sanguimancers as having names, or a past, or anyone waiting for them to go home. It dredged up the salt in my eyes and made the conspicuous stickiness of my fingers feel like an accusation.

Facebook, though. That was an idea. Jaesung had the app on his phone. I didn't have an account. Before coming to Minnesota, I hadn't had friends to share it with.

I made it to the back side of the grain elevator and tucked myself into the shadows. Pulling up the app, I ran a search on Jaesung's name.

There were a few in South Korea, more scattered out across the US. I scanned the pictures, the cities, the Universities, and found him about six people down. His profile picture was Poo-Stank in a snap back and sunglasses, tongue lolling out. I tapped it, finding nothing more than profile picture changes. Everything else was locked down.

A noise near the front of the farmhouse had me scrambling to turn off the phone.

"-don't know, hun. I don't see it," a man's voice said. "Want me to go look? Jeepers. What's going on at the Fergusson's?"

I could have cursed. Clumsy. I'd thought it too late, too dark to see me. But the light from the cell phone must have been visible around the edge of the silo.

"Think that's what the sirens were all about?"

Shoes crunched on gravel. I breathed out slowly, knowing I looked suspicious. I didn't want anyone to see or connect me with the destruction at the other farm house. I glanced at the ladder. It had been so hard to climb this far. Still. If I could get up on it, I could see anyone coming for miles. And this was a lot of metal to amplify spells.

I shoved the phone in my coat pocket, grasped the ladder, and climbed. Within a few rungs, I knew it would be hell. The movement pulled at all the painful places on my ribs, opened the scabbed fronts of my thighs. My hands stuck to the rungs.

Headlights of a truck started up below. I nearly slipped from the ladder. A truncated gasp, and I caught myself, hugging close to the metal, terror throbbing in my ears. The truck pulled around the grain elevator, onto the long driveway between fields, and trundled off down the road.

They were checking on the neighbors. They hadn't seen me.

I was dizzy, out of breath, and on the verge of vomiting again. I clung to the ladder for several long moments, catching my breath and letting the dizziness ebb. I reached for the next rung, and the next, until I hauled myself onto the cross-hatched metal catwalk and curled, shivering, into a ball.

It took a few minutes to pull the phone back out. It was still on Jaesung's profile. I tapped on the message option.

It's Hel. Grabbed a phone.

I stopped typing, unsure of what to say next. I wasn't okay and I wasn't safe. I was freezing and beaten up and I didn't think I'd be able to get off this grain elevator by myself. If I stayed out here much longer, I wouldn't have the option. My fingertips were clumsy.

A set of ellipses formed at the bottom. Then words.

WHERE THE FUCK ARE YOU?

Before I could respond, three more messages appeared in quick succession.

Are you okay?
You disappeared and no one knew where you'd gone or what
happened.
Jesus Christ, where are you?

My eyes burned, blurring the touchscreen keyboard as I typed out a shaky reply.

Temp safe.
I'm where we watched the Leonids.
I got away.

I wanted to add that I was cold and battered and tired and that all I wanted was to curl up under his electric blanket and forget anything else existed.

On my way.

My hands shook. Jaesung was coming. I was ashamed at how much I'd hoped to read those words. The relief washing through my chest sent the tears out in full-force, carving hot lines down my frigid skin. My nose ran, and as I sniffed, I tapped out another message.

Don't bring Kris.

She's with Anita.

Ellipses came up again. I watched them, desperate for the words, my lifeline to him.

What's the number on the phone?

Nvmd. Call me.

He typed out his number, which came up underscored in blue.

Can't. Ppl awake.
There's a fire down the road.

Stay there.

I imagined him throwing himself in his pickup, cussing and still in the vestiges of his suit. His hair a wreck, that familiar fusion of anger and worry plastered over his face. *Jaesung is coming.*

I'm not sure when I fell asleep, or even how I managed it. All I knew was the cold, finally seeping through my skin, reaching down to bone. Chill fingers curled into my brain, sinking into the grooves, and held me under.

Until a hand was on my face. Hot palm, pushing aside my hair, skating over the wounds.

"Hel," he said. "Come on, baby, wake up. Come on. I can't carry you down."

It was like being drunk. I obeyed commands, opening my eyes and pushing myself upright. I swayed, and he was there, arms around me, cradling me to him.

Rough nylon harness scratched against my chest. I sank back into a half-sleep against his chest, ignoring the words in favor of the sound of his voice vibrating against my cheek.

Then he was working straps around my back, under my arms. Clipping me to him. He pulled me toward the edge of the catwalk. Every limb was weak and stupid, refusing to follow my commands. Somehow, I turned myself around, clung to the ladder as Jaesung held on behind me. He guided us down rung by rung.

I slipped four times, jerking Jaesung off the ladder twice. We swung, at the mercy of the safety line he repositioned every three rungs. When we made it to the bottom, I slumped into the wall of the grain elevator.

He gathered me in again. Words still made no sense. His hands closed around my face, cupped it so he could look into my eyes. I saw him take in the wreck, watched as he confirmed the worst. If my heart had not been as frozen as the rest of me, it might have broken.

"Let me take you to a hospital," he said. His voice was unsteady, like there was something in his throat. Like he was about to cry.

The words took a while to process, and when they did, I shook my head. "They'll find me," I tried to say. It didn't come out right. He didn't understand the words, but the head-shake was enough.

His hands went gentle on my face again, tracing along the cuts beneath my eye and the sticky mess on my chin. I saw the single heave of his chest before he turned away, scooped me against his side, and half carried me to the truck.

We rolled in silence down the main road, headlights dark. The heat was on full blast. I slumped against Jaesung, shivering and grateful for the solid warmth of another person.

No. Not *any* other person. Him. I'd wanted him. I couldn't keep lying to myself, thinking I could keep from loving him by refusing to acknowledge it.

He kept an arm tight around me and said nothing. Another firetruck and a police car passed us as we made our way back toward Henard. Finally, the town emerged from the darkness, street-lights filtering through evergreen.

"Not home," I said. He must have understood me this time.

"I'm not taking you home. They know where it is, I'm guessing, if they knew where the wedding was."

I nodded, fresh misery rolling into my head. I reached under his wool coat, desperate to get at something that felt less like padding and more like him. My fingers curled in his shirt.

He tightened his arm, and I pressed my face into his neck, which was hot against my skin. That's where I stayed, ignoring the stripes of streetlight and stoplight that flicked across my face.

We pulled into a parking lot behind a long two-story building. At Jaesung's urging, I slid from the car and into the frigid air. The heat had made me feel more human, but my extremities were still numb. There might have been frostbite on one of my feet, but I didn't have the strength to look just now.

I limped around to the back of the building, to a gray steel door, which he unlocked. Why did he have a key to a place like this?

"Where are we?" I asked.

He pulled open the door and helped me in. "Dance studio."

The place was dark, and smelled like old, dusty fabric. When Jaesung flicked on a light, I saw why: racks of costumes hung all around. Several lightbulb-surrounded mirrors set against the far wall, counters and chairs separated by flimsy dividers. Some of them had mannequin heads with wigs atop them. Others held boxes of makeup and taped pictures or handwritten notes.

I saw myself in one of those mirrors. Blood streaked my face. My hair was dark with all the blood and dirt and grease in it. The brown coat hung open, revealing the wrecked dress.

Jaesung seemed to notice only now it was covered in blood.

"Oh my god," he whispered. I sank into a chair, and he pushed the coat from my shoulders—a gentler echo of the way I'd undressed him earlier.

The suspenders were still on under his coat. I'd felt them.

"It's mostly not mine," I managed, but he seemed not to care. The scents of iron and gasoline and fire clogged my nose.

He kissed me. It was soft, lips barely brushing, but I felt his ragged breath. Long fingers brushed back into my hair, stroked my ears, my jaw, touching me with a restrained desperation he couldn't unleash.

"Jae," I whispered, almost afraid to startle him.

He caught my lips more securely. He had to be tasting blood. I had a missing molar.

"Jae," I said, firmer this time. I leaned back in the chair and he released me. A small streak of red had caught on his lip. He stared at me, brows knitted, face drawn and worried.

"Helena," he whispered. "I don't—what am I supposed to do?"

I shook my head. He slid his hands down my arms, catching my fingers in his. They were as stained as my face, maybe worse. A fingernail had split. Red seeped from the cracks.

I tried memorizing his face. Maybe Deepti was wrong and the image would stay with me, non-eroding like those memories from my childhood. I wanted this—something good to hang onto if the realization working its way to the surface destroyed us.

I had to tell Jaesung the truth. All of it. Which meant changing everything he knew about the world.

"I still have stuff to tell you," I said. My teeth were chattering.

"You don't need to tell me right this second. Let me.... Shit." He'd just put a hand on my scraped up thigh, eliciting a hiss of air through my teeth. Jerking it back, he grimaced, brushing his fingers over my shoulder instead. "Let me get you cleaned up first."

He trailed off, staring at my shoulder. For just a moment, I couldn't understand why. Then I saw the Hellhound bite. Horror kicked me in the chest. It was healed. Like I'd gotten it months ago.

Jaesung's face went gray. He looked from my shoulder to my face, dark eyes transitioning from confused to disturbed. He pulled his hand away.

"Jae," I tried to catch his hand and missed.

He shook his head, stood up, and stepped back. The room's air thickened. It was hard to breathe. He stared at me, expression closed, every muscle tensed.

"Jae, don't—just—I can-"

"What the hell is going on?" The question came out on a ragged rush of breath. His hand shook as he pointed to my scarred-up shoulder. "That was a wreck. Just a few hours ago. How the hell?"

"Sit down."

"I don't think.... But I touched it. It wasn't faked."

"Jae!" He snapped his eyes up, startled from the panic spiral. "Sit down," I repeated.

He was sucking in shallow breaths, shaking like I was back on that grain elevator. He reached for one of the vanity stools and sank into it, not taking his wide, frightened eyes off me. My chest ached, seeing him look at me that way. Then again, I'd killed five people tonight, one of them with a boxcutter to the trachea. Four with magic. He should be afraid. This was so far beyond his world.

"I was healed by magic."

No need to sugar coat it. It was better to get the truth out as quickly as possible, before he ran.

He didn't. Elbows to knees, he leaned his mouth against clasped hands and watched me over his fingers. There was no change to the expression in his eyes. Possibly, he was waiting for me to make sense. I took a breath, knowing it would only get weirder.

I told him. Clumsily, with several forays backward to add details I'd forgotten. He didn't move, didn't talk, and I could feel his opinions of me changing. He had to think I was crazy. Maybe it would be better to let him think it—a cleaner break. I'd be a dodged bullet. No one worth missing.

But I couldn't stand the idea of him thinking me crazy. Dangerous? Fine. I was dangerous. But I wasn't crazy. It was important he understood that.

"I can prove it," I whispered, when the silence became too much.

He leaned his face into his hands and rubbed it. Voice muffled, he spoke.

"Let's get you cleaned up. I don't know what all we have besides lambs wool and tape, but...." He stood, heading for a closet with yet more racks of costumes and supplies.

He didn't believe me. Of course he didn't.

"I know this sounds insane, and it's easier to write it off than change what you know of-"

"It doesn't matter," he said. He sounded exhausted.

"It does!" I insisted, forcing myself to stand, despite the pain in my body. "I've got to leave. The Guild wants to lock me up and the Lochlys want me dead or enslaved. I'll be out of your life—don't worry. But I can't stand you remembering me as a crazy person. I want you to know the truth, so you know I'm not leaving because I want to."

He paused, and I watched the tension in his back. He took a deep breath, shook his head, and went back to the boxes of markers and makeup and canvas shoes.

Something in my core cracked, fissuring out like the floor of the auto garage under enemy spells.

Jaesung had wanted the truth for months. I'd known it would be too much, but I couldn't let him go on without knowing the danger forcing me away.

I let him dig for his lambs wool and tape. There was no graceful way to prove this, so I would have to do it ungracefully. I reached behind me, unzipped the dress to my waist. Had things gone differently tonight, it might have been him doing that instead of me. We might be back at Ruff Patch, under his electric blanket, or warm enough not to need it. Not in the costume room of a dance studio.

I still had power left. I'd used the bounty hunters' blood, not my store. Not all of it, anyway. I clenched my teeth, and the ruined dress slipped to the floor.

I sent power into the tattoo on my good shoulder and braced for the discomfort of transforming injured. The scabs on my legs cracked, and the ripples of fur shooting from my skin stung like a bitch. I fell forward onto fingers that shrank back and thickened into paws.

When it was over, I shook out of underwear and boots. I could taste Jaesung's anxiety, and I knew I was only about to make it worse.

When he turned around, he jumped, dropping the box in his hands, and backed up into a shelf.

"What the f-" he looked around, as if I might step out from behind one of the costume racks.

I barked, nudged the dress, and picked it up in my teeth. With a soft whine of pain, I transformed back, clutching the ruined dress to me the second I had hands. That bit was more for Jaesung's comfort than mine. Considering the transformation itself, I wasn't sure throwing naked girl into the mix wouldn't send him over the edge.

I'd been ready for him either to pass out or throw up. Instead, he sat down, right there in the supply closet next to a rack of costumes labeled "Midsummer Night's Dream". He covered his face with his hands, breath unsteady.

I took a step forward, but his hand shot out, palm toward me to keep me back.

It hurt, but I understood. Gang member was one thing. Shapeshifter, stuck in the middle of a magical game of Cops and Murderers, was different.

I couldn't make myself put on the dress. Luckily, there were more than just costumes on these racks. I found a pair of leggings and tugged them on, pulling an enormous renaissance-looking shirt overtop and belting it with shaky fingers. No socks, but I found leg warmers and shoved them into the boots with my feet, then pulled the brown wool coat back on.

Jaesung shifted to his knees, then climbed shakily to his feet. I froze, unsure of whether to say anything, or even what to say if I tried. After all that explanation, it seemed I'd lost my command of words.

He still trembled, probably in shock, but when he finally met my eyes, the fear was gone. We looked at each other, for the first time completely aware of who we were looking at. I felt more naked than I had before pulling the clothes on, but I refused to let myself regret telling him.

If he accepted me, it would be with all the facts. If he didn't, at least I knew why.

Finally, his arm moved. In a halting gesture, he lifted the backs of his fingers to my jaw, brushing over my bruises. I saw him swallow.

"I know where you can go."

CHAPTER TWENTY-EIGHT

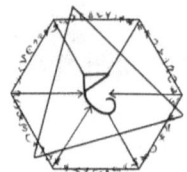

The streets were too empty. I settled low in the passenger's seat of Jaesung's truck, wincing with every bump and turn. Outside, sallow streetlights bled onto sand and slush, and black pines striped the sides of dark-windowed buildings. Snow still lay thick on the borders of the road, eerie and unblemished.

I didn't like the quiet. Something about it felt volatile, like there was danger in the shadows, holding its breath. The first familiar landmarks only set me more on edge.

"They'll have someone watching the house," I said, resurrecting the argument we'd had climbing into the car. "Or they will, if they're alive."

"Which is why I'm grabbing stuff, not you," Jaesung said. He put a hand out, waving me lower in the seat. "Might need to get on the floor in case they're up high."

"That sounds easy and not painful at all." I unbuckled and shifted forward. The scabs forming on my legs cracked, bleeding into the lumps of lambs wool taped across my thighs. The floor was wet with melted slush from my boots, and it soaked through my leggings in cold splotches.

I wrapped my arms around my knees and huddled in the coat. Jaesung's legs stretched beside me, foot moving on the gas pedal. He hadn't even changed out of his stupid, shiny shoes. For some reason, this set my eyes to burning.

I hadn't touched him since telling him the truth—I'd left the question of contact up to him. This time, I couldn't help it. I snuck a hand across the seat, putting it just above his knee. He didn't pull away, and I could only hope that was tacit welcome. It was comforting just to confirm the existence of another person with touch.

His muscles flexed under my palm as we accelerated and slowed, until he pulled into a parking spot down the street from Ruff Patch. With a low, "be right back," he slipped from the truck and locked the doors behind him.

I huddled in the footwell, out of sight, and tried not to listen to the whisper of my own thoughts in the silence.

Chicago. My only impression of it was wind, tracks, and concrete, plus the big station where I'd cried for Mom so many weeks ago. Jaesung planned to take me to the suburb where he'd grown up, since his mother was in Henard for the wedding. I could crash and recuperate, gather my resources and form a new plan. On the other hand, potentially leading the bounty hunters to Jaesung's family was a stupid risk, and one I shouldn't have been willing to take.

Shouldn't, only here I was—doing nothing to stop it. I could have hot-wired the truck. It was an old fucker, and though I was now short one boxcutter, Jae kept a box of tools behind the seats.

I wanted him with me. I'd finally gotten too weak to deny it. The thought of facing the next days alone made me want to return to the farmhouse and toss myself onto that burning car, just to stop the ache.

Time crept by, and though I leaned my head into the seat, I didn't dare let myself doze. I couldn't afford to let sleep slow me down if we got attacked. But twenty minutes went by without Jaesung. Then thirty.

By forty minutes, he hadn't answered the two texts I'd sent him.

Either he was spending way too long picking out which boxers he wanted to bring, or something was wrong. Or maybe he was just calling the police to let them know there was a crazy, magic-wielding shapeshifter in his truck.

I unlocked the doors and slipped out, skulking through the shadows as well as my injuries allowed. My neck prickled, though I could no longer tell whether it was from cold or uneasiness.

I pushed open the office door and slipped inside.

A low, soft rumble vibrated in the dark—a growl. My hand went for the light. Panic shot up my spine as I bent my knees, prepped for another bounty hunter.

The light flooded on, earning a bark from one of the smaller dogs. Poo-stank growled in his kennel, standing over a dark-clad form, slumped against the bars.

Jaesung, gagged and handcuffed, shouted something muffled just in time.

A spell shot from the darkness.

I dropped into a crouch. My legs screamed. The sapphire mandala splashed against the wall and solidified into a net of energy, trapping a metal pencil-holder.

"I've got a proposition for you, sweetheart."

The familiar voice only made me drop my guard a trifle.

Isaac stepped from the shadow of the stairs and into the disc of light pouring through the plexiglass circle above. His face had a long streak of blood across the jaw, and most of his left side appeared to have been recently on fire, but the gun leveled at my chest was steady.

"You usually do," I said. "And I usually say no. But why not—let's hear it."

He didn't look amused. In fact, his face was sourer than I'd ever seen it. "Heard you were skipping town. Thought I'd come along."

"No."

"Let me rephrase," he said. "I'm coming along, or I'm explaining to Deepti that you used sanguimancy to kill those four rogues."

My mouth went dry, but I could think of nothing to say to that.

"You know it leaves a residue," he said. "It was all over that farmhouse."

Poo-stank growled louder as I rose from my crouch. It was ten feet across to the first kennel, and only if I leapt straight over the examination tables. The likelihood of me getting to Jaesung before Isaac shot was slim to none.

"This doesn't have to be another fight, Martin. You've got bigger problems than me. Gwydian is coming, and he won't stop coming till you're dead. You're gonna have to face him, and your best weapon is in here." He tapped his head. "Which means you need more spells and—if the state of that fire out in the county is any sign—control."

"So Deepti sent you to babysit?"

"Call it what you want. You need my help. Especially if you're taking Tinkerbell over there with you."

Jaesung gave a slow, unimpressed blink.

I narrowed my eyes at Isaac. "Put away the gun and we'll talk."

He thought about it a moment, then stowed the weapon in a side-holster.

"You said I need more spells," I said. "Are you going to show me?"

"I figure you ought to learn something that isn't a fire-geyser."

I gave him a wary look. "And you're, what, expecting me to let you tag me first?"

Isaac rubbed at the ridge of his eye socket, heaving a sigh that was half growl. "We thought we'd have enough time for all that. Turns out we don't. We can't guarantee we'll protect you from Gwydian. He's pointed his whole network at you."

Dread swooped in my belly. "That's a lot of bounty hunters."

"Yeah. And according to Guild Hunters spread out down the coast, your friends from the other night weren't the only ones with a pet Hellhound."

I winced, forcing the implications of that to the back of my mind. My pack couldn't be priority right now. I had to think about my own survival.

"So. You're suggesting we skip town and go all master-apprentice until Gwydian catches up?"

Isaac shrugged, but his gaze slid sideways a fraction. I narrowed my eyes.

"That's not why, is it? Ah." I nodded, a bitter smile curving onto my lips. "I get it. Teaching me is a cover—that's why you're not worried about tagging me yet. I'm not the goal right now. I'm bait."

Isaac watched me, arms crossed. He seemed to consider me, deciding what amount of truth would be just enough to placate me.

"I know how this works," I said. I glanced at the kennel, where Jaesung had quieted Poo-stank and watched us with a sharp, suspicious look. "We leave them out of it, except for someone to keep them safe. I've dragged these guys into enough trouble. It stops now."

Isaac sucked in air through his teeth. "Actually, we're taking Tinkerbell with us. Insurance."

"Like hell you are." I tried to duck around the steel table, but the movement was too much for my weary legs. Isaac blocked me.

"Easy, Martin. Like you said—you know how this works," he said. I kicked. Pain made me slow and the movement left me off balance. I wobbled, and Isaac caught me across the chest as I overbalanced forward.

I grunted, pain sparkling behind my eyes. Thin, cool fingers found the nape of my neck, traced a mandala there. I worked on my breathing, relatively certain the mandala he drew would heal, though it was hard to discern the exact glyphs.

Jaesung grunted something. His voice sounded worried. Not for himself, but for me. The idiot.

"I'm fine," I whispered. A moment later, when sapphire magic made a brilliant glow, silhouetting me and Isaac against the wall, it was almost true.

"I'm not the healer Mia was," he said. I clenched my teeth at the past-tense. "But that's got you a few days along—whoa, kid. Yeah. Forgot to mention it'll take it out of you."

My knees had given out. Isaac's arm across my stomach was all that kept me upright. I shook all over, vision swimming, gut as empty and ravenous as a Hellhound. He lowered me to the concrete. I slumped back against the column.

The pain had faded. My face no longer throbbed, and the tightness of scabs across my thighs told me healing had begun there too.

I forced my head up. It took a lot of effort to open my eyes and glare at Isaac.

"You did that to weaken me."

He smirked, and I knew I was right. Then he turned to the kennel, fishing a key ring from his coat pocket.

"Leave him out of it," I said, voice tremulous with exhaustion. "I already said I'd go along with it." An image had swum up in my mind. Dad, stepping into that enslavement circle because Gwydian had Mom and me. Would I go back to that life—or worse—if he had Jaesung at his mercy?

Then again, if Gwydian already knew about my friends, would they be safer left behind with a few Guild protectors, or with me, and the larger force of Sorcerers?

"Hel, don't." Jaesung must have gotten free of the gag. I tried to look up, but my head weighed a thousand pounds.

"It ain't like she can argue with you right now, Sugar Plum," Isaac said.

"Unlike some people, I care what *she* wants," Jaesung said.

"Bitch is K.O. What's she gonna do?"

"Call her a bitch again, *bitch*."

Isaac raised an eyebrow and pointed back and forth between himself and Jaesung. "Which one of us is handcuffed in a dog pen?"

Jae had no witty response for that.

Isaac unlocked the kennel. Poo-stank had been leashed to the back, because he lunged at Isaac and came up short.

"Stanky, hey! Stank!" Jaesung said, and gave a sharp whistle. Poo-stank backed up, head low and ready for the attack. He still growled, shoving his furry body into Jaesung's as if to herd him behind.

Jae stood, the chain connecting his cuffs rattled against the door.

For the second time, he glared down at Isaac, contempt twitching his lip.

"S'matter, Tinkerbell?" Isaac said, unlocking the cuffs. He seemed unperturbed by the height disparity, and that Jaesung was making threats with his whole body. One cuff sprang open, and Jaesung freed himself from the kennel door, rubbing his wrist.

Isaac jerked his chin in my direction, and the next moment, Jaesung was there, long legs bent as he knelt in front of me. His hands went to my face, brushing back hair and checking injuries. My breath was coming short and fast as I fought to stay awake.

His thumb dragged across a lip that had been split five minutes ago.

"See?" Isaac said. "Didn't hurt her. Now you can grab all that shit you packed and come on. You said Chicago, right?"

"Yeah," Jaesung said. His dark eyes met mine, and I shook my head, trying one last time to warn him off. "We can't go just yet, though."

Isaac lifted his hands and dropped them in frustration. "What the fuck is it now?"

In one graceful movement, Jaesung stood, pivoted, and brought his fist across Isaac's face.

The Sorcerer went down, twisting with the force of the hit. He landed on his hands and knees, conscious, and undoubtedly wishing he wasn't. Jaesung shook out his hand, grimacing even as satisfaction rolled off him. "Now we can go."

When he bent to slide an arm around my back, I clenched a fist in his shirt and tried for a smile. A flicker of a return smile ghosted his face.

I knew I should tell him to run, to leave while Isaac was down, not willingly come along as collateral. But the truth was, I wanted him with me.

He finally knew everything. He had proof I was a shape-shifter, a magic-user, and a fugitive from two separate groups of deadly Sorcerers. His whole world had changed in the past few hours, and still he pulled me against his side, supporting my unsteady shamble all the way back to the truck.

I couldn't believe Jaesung wanted to stay with me, but he did, and that changed everything.

~

I slept almost the entire drive to Chicago. Wedged as I was between Jaesung and Isaac, it should have been more uncomfortable, but I was used to Jaesung's smooth driving, and his arm around me was the anchor I needed to feel calm. As much as I hated to admit it, Isaac's presence helped. He was grumpy, and likely disposed to letting Jaesung get singed were it to come to a magic battle, but I wouldn't have slept so soundly without someone there to keep an eye out for sanguimancers.

We stopped at a gas station in Eau Claire, Wisconsin, where Isaac forced two cokes and a rubbery breakfast burrito on me, followed by a bag of powdered donuts.

I don't remember how many I made it through before the tears leaked out, but the last several tasted like salt. Jaesung's hand rubbed my arm, hugging me to him as we pulled onto the highway again. I slept.

The next time we stopped, the world sounded different. The loud hum of highway and bright slash of passing headlights were absent. Instead, I opened my eyes to a garage door creaking open, and the muted sunlight of an overcast morning.

My throat was dry. I sat up, woozy and with a mouth that tasted like lambs wool. Isaac, one elbow pressed against the window, blinked heavily. Had he fallen asleep? It made sense—he'd fought too.

"Home sweet home," Jaesung said. He slid out of the driver's seat. I scooted over and waved off his help. I needed to show Isaac I could stand, even if doing so made me nauseated.

We climbed the small set of stairs into the laundry room of what turned out to be a tiny two-story townhouse. The kitchen and den were a single room, with just enough space for the standing piano where Jaesung's mother taught lessons.

Isaac lifted his eyebrows. "This place is too clean."

Jaesung shrugged, but I privately echoed the sentiment. There were fresh vacuum tracks in the carpet, and the pictures lined up on the back of the piano seemed to have been dusted recently.

Across the living room, I couldn't quite see the smaller pictures, but there was one of a younger Jaesung in a basketball uniform, and another of him as a kid, looking mischievous while wearing what I could only guess was a school uniform. The street behind him in that picture looked strange. There were wide, brick sidewalks lined with potted greenery at regular intervals, and far too many power lines criss-crossing above. Then I spotted the yellow and white symbols painted on the street behind him. They were in Korean.

It must have been a street in Seoul. The little uniform, with its plaid shorts and white-piped navy blazer, might have been the cutest thing I'd ever seen. It was weird to look at those pudgy cheeks and slightly evil grin and compare it to the lean, dark man beside me. He hadn't worn glasses at that age. He was still wearing his contacts now. I missed his glasses.

Jaesung dropped his keys into a dish on the kitchen island and ran a hand backwards over his head. A pang of guilt stabbed my chest as I noted the dark shadows under his eyes. He'd been up for more than a day. After all the intensity of the wedding, then worrying and looking for me, having his understanding of reality shattered, and driving six or more hours from Henard to suburban Chicago. I bumped his arm with my shoulder. He wound it around me.

"You look like shit," I said.

"You're welcome," he replied, correctly interpreting my meaning.

Isaac popped his neck and drummed his fingers on the kitchen counter. "I'm gonna set wards. You got any salt?"

Jaesung stifled a yawn. "Like, table salt?"

"Sea salt works better, but table salt's fine."

"Cabinet over the stove. Knock yourself out."

Isaac grunted and went to the range. Jaesung turned his head toward me and mouthed, "Salt?" I shrugged. Salt-water worked to amplify magic, but I wasn't sure why, or how to explain that to Jaesung.

He dragged me to a narrow set of carpeted stairs lined with more pictures. I caught flashes of family members and pictures of Jaesung in a variety of costumes and ballet poses. The most striking appeared to be a page from a magazine.

The photographer had caught him mid-leap against a black background, legs at full extension. He looked out along the line of one arm, with the other curved strong over his head.

He was shirtless and barefoot, the tights leaving no curve of muscle to the imagination. Even young, his legs were powerful, chest and shoulders only slightly thinner than they were now.

The bottom corner had a small caption that read: *Jae Sung Park, 17 - Chicago High School for the Arts.*

They'd photoshopped out his scars.

I didn't have time to dwell on the feelings that surfaced when I saw the smooth shoulders, the struggles they'd erased, or why I found it so offensive. He was continuing up the stairs ahead of me, drawn by the siren song of bed.

At the top of the stairs, he turned left, and opened the door into a tiny bedroom. I followed him in, taking in the neat twin bed with its gray and red comforter, the bookshelf that held basketball and track trophies wedged between sci-fi paperbacks. His desk was empty except for a picture frame and a small, potted cactus.

"You want a shower?"

His voice was startling in the quiet. I nodded. Being clean right now sounded like the best thing in the world. He motioned me down the hall to a small bathroom, pulled a towel from under the sink, and gestured to the tub. "Toothbrush and stuff is downstairs. I'm... gonna crash, I think."

"Okay. Do you want me to..." I searched for the right way to ask where he expected me to sleep. "I mean, I don't want to wake you up coming in."

He shook his head, hand twitching dismissively. "It won't matter —I'll either be dead to the world or freaking the fuck out, so just come in when you're done."

There was still a slight bruise on his wrist from the handcuffs, and I touched it. "I never meant to drag you into my mess."

"I know."

"I was going to leave."

"I know."

"If you knew the truth, I didn't think you'd want me to stay."

He sighed, and I glanced up. Weariness hung on his face. His eyes were serious and uncertain. "*You*, I want. The rest of it... is sort of on lock down. I'm not dealing with it right now; it's too big."

"Yeah." Without command, my hand drifted to his chest, where his heart pulsed against his sternum. The warm depression between muscles fit my hand. I wasn't used to wanting to touch people, or giving in to that want.

He pressed his hand over mine, cupped the back of my head in his other, and bent. I rose to meet him, and though the kiss was soft and over far too soon, some of the anxiety in my body settled.

I spent an eternity in the shower. The water ran black and red around my feet. It took several applications of shampoo to get the smell of charred car from my hair. Shreds of lambs wool stuck in the scrapes on my thighs, which, thanks to Isaac, were shedding the scabs in favor of new, pink skin. I had to sit on the side of the tub and rub with a wash-cloth, wincing and hissing, to get them all, but once my skin was clear, I felt better.

Jaesung forgot to pack me anything to sleep in. I dug out a pair of his pajama bottoms and pulled them on with a sweatshirt. I brushed my teeth, wincing as the bristles delved into the gap where my missing molar had been. It had been too cold for my face to swell, but I still had bruises. The pallid girl in the mirror was little more than a wraith of my former self, and I couldn't look at her long.

I slipped into Jaesung's room like a cautious cat. His blinds were drawn against midday sun, casting the room into artificial dusk. I couldn't tell if Jaesung was asleep, lying there with one arm over his eyes. He didn't fit well in his bed. The mattress was too short for him, and the comforter struggled to stay on his feet.

I crept over and lifted the covers. He stirred, then moved toward the wall so I could slide in. My legs ached, and my ribs felt worse. A deep twinge in my shoulder said there were far too many parts of me still recovering from the Hellhound fight to have suffered a second round of injury and healing.

As I scootched into bed, his arms came around me. I settled into him. My head rested heavy against his shoulder, and his chin pressed into my forehead.

It was not romantic. Not really. There was something desperate and afraid in the way he clung to me, heart thudding against my cheek. I reached for his hair, drawing my nails across his scalp like I would for any of the dogs that needed calming. His breath stayed shaky for a long time. When it relaxed, the tension in his body slowly followed suit.

I thought he'd fallen asleep. Then, into the motes of dusty sunlight creeping up the wall, he spoke.

"You know how you said the world needs more good cops?"

I nodded. His hand found my damp hair, fingers grazing the back of an ear. "I think the world needs more good Sorcerers."

CHAPTER TWENTY-NINE

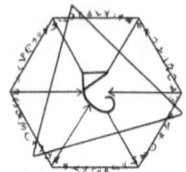

I woke around five in the afternoon. Cool dusk light had replaced gold, and my wet hair had halfway dried, leaving a humid spot on the pillow when I lifted my head. We'd moved apart in sleep, seeking more comfortable resting positions, and Jaesung didn't stir as I extricated myself from the tiny bed.

I dug through my duffel, pausing as my fingers fell on something sharp-edged and hard. I tugged it out. It was the picture of my parents. I sucked in my lip and withdrew the sketchbook from Krista, the sweater from Sanadzi and Eugene, and my little piece of sea glass.

My throat throbbed. How had he known exactly what to grab? It made me wonder what he might take if he knew he might never come back. Family mementos, necessities? I wanted to call it sentimental, and maybe it was, but I would have hated to lose those things—my touchstones to friends and family I'd lost or might lose.

The scent of frying meat wafted up the stairs, setting my mouth to watering. I pulled on jeans and the sweater and slipped downstairs.

Isaac might have been an asshole, but he was an asshole with an unexpected talent for food. Stepping into the kitchen, I was greeted by the sight of skinny, freckled arms slinging a spatula. Bacon draining on a paper towel-covered plate.

He glanced back at me and jerked his bruised chin in greeting. I quirked an eyebrow at the sweet smell of whatever he was frying now.

"French toast?" He sent me a thumbs up. I leaned against the island and filched a piece of bacon. "But you're wearing a Marilyn Manson tee shirt."

"What, so I can't like good food?"

"There's powdered sugar on your jeans."

He shrugged, attempting to dust the white handprint from his thigh. "Given the amount of magic I use on a daily basis, I had to learn to fucking cook or spend all my money on fast food." He poked a slice of bread swimming in a pan of some yellow, eggy mixture by the stove. "Also, fun fact: magic doesn't cancel out cholesterol."

"Noted."

We were silent for several minutes during which he fried more toast and I peered out the kitchen window into the back yard. It was snowing again, gentle flakes fluttering down to collect on the windowsills and birdhouses next door. It was awkward, being alone with Isaac, and from the tension in his back, he felt the same way.

"So, what are you going to teach me? Is this going to be boot camp, or a wax-on, wax-off sort of thing?"

Isaac snorted, sliding French toast onto a plate and shoving it onto the island. "Neither. It's a sit-down-and-memorize-shit thing. Maybe a little of practical application, but there ain't much of a back yard in this place."

We ate, and I accepted an iron pill. Just as I was contemplating hunting through the cabinets for something caffeinated, Jaesung appeared. He'd showered and changed into track pants and a loose gray shirt. He and Isaac met eyes, but didn't speak, even when Jaesung helped himself to the leftover French toast and the two slices of bacon we'd set aside.

"Mom doesn't buy bacon," he said at last.

"I had a delivery," Isaac said, gesturing me to the couch. "Got your sketch pad, Martin?"

I retrieved it and joined Isaac leaning over the coffee table. To my surprise, he leaned back and looked at Jaesung, his face blank.

"You Chinese?"

The question startled me but Jaesung didn't look surprised by it. Annoyed, but not surprised. "Korean," he grumbled. "What are you, a leprechaun?"

"But you use the Chinese characters, right?"

Jaesung looked at me, his expression somewhere between confused and annoyed. "We have our own phonetic writing, but we use them, yeah."

"Cool, so the order of strokes in the characters is important, right?"

"Ostensibly. Not everyone cares."

"Where do you think that comes from?"

Deadpan, Jaesung answered. "A pathological need for control achieved through a culture obsessed with organization."

Isaac blinked.

"He's a sociology student," I said.

"Magic," Isaac said. "The Chinese were some of the first to figure it out."

Jaesung lifted a hand. "Is anyone surprised?"

Isaac motioned for me to open the sketchbook. He hunched over the pad and drew a trio of vertical lines. "Each stroke shows the magic where to go, what form to take, and what direction to leave. Take this one." He glanced back at Jaesung, pointing the marker at the character.

"*Cheon*," Jaesung said. "River."

"It goes at the middle of a mandala that's built like a circuit—keeps magic flowing through it." He drew a circle next, with a line through the center. "This one means sun."

Jaesung grimaced. "Like a thousand years ago. It's changed."

Isaac waved a hand at him. "Shut up, Park. Anyway, this one is in a bunch of the mandalas we use to cast light or heat."

"Maybe people without magic simplified things," Jaesung said aloud. "After all, we muggles don't need that many strokes. God. Taiwan must be full of Sorcerers."

Isaac cast a glare back over his shoulder. "Can I continue my lesson?"

"Depends. You owe, like, twenty bucks to the racist jar."

Isaac rolled his eyes. "I don't have time to pamper your injured feelings. In case you missed it, there's a sanguimancer from a murderous family of Scottish druids after your girlfriend."

"Can you both stop?" I said. "Isaac, stop being a dick if you can. Jae, I know he's a dick, but it's hard enough to let myself listen to him without you antagonizing him into new heights of assholery."

Both of them scowled, and Jaesung looked liked he wanted to argue. Instead, he lifted his eyebrows at Isaac and set about loading the dishwasher, loudly.

Isaac rubbed one tattooed forearm and jerked a thumb back at Jaesung, dropping his voice to a murmur. "Is it cause he rescues dogs?"

"Huh?"

"You actually like Tinkerbell over there."

It wasn't a question. I sat straighter, gripping the marker tight, uncomfortable with the thought that Isaac wanted to know anything about my private life.

"Yeah," I admitted. "I do. Unlike some people, he's not trying to kill or enslave me."

"You women and your impossible standards."

His grin was a slash of mockery. "Are you going to teach me mandalas or not?"

He flipped to a new page in my sketchbook. Freehand, he drew a nearly perfect circle.

"Mandalas are constructed to direct the flow of power toward the middle. The outer ring denotes the edges of the circuit, and the cardinal points," he drew four smaller circles at north, south, east, and west, "anchor the power within that circle. The shape of the effect is always determined by the glyphs within this outer circle. I'm sure you've seen spells fly in bolts or in discs or shards."

I nodded. Isaac continued, "The pattern is created by the way power flows inward from here to light up the next ring."

"Okay, so if that were the case, shouldn't most mandalas look the same on the outer rings?"

Isaac nodded. "You'd think so. Unfortunately, people got their own ways of creating effects. It's like how everybody figured out that sharp things on sticks made good weapons, but nobody made them the same fucking way. And bitches got to tinkering. Anyway, the effects of the spells responded better to some techniques than others. It's pretty much impossible to figure out without some serious theory."

"And that's why it's so hard to figure out spells just by looking at them. Because there are thousands of ways they could match up with the inner glyphs."

"And thousands of ways they could blow you to bite-size for a maggot."

A dish clanked loudly in the washer, followed by a quiet curse. Isaac quirked an eyebrow, shook his head, and drew another circle inside the first.

"The middle rings, however many there are, are like the spell's DNA. They decide the medium the power will take, whether that's an element or a different kind of energy, and how it will affect the target. For something like fire, you wouldn't have to specify that. Fire burns. No shit. But say you want to transform a girl into a big-ass dog?" He flicked my shoulder. "That's gonna need some intricate coding."

I leaned away from him, bristling at the touch. He lifted his hands in a placating gesture.

"So the middle is where you specify direction?" I asked, ready for this part of the lesson to be over.

Isaac looked surprised. "You know this shit already?"

"No, but it makes sense to give yourself a way to aim."

"Clever girl," Isaac said. I gave him a sour smile. "You can think of the middle like crosshairs on a scope. You line up your target. It you want the spell to shoot out as an attack, you draw it in the air, make this mark-" he sketched a shape "-and overload the circuit. The power will take the exit you give it. If it's an embedded spell like a ward or a shapeshifting spell, you push power into the circuit until it's at capacity, then close it off with a central glyph. Remember river?"

I sat back against the couch, absorbing the information. The construction of mandalas had always been a foreign language, one where I knew a few words but not enough to speak or understand. Now, as I recalled the forms of the spells I'd memorized, I could analyze their parts.

"It's all about the order of flow," Isaac continued, sketching a simple, three-ring mandala. "Like a human heart—you've got your chambers and valves and veins and arteries, and if just one thing messes up, the whole system stops working right. Spells are like that."

"Speaking of ways to die," I said. "Is this really the way we should go about this?" I waved a hand at the sketchbook. "Shouldn't I be practicing spells or something?"

"On what, the neighbors?" Isaac's brows knitted, knee jittering as he spoke. "Nah, there's not enough space around here, especially with some of the spells I'm giving you. And I don't want you wasting your magic by firing at trees."

"So I'm going to spend the next however many days...?"

"Memorizing the mandalas I give you, eating lots of meat, and generally making your peace with the idea of maybe not dying."

I didn't want it to, but that made me laugh. Partly because it was so true. I hadn't really considered life after Gwydian, and the thought of it even now felt forbidden. My smile faded.

The possibility of making it through was slim, and the idea that even Isaac was trying to give me hope just convinced me it was unlikely.

"Yo, Park," Isaac said. He'd stopped calling Jaesung Tinkerbell to his face, probably due to the bruise still dark on his freckled cheek.

Jaesung looked up from filling the kettle.

"You got any old silver jewelry?"

"Old... what? Not that I know of."

"Come on, your mom's got to have something."

Jaesung set the kettle on its base and flicked the boil switch. "Why?"

"Because I'm casing the joint for a low-level robbery. Nah, see these?" He held up his be-ringed fingers. "They've got spells etched into them. Some are personal shields, and some let me fire off certain spells faster. Martin doesn't need the latter, but we usually tattoo the shielding spells. Figured she doesn't want a sewing-needle tat."

"Not so much," I confirmed. Jaesung dug out his high school ring which, despite being bulky and half black with oxidation, seemed to suit Isaac's purposes. I drew mandalas over and over, my stomach growing tighter as I tried not to imagine what I would see when Gwydian showed up.

How many members of my pack had he recaptured? Had any of them been re-enslaved like Morgan, or had he turned all the rest into Hellhounds?

And then the questions Isaac had evoked: could I survive this? And what the hell would I want if I did? There was no way I could settle into a normal life. As much as I wanted what my friends had, there was too much instinct anchoring me to the life I had now. Even if I killed Gwydian and, by some miracle, survived, the Guild would never leave me alone.

And now, I'd made it impossible for Jaesung to go back to living in ignorance of magic.

I remembered my first impression of him—that day on the train, when he and Krista had been scoring passers by. He'd seemed harm-less, way too clean and way too normal to ever be a part of my life. And yet here I was, sitting in the living room of the home where he'd spent his teens, preparing to meet Gwydian head-on.

If I made it through this, I would have to make it up to him.

CHAPTER THIRTY

W hen Jaesung's phone rang the next morning, all of us were slumped in the living room, preparing. Isaac was filing off the raised date on Jaesung's ring, I was memorizing mandalas, and Jaesung was fiddling around on his laptop.

We all looked at the phone vibrating toward the edge of the coffee table. The displayed name was in Korean. Jaesung lunged for it.

"*Yeboseyo?*" he said, voice falsely calm.

I heard the shouting from three feet away. Jaesung jerked the phone from his ear and held it away, eyes going wide at the onslaught of enraged language. He tried to interrupt several times, but the woman on the other end spoke over his frantic Korean until, at last, he switched into English.

"Jesus, Mom. No, we did *not* elope!"

I jumped, and Isaac laughed. Jaesung covered the receiver, shooting him a glare as the shrieking started off again. "Mom? Mom!"

He gave a frustrated groan and set aside his laptop, taking the phone with him upstairs.

Isaac cackled. "Lover boy's in trouble."

"At least he's still got a mom," I snapped back.

Isaac went back to filing the ring.

It was twenty minutes before Jaesung came back down, and I could tell by the state of his hair that the conversation had not gone well. I winced in his direction, trying to express how sorry I was to have fucked things up without saying it in front of Isaac. He caught my eyes, gave a little shrug as if it was no big deal that he'd ditched a wedding and disappeared, and dropped into the chair he'd vacated earlier.

"Are we married?" I asked.

He tilted his head against the back of the chair. "Jury's out."

"Okay," Isaac said, holding up the ring. "Time to etch this fucker."

I'd wondered how he would do it. He chose a fine-tipped sharpie from the pile of writing utensils and, with a steady hand, drew a tiny mandala on the broadest part of the band. The messenger bag he'd brought contained a small bag of crystals that looked like drugs, but emitted a metallic smell in water.

"Ferrous nitrate. Don't touch this shit—it's acid," he said, and dropped the ring in.

"The sharpie works?" I asked, leaning away.

"Yep. It's a resist coating. Protects the metal. Thank you studio art degree."

Jaesung gave him a sharp look. "I find it suspect that you call me Tinkerbell when you have a liberal arts degree."

Isaac shrugged. "All the dance majors I knew sucked cock no matter what they had in their tackle box."

"Now you owe the homophobia jar too. You're really racking up debt, Ike."

I pressed the heels of my hands against my eyes and willed the boys to shut up. I was no longer used to broken sleep and strange hours—the past few weeks had spoiled me in that regard—and the last few hours of memorizing mandalas had transformed my brain into a fried mess. My eyes throbbed in their sockets.

"We should call it a night," Jaesung said. "Eat something, head up to bed. I can't make French toast, but I can boil a mean bowl of ramen."

I sank onto the couch as Isaac stepped outside for a cigarette, leaving Jaesung and I to sip at our ramen. Jaesung had added frozen peas and carrots, a boiled egg, and a drizzle of spicy oil.

I finished my noodles and the egg first, then sat sipping broth and letting it warm me all the way through.

"I've been thinking," Jaesung said. With those three words, my stomach dropped. No one ever started with that if they had something good to say, and my mind was coughing up a thousand scenarios in which he left me behind, or asked me to leave when it was all over.

I took a sip of broth to wet my suddenly dry mouth and tried to sound casual.

"Thinking?"

"Yeah." He took a breath, leaning his forearms on his thighs. "The spell. The one on your shoulder. That's the one that lets you... turn into a dog, right?"

I hadn't expected that line of inquiry, and it surprised me into honesty. "Yes."

"And that book you took from Gwydian-" God, it was weird to hear Jaesung say that name "-had that spell in it. That's one you memorized that the Guild wants, right?"

I nodded again, unsure of what he was getting at. His brows drew low, nostrils flaring.

"I'm not staying behind when you go to fight Gwydian."

I set my cup down. "You're...you can't go. I'm *bait*. Part of my deal with Isaac is that the Guild keeps you safe."

"I didn't make that deal."

Fear wound through my chest. "No, Jae. This isn't...this isn't like...this is *magic*. You literally have no defenses. I'll have a hard enough time protecting myself to worry about you as-"

"Then make me one!" His clasped hands popped apart, holding

the air as if it weighed a hundred pounds. His eyes were hot, and he seemed to hunch under the weight of his own decision. "You know the mandala—you can do it to me."

I stared. Jaesung—a spell-hound. I imagined him sprawled across a mandala, Poo-stank's body bleeding out at his side.

"You don't want that," I said, shaking my head.

"What I don't want is to stand by and do nothing. I don't care if I'm throwing rocks—I'm going with you."

My hands fisted over my knees. "I don't need you to protect me."

"I know." He slid off his chair, settling on the floor between my knees and reaching for my hips. My hands, the traitors, went straight to his shoulders, seeking the heat of his neck and collarbone.

"You're angry as hell," he continued. "And reckless, and your life has gone to pieces, and you're still so fucking strong. Of course you don't need me."

"I'm not strong."

"You don't feel that way, maybe, but you're still facing Gwydian. You haven't given up or let anyone make you do anything you don't want to."

"Except come here with you as Isaac's hostage."

Jaesung smirked. "Bullshit. You'd have found a way to get out of it. You wanted me."

I couldn't deny it. His hands tightened on my hips and I let myself be drawn forward off the couch, into his lap. My stomach gave a pleasant flutter as our chests pressed together. Jaesung nudged my nose with his, and I nudged back. Finally it was just the two of us. The world disappeared as our breaths echoed in the inches between our mouths. His forehead leaned against mine.

He'd found an old pair of glasses, outdated in prescription, but good enough to work. I'd missed them, and they made my heart thud warm and fast. Or maybe that was the product of being trapped between Jaesung's chest and the base of the couch.

"I'll go nuts if you leave me behind," he said. "I need to be there. Even if I'm just in the background like the guy with no hit points."

"I don't know what that means," I murmured, but I didn't care. His fingers were sliding under the back of my sweater, making warm circles along my spine. "Also, you can't seduce me into letting you go with us."

"Can I try?"

Both of our mouths split into grins, and, though I denied it to even myself right after, I giggled. He brushed a hand through my hair, caught a handful at the back of my head with a gentle, sigh-inducing squeeze. The muscles in my back relaxed.

"You're the strongest person I've ever met," he said. "Hands down. Badass. You'll probably call me an idiot, and I probably am with shit like self-preservation."

"Cell towers," I said.

"Cell towers, yeah. But even cell towers haven't scared me like you."

"You shouldn't want to be with someone who scares you."

I said it without conviction, the tip of his nose tracing up the length of mine. His lips pressed between my eyebrows, not quite a kiss.

"No, that's..." His breath flushed warm on my face. "*You* don't scare me. What scares me is the thought of letting you walk into a trap with the people who failed to protect you last time. It scared me when you disappeared from the wedding, and it scared me when I found you beaten up. Before that, it was the shoulder and the ice and leaving you alone at the train station. But not because of what you did or what you were. It scared me because I am completely in love with you, and I can't do a damn thing to help."

It took a moment for the words to hit. At first, I didn't really feel them, just recognized that he'd said it. I'd thought it myself a few times, that I loved him, or at least felt for him the closest thing to love I understood. Weirdly, I didn't expect him to feel it back. I'd imagined myself a charity case for all of them, subject to first concern, then suspicion, and finally pity. I was the stray taken in, not because I was wanted but because the effort of saving me created its own bond.

And now he was telling me I was wrong.

Heat flushed across my chest, working its way deeper, curling in tendrils between my ribs toward my heart. His fingers still tangled in my hair, his mouth still pressed against my forehead. I was grateful not to have to look into his eyes—I didn't think I could.

"You're right," I whispered. "I think you're an idiot."

I felt him smile against my brow before he tipped his forehead to mine again. "As long as I'm not the only idiot." His arms slid around me, hugging me into his chest.

I laughed, but the sound was breathless with shallow panic. I closed my eyes, still afraid to look at him.

"You're not."

I felt the reaction in his body, the swift tense and release of all his muscles feeling the impact. His breath reflected off my lips in a shudder. I was dizzy with fear, with the feeling of his belt biting into my thighs and the heat of him against me.

I couldn't imagine life letting me have this. The thought was a barb to the chest. It would do just as much damage to remove it as to leave it there, festering. My breath hitched, Jaesung's hands warm at the small of my back.

I pushed forward, pressing my cheek against his and winding my arms tight around his neck.

"That's why you can't go," I whispered. "I've lost... I have no one else left. You said you'd go crazy if you didn't know what happened, but if anything happened to you I... I wouldn't... I don't think I could live with it. Without you. I can't lose everything again."

"Hel-" The patio door opened and cut him off.

"Bad news, kids," Isaac said. He made no snide comments at finding us sitting entwined on the living room floor. The news must be worse than bad.

I leaned back, though Jaesung's arms didn't withdraw from around me.

"Gwydian's on the move. Miami Guild found his place empty, and Atlanta reported a spike in corruptive magic."

"You have a sensor for that?" Jaesung asked.

Isaac tapped his chest. "We can feel it. Hel probably just thinks it's normal, since she grew up with it, but the rest of us can tell."

I shivered. "How long do we have?"

"Assuming big-bad has to stop for pee-breaks? Two days, maybe."

My arms were going stiff with suppressed adrenaline. The blood thudded thick through my veins. I looked down, focusing on the ChiArts logo on Jaesung's shirt. Two days.

"Get some sleep," Isaac said. "Let those mandalas sink in. Park. I need to talk to you."

I extracted myself from Jaesung's lap, no longer feeling warm. My walk upstairs was mechanical, and I crawled into the narrow bed already shivering. I didn't sleep. Mandalas swam behind my closed eyes, along with flashes of that night on the yacht. I could still hear him, soft voice in my ear as he told me to come "home".

I thought of Morgan, of Eamon, of Zenia and Rodolfo and Cai. All the people I'd loved who were either gone or forced to turn against me.

When the door creaked open a long while later, I sat up, startled. Jaesung froze in the doorway for a second before slipping inside.

"It's just me," he said, pushing the door closed behind him. "I brought this." He held up the ring. "Isaac said all you have to do is prime it, whatever that means."

I pressed a palm into the mattress and shifted myself up. Jaesung sat on the edge, taking my other hand.

"This feels weird," he said, sliding it onto my middle finger, where it rattled loosely. He moved it to my index finger. "Like, 'I love you, have a ring with a spring-loaded spell'."

I found a smile. "Your mom will never believe we didn't elope."

He snorted, checking the tightness of the ring. "Still loose. Maybe you can wear it on a necklace. Actually," he looked up at me. "That's a better idea anyway, in case you have to change into a hound."

"I hadn't thought of that," I admitted. "I never wear jewelry."

He made to stand up, looking for something to thread through the center of the ring. My belly twisted, that gut-deep dread pushing its way into my chest.

I caught his sleeve. "Jae?"

He sat back down, looking uncertain and a little harassed. "What did Isaac want to talk about?"

He put a hand on my leg, patting it through the covers. "Basically? How not to get myself killed when Gwydian attacks."

"Specifically?"

His gaze flicked away from me, and he took a moment to gather his words. "He showed me how to load and use his gun. I can't make the bullets do fun magic things, but..."

I nodded. "Yeah."

Jaesung with a gun. I bounced off the idea hard, but the survivalist in me recognized it as smart. He needed a way to protect himself in all of this. I couldn't deny him that.

"I guess I should learn to use them at some point, if I go into law enforcement."

"Yeah."

His hand tightened where it rested just above my knee. "Hey, it's-"

"Don't say it'll be okay."

He scooted closer, brushing my half-assed braid back over my shoulder. His palm moved down my arm and he took my hand, running a thumb over my wrist. "You never know. What if it surprises you and you have a frustratingly long life?"

"I can't stop thinking about it," I said, staring at our linked hands. "I can't sleep. My brain is going too fast." He nodded. "Thinking of the future forces me to think about a thousand possibilities, and none of them end with happily ever after."

I thought of Eamon's hound form, engorged muscle splitting through shredded skin and fur, his teeth in my shoulder. How many more of my pack would be like that?

My whole body clenched around the despair. I pressed my hand against Jaesung's chest, felt the warmth of his skin and his beating heart, and considered the possibility of never feeling it again.

I stood, certain I was going to vomit, and stumbled to the bathroom. Jaesung knelt beside me, and though he didn't listen at first, a few choked out words sent him back into his room. I knelt there in front of the toilet, trembling, waiting for the distress to heave its way up my throat.

Nothing came. I brushed my teeth anyway.

When I returned, Jaesung sat on the bed, head in hands. The ridges in the hardwood floor scraped at my bare feet as I slunk across. Jaesung didn't lift his head until I stopped in front of him, the bed frame cutting into my shins where I stood between his knees. His thighs pressed in against mine, two points of heat in the chill air.

He tilted his head back and met my eyes, helplessness drawn in the downturn of his mouth. I reached out, and the backs of my fingers grazed his jaw. It was rougher than it looked.

"Distract me," I said.

The tendons in his neck flexed. I watched him consider me a moment, confirming my words against the physical signals. Slowly, he straightened. Both hands found my waist, and he pulled my stomach into his shoulder. A mix of relief and anxiety weakened my legs as his head tucked against my side, both arms going around my hips. There was something at once vulnerable and protective in the gesture, like he was trying to comfort both of us at once. What connection had he just made?

I stared down the line of his back, cradling his head against my side. We stayed that way for several moments. Then his hands found my skin. Callused and warm, they slid up my back. I hadn't put on a bra after my shower, and his fingers slid, unobstructed, into the grooves of my shoulder-blades. Those hands that soothed dogs and tied knots in climbing gear, that flew across computer keyboards and video game controllers, and held his friends when they were weak. I imagined I could feel all of that in the fingers caressing my skin.

My legs weren't working right. He moved his hands back to my hips and glanced at me over his glasses.

Now that I knew him, he looked different. I understood the way his mouth moved, the story behind the tiny white scar hidden under his lip. It was easy to imagine the way his eyes looked when he laughed, when he was angry, sad, exhausted. I knew where his face would wrinkle someday, and why.

My throat was hot, and my hands drifted up his neck. I grazed my thumbs over his ears, watching the quality of emotion in his gaze change. I no longer cared if he saw what was in mine.

"Okay." His voice, low and smooth, vibrated through me. And then he leaned through my hands, pushed up the hem of my shirt, and met my skin with a kiss.

His mouth was a hot contrast to the cold air. My breath shuddered out, and everything under his mouth melted. He hooked an arm around me, holding me steady as he worked his way toward the angle of my hip.

The effect radiated down the backs of my thighs, tendrils pushing into the crevices of my body. It had happened so slowly I'd barely noticed, but the months at Ruff Patch had changed the geography of my heart, made it struggle against all I'd told myself was impossible. Feelings I'd paved over long ago had cracked their cement seals like roots.

Now, Jaesung was bringing them to life. The sweep of his tongue undid me. The room, the cold air, and the threats living in the night beyond vanished. All I needed, and all I cared about was the man in front of me, making everything ten times more complicated and a thousand sweeter.

He slid his free hand down the back of my thigh, and I knew he could feel it shaking as he kissed a scar just above the hem of my jeans.

I sank onto his knee; his hand found my neck. I leaned into him even as he drew me in, and we kissed like we'd never been interrupted.

It wasn't enough. Not for either of us. He half rose from the bed, turning with me in his arms. My back hit the comforter. I drew him over me. Long bones and powerful limbs made him heavy, and his weight pressed me deeper into the bed. This didn't inspire the visceral fear I'd experienced with guys before. I smelled him, I recognized his touch. My body knew it was Jaesung.

It was safe to let down my guard, safe to let myself feel the surge of lust and pursue it. His mouth burned my neck. I untangled my arms from his shoulders and tugged his shirt up his back. He stopped kissing me long enough to duck out of it. His chest shook with a quiet laugh as his glasses got stuck.

I leaned up and kissed the hollow of his throat. He could worry about his sleeves. Pushed up on his elbows above me, he looked even better than he had in the picture on the stairs.

I studied the furrows of muscle, the way his abs flattened between his hip-bones, disappearing beneath the wide elastic waistband of his boxers. It wasn't the perfect definition models had, but the natural shapeliness of an athlete. Part of me wanted to push him flat against the mattress, savoring-the-moment be damned.

He caught me looking. "Are you objectifying me, Miss Martin?"

"You enjoy it," I said, running a hand down his chest to prove it.

He snorted, tucked an arm around my waist, and pulled us tighter together. I inhaled, arrested by the desire in his dark eyes. "I can play that too."

I bit my lips against a silly, flushed grin. He shifted his hand between us and pushed up my shirt's ragged hem. It joined his on the floor. Then there was just the skin of his chest and mine.

His hips rocked down. It was controlled, firm. Intentional. I gave a sharp gasp, shock and pleasure fizzing through my nerves. My body moved instinctively. I wrapped my legs around his and grasped his hips, holding him in place. Everything in me had gone hot and pliant, every nerve ached for touch. He stroked up my side and found my jaw, drawing me into a kiss softer than I expected.

I wasn't sure which of us was trembling. Maybe it was both.

"I want you." I couldn't recall thinking it, or giving myself permission to say it. He shuddered, and for once he didn't seem to have anything to say, just shifted obediently against me. I lost my breath, lungs crushed by the sweet ache expanding inside me. He groaned maddeningly in my ears. We pushed off the rest of our clothes, discarding them with all thoughts of the future.

CHAPTER THIRTY-ONE

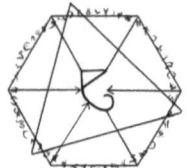

Jaesung and I woke again late that evening, pulling on our clothes in the cold shadows of his room. Neither of us turned on the light, as if it might break the spell of intimate safety we'd conjured. I spent the evening buried in spells while Isaac and Jaesung retreated to the backyard to practice firearm basics. I tried not to watch. The gun wasn't loaded, but just the sight of the mandalas carved down the barrel unnerved me.

I avoided thinking about Mom. The fight was no longer just about me and my desire for freedom or revenge.

I organized spells in my head by type, and when the boys came back inside, cheeks red with cold, we broke for food. Tension kept us quiet, and by the time dawn came again, my back and neck were knotted. I settled into bed next to Jaesung, but could only bury myself against his back. He didn't push for more. It seemed imperative right now to run scenarios, prepare for the worst even as my heart ached for some sliver of hope. I held onto him, an anchor in the chaos.

I don't know when I fell asleep, but when I shifted up onto my elbow, amber streaks of sunset painted the wall. Jaesung stirred and turned on his back toward me. Heavy, sleepy arms drew me into a kiss. I lingered, savoring the unguarded sweetness of his sleep-clumsy mouth on mine, then slid into the chill of the room.

I showered, rinsing away sweat, soapy hands working at the knots in my neck and shoulders. There was nothing I could do about the nausea, or the anxiety buzzing over my skin like a low-level electric current. I dressed, stretched out my aching back, and pulled my damp hair into a braid.

My own eyes looked back at me from the mirror—hazel and sunken in sockets much deeper than they'd been a few days ago. I was too thin—the effect of magic, probably, though I'd only flirted with it around the edges of the mandalas. I pulled the ring from my bag of toiletries. Jaesung had cannibalized an old cowry necklace he'd gotten on a trip to California and given me the cord. I tugged it over my head and dropped it down the front of my shirt, where it settled cool and heavy against my sternum.

The house was silent. I slipped down the stairs, my hair smelling of Mrs. Park's flowery shampoo.

The drawn curtains glowed with the sunset, letting a muted suggestion of light slip across the living room. Isaac's head was silhouetted over the back of the chair, hair nearly the same color as the light peeking in.

It took two steps for me to realize that the room was too quiet.

Just as I thought it, I smelled something rich and metallic. Alarms went off in the back of my head, and my fingers curled into fists even as I identified the scent of blood. And the silence was wrong because Isaac, skinny as he was, snored like a broken cello.

"Isaac?" I whispered. A frisson of horror slid down my spine. I stepped forward, wanting not to look.

Isaac's eyes were open. Blue and staring at the far window, as if surprised by the sunset. His skin was gray down to the open gash in his throat. Below that, red. His shirt was dark with it. The color pooled in the creases of his jeans, sunk into the upholstered cushion below. His arms, tattooed and freckled, hung stiff against the arms of the couch.

I stifled a gasp of horror, stepping back. That gash was deep and wide, made with a single firm slice. The blade would have been sharp and substantial. Like a hunting knife.

My senses blew wide with fear. Where was Jaesung—still upstairs? Why hadn't Isaac's wards worked? Where was the attacker? Who?

But I knew the answer to that last question, even before the broad figure came barreling out of the darkness. Morgan ducked around my kick, and I turned just in time to avoid his left hook. He slammed into me, and we fell back against the stairs.

I screamed, wild as an animal, and clawed at my cousin's face. His hands were rough as he struggled for purchase. His intent was capture, which would have given me the advantage with anyone else. But this was Morgan; I couldn't fight to kill. I struggled to call up a mandala, but only vicious ones sprang forward. Wind. What was the wind one?

It popped into my mind. An instant later, a gale ripped Morgan away from me. The gust sent him crashing into the back of the chair, spilling Isaac onto the floor as it overturned.

Breath knifed into me. I struggled to my feet even as Morgan lunged for me again. I ducked sideways, crashing to the floor, and came up on one knee to see him struggling to right himself on the stairs.

This time I was ready with the mandala, blasting him back into the kitchen.

Morgan. Jesus, Gwydian must have sent him in when no one else could get through Isaac's wards. It had to be something about Morgan's lack of magic...

There was no more time to think. Morgan withdrew something heavy and dark from behind him, and I had only an instant to move out of the way.

A gun. A familiar black Beretta, which I'd last seen when I handed it to Morgan in the warehouse, months ago.

I hurled myself to the carpet just as the shot fired. Something punched my thigh, and an instant later, the pain hit. I screamed, Isaac's blank eyes looking on from under the chair.

There's no pain like being shot. It differed from being stabbed or punched, or even from breaking a bone. I'd done all three, and nothing could have prepared me. There was no way to hold back the scream. The burn of it was almost as bad as anything else—everyone is so focused on the punctured flesh that they don't stop to think about the fact that bullets are hot. They sit against your bone and sear into you without mercy. At least, this one did.

Panic sent me struggling to my hands. I dragged myself forward, painting a bloody streak across the carpet. Behind me, Morgan stalked forward. The look on his face burned as much as the bullet.

His expression was stony as ever, but behind that grim mask, his gray eyes were alive with horror. He lifted the gun.

I had to stop him before I lost too much blood. Before the shock I could already feel working its way into my core took away my ability to cast. I lifted my hand, calling up the mandala for knives of ice. His hand shook. He was fighting the enslavement spell.

"Morgan...." I choked on his name.

And then I saw the shadow on the stairs. A second later, a hockey stick slammed into the side of Morgan's head. A bullet streaked past my shoulder. I heard glass shatter.

"Jae, NO!" I shouted. "Run!"

But there wouldn't be time. Morgan staggered upright, blood streaming from his temple. Jaesung swung again, but there was no world in which he was a match for my cousin.

Morgan caught the stick and twisted, jerking Jaesung toward him. It took a split second. He kicked, and I heard the grinding crack of bone. Jaesung let out an animal roar and went down. Morgan lifted the gun.

This time, I didn't hesitate. I blasted the spell straight at the gun.

It sliced through the barrel, through the chamber, and the long finger on the trigger. Those slicing blasts slammed back into the wall, the energy sizzling through.

Morgan turned cradling his bleeding hand, and something in his face shifted. I knew that look—the gleam in the gray eyes that meant he'd had a revelation. Something in the order's interpretation gave him an opening.

He ducked, heaving Jaesung to his feet. I watched in horror as he locked an arm around his neck and hauled him toward the garage.

"No..." I said, and shoved myself onto my knees. My leg screamed, but I forced the pain into the back of my mind. He couldn't take Jaesung. Gwydian would kill him. Gwydian would hold him hostage like he had me and my mother. And I would go.

Damn Isaac, this was the entire reason I'd wanted to leave Jaesung behind. Damn me, for letting him come anyway.

I made it two steps and fired off a wind spell that slammed several pictures off the wall but did nothing to stop Morgan. The next moment, I was on the linoleum floor, arm outstretched toward the door.

"Jae!" I screamed, dragging myself after them, desperate to get to him. His leg was broken at the knee, dragging behind even as he scrabbled at the door frame, trying to hold on.

"Helena!" It sounded like a warning, not a plea.

I didn't care. I pulled myself up on the island and scrabbled for the knife block. My vision was going dark around the edges. Morgan shoved Jaesung's head hard into the door frame. He dropped, caught only by my cousin's powerful arm. "Morgan, no. No!" I screamed. "This is worse! NO!"

My clumsy hand hit the knife block. It toppled to the floor, scattering blades across Ms. Park's spotless kitchen. I was too far gone for fine movement. I threw myself at Morgan's back, hit the edge of the closing door, and crashed backwards into darkness.

A slap across the face drew me from the black. I swam for a moment, drowned in the deep bottom of a chill sea, and contemplated staying.

I didn't want to face what waited for me at the surface. Broken moon-light, a world much less restful than the slow-shifting sand and cold oblivion of unconsciousness.

A second slap, and I groaned, waving an arm through the chill current, pushing away the shark. It didn't matter that I could breathe —of course I could. The bottom of the ocean was where I lived. Where I belonged, with the rest of the creatures that had never known light.

"Shock her."

Fire lit the water, branching through my veins. I sat up with static in my hair and a shriek on my lips, smelling blood and ozone. Strong hands grabbed my shoulders before I could fall back, and I opened my eyes to terra-cotta skin and fierce golden eyes. Deepti. I tried to twist away, but found a forest of legs circling me. I looked around, wild with anger and desperation, and counted twelve Sorcerers, including the Guild Mistress herself.

"Where are they?" I said. "How did he get through Isaac's wards? How did you get through... what-" I lifted a hand to my head, which swung around in dizziness. Deepti steadied me with a hand.

"Isaac's wards died with him. As far as we can see, he set protec-tions for only those with magic. The one who attacked was not a sanguimancer, but a man."

"A spellhound," I corrected. "Morgan. My cousin."

Deepti's brow furrowed. "Your cousin?" For a glimmer of a moment, she looked hopeful.

"Oh my mother's side," I said, angry that, even now, she was more worried about my genetics than my humanity. "He took Jaesung. He knew I'd..." I twisted around, and this time I did heave up everything I'd eaten. Deepti combed back my hair, holding it aside as I coughed and expelled a second stream of watery bile onto the floor. When I looked up, eyes watering, the Guild Mistress was making subtle hand signals to some of the Sorcerers behind her.

"We've got a tail on them," she said. "You're very lucky."

"Lucky?" I choked on the word.

"Yes. The bullet nicked your femoral artery. You would have been dead within minutes if Eric had not been near enough to stabilize you."

"Too bad Eric wasn't near enough to keep me from getting shot in the first place."

A deep voice behind me grunted, and I heard the creak of fabric as the owner of that voice knelt at my back. "Your cousin's good, Martin. I think you know that."

"Eric was an officer before he joined as a Guild Enforcer," Deepti said.

"Yeah, well, there are some shitty officers," I snapped, prodding gingerly at the bandages around my thigh.

"I am adept at healing," she said, motioning for Eric to take my shoulders. "But I fail to see why I should bother at this point. You are compromised—Gwydian has your cousin, the boy you love. Like your father, you would give yourself to him to save their lives. The only clear course of action on my part is to see you restrained."

I bared my teeth as if threatening to bite her and even lunged forward. The hands on my arms restrained me. "Fuck you!" I jerked against the grip, kicking out with my good leg as I tried to kick the woman before me.

"Miss Martin!" she called, forcing her voice out louder than my impotent growls. "I am prepared to bargain!"

"Of course you're fucking prepared to bargain, you bitch! You've got all the power!"

"Says the woman who can cast spells with her mind."

I stopped writhing, breath coming fast and short. Seven separate mandalas flashed into my mind, every one of them deadly. Bodies around me tensed, the hands on my arms went tight. I glared up at Deepti, hesitating only because I knew, with a sinking sense of dread, that I could never save Jaesung and Morgan, let alone kill Gwydian, without her help.

But the deal she had offered me was only marginally better than Gwydian's. Let the Guild mark me, keep track of me. With a kill switch on me, they could demand anything they wanted, and I would have to do it. It was almost worse, to make compliance a choice rather than a compulsion—if they asked me to kill, it would be me.

"What do you want?" I growled.

Deepti's lips tightened, but there was no triumph in her golden eyes. "Make me an offer."

My nostrils flared. "I'll give you two years. I'll work for the Guild."

"Ten," she said. "It will take me three to train you."

"Five. Three to train, two to work. After that, you take away the kill switch and leave me the fuck alone. Forever."

She crouched. Blood stained her knees, soaking into the camel-colored trousers. It streaked up over the delicate bones of her wrists, lingered under her fingernails.

Mine, or Isaac's? I shuddered.

"Five," she agreed. "And the enslavement spell. We must subdue Gwydian."

Breath whooshed out of me, half laugh, half disbelief. I stared at her, the refusal trembling on my lips, even as a dreadful certainty spread in my mind. If I said no, she would make good on her threat to lock me up, far from any hope of saving Morgan and Jaesung. She'd told the truth, when she'd said I had surpassed them in importance, but that didn't make them any less valuable to her. She'd never given up on those spells.

I saw my mother's face all over again, slack in surprise, going gray in death. The blood seeped into her hair, her bright eyes cold and empty.

To say yes would feel like a betrayal.

But Morgan was still alive, and Jaesung. I almost felt his hands in my hair, his mouth on my neck. His laugh vibrating my chest, where a length of cord suspended the heavy silver high school ring with Isaac's protection spell.

"If I give it to you," I said, heart thudding in my throat, "you have to swear that the first priority—more than killing Gwydian—is to get Jaesung out alive. He was never a part of this."

Deepti rolled the idea around a moment before nodding. "Very well. Taking Gwydian, dead or alive, is our second priority. Your cousin is too dangerous to guarantee."

It hurt to nod, but I understood. Morgan had nearly killed me. He'd kill any of the Sorcerers that got close enough to let him.

"And you will give five years to the Guild. Three as my apprentice, and two in the field."

It felt like closing shackles around my ankles, but I nodded. "Fine."

She stretched out her hand, and the circle of Sorcerers moved, passing her a familiar sketchbook. When I took it in my fingers, I left rust-colored smudges across the cover. I opened, flipping past the pages of mandalas Isaac and I had drawn. It smelled like sharpie and powdered sugar.

"Does he have family?" I asked, accepting a slippery pen.

Behind me, the low voice answered. "A sister. She's with him. She's a Guild Tracker too."

I lowered the sketchbook into my lap and swallowed back an unexpected surge of pain. I hadn't even liked Isaac, but he'd been trying to help me. Given time, I might have gotten past his abrasiveness and actually....

I choked back a sob and opened to an empty page.

CHAPTER THIRTY-TWO

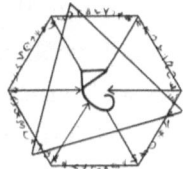

Naked branches stretched across the windshield like fissures, spilling in light from Orion, Taurus, and Canis Major. I traced over the shapes to keep myself calm, ignoring the crackling static from Eric's police radio along with the spaceship's worth of computers and blinking lights in the front seat of his cruiser.

I sat on the passenger's side with my legs pulled up, chin on my knees. The floor was a mess of balled up hamburger wrappers, plastic soda bottles, and other artifacts of our three-hour drive to southern Illinois. My leg throbbed, despite the rudimentary healing job Deepti had done, and my body felt drained even with another bag worth of transfused blood.

I stared at the trees, willing myself to see far enough through the winter-stripped trunks to find Gwydian, and therefore Morgan and Jaesung.

Fortunately, Eric was a man of few words. Nothing I said would make the waiting easier, so silence stretched between us as if by mutual agreement.

We'd pulled off the side of a highway onto a snowy shoulder by the edge of a thick pine forest. The forest, belted in by a five-foot wire fence, came up as a privately owned campsite on Eric's GPS. It was to here that Deepti's people had followed Morgan, confirming his presence with a photo of Jaesung's truck parked in the campground's abandoned lot.

I'd been surprised to find Deepti receptive to my ideas. Apparently, my evasion of her people over the past months had been sufficient proof that I could handle myself. Plan in place, we'd split into teams of two and scattered around the campground's perimeter, waiting for the confirmation that Gwydian himself was in the camp.

"This would be a lot easier with a drone," Eric mumbled.

I snorted. "Because that wouldn't tip him off."

He shrugged, and the movement displaced the bullet-proof vest under his uniform. Eric was a big man in his thirties. Not tall as Morgan or Jaesung, but broad-chested and padded out with the muscle I'd learned not to expect from a Sorcerer. Then again, given the number of burger wrappers he'd chucked at my feet, he had to eat four times the amount of a normal man just to stay his size. The uniform itself was black, with gray accents and a gold badge proclaiming him a Sheriff's Deputy.

We weren't in the right county, but I doubted anyone would question him.

The scanner crackled and squealed, letting out barely intelligible words and numbered codes. The static filled the car, setting my ears to vibrating. I wanted to get out.

"Amelia will be back soon," he said, as if reading the tension in my posture. "In fact..."

A ripple at the edge of the trees had me lowering my feet to the floor, leaning forward to peer through the windshield. A sparkle of light along the snow seemed to zip open around the edges of a mandala, which faded under the footsteps of a petite woman. She couldn't have been any older than twenty, with a chin-length black-dyed bob and a pixie thin frame. She hurried over to the police car, breath puffing out from the fur-lined hood she'd pulled tight to her face.

Eric unlocked the doors, and Amelia heaved herself into the back seat. "Holy Icicles, Batman!" she said, slamming the door shut and stomping her feet clean of snow.

"Did you leave tracks?" Eric demanded. He handed a bag of room-temperature burgers into the back seat.

"What do you think this is, amateur hour?" she demanded, snatching the bags. "Did I leave any tracks? How long have I been doing this shit? Longer than you. Shut up."

She crammed half a cheeseburger into her mouth.

"Amelia specializes in espionage," Eric explained. "She's what the Guild calls a cloaker."

"Great," I said flatly, my eyes riveted on Amelia. "What did you see? Are they down there? Is Gwydian down there?"

She nodded and chewed, stuffing the rest of the burger in her mouth before replying. "I got a pretty good look at Fuck-face number one. No one told me dude was, like, thirty. I thought he was a geezer like Eric."

"I'm thirty nine."

She swallowed her burger, fished out another, and unwrapped it. "Anyway, he's down there. I counted twelve sanguimancers with him, six at the site and six on sentry. There are four other non-magic body-guard-types, including the Viking, and eight Hellhounds."

My throat tightened. Eight. That would mean most of my pack, if not all of them.

I refused to let their faces come to mind. Grief would come later.

"And Jaesung?"

She nodded. Eric flicked on the overhead light, using the time to double check his guns, and I got a good look at the girl in the back seat. She had bright green eyes and there was a border of lighter-colored hair at her hairline, suggesting she'd dyed it black. There was something familiar about her face, too, something about the arch of that pierced brow.

"Are you Isaac's sister?" I asked.

She stopped chewing, nodded, and started again. Something in the flash of her green eyes told me not to tell her I was sorry for her loss. My chest hurt for her, and I thought of how it had felt to lose Dad, and Mom, and Cai, and Eamon. I gave her a nod. She dug into the next burger.

"You ready, Martin?" Eric asked, sliding his spare gun in its holster.

I would never be ready. But I opened the door, stepped into the icy air, and folded into a transformation. Within a few seconds, I was shaking off my sweats and boots. Eric bundled them, slung a length of chain around them, and hooked it around my neck beside the cord bearing Jaesung's ring.

I padded into the woods, nose to the earth, following Amelia's scent-trail back. Her cover-up job had been impressive—my paws cracked through what seemed to be unbroken snow, though the scent of coconut shampoo told me she'd been here. Smell was different as a dog. I didn't so much get an overall sense of a scent as a dissection of them—elements of pine and chemical and perfumed oil, animal musk and sap.

I paced through close-growing trees for about a mile, sighting through the black trunks. None of the deciduous trees had leaves left, and visibility here was too good for my liking. It might mean I could spot the Sorcerers easily, but it also meant they could see me. Still, I had the advantage of being low to the ground and having a good path to follow.

Amelia had chosen a route that took advantage of a dried up riverbed, and the uphill slope gave me decent cover until I reached the top.

At which point I had a clear view down the far side of the slope, through the legion of stark black trees and into the campsite.

An enormous bonfire rioted at the center—a tower of flame several stories tall. It made the blaze I'd conjured to destroy the grimoire seem pitiful in comparison. My hound's eyes were attracted to movement around the fire. I was too far to make out necklaces or tattoos to confirm they were sanguimancers, but enough of them looked well-fed that I assumed they had to get their energy from an outside source. Not everyone could eat like Eric.

Four of them were short and brawny. They stood together, conferring outside a large gray tent. It took me a moment recognize that one of them was actually wearing a kilt.

Wonderful. Capturing me was apparently cause for a Lochly family reunion.

That was when I saw the campers. There were two of them, a man and a woman in jeans and boots and shredded North-face jackets. They hung by their ankles from a sturdy branch, throats cut, bleeding into a large blue camping cooler.

Maybe I'd been away from it too long, but the sight revolted me, sent my hackles up and my whole body to shaking with the need to fight. To hunt.

I heard footsteps far to my left—one of the sanguimancers walking the perimeter.

I melted back into the shadow of gathered trees. The best thing would be to take out as many sentries as possible without them sounding the alarm. I wouldn't be able to do that as a hound—people with teeth in their necks tend to at least try to scream.

That was why I had the chain. I pawed the bundle of clothes over my head and transformed, trying to stay silent despite the stinging chill of snow under my feet. Quietly as possible, I rooted through the bundle for the walkie-talkie and stayed, crouched naked behind the trees, wiggling my toes into boots.

The man appeared. He was another stocky one, with the same dense curls as Gwydian and a mandala tattooed on his throat. There was a keen look in his light eyes, and for just a moment, I could swear he was sniffing the air.

I tossed the walkie-talkie high, sending it arcing over his head to land on the declining slope. He jerked toward the sound of it landing. Two steps later, he had his back to me. I wound the chain around both hands, lifted off my heels.

I saw my path through the snow and undergrowth. The snow

muted my steps. He paused, peering into the blue snow for sign of movement.

I dashed. Three long steps and I launched myself onto his back, looping the chain around his neck. He gave a strangled sound and slid on the incline, falling backwards. My bare back hit snow and the brittle wire of ivy. Air shoved out of my chest, but I clung on. He scrabbled at my arms, digging in nails, drawing blood.

Sanguimancer. He could use that blood. I gave the chain a ruthless jerk, heard the crack of bone and cartilage. He thrashed, and I held on like a gator drowning prey. Slowly, his struggle ceased, and he went still.

Shivering, I shoved him off me and unwound the chain. It had dug deep into my fingers, leaving indentations. I couldn't look at the man's face as I retrieved my walkie-talkie and scampered back up to the top of the hill.

On went my sweatpants and thermal shirt. I wound the chain back around my left hand and gave the walkie-talkie's button a double-click. Two double-clicks back. Eric was on his way with Amelia.

"It's a family reunion out here," I whispered into it.

"No kidding," came his reply. "Amy's gotten three of them ID'd as Lochly."

"I hope all of them aren't sanguimancers. I took care of one."

"Dead?"

"What do you think?"

I wasn't sure if I was angrier that Eric had to confirm, or that he was reminding me. My hands were shaking. Killing like that was different from what I'd done before, under Gwydian's command, or in the midst of a fight. That had been calculated. Cold-blooded.

I snuck off the way the Sorcerer had come, dropping my footsteps into his to hide my tracks. My eyes and ears were sharp for any sign of another perimeter guard. I made it to the North side of the valley and glanced back down into the camp. A gap in the trees gave me a good look at what was on the back side of the bonfire. A blue pavilion crouched over a pile of gear, but from this vantage, I could only see about a foot beneath the roof. Still, it was the most logical area to find Gwydian.

Of course he'd be in a pavilion, sitting there like some medieval king, maybe with Morgan standing at his shoulder like a royal guard.

I hoped Jaesung was somewhere else, but I got the feeling he wouldn't be that lucky. I moved, hunching low and scuttling along the edge of the slope, wincing at every slush of unexpected leaves beneath the snow.

A wet crunch froze me in place. It had come from the other side of a jut of trees, down in a snow-filled gully. I strained my ears, dissecting the whistle of wind and the distant roar of flame, but the sound was too quiet to identify.

I stalked forward, preparing a spell in my mind in case it was another Lochly family member, and peeked over the edge into the gully.

A bear-sized monster bent over a man, muzzle deep in the viscera of his abdomen. Its once-shiny brown coat split over bloated muscle, its razor teeth bulged from a mouth almost too full of fang to chew the sanguimancer's flesh.

I barely recognized the bastardization of Zenia's hound form. Horror heated my brain. I'd told myself this was likely. I knew.

At least she'd fought back. Her sanguimancer guard had lost control of her spell, and ravenous beast that she'd become, she turned on the most convenient source of blood.

"Go Zen," I murmured. Then I locked away my feelings and crept backward, quietly as I could. The Hellhound's meaty rending covered my retreat.

I could have killed her, but I didn't want to use magic on the slope if I didn't have to. Any flash of power would alert those in the valley that there was something wrong. Besides, an uncontrolled Hellhound might be just as bad for the sanguimancers as it was for me.

When I was far enough from the Hellhound not to be heard, I

lifted the walkie-talkie. "Steer clear of the North perimeter. One beast is off the leash."

Eric clicked back an affirmative. Three more affirmatives clicked back.

I continued down the trail of guard footprints, wary of shadows in the black trees, and came to a place where the footprints widened into a flat area. It looked like several people had been here—there were two or three different boot treads that had stamped the snow down thick and glossy.

There was also blood, spattered in an arc across the trampled area. A frisson of fear zipped down my ribs, and I lifted the walkie-talkie.

"Who's in the northeast area?" I said, keeping my voice low. I couldn't see anyone, or hear anyone, but that didn't mean they wouldn't see or hear me. "There's been-"

Light shattered the ground beneath me—acid green and searing like chlorine into my eyes. I jerked sideways, but it was too late. The mandala sent up streamers of magic, which lashed around my legs and held me fast in place. Someone laughed from a few feet away, and the dark forest unzipped. A man stepped out of the cloaking spell, the mandala beneath his own feet fading as he paced toward me down the path.

An acid green mandala blossomed into a shield before him, but I got a good enough look at his face to recognize him. It was the man who'd been with me on the ice. The one whose spell had trapped the border collie. The first sanguimancer I'd noticed.

"I figured it was you," he said. "Paw prints turning into girl's feet. I mean, who else?" He asked it like a joke, grinning as his breath clouded out in front of him.

"Could have been your mom. I heard she's a bitch too."

The sanguimancer's smile widened. "Thanks to you, I might just get a big enough payoff to set mama up in the Caribbean."

My walkie-talkie clicked and before I could move a finger, the sanguimancer opened his hand on a nasty looking mandala. It sprouted from the tattoo on his palm like a deadly flower. "Drop that."

I did, figuring my silence would be signal enough for Eric and the rest to know I'd been caught. The second part of the plan would begin without me.

As the sanguimancer swapped the threads of his mandala from my legs to my wrists, I tried not to think about all the ways this could go wrong.

CHAPTER THIRTY-THREE

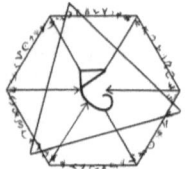

There was a massive amount of shielding around the pavilion. It shimmered in several colors, almost pretty with the mandalas tiled beneath it, except that Gwydian sat behind those shields almost exactly as I'd imagined. Morgan at his left shoulder, a camp chair draped with several wool blankets serving as a makeshift throne. Before him, a blue tarp draped several human-sized mounds. The sight of them nearly took me out at the knees.

It couldn't be Jaesung. Or, if it was, he would be alive—Gwydian would not use his best bargaining chip like that. But there were too many shapes underneath that tarp—one more than I'd expected.

My gut lurched as I envisioned Krista, Sanadzi, and Eugene all in quick succession.

Gwydian stood from his camp chair, gesturing to the kilted quartet flanking the pavilion. All but one of the colored shields dropped.

"I was hoping you'd accept my invitation," he said, in that soft, evocative brogue of his.

Stubble shaded the flat planes of his face, making his blue eyes stand out. He was not in his Crime Lord suit and tie today, instead favoring something earthier, perhaps to celebrate what he thought was a victory for the Lochly clan. A cognac coat, dark jeans, and hiking boots, with a tartan scarf tucked around his neck.

"I took the liberty of dis-inviting a few of your cousins," I said. "Hope you didn't like them much."

His expression didn't flicker, though a few of the Lochly fists tightened. The sanguimancer at my shoulder snorted. "I understand you've burned my book. That was a very important family heirloom, Helena, and the clan isn't happy with you."

"Or you, I'm guessing?"

His smile gave away nothing, nor did the stony expressions of his family guard. I glanced at them again. The two on my left were probably father and son—they had the same crooked nose and receding hairline, which only seemed to open their pale eyes. They didn't seem to be cold, with their bare, crossed arms covered in tattoos. On the right was a pair of dark-haired men with thick jaws and ham fists, guns ready at their hips. They'd be the non-sanguimancers.

"It's time to discuss your options, Helena," Gwydian said. I restrained a wince. There he went, saying my name again, like a father or beloved teacher. It made me sick.

An instant later, I didn't care. He'd reached down, flicked back the edge of the tarp to reveal the outer ring of a mandala. It was drawn in bright cerulean sand, and underneath its twisting designs was another mandala in black sand, and another in red. My throat tightened.

"You won't have seen this before, but I'd imagine some of your friends in the Guild have. That Hindi girl is still leading up here, isn't she? She would know it."

I didn't like the way he said 'girl' about Deepti—as if her age and power conferred on her no right to be called woman.

"You still have so much to learn, Helena. They've told you, I expect? About your father's family?"

I clenched my jaw and didn't answer. I nodded to the tarp instead. "What's under there?"

Gwydian's smile was soft, and he shook a finger at me as if I were a misbehaving child. "Now, now—you have to wait for that. I still have questions."

I didn't feel much like waiting. My favorite mandala—the gust of wind—appeared in my mind. I hurled it at the edge of the tarp, just outside the glitter of Gwydian's shield. It caught the blue plastic sheet and ripped it aside.

I made a sound in my throat somewhere between a growl and a cry. Jaesung sprawled across the mandalas, his shirt torn open at the chest. A familiar tattoo inflamed the skin. Next to him lay a wolf. Dead, its head resting on his shoulder like Poo-stank might have done.

I lost the strength in my knees, and the sanguimancers let me stagger toward him. I stopped, just at the edge of the sandy mandalas. His chest rose and fell, shallow and quick.

He was a spellhound now.

Gwydian had done to him the same thing he'd done to my mother and me. My last hope of restoring him to a normal life was gone. I'd now made an indelible mark on his future, changed not only his outlook, but the makeup of his mind and body. Even if we survived this, he would be subject to the same prejudice as me. The Guild would want its own mark on him.

Maybe I could trade another two years of service to keep him out of it.

Gwydian's boots appeared at the edge of my vision. He crouched, knees close to my head. I looked up, fear and anger shuddering through me. That damn shield. It had taken the Guild so much power to get through it before. I couldn't do it now, not and ensure Jaesung's safety. I glanced back at Morgan standing by the camp chair. His right hand was wrapped in a bandage that didn't look nearly bloodstained enough to account for missing fingers. Someone must have healed him, which meant Gwydian had wanted him here as a threat. If I pulled anything cute, he would be forced to kill Jaesung.

I had to stick to the plan.

"Now, we can make this easy," Gwydian whispered, flicking into the collar of his shirt. He pressed his fingertips to the edge of a tattoo —the same tattoo I'd once had on my shoulder. "Or we can go through the obvious tedium."

Morgan stepped forward, cocked the gun he'd taken from Isaac's corpse, and aimed it down at Jaesung's head. I tensed, even though I'd expected it. Fear was a writhing mass in my gut as I met Gwydian's pale blue eyes. He was so close—without that shield, I could have punched him. Or transformed into a hound and ripped his throat out.

"Let him leave," I said, nodding toward Jaesung. "There's a police car about two miles through the woods. I saw it on my way here. Let him get in that car and I'll step onto that slave mandala without a fight."

I nodded down at the white mandala, which I thought I recognized beneath the lines of the blue one.

Gwydian twisted his face into a skeptical look. "Come now, do you really think that's how this works? After I've gone through the trouble of making him a hound like you?"

"You'll have me. Or you'll kill him and you won't have either of us."

Gwydian's eyes met mine, and I hoped he would see how dead serious I was. His kind face tilted, and I saw the consideration in the set of his lips. He nodded once. "Kill him, then." He gestured at Morgan.

I lunged, throwing myself on Jaesung even as I shoved power into the ring dangling over my sternum. The shot cracked, and a bullet slammed into the turquoise mist around us, hovering in a lightning-strike of power before it dropped to the mandalas below.

I could not stay on these mandalas. I shoved the cord from

around my neck and onto Jaesung's, then twisted, sweeping a leg at Morgan's feet. He dodged, but it was enough. I pivoted to my feet and grabbed the gun, twisting myself inside his guard just like he'd taught me.

My hands on the barrel, I wrenched his arm up, and the shot he fired hit one of the broad Lochlys in the chest. Another twist, and I had it out of Morgan's hand and pointed at the second broad Lochly. I shot him. Bounty hunters shouted from the other side of the fire, accompanied by the chilling howl of first one, then several Hellhounds.

Morgan had me, an arm around my throat, and I had to drop the gun to grab him. I reached back, seized his jacket, and bent forward. With two fingers gone from his right hand, he couldn't grab my waistband to upset the move. I tossed him over my shoulder, onto the shield still crackling over Jaesung.

Gwydian slapped a tattoo on his arm and it lit up, the pattern of light flipping like a coin into the air before expanding, its center targeting me. I saw the spell coming, but my brain was empty.

A golden mandala blossomed in front of me, and Gwydian's spell shattered against it. The gilded light sparked and shuddered, exploded in a series of small fireworks as it expelled the energy of the attack.

Spells arced from the woods, slamming into bounty hunters and other mandalas, turning the valley into a pandemonium of deadly color.

Gwydian was on his feet now, his expression calm but for a familiar heat in his blue eyes. Dread dropped my bowels into my feet, but I scraped together my concentration. Beside me, Morgan was struggling to his feet.

I pictured a vicious mandala, let it glow bright in my mind's eye, and shot a jet of molten heat straight at Gwydian's stomach. His shield caught the attack, and he staggered backward as it sparked like a speaker doused in water.

He growled something in another language and ducked away,

between the father and son sanguimancers now drawing a pair of their own mandalas. I sent two more jets their way, missing the son but hitting the father in his naked knee. He howled, and his son leapt for him, just as I'd hoped.

Then I was after Gwydian, running like I had the teeth of my hound form, like I could tear him to pieces. Bullet-cast spells flew over my head, and I was nearly impaled by a spear of sapphire flame. Eric roared a warning just in time and I hit the mud, skidding in the slurry of deadfall, dirt, and melted snow. Gwydian slapped his arms and fired off two spells in my direction, one after another. I rolled away from the first and heaved a shield up just in time to catch the second.

My shield exploded, sending hot sparks of energy into my face. I screamed, slapping at the burns as if they were cinders I could put out. Then I realized where Gwydian was headed, and the pain no longer mattered. I lurched to my feet after him, skidding on mud as I rounded the fire just in time to see him kick over the cooler beneath the two strung-up campers.

A wave of blood. It stood out bright on the remaining snow, glinting in the firelight as Gwydian skipped over the cooler and landed in the spill. His boots splashed, spattering his jeans, and he dropped to a knee, digging his fingers into the blood and mud.

I rushed forward, calling a spell up in my mind—all I needed was to break his new shield. Break it, and the others would help me kill him.

A dark shape hit me like a train.

I felt the crack of ribs as it slammed me back, sent me sprawling back into the mud. My shoulder hit rock, and the hand I put out to steady me got a hot streak of bonfire.

I screamed, whipping out my hand, which was already blossoming into deep red. Then the Hellhound was on me. Not Zenia, but another, this one too disfigured to recognize. I had no knife with me this time. Nothing but spells. It howled over me, serrated jaws spreading wide as it reared back to strike.

And jerked, staring for a moment with malevolent violet eyes. A violet mandala sliced out of its forehead. The beast shuddered, and this time I was fast enough to scramble out from under it before it fell.

I swung my head toward the gunshot.

There, slumped at the edge of the pavilion mandala, was Jaesung. He was awake, Isaac's gun in his hand. I didn't know how he'd primed the bullet, and I didn't care. He was awake. He was alive and clutching the ring Isaac made over his inked chest.

I didn't manage a smile but it wasn't exactly the moment for thank-yous. That could come after I'd made Gwydian pay.

But as I looked on, the red mandala beneath Jaesung went bright with light. He went rigid, then twisted in on himself.

I started toward him, dodging the Lochly son's spell.

No. With the mandala lit up, I knew what it was, and I felt stupid for not guessing. Stupid for not shoving Jaesung off the mandalas when I'd been over there before. His bones were shifting, flesh changing as the mandala forced him into canine shape. He screamed like it hurt, though it shouldn't.

I stopped running, realizing then exactly what the campers had died for. What Gwydian wanted.

I whirled back to the fight. Eric dropped one magazine only to slam another in his gun; Deepti, her movements fast and sharp, made her way toward Gwydian. He was holding a shield against her golden spells, power arcing up his arms and in sparkling webs across the ground to the red mandala.

That Hellhound spell was meant for me. I'd evaded it, so Gwydian was doing the next best thing—changing yet another person I loved into a monster. I would not let it happen again.

My mind opened like it had that night at the farm house, searching for the source of blood and power. Metal glowed bright in my senses—silver and gold and steel and iron. It was everywhere, conductive to energy like nothing else. I stoked the turquoise flame in my chest and sent it out toward those metal beacons, felt it resonate and catch, and amplify.

The mandala was in my mind even as I ran toward Gwydian.

Deepti had harnessed the great bonfire, sweeping flames around her to ward off the attacks of the three remaining Hellhounds, even as she concentrated the shots of her pistol at Gwydian. His shield was so bright I could barely see his bared teeth through it. It didn't matter. My hands crackled with power. I felt it vibrating my chest, felt the cruel joy of sanguimancy flow into me, for some of the iron I'd found had been in blood.

I shot out the spell, felt it tear through me like a hurricane. It hit his shield, and I ran toward it, trusting in the power that poured from me to be enough.

This was the man who ruined my family, who took away my childhood and made it so I could never have a normal life. But normal or not, I would live despite him, despite the monster he had made me.

I leapt toward him, shedding my human skin even as I shed all thoughts of past and fear of future. The shield trembled in my vision as I ran, leapt, and shattered through it.

My paws hit Gwydian's chest, bearing him down to the blood-soaked ground with a mighty crash. I lunged, my teeth in his neck, and halted. A battle raged around us, and for a moment I stood there, hot breath clouding from the jaws I had around the neck of the man who had single-handedly destroyed my family.

I could have killed him. Most of me wanted to. Instead, I drew on the power of the blood spilling from under my teeth, and sent a surge of turquoise power into the mandala on his chest. He gasped, writhed under me, and I clamped my teeth harder. I lit up the mandala on his chest, lifted it out, shoving out the violet magic that claimed it.

The master spell was only different from the enslavement spell in the center, where it directed all power to the wearer. I bent the center glyph, twisting it so the spell focused outward, and drew the arcs of leashed spells out. They snapped, freeing the slaves still held to him. Some of those were Hellhounds, which backed down from the fire and scattered, searching for weaker targets. Somewhere behind me, though, one of those tethers was no longer attached to my cousin.

Gwydian screamed, tracing half mandalas on my skin, in the ground, stopping each time I let up and returned pressure with my teeth. I growled, dragged the last surge of magic through a brain now burning like the flames in Deepti's hands, and hurled the leash to Gwydian's enslavement spell to the waiting tattoo on Deepti's wrist.

CHAPTER THIRTY-FOUR

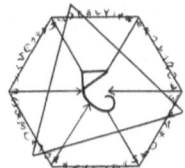

Smoke drifted across the stars. I staggered past a charred fire circle, my head empty of anything except the two men on the other side. Men. One of them was a man, the other a dog, only not the right ones. A low-level hum drowned out all but a few muffled sounds, the whoosh and rip of spells dying off as sanguimancers attempted to run.

Without Gwydian, they didn't stand a chance.

A man in a dark uniform appeared at my side and lifted some of my weight. Maybe all of it. I wasn't sure. All I knew was that the distance between me and the crooked pavilion was getting shorter.

A few yards away, the man rose. He crossed the last steps between us, reaching for me with a hand that was missing its first two fingers. Eric relinquished me into Morgan's arms, where I stayed, wrapped up tight.

There were no apologies. Not from him, or from me.

It wasn't until I heard the canine whimper that I found strength to push away from my cousin's embrace. I sank to the mud beside the silver and black form of a wolf, whimpering in distress.

"Jae," I said, before the wolf's muzzle was in my chest. I wound my arms around him, burying fingers in his thick guard hairs, and felt the rumble of his voice as the whine became louder. I rubbed behind his ears just as I might have with Poo-stank. "It's okay," I said, unable to grasp the urgent thought floating just out of reach. "It's okay."

Morgan knelt, putting his uninjured left hand on Jaesung's back. "You want to change back?"

Jaesung's response was half growl and half whine, the frantic canine equivalent of 'no shit'. I kept my fingers in his fur, even as Morgan spoke in cool, even tones, like there hadn't just been a blazing magic battle around us all. I let my mind drift, let the dizziness and hunger take over until the fur beneath my fingers retracted. I opened eyes I didn't remember closing and held Jaesung's shoulders steady as I could.

He whined like it hurt, though it didn't. It wasn't comfortable, though, and when the whine transformed into a human-sounding groan, I knew the worst was over. Scar-striped skin settled under my fingers, and silver-gray fur darkened and retreated up his spine. Moments later, he was Jaesung Park. Tall, tan, and naked on the blood-soaked ground. He collapsed back into my chest, and though my own strength was giving out, I held on, bending my face to his shoulder.

This time I did apologize, whispering it over and over into the short hair at the back of his neck. He grunted, but didn't seem to have the energy to form actual words. He'd been forced through two changes in one night and probably hadn't eaten since the ramen we'd downed the day before. A coat appeared from somewhere, tucked around him.

"Let me look at his leg."

The voice had me looking up, shocked to find there were other people standing around us. Guild Members, massaging tattooed arms, holding up injured compatriots, texting or talking on cell phones.

Deepti crouched beside me with her slender hand extended toward Jaesung. For a moment, I wanted to growl. But then she twitched aside the coat, and I saw the black and red mess of his knee where Morgan had kicked him. I didn't need to be a doctor to tell that it was badly broken.

Heat rippled up my throat, and for a moment I thought I would vomit up my guilt. Instead, I heard myself give a soft sob. My eyes burned, and I pressed my face into Jaesung's neck again until I'd controlled myself.

Someone sat behind me, pressing his back against mine. I felt the tickle of blond hair across my shoulder and swallowed.

Jaesung groaned, and the golden wheel of Deepti's spell flamed high and bright.

Other Sorcerers still cast spells around the campsite, washing away the char and blood, sweeping in snow from the woods to settle over the place. Eric stood on the blue cooler, sawing at the rope holding up the second dead camper. The first was a limp cocoon at the base of the tree.

"Where's Gwydian?" I murmured. It didn't come out clearly, but Deepti seemed to understand regardless of my slurring.

"Sitting in a police car with Amelia. We have a flight to catch in the morning. The Tribunal awaits him in Istanbul." She rocked back on her heels then, looking gray. "That is all I can do for his leg just now. He will need a real hospital."

I nodded, not sure how we would get to a hospital, or how we would explain Jaesung's leg. Or his tattoo. Or his mother's living room.

I glanced at the twist of fabric that was his clothing, wondering if his cell phone was still in there by some miracle.

"Deepti, I have to call in the campers," Eric said, leaning down so his salt-and-pepper head was visible beneath the sagging edge of the pavilion. "The Lochlys are crazy enough to admit to what they did to regular law enforcement."

Behind me, Morgan stiffened. I turned my head to look at him, and he mirrored my movement.

"We should go," he said, and I knew without having to hear him say it that those campers had died at Morgan's hands.

I tightened my hold around Jaesung's shoulders. "We need to get him to a hospital."

"He's calling law enforcement." Morgan nodded toward Eric. "There will be ambulances."

I fought through the fog in my brain, trying to figure out what Morgan was saying. "Go...where?"

"Canada. You delivered on your side of the deal," he said, nodding to Deepti. "They promised to let us go."

Deepti lifted an eyebrow. "You have missed a great number of bargains while you were under Gwydian Lochly's control."

"I don't care." He shifted forward, the support at my back disappearing. I had to hold tighter to Jaesung to keep upright. "Helena? We have to go."

"No."

Morgan's gray eyes focused on me, blank with confusion. "We can't wait for the police to get here."

Eric raised his hand. "This badge isn't plastic, buddy. And we've got to come up with an explanation for all of this-" he swept his arm around the partially reconstructed campsite. "-and the mess you left back in Chicago. Preferably one that doesn't involve magic and keeps all the right people out of jail."

"You don't need Helena and me for that. We've already got somewhere in Canada to-"

"I don't recall giving you a ch-"

"I said I'm not going!" My voice was loud enough to silence the two men arguing above me. Deepti met my gaze over Jaesung's head. I clenched the coat tighter around him, but he was shivering in my arms. "I'm not going to Canada, Morgan. I made a deal with the Midwestern Guild."

Morgan stared at me, his brow drawing in. He'd always been obedient—following plans through to the end. Changing the rules wouldn't make sense to him. Or, I didn't think it would, until his gaze flicked to Jaesung's slack face, then back to mine.

"I'm not going," I repeated. Then, softer, "But I don't want you to go either."

Morgan swallowed, and with a curt jerk of his head to show he'd understood my plea, turned his back and strode across the campsite. I watched his broad shoulders, the sway of his blond ponytail as he vanished up the slope.

"Will he go to Canada?" Deepti asked.

I shook my head. "He might. But he'll come back if he does."

The Indian woman nodded and stood. "I have an early flight. And I think the two of you need a hospital."

I was about to protest when the understanding hit me. I could go to the hospital. No one was chasing me. The Guild was, for the moment, an ally. I didn't have to avoid the police. I could register an address. I could take a driving test. I could go to college.

It was over.

A violent rush of some emotion too strong to identify washed through me. Grief or relief, anger or hope, I couldn't say—maybe some combination of all of them. I might have been crying, but I didn't care if I was, or who saw, or whether it made me look weak. I held onto the boy in my lap and let the current sweep me away. For the very first time in my life, the future opened up—mine to decide.

CHAPTER THIRTY-FIVE

"Stanky, get out of the chips!" Jaesung yelled, holding onto the open hatchback. He balanced on his good leg, prodding his crutch at the hyperactive German Shepherd without conviction. Poo-stank, thinking it a game, snatched the end of the crutch and tugged until Jaesung lost his impeccable balance and fell onto the stack of duffle bags next to the SUV.

Poo-stank took off with the crutch held triumphantly in his jaws, tail waving in anticipation of a chase. But Jaesung wouldn't transform into a wolf to play tug of war with his own dog. Not in broad daylight.

Krista dropped her armload of travel-pillows and took off after the crutch, somewhat hindered by the fact that she was laughing too hard to breathe.

I reached a hand to Jaesung, who was disentangling himself from my duffel bag. He snatched up a bag of chips with a half-gnawed corner and threw them at me. I caught them, reached down to grab his hand, and hauled him up. His arms went around my shoulders as he regained his balance.

I steadied him with a hand on his ribs. "How's the leg, Tinkerbell?"

"Fine, thanks for asking."

"You gonna keep packing, or do I have to do that as well as drive?"

"Oh, I see how it is," he said, turning back to the stack of luggage.

I stepped into his back, winding my arms around his chest. Because I wanted to. Because I could.

"No, no, I understand," he pushed my hands away. "I'm the workhorse."

I grabbed him again, and this time he turned in my arms, bending his forehead close to mine. He gave me a mock stern look, which would have been more convincing if the closeness hadn't made him look slightly cross-eyed. "Are you going to let me pack?"

His lips twitched. I licked them. He snorted and shoved me toward the pile of bags. "Be useful."

By the time Krista returned with Poo-stank's collar in one hand and a crutch in the other, we'd shoved all but my ragged purple backpack into the trunk.

"Here you go, Limp McCrutchy," she said, extending the crutch. Jaesung took it with an exasperated look on his face.

"Are we going to need an Ableism jar? I will fucking make one."

Krista jerked up straight, her blue eyes wide. "Wait a sec, I forgot the jar! No! That's my Mickey Money!"

As she scampered back through the open garage door of Ruff Patch, I called out behind her. "You know Disney isn't anywhere near Miami!"

"IT'S ON THE WAY!"

"She won't give up on that." Jaesung rolled his eyes and shepherded Poo-stank into the back seat. I climbed into the driver's seat and Jaesung hitched himself up into the passenger's seat beside me. "We might have to stop on the way just to get her to shut up."

I tossed my backpack into the space between our seats. "I don't think Mom would mind."

His slightly harassed expression softened. He nodded, and then his hand extended toward me. I took it, the hennaed mandala standing out a dark reddish black against my skin. Jaesung swept a thumb over it.

"Deepti won't get mad at you for leaving Minnesota, right?"

I shook my head. "I'm not exactly under house-arrest. And anyway, I texted her. She seemed to think it was a good idea, though I think she's concerned I won't come back."

I thought of Morgan, who hadn't shown back up these past three months. A postcard from Toronto hung on the fridge. There'd been no message attached, but I recognized his writing in the address.

Jaesung's fingers tightened on mine. "Did you tell her she has nothing to worry about?"

There was a note of concern in his voice, like he secretly wanted me to tell him the same thing.

I twisted in the driver's seat, looking over at him. He rolled his head toward me along the back of the seat, meeting my eyes. His hair had grown out a bit. The sides were no longer as short and neat, and it had taken him more product to get the long top strands to keep away from his face.

I thought about it. I had no idea what would happen when I went back to Miami, whether I would be struck with disgust or nostalgia at the familiar sights. I was going with the intention of saying goodbye.

"Scared?" I asked.

"Starting to wish I hadn't suggested it," he answered. Then he squeezed my hand. "Nah. Not really." He squeezed again. "Okay, slightly."

Poo-stank chose that moment to whuff softly in the back seat. We looked over to see Krista hurrying toward us, waving over her shoulder at Sanadzi.

"Don't," I said. "Miami was never really home."

He nodded, and when he glanced at me again, there was a bright look in his eyes that made my stomach tighten. "So," he said, lips curling. "I don't mean to be funny, given your—well, our—condition, but...."

I quirked an eyebrow suspiciously. "Yeah?"

He leaned across the space, tugging my hand until I leaned in too. His breath was warm on my lips, and I saw the crinkle of his cheeks as he grinned. "Stay."

I wasn't sure whether to smack him or give in to the twitch of happiness in my chest. Luckily, Krista chose that moment to swing open the passenger's door and hurl herself inside.

"ROAD TRIP, BITCHES!" she screamed, tossing a huge jar of cash onto the floor in front of Poo-stank. "I am ready to go meet Harry Potter and eat a giant fucking Turkey Leg. Poo-stank wants one too, don't you Poopoo?"

Jaesung twisted back around. "I don't think they let dogs into Universal, Krista."

Krista grabbed Poo-stank's furry cheeks and wobbled them back and forth. His tongue lolled out, licking her wrist. "Who could say no to that face?" she cooed, then leaned in to receive kisses. "Nobody says no to Poopie. No. Hey, I brought music! Turn on the car and go to bluetooth!"

Jaesung looked at me, cringe-smiling under her enthusiasm. "Are we there yet?"

I turned the keys in the ignition, blasted the music, and pulled the SUV onto the street. I thought about checking the rearview mirror, getting one last look at Ruff Patch, just in case, but I didn't.

I would be back. After all, it was home.

DEAR READER,

Helena finally found belonging.

But there are consequences for everything.

Are you ready to find out how the Guild really feels about having a Spellhound in their midst?

Or how Jaesung processes his traumatic new powers...and shaky future as a dancer?

When Helena uses sanguimancy to save her mentor's life, the Guild calls her to trial—with potentially fatal circumstances.

She can only see two paths:

1. Return to a life of running—tearing Jaesung from everything he knows, or...

2. Turn herself over to the Guild to protect him, and pay their deadly price for blood magic.

CLICK HERE TO READ IT NOW.

www.ingramcontent.com/pod-product-compliance
Lightning Source LLC
Chambersburg PA
CBHW051329250626
47155CB00007B/2514